SARAGOSA
PRIME
A STOLEN WORLD

Kenneth E. Ingle

BooksForABuck.com

2008

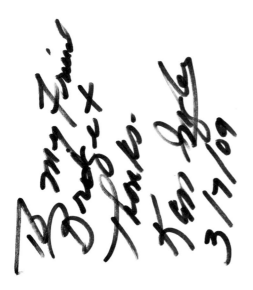

SARAGOSA PRIME:
A STOLEN WORLD

Kenneth E. Ingle

BooksForABuck.com
November, 2008

ISBN: 978-1-60215-088-1

A WORD OF THANKS

As with most books, it takes more than the writer. In my case, a number of people read this work and contributed mightily and for that I am grateful. Ann Marie Hardin read and reread chapter after chapter and kept me honest. Writers tend to stray. Ken O'Toole (you may remember him as creator of Denton Dodge) Leslie Turner, Bob Henry and Pat Snyder all kept after me to get it right. I learned a great deal from the DFW Writer's Workshop.

Coming out of the business world, I had to unlearn what I thought I knew about writing. It was a complete revelation in my case. I had to start over. It wasn't easy for me or my critiquers.

PROLOGUE

FTL travel has existed for a little over one hundred years, allowing exploration and conquest of planets and systems within three hundred parsecs of earth. The Federation of Aligned Worlds has replaced the failed United Nations but lacks the power to govern. Reminiscent of the old six sisters who ran mass media two centuries earlier, six conglomerates effectively control space. The new conglomerates are deadlier and much larger. Over one thousand planets, moons or asteroids had been colonized, mostly for commercial purposes. Mixed among these are a few religious groups who somehow managed to get transplanted and form havens for those of a like mind.

Commercial interests vie to do business following the standard adage that money knows no sovereign boundaries. Each conglomerate strives to be independent, each must provide its own security and all have professional Marine, and Naval forces. Those interested in conquest have standing armies. The cost of space travel and colonization is so high collaboration is the order of the day. Security alliances, like commercial associations do make for strange bedfellows.

And then there are the renegades and pirates. They rule by terror and no one is immune.

The problem of FTL communication remains unsolved. Messages travel no faster than the fastest space ship.

White Mining Corporation (WMC), one of the first companies to venture into deep space, claimed planet, Saragosa Prime, in the Vega region on the edge of the Galon Sector. It fell to the grandson of the founder to make good on promises to give Saragosa Prime political freedom.

Winner White IV has a reputation for keeping his word. Once he decides to do something, time is the only factor in doubt. He matured in the cunning world of a fighter test pilot and Navy SEALs. However, being the new head of smallest of the Big Six conglomerates, he's found little peer support and even less respect.

CHAPTER ONE
The Invasion

Winner White tried to sort out his emotions. Fired as CEO of White Mining but still head of the Navy, Marines and Security, he cleared the perimeter guard post and stopped at the spaceport terminal. Standing under the curved canopied entrance half a dozen people waited for his arrival. As Commander-in-Chief, (SCIC) and heir apparent, he still carried one hell of a lot of clout.

"Mr. White, I am Fenn Ashcroft, Captain of the Galactic Star. I serve at your pleasure."

Winner nodded, returned the salute and extended his hand. "Captain, we should have met sooner. I owe you an apology."

Ashcroft smiled. "Sir, may I present my Executive Officer, Commander Clayton Davenport."

"XO," Winner said, returning the salute and again extending his hand. Thirty minutes later, he boarded the shuttle for Galactic Star—once a cruiser but now recommissioned as a passenger liner.

Winner waited for the all clear to enter the shuttle. He had read the performance data on Galactic Star that Ashcroft earlier sent him. Half out loud he said, "Registration: Galactic Star; fleet name: Galactic Star; Id number three-eight-two; empty weight/mass, one million, one hundred fifty-five thousand ton-mass; Width, three hundred meters; length, one thousand meters; height (excluding externals) two hundred seventy meters."

Ashcroft looked impressed. "Guess you weren't too busy in the executive suite to learn about the pride of our fleet."

"What about armament and hyper drive?" asked Winner.

Ashcroft nodded. "Sixteen energy canons; Twenty-four torpedo tubes; Thirty eight short range photon turrets and forty fighters; rated speed high end of Eta band; Th. possible"

"Does the Th mean what I think it does?" Winner asked.

"Probably." The captain smiled. "If you're thinking theta band. The ship's structured to that speed."

Winner was impressed with Ashcroft's recitation. But then, a good captain should know every asset he has available.

"However," Ashcroft continued, "the touring passengers will not see or know of any of this. All of the tourist facilities and areas are unquestionably civilian, even to the dress code for the crew that serves them. But, once into the crew only area, Galactic Star is still a warship."

Winner smiled. Even the banks didn't know Star had remained battle capable. He'd made every effort to keep the true nature of the ship quiet. It seemed to have worked to perfection.

Winner changed into his full dress whites. He'd been through enough of these sideboards to last a lifetime but this one was different. The passengers expected to see the full pomp of the CIC boarding. Most didn't know he'd been relieved as CEO and probably could care less.

Saragosa Prime

* * * *

Three months later, Winner hunched down in the alley next to a mountain of rotting garbage. Destruction littered the streets with the gaps between buildings almost impenetrable. What had been the magnificent skyline was now laid waste, burning and smoldering, a victim of space bombardment.

His fists clenched at the foul nauseating sweet smell of death that mingled with the sulfur-tainted air. On the run for two days, tired, sleepless, wet, hungry, thirsty and dirty, his aching, bloody body cried for relief. But his body's suffering was only a small part of the pain. He had betrayed the trust of the people of Saragosa Prime.

Zed Bartok's forces occupied the planet, all due to Winner's failure to prepare for such an eventuality. Most of the commercial buildings, once the proud Saragosa City, lay in ruin or abandoned. Bartok's soldiers and mercenaries patrolled the streets, hunting for the few who dared resist.

Winner told himself he had to survive. Under Bartok's rule, Saragosa would never gain the independence Winner had promised the citizens. Certainly none of the other conglomerates cared whether Saragosa remained free or fell captive to corporate interests. Survival, however, would be a challenge. Winner had to get his hands on a weapon. So far, the smallest enemy group he'd seen was a six-man squad.

Cautiously, he maneuvered a large trash filled box in front of a hollowed out area and made his hideout. Night was already descending. The air reeked with the stench of three days of death and destruction. It stifled other odors and clung to him like a greasy film. Fumes rose from the putrid debris, mocked his mind and made worse the haunted days on the run. He wanted to vomit but he'd not eaten. If he didn't get food and water soon, starvation and dehydration would do what his enemies hadn't. He needed sleep. Constant running and hiding left little time for finding food or a safe place to rest.

Slowly, the sun crept lower. Winner, exhaustion almost complete, needed to get out of the city and to find friends. Nothing else mattered if he didn't get some distance from those who wanted him dead.

After three days of killing and destroying, Bartok's drunken soldiers looted the city.

Winner crouched in his hideout, ready to flee or fight although both would bring the same end. He couldn't believe that his decision to grant democracy and an elected government to Saragosa Prime had prompted the invasion. Bartok was a renegade businessman who had earned the reputation of taking what he wanted. Saragosa's entry into the deep space protein market threatened Bartok's corner on that business. That was probably all the reason the bastard needed, but the bankers and the other conglomerates probably looked away because they feared the example of an independent planet.

Bartok's field commanders ordered daily public executions. Resistance of even the most remote kind meant quick death. Every soldier or mercenary was judge, jury and executioner. The cities, highways, mines and processing plants were firmly in the hands of Zed Bartok's troops.

Winner wondered if Bartok had enough force on the ground to take the mountains and wooded foothills that stretched from the outskirts of Saragosa City to just short of the mines, three thousand kilometers away. He'd have to make his way to the hills in the north and find out.

He jolted awake, pushing his matted black hair from his face. "Damn."

As tired as he was, sleep was no longer an option. He reached for his wrist searching in vain for his chronometer, and then cautiously stood to see what had awakened him.

Nothing moved in the darkness.

Maybe the disturbance was his sub-conscious mind trying to keep him alive —a lesson his conscious mind needed to learn in a hurry. He was as close to dying as he'd ever been. As a Marine and test pilot, he'd faced death for seconds at a time. Now, though, it was his constant companion.

Being one of the wealthiest men in the universe didn't help him a bit right now and did nothing to sweeten the foul smell that permeated the air.

Finally, the sound came again—a soldier's boot squeaking.

Then the sharp command of the guard standing in the shadows shed by the corner streetlight pierced the quiet night, "Get you ass over here."

He watched from behind the pile of trash.

At the alley entry, not twenty meters away, a beggar faced his interrogator. Lighted by the soldier's flashlight and a dim street lamp, Winner thought he recognized the slender outline of the young scientist, Phalen Derka, whom he'd met shortly after his arrival on the planet. His dark lithe slender body, anything but fragile, reflected Indian genes. His name was the product of an Irish mother and Indian father. Disguised as a crippled beggar, the man dragged a lame leg, asked for a handout and offered a twisted hand that looked more like a claw.

"Get away from me you spastic bastard. And get your crippled ass off the street. If I see you again, I'll put you out of your damned misery." Using the butt of his laser rifle, the heavier, taller, body armored clad soldier shoved the beggar.

Winner watched as Derka hobbled aside and the guard went on his way. Could he get Derka's attention without giving himself away?

The young man gathered his ragged clothes about him and turned up the alley. Winner's pulse quickened as the scientist pushed toward him, past the mounds of trash.

"Derka."

His whisper brought the young man to a halt.

Doing nothing to show alarm, the would-be beggar scrounged in the trash. "Who is it? Where are you?"

"Over here. To your left." Winner stayed covered, waiting to see if their actions attracted unwanted attention.

He watched until the young man was almost next to him. Satisfied they were alone, he stood.

In an excited whisper Derka said, "Mr. White! Finally! We've been looking for you."

Winner felt a momentary sense of relief. At least there was some organized resistance on Saragosa.

The young man continued. "Quickly, follow me. We must get out of the city."

In one stride, Derka shed his assumed physical defects and started a slow run down the alley toward the street, Winner close behind. As they moved down the passage, Derka pulled night-vision goggles from the backpack that moments before, had been a part of his hunchback disguise.

Each street crossing offered to expose them. Phalen halted at every intersection and cautiously inspected the area, often waited out passing squads of drunken soldiers and mercenaries.

Exhausted as he was, Winner found the strength to keep pace with the young man through the darkened narrow passages. In less than an hour, they reached the outskirts of the city.

The terrain changed to hills, trees, narrow arroyos and rocky slopes as Derka sought out hidden paths. Winner labored to match his young advocate's strong pace.

They climbed the foothills for over an hour and then rested in the crags.

Derka gestured at the low shrubs that provided what cover was available. "Looks like some of the terraforming the company did over the last hundred years is paying off."

Winner nodded. He was thankful that effort, never meant to provide sanctuary for fleeing citizens, now gave him shelter and maybe saved the lives of people, including his.

Derka soon had them on their feet and moving, hour after hour.

Just as it seemed they'd never stop, he abruptly halted, stood silent among the boulders and waited until their breathing slowed. No breeze passed through the trees, but the cool night air made the exertion tolerable. The faint glow from Luna I lighted Derka's face—another hour would pass before Luna II would break the horizon. He placed a finger over his lips and listened intently.

No sounds betrayed the silence. Saragosa was home only to a few imported animals—those brought from Earth over the years. Only a cross between the Texas Longhorn and range Buffalo had proven capable of withstanding the rigors and diet offered by the planet's native flora.

Peering through his night goggles, Derka surveyed the surrounding area. Satisfied they had gone undiscovered, he motioned Winner to follow and a few minutes later stepped between two rock outcrops. The collapsed boulders created a tunnel opening into a hidden natural passageway. Over one hundred meters into the hill, it opened into a large dank, musty smelly cavern. In the dim light of electric lights strung overhead and above on a ridge that ran the circumference, Derka faced a small group and announced, "I found him."

CHAPTER TWO
The Cave

About fifty people, some in tattered cloths, closely divided between women and men, gathered around the two men. Thankful to be alive and back among friends, Winner strained against the dim light and saw the surviving population of what had been one of the largest and wealthiest mining planets. He took a deep breath and forced himself to hide his despair. He'd let them down. Yet pride and determination filled their tired, anxious faces.

The cave, over one hundred meters long and thirty wide arched some twenty meters high. A hard smooth dirt floor offer up occasional small puffs of dust as people moved about. Stacks of supplies and the few weapons lining the walls gave some semblance of permanence. Flat rocks set against the walls provided what passed for chairs.

Winner silently released a tired breath. He would show strength and resolve. Unworthy though he was, these people looked to him for guidance.

Finally, he broke the quiet. "How many more of us are there?"

He gritted his teeth waiting for the answer. This might be all that had lived and were able to fight. He wanted to make sure they understood he was there to see them through whatever lay ahead. If they would accept him.

Derka responded, "Fifty people here so far and only about fifteen are physically capable of fighting. Beyond these few, we don't know. I saw maybe one hundred or so while hunting for you. We'll start a thorough search in the city shortly."

Winner asked, "Company leaders? Are any still alive?"

Derka answered, "No. The first salvo from space was directed at the corporate headquarters and the Governor Generals offices. Demolished. No survivors. Where were you?" His question wasn't accusatory.

"Visiting my mother at her villa." Winner took the question without hesitation. Located a kilometer west of the headquarters, the ornate building was scheduled to become Earth's embassy. "She escaped with Daker Smithe. I saw them head north toward the hills." Smithe was White's personal envoy overseeing the elections. "He doesn't know the first thing about surviving out there." He tried to put his best face on it. "I took off for the Marine barracks. Got within half a kilometer before it took a direct hit. Nothing left standing."

Winner followed Derka's eyes toward the back of the crowd. He let the moment pass and asked, "What have we got in the way of food and water?"

A deep voice recited what supplies their cache included. "We could feed the fifty already here for months; five hundred for a month."

Winner looked into the glistening eyes and weathered face of a huge solemn man dressed in the characteristic dark blue coveralls most men of Saragosa wore. Long strides carried him through the group. Furrows lined his forehead and large bushy eyebrows, streaked like salt and pepper that matched his steel gray eyes added to a natural cheerfulness now subdued.

"I'm Vladislov Hrndullka." A thick slice of Nordic inflection tailed on the end of each word. He extended his hand. "My friends call me Hulk. You could use some different clothes."

Winner glanced at Hrndullka's ragged clothes, grinning past his tiredness. "It's easy to see why they call you that. My friends call me Winner."

His hand disappeared in the giant's grip. He was a good head shorter than Hrndullka and considerably lighter.

Casually the big man responded, "Winner it is. I'm, or was, superintendent of mine number three and the main processing plant at First Run. Up until five days ago, I worked for you. Now I'm ready to fight for you." The resoluteness in his voice seemed to translate to the group. This man was their leader—by choice of the group or through position within WMC, Winner had no way of knowing.

He sensed a swell of pride from the crowd. "I'm glad you're on our side." His sober expression changing to a grin. "Did you get these people together?"

"If you're concerned about their trustworthiness, almost everyone here lost family to the killer invaders. All we have left is on our backs. Bartok will get no quarter from us."

Winner looked at the shabby group. They could never stand up to Bartok's trained soldiers and mercenaries. He said what his soul felt. "I'm sorry you've lost loved ones and your homes."

He needed to do something physical, let off some of the frustration that crowded his chest. The weariness in his bones and the agony he felt for these people added to his sense of despair. A rock protruded from one wall and he heavily sat. The faith these survivors showed toward him added to the remorse he felt for not taking more seriously the threats against him and the corporation over a year earlier. Caution might have forestalled others wishing to bring him down.

A young lady brought a plate of food and drink, which he gratefully accepted, eating with relish his first meal in three days.

Exhaustion replaced hunger as he consumed the food, yet Derka had done the same for him. Every day he'd been on the run, Derka had hunted for him. It wasn't until Winner ate and lay down to sleep that he saw Derka do the same.

He awakened long after the rest of the group was up and had breakfast. He had no idea how they'd come up with food and didn't ask. A basin bath and clean clothes did a lot to restore him to humanity.

Hrndullka spoke determinedly. "I can speak for all of us. We're ready to follow your lead, Mr. White."

Winner acknowledged his words with a nod. "What kind of help do we have?"

He didn't want to have to guide these people, but he could not leave them feeling abandoned.

"Combat training and hyperwave communications?" Hrndullka demanded. "Do we have anyone that's familiar with com equipment and knows what's available on Saragosa?"

Winner was pleased. Hulk didn't hesitate to take control: a natural leader. He asked, "Any volunteers?"

"I can handle the communications," Derka almost shouted.

His exuberance brought a laugh from the huge man.

Six others stepped forward, two in civilian clothes, the rest in fatigues.

"Marines." An air of pride seemed to take Hulk. "And hopefully more will find their way to us in the next few days."

Winner motioned Hulk, Derka and the Marines to one side of the cave. He would be more effective if he didn't have to provide day-to-day leadership. He needed to establish some form of command structure. "Hulk, I'm naming you Governor General. You are to take command of everything on Saragosa Prime." These people already looked to the giant as their leader. He called the group to join around him and told them of his decision. The enthusiastic applause bounced off the cavern's walls. Their faces told him it was the right decision.

Winner shook Hulk's hand. "We're going to get rid of Bartok." That brought nods and smiles from the survivors even though he had no plan of how to do it. He hoped it didn't sound like useless bluster.

Hulk faced the people and quiet settled over the room. "We won't be able to use this cave for long. As Bartok's reinforcements arrive, his men will scour the countryside. With fifty people here, the chances of this place going unnoticed are nil. I want you to filter back into the city starting tonight. At least food and shelter are available there. Stay off the streets as much as possible. You know how to maintain contact with each other. Don't do anything to attract attention. Don't break any rules—that should help keep you out of harms way."

Winner made sure his doubts remained behind his mask. He wasn't the least bit sure of that but had no other plan to offer. This cave would be discovered before long—abandoning it was a sound idea.

Hulk continued, "We'll disguise the entrance, maybe we can hold onto it for storing supplies. Remember, our time will come."

Winner took the giant by the arm, leading him to the back of the cave. "Give me a quick briefing on what equipment and armament you have. Then issue provisions and weapons to our Marines." He managed a smile but there was little to justify that. Giving these people hope was one thing, sending them to their death left little reason for amusement. He tried to put the thought behind him.

Hulk described their weapons and equipment—a distressingly short list.

That finished, Winner clapped Hulk on the back. "Let's meet these Marines."

None of the six had insignias of rank, but they formed at attention in front of him, armed and provisioned.

Searching the face of each, Winner said, "Stand at ease. Our lives are dependent on each other. We need to know what each of us brings to the group so give a thumbnail sketch of your background. I'll start it off: SEALs, close combat at Farside—graduated; combat four times, space flight school, two years patrol; four years flight test star fighters Gorman Spacecraft Company. CEO of WMC three years." He looked at the first Marine.

"Nothing as spectacular, Sir," her eyes sparkled. A blush followed.

He masked a slight grin and hoped he didn't come across as arrogant.

"Sorry, Sir. That wasn't meant as a commentary."

He nodded, recognizing that this lady spoke her mind.

She stiffened and brought her lithe, sinewy one hundred seventy centimeters to full attention. Her red hair, cut short military style, made her eyes come alive with dark green fire set against her clear complexion. A small mouth in a square jaw finished a recruiter's poster picture. "Lt. Melissa Graves. Trained at Farside—graduated. Stationed at Nimitz Crossing when the attack came on Saragosa. On the first assault craft to counterattack. I don't know if anyone else in my unit survived. Single, age—military secret."

Winner laughed, glad for her sense of humor. She'd need it. Melissa was taller than most women with reasonable muscular development. Having been through the close combat school himself, he knew looks didn't mean a damned thing. Farside graduation was by combat and they had never graduated a loser. If you won, you graduated. As a lieutenant, she would have led one of the squads coming in from Nimitz Crossing involved in the landing. He did want to know how she lost her command but that could wait. He nodded to the men next to her.

The five remaining, all men offered varying experiences. The essence was the same for each, however. As one said, "A Marine grunt is a Marine grunt is a Marine grunt."

Winner understood. "Lt. Graves, these are your people. See to them."

"Aye, sir." She snapped of a crisp salute and motioned the men to withdraw.

Winner waved for Hulk and Derka to join him, and then walked to the sunlight drenched cave entrance. "We can't help ourselves here on Saragosa. We have to find some way to get off the planet and find Galactic Star. We can't wait the six weeks for a communications signal to hear Earth tell us they won't help.

"When word of this gets to Earth, maybe help will come but we can't count on it. At least not in time to be of any use to us. We must get the forces and armament we need here in the Galon sector. The Galactic Star should be the centerpiece to our resistance, but all I know about her location is that she's on tour somewhere in the Vega System with three thousand civilians on board."

Hulk, arms crossed his chest, one hand rubbing his chin, doubt evident, said, "We don't know what Bartok and his friends attacked beyond Saragosa. We have no way to contact Nimitz Crossing or Minns Station; they may or may not be ours."

Winner liked Hulk's scope of thought. "We have to consider both locations may have been compromised. Bartok slipped past our outpost's defenses undetected. There should have been ample warning for Saragosa to mount some defense. The failure of the outposts to meet their mission requirement as

13

early warning stations cost many people their lives and all their freedom." There were insufficient troops to stop Bartok, but it wouldn't have been a walkover if they'd had warning. With any warning at all, many civilians could have escaped harms reach and would still be alive.

"Any word on Colonel Ziron?" He suspected he knew the answer.

Hulk ran his hand through his snow white bushy hair, "Executed, the first day of the invasion. It was a mopping up operation for Bartok's men after that."

"Ziron's two hundred military police never had a chance against Bartok's soldiers and mercenaries. And the two hundred Marines from Nimitz Crossing only meant more losses for us—a terrible waste of lives and resources. The enemy had planned well and picked his time perfectly."

Hulk simply nodded.

"Hulk?" Winner looked around to be sure no one could overhear. "Is there any word on my mother? Is she still alive?"

CHAPTER THREE
Zed Bartok

Zed Bartok strode into the Namaycush spaceport, the echo of his white jackboots reverberating off the light gray plasticrete floor and walls. "Is my shuttle ready?" His roar almost lost in the noise of his boots against the deck plate. "I want to get under way, now!"

His round smooth head, hairless except for black bushy eyebrows, glistened in the bright lights surrounding the loading ramp. His face carried a permanent frown. At over one hundred eighty five centimeters and massing a hundred kilograms, Bartok's height and bulk dominated those around him.

He added to his impact by wearing the latest in military fashions, provided they projected the macho image he cultivated.

Dispersed around his launch, ten menacing looking men clad in body armor with flechette and pulse rifles made up his armed guard.

Those trying to please or feared him scurried to satisfy his whims. "I've taken Saragosa. In fact," his laugh not directed at anyone in particular, "I got Saragosa and next all of the Galon Sector. Who knows? The Vega System might be mine too. And, I'm going to kill Winner White myself." He'd made that boast many times before. He didn't mention that Winner White had eluded his troops and was still loose on the planet. He smacked his hands together in jubilation all the time his eyes stared over the workers and guards.

Namaycush, Bartok's home planet and headquarters, the namesake of a Canadian fishing village, was the galaxy's major producer and exporter of processed and live food fish. Saragosa with its vast oceans would be ideal for expanding his business. Over the centuries, the sterile, sulfur-tinged oceans on Saragosa rejected all but highly specialized amoebic life. After ninety years, the best scientific and engineering minds within WMC had come up with the solution that would made the oceans a viable food-producing source, transforming the planet's economy into much more than mining.

"White got Saragosa ready for me," Bartok laughed; the launch crew copied their master.

Wanted on Earth and most other jurisdiction for a host of grievances including murder, Bartok dared the spineless Federation of Aligned Worlds or the conglomerates to come after him. So far, none tried. Until three days before, his holdings consisted of four planets, two taken by force. Now he could add Saragosa Prime and soon the rest of the Galon Sector.

The air car skidded into position to receive the volatile leader for the trip to the launch pads. "Move it," he ordered.

The car eased forward and soon sped at treetop level toward the space drone. The rear window opened and Bartok leaned back in the seat to enjoy the breeze. Silently he cursed the dark gray cloud cover. It was the only thing to mar his departure. He was as close to total satisfaction as he'd ever been.

Skillfully, his driver headed the air car for the Namaycush launch pads.

Bartok's entourage scrambled into waiting transports, not wanting to fall behind and earn the wrath of their volatile leader.

The launch site came into view and the air car slowed, dropped to just above the ground and landed at the terminal. Bartok climbed out and stomped up the ramp toward the waiting shuttle. The trailing cars headed for the remaining orbital launches parked around the tarmac.

His manners were crude, but his planning was anything but. The launch area, meticulously laid out, was immaculate. The gangway guard snapped to attention. Bartok's glare fixed on the seductive woman standing next to the boarding hatch.

"Hi lover. I was beginning to think you'd changed your mind. You promised me—" she smacked her gum as she spoke from the top of the ramp.

"Promised what?" Bartok stopped in front of her, hands on hips, his mind completely absorbed by the victory over Saragosa.

Her dark complexion highlighted ruby red lips that formed a pout. Her silver sateen jump suite glinted as she started toward him, "You've forgotten already?"

The big man retaliated. "You're dumb beyond belief. I've got Winner White on the run and I ain't takin' time for you. Now don't give me any of your trite cute shit. Get aboard."

"Well, you can go to hell!" Her face glistened with anger then with hurt.

Eyes wide and wild, he lashed out, his fist striking the beauty below the nose. The blow drove her back, head hitting the titanium alloy edge of the hatch opening.

"No! No! I'm sorry." She threw her arms over her face but it did little to stop Bartok's powerful fist.

Blood spurted out of the gouge as his large, diamond-studded ring ripped her lip, leaving teeth protruding through the tear.

She dropped, unconscious before her head thudded against the deck. She rolled almost to the bottom of the ramp; a crimson trail marked her path.

"Dumb bitch!" Bartok looked at his ring, flicking off an offending piece of skin. A quick brush of his palms took care of anything that remained all the while guarding against any stain to his immaculate white uniform.

A guard at the bottom of the incline rushed forward and carried the unconscious bleeding woman clear of the ramp onto the loading dock.

"Put her on the shuttle!" Bartok ordered.

Risking a similar fate the guard said, "Sir, she needs medical attention and you don't have it on the shuttle."

Bartok, still in a rage, grabbed for his laser pistol and seemed surprised when his hand came away empty. Only the fact that he didn't have a weapon strapped to his side saved the man. The soldier had knowingly placed his life at risk by helping the woman and defying his leader. Bartok could not tolerate that from a subordinate.

"Put her on the shuttle!" his lip curled in a snarl, malice laced his voice; his steel-toed boot poised to strike.

The port master, waiting inside the launch, rushed forward, momentarily stopping everyone where they stood. He helped the guard carry the unconscious girl to the pad below. "Mr. Bartok, with your permission we need to get her to a hospital."

His rage ebbing, he answered, "Go ahead." It wouldn't look bad letting the ground boss have his way—this time. "Get her out of here and let's take off."

He had other women, smarter women, waiting to replace her. Until then, one of the galley girls would do.

The crew moved quickly making ready to get underway, the boson finally securing the hatch.

Bartok watched the ramp withdraw and signaled the cockpit all clear for lift-off. Immediately the air scrubbers kicked in and a slight breeze wafted through the passageways followed by the roar of the powerful lift engines. One hour later, they rendezvoused with Vengeance II on orbit.

Hunkered next to a porthole, Bartok fixed his gaze on the silver colored starship a mere dot still one thousand kilometers away. He smiled and nodded. With this ship, he would conquer what he wanted and get rid of Winner White.

He'd lost Vengeance I at Nimitz Crossing three years earlier. He'd bragged he'd killed Winner's father in that battle; even at that, he didn't consider it an even trade. Vengeance II's design had to satisfy only one criteria—speed. Every ounce of weight not given to armament or electronics went to speed. She was the most sophisticated, fastest, maneuverable hyperspace destroyer in space. She boasted the best in electronic targeting, latest navigation equipment and cloaking were part of the original construction, in part to help keep the crew population below two hundred fifty people, that in itself helped speed. Vengeance II couldn't match White's Galactic Star, a heavy cruiser, in destructive force. Fortunately, though, that didn't matter. White had foolishly refitted that ship to make tourist runs. Converting her back to a warship would take months—months Bartok had no intention of giving White. Even at that, Bartok plans didn't include a face off with the larger more powerful starship. There were other ways to take out Galactic Star. And he would pick the time.

He stomped through the narrow passageway to the bridge.

Laid out in a semi-circle, the command center was a model of efficiency, no space wasted. The navigation console centered at the nose of the ship with the captain and Bartok's chairs immediately behind. Astrogation was on the right with fire control communications to the left. Vengeance II was everything he'd ever wanted in a fighting ship—and he planned to make the best of it. He had to. Conquest was costly. His finances were worse than when he seized Namaycush. Some of his creditors hinted he needed to get his accounts current. Bartok had hinted back that they just might get a visit from Vengeance if they didn't back off.

"Set a course for Saragosa," Bartok ordered. "Get there as quickly as possible."

Captain Blaine, in his quiet command voice, repeated the order from his bridge chair. Bartok liked his captain's immaculate dress, but his poise and bearing drew Bartok's envy and ire.

"Aye, Captain," the astrogator responded and added in response to the speed order, "Vengeance can travel in the Epsilon band for four hours."

"Jump it up to the Eta band," ordered Bartok as the familiar hum of the gravonic engines filled the air and vibrated through the structure.

"Not a good idea, sir," Blaine said. "The hull and engine can take it but the crew can't. Over one hour and we'll all be heaving our guts out."

"How much time can we cut off the trip if you kick it up?"

Blaine nodded to the astrogator.

"Each band doubles over the previous. So, I'd estimate two-thirds. From six days standard to two," the operator answered.

Bartok turned to Blaine. "Issue the goddamned vomit bags and take us up to the Eta band."

Every person on the ship knew what would happen if they didn't have their gag bag handy when they got sick. It wasn't a pleasant thought.

He knew the captain's reputation when he hired him. Known as his own man, a less than desirable characteristic for Bartok, he also had the reputation as the best destroyer tactician. They had already had it out about command. Blaine let him know Bartok was not to countermand any orders or go around him. Bartok could pilot himself but only a fool would tempt hyperspace in a starship with anything less than a skilled captain. He wasn't about to put Vengeance in the hands of an incompetent skipper, so Blaine remained at the helm.

Bartok stomped to his quarters immediately behind the bridge, his retinue of bodyguards having dispersed throughout the ship. Smallish and stark barren, his titanium alloy cabin verified the commitment to speed, armament and technology. A fold down bunk, tiny sonic shower and smaller closet lined one side of the three-meter room. A communication terminal, desk and chair filled the other. His only perk a small porthole.

"Computer," he ordered. "Messages."

'Three messages. First received on tight beam. Decryption code not available for entire message.'

"Play it." He sat down at the console table and withdrew a small book, one of his few concessions to ancient technology, to decode the message. 'Secured transmission from WMC Laboratory to Winner White, Saragosa Prime. Unable to decipher attached encryption.'

"Next," he ordered. He'd deal with it when he got to Saragosa.

Fonso Carrel's image appeared on screen, 'Bartok, my fleet will arrive at Saragosa in two days.'

"Computer stop. Date and time of Carrel's message."

'Message received at 0200 this date.'

"Good! Good! Same time as I get there!

"Resume."

Carrel frowned on the screen. 'Don't take my involvement as a given. I'm not crazy about risking my fleet without some specific goal and a clear exit strategy. If it was anyone other than Winner White, I doubt I could justify any losses to my board, particularly since you're involved. I'll tell you this much, they question your rejection of an experienced military officer to head your army and the hiring of Colonel Masten. The guy's a psychopath. What in the hell do want him around for? If there's something that tips the scales in your favor, you need to make it known.'

Carrel's image disappeared from the screen with no salutation.

A smile crossed Bartok's face. "Have I got a message for you." He got a bottle of bourbon, and toasted the empty screen. They were his, he gloated; he could hardly contain himself.

"Next."

Kirk Filbright's image appeared. All he needed from this guy was his starships. Weak, the man would grovel after whatever scraps Bartok offered. He wouldn't waste time thinking about this slug. Before the message started he ordered, "Stop."

Bartok slumped in the form-mold chair. A foreboding, not about Carrel but Winner White nagged him. He needed to shake it. Yet, at the same time, he could hardly contain his exuberance at the thought of killing his nemesis himself. As if he needed the assurance, he said to the empty room, "There's no way for him to get off Saragosa and no place to hide."

But he couldn't get rid of the ominous feeling.

CHAPTER FOUR
Hope

Derka stood aside as Winner leaned his back on a large rock. The scientist had replaced his street rags with a blue jumpsuit. "I've got to get to the lab. They're going to need someone to run it and I can't think of anyone better than me. Besides, if you can steal a sub-orbital launch we may be able to capture one of the spaceships on orbit and get out of here. I may have a way to hide us from detection while we do it."

"Don't go over to the enemy," quipped Winner. "Stealing a launch craft may not be much of a chore—keeping it and not getting shot will be."

"I hope they think I've given in to the inevitable. One way or another, I need to get some time in that lab."

Winner stood, clapped him on the shoulder, and wished him success. He didn't ask Derka exactly what he had in mind or if he even had a plan.

He followed the young scientist to the adit to see him off and for a breath of fresh air.

Derka nodded to him, and then climbed the rock wall that fronted and hid the cave.

Maybe everyone that met the young man might misconstrue his seeming frailness. Winner had. This man was anything but fragile. A more apt description was lean and mean hidden behind a boyish smile, charm and tremendous intellect.

* * * *

Derka scanned the area around the entrance. Nothing moved. Quickly, he covered the open area to the surrounding trees and made his way toward town. Following a circuitous route, he cautiously moved from rock outcrops to trees, all the time checking his back trail, finally entering the outskirts of the town as the sun rose.

Night gave way to the orange dawn. He stayed to the residential area avoiding the industrial buildings fearing most of Bartok's guards would be watching for saboteurs.

Once in the business district, Derka followed a direct route to WMC Laboratories located on the western outskirts of Saragosa City. Few people, mostly guards, were on the streets. He was stopped only once by a roaming patrol. Not all of Bartok's men were renegades and criminals. Some were professional soldiers and they conducted themselves as such. Once told he was heading for the laboratory to offer his services, the patrol hurried him on his way unmolested.

Derka entered the lab grounds, stopped and intently surveyed the buildings and noticed the antenna atop the garage, off its mounting. He approached the lab, his stride confident. Bartok's bombardment and assault plan had avoided attacking the research zones. It was intentional—you don't destroy what you need.

He walked to within a few meters of the first guard he spotted and stopped. "Good morning. Are you in charge?"

The sentry seemed to swell with the question, just the reaction Derka hoped for.

More of a grunt than laugh came from the guard. "No. Step through that detector. If you're clean, you can go inside; someone will take care of you. If not, I'll shoot you."

Derka glanced at the flechette rifle hanging from the guards shoulder. In the close environment like hallways, the needle/knives could do indescribable damage to the human body's soft tissue.

Without hesitation, he stepped through the detector. He shot a forced grin back at the sentry and entered the lab.

Spared looting and destruction in the first five days of war, the dark red plastibrick building was in pristine condition. Destruction of any part of the science complex would have been a major blow to whoever controlled the planet. Maintaining correct chemical balances of the planets air, water and foods was a major part of the scientist daily routine. A necessity on most planets, it was of paramount importance on Saragosa.

A guard stood just inside the door, his black uniform in stark contrast to the white halls. He motioned Derka toward an office.

Derka entered and waited for the officer seated behind the desk to acknowledge his presence.

"Name!" The command in an almost serene voice.

"Phalen Derka."

He assumed the eagle on the soldier's collar meant the same in this army as any other, a colonel. Without looking up, the officer keyed the desktop computer. Apparently finding what he was looking for, his attention remained focus on the screen.

"Sit down. I am Colonel Masten.

The officer seemed relaxed, exhibiting the demeanor more often seen on a college professor. His slightly mussed black hair, showed light gray at the temples. His black and tan uniform, pressed and neat, appeared tailored to his athletic frame. Eyes fixed on the monitor he said, "You were a scientist in this lab. Computers. Why are you here?"

"I want my job back."

"Just that simple. You want your job back." Raising from behind the desk his fingertips rested on the surface. The colonel leaned forward putting him at the smaller Indian's eye level.

Derka inwardly shuddered as he looked into an abyss—the colonel's eyes were vacant, completely void of any human emotion. Coldness seemed permanently embedded in his face.

"I suppose you're a scientist not concerned with political questions. Do you really expect me to believe that?"

"Yes." He hoped he was convincing enough.

The officer's black eyes stared at him for a few seconds—no emotion reached his face to betray his thoughts. He looked back at the monitor. "It says here you're just that; you've never shown any interest in anything but your work. Maybe we can be of use to each other. I need someone to run this place. Are you up to it?"

"Yes. It really doesn't require much administrative effort. Everyone knows their job so most of the director's chores mean allocating resources. You know, who gets to use which instruments or piece of equipment next, that kind of thing." Derka felt his temperature rising, not from anger but anxiety. Did the man believe him? He forced himself to remain calm. "How many scientists have report so far?"

The Colonel ignored the question. "Come with me." He motioned toward the hall.

Together, they walked down the passageway to another office. The door opened—it seemed automatic until Derka saw the guard standing inside next to a brain scan machine.

Despite his efforts, the young scientist's anxiety overtook him. "Do I have to submit to this?" He let his voice rise abruptly. He recognized the heavily wired insulated chair. It was the prototype design. In the early stages of development, it had killed several men.

"I can shoot you now." Masten's voice left no doubt.

Derka had expected some form of truth test and the scanner would be it. The laboratory director had ordered the tests stopped a month earlier and all the equipment destroyed. From somewhere, somehow, Masten had found the original test equipment. It looked ominous. Most breadboard models are flung together without concern for form or appearance. At the prototype point, scientists are just interested in trying an idea or testing a theory. Since Derka had written the computer programs and proved them on this machine, he knew its flaws and weaknesses.

"Sit down," Masten ordered. He stood next to the control panel, the passive look he'd earlier shown replaced with what seemed intense anticipation. The guard took a position behind the console.

To get through this, Derka would have to exploit the machine's flaws. He had to work himself into an excited state before the scan started and maintain it throughout the test, but without Masten noticing. The fact that Masten had the machine meant that someone who worked in the lab nominally as a White employee had informed. Had they told him of its deficiency? Nothing seemed to indicate that.

He set his mind to the task—to deceive Masten and the machine. All that assumed Masten hadn't reverted to the earlier configuration or the damned thing would fry his brain.

Derka decided not to say anything about the settings. If the Colonel thought he knew anything about the machine—no matter what, he was dead. If Masten had tampered with the machine—dead. If he was caught tricking the machine—dead. If he failed the test—dead.

Derka conjured up an image of rats. He loathed rats. He concentrated on his early youth in the rat-infested back streets and alleys of Calcutta while maintaining a passive facade.

He envisioned every rat he'd encountered as a child—and there were many. He pushed each image and kept the rage building. It was his only hope to beat the machine. It was his only chance to avoid scrambled brains or be exposed as a liar.

But he had to say something and decided to risk Masten's suspicions. "Do you know this thing can kill people if not properly set?" He added a nervous tic in his voice adding credibility to his lying.

"Shit happens. I have no choice, not that it matters. Mr. Bartok says use it before we put anyone in a responsible position."

He hoped the colonel didn't know the machine defaulted to normal when confronted with an extremely high stress situation. He'd programmed it to react that very way to avoid mind wipes. People under extreme stress, mental and physical, were particularly vulnerable. Now that stress became an asset, he meant to use it.

"Sit down. Relax. This won't take long. We've learned enough to know how the proper settings. We don't damage anyone again."

Derka could only wonder who had become a victim in the last day or two. The heavy wooden timbers made the chair loom even larger before him. He couldn't run—he'd never get out of the building. He encouraged his anger, imagining the people who died in its initial testing. Anger was the advantage his knowledge could bring to the test.

The guard moved to buckle the sweat-stained wrist straps.

Derka objected, "Hey, you don't need these. The headband and body sensors, yes, but not the wrists." He realized too late his mistake, admitting he knew about the machine. Maybe Masten wouldn't pick up on it.

The guard shoved him back into the chair and held him there buckling his wrist firmly to the chair. A smile touched the corners of Masten's lips.

The operator strapped sensors to Derka's head and palms, and then stepped to the control console.

The soldier moved the controls as the colonel said, "I'll ask you a few questions to establish a baseline. You are to answer yes or no."

Derka blinked.

"Is your name Phalen Derka?"

"Yes."

"Are you twenty seven years old?"

"Yes."

"Do you,— disregard. Did you work for WMC Labs?"

"Yes." Derka answered and noticed the wry smile formed on the man's lips. He was thankful the colonel had changed the question."

"Do you know Winner White?"

"Yes."

Masten leaned into the next question his eyes intent. "Do you know Winner White well?"

"No," And Derka hadn't lied. What little he personally knew about Winner White he'd learned in the last few days. What he'd learned as an employee over the last few years was just hearsay.

CHAPTER FIVE
The key

His attention riveted on the instruments, Masten asked his final question, "Do you know where Winner White is?"

"No." Derka had lost track of the times he'd lied. He didn't know if that helped or hindered but suspected the former.

The Colonel signaled the attendant to turn off the machine.

Derka stood, and straightened his blue jump suit. "Do I get the job?"

He was relieved to out of the chair and braced himself for the answer. He met the officer's cold eyes and concentrated to keep his pretense intact.

"The machine says you're telling the truth, but I've got a gut feel that you're a very clever and skilled liar." His voice hardened. "I'm seldom wrong."

There was a long pause, as his eyes seemed to probe Derka's soul.

Finally, Masten's demeanor changed. "Anyhow, I'll be the director of the laboratory, at least for the time being. I have my doctorate in biochemistry. If you're wondering why I'm not in Bartok's army but here in the Lab, the big man says I'm a psychopath and a better scientist than soldier. He says I enjoy killing too much—even more than he does." His smile was pleasant, almost reassuring, as he added, "He says kill only if it makes him money." His eyebrows raised and an ominous smile crossed his face. "Bartok just wanted to lead the army."

Derka didn't outwardly flinch at Masten's disclosures but his insides crawled. He didn't know if it was true and didn't want to find out, but knew he'd have to exercise extreme caution. He didn't know what the colonel had noticed but he'd gotten all the warning he needed and realized this man could change moods without the slightest provocation. He couldn't afford to relax for an instant.

Masten's face went grim. "I'll establish project priority and protocol. You're not to be concerned with any judgments, even if they offend your sensibilities or morals. Those determinations will be made by others, not you. Report to your lab. You're not to leave the building without my approval."

Derka was still shaken when he reached the office and put on a white lab coat. Masten hadn't given him orders on what to work on, so he keyed the computer to see how many people were on board.

Only ten of the scientists had reported, with Derka by far the most senior. He recognized all of the names, had once thought of them as his friends. At least one of them had told Masten about the lie detector and was a traitor. Maybe more. For the time being, he could trust none of them.

He started to leave the terminal when he spotted the security note tucked in the corner of the screen. Quickly he scanned it—a coded message for Winner. He knew better than try to access it. Alarms would go off all over the place.

He vidcomed Masten. "Colonel, has anyone been in this office?"

"Yes, I have. Why?"

"A message to Winner White from two days ago is logged on the terminal."

A long pause followed. "See if you can do something with it. Nobody's been able to break the code."

"With his money, it's probably just a financial report."

Masten keyed the mike, his voice laced with caution, "I'll authorize your access."

The approval appeared on the screen.

Derka was ecstatic but disguised his feelings. "I'll keep you posted."

Quickly he opened the message on his screen. In seconds, it was clear the code was specific and probably not breakable without the key. Now he faced another problem.

He keyed Masten, "Colonel, the message is quite long. Is a printout permissible?"

"Yes, but it doesn't leave the building."

"Okay, understood." Derka entered the commands to get the hardcopy. He looked up as a guard walked into his office.

"The Colonel says you're to give me whatever you've got when you leave."

Derka nodded and continued at the keyboard. A printed copy splayed out. Ignoring the guard, he returned to his desk and set to work on the document. Five hours later he said to the sentry lazing in the outer office, "I've done all I can with this. You can have it." The soldier accepted the sheaf of papers and left.

Casually, he walked into the outer office and stopped at the attendant's desk. Opening the drawer, he removed a small vial of white nail polish. Despite Masten's warning, he left the office and walked along the brightly lit passageway to the equipment service lab, two halls away. A cursory scan of the area showed he was alone. He took a sub-space transceiver from the shelf and quickly altered its configuration. He carefully pulled a phase shift inverter from the shelf, made a minor adjustment, and returned both to their proper places. Derka impressed himself with how cool and calm he was—at least it seemed that way. He walked to the next aisle, again making sure he was alone. He pulled a hyperwave crystal container, used by a large starship for its communications and detections systems, from the rack. Quickly he unscrewed the base housing and slid the two pieces apart exposing the crystal that served both the communication and detection systems.

Careful to leave no marks, he pried off the cap revealing the crystal and the highly polished surface that maintained spectrum separation. Taking the vial from his pocket, he coated the inside of the cap then reinstalled it. He placed the unit in its original location and headed back to his office, checking the chronometer as he returned the bottle to the desk. He'd been gone less than five minutes. He hadn't seen anyone while he'd been out of his lab and could only hope Masten wouldn't check the automatically created security logs. Now all he had to do was figure out how to get the equipment installed on the largest ship on orbit. This was all they needed to give him and Mr. White a reasonable chance to escape.

To complete the subterfuge for getting the coded message out, he keyed the computer and went to work developing an algorithm—but this one had to be special, the best he'd every concocted. When it'd done its job, it would command itself to erase and leave no tracks. Mentally, he retraced every action he'd taken. If everything went right, even Masten wouldn't know what he'd done. He shook his head. It all seemed too improbable. But he'd done his part. He faced the guard and then stepped through the detector. It revealed nothing and he was allowed to leave the lab.

With an air of what he hoped wasn't misplaced confidence, he headed into Saragosa City.

Noon was still an hour away. The sun partially hidden by clouds had slowly warmed the land. Sulfur tainted dust devils danced in the breeze that wafted across the streets. Shortly after leaving the lab, he altered his direction, skirting the city's north side.

He needed to reach the rock outcrops and nearby cottonwood trees unnoticed. Once there, he could easily make the cave without being detected.

For the next five minutes, he stood in the deep shadows cast by a building. One patrol had passed and no one was in sight. Five hundred meters to the rocks. Run or amble across? Amble he decided and started to walk.

About fifty meters from the trees and outcrops, he heard the unmistakable roar of a personnel carrier. He dove to the ground and lay still.

It passed within one hundred meters but no one looked his way.

Derka crawled the remaining distance. He continued his circuitous route, constantly checking to see if anyone followed. He made the cave one hour later.

Derka deferred changing out of his dirty clothes until he'd given Winner his report.

Winner tried to hide his skepticism. "Very risky. Everything hinges on that one piece of equipment getting installed on an orbiting spaceship." He adjusted the reflector on one of the phosphor luminous lamps lighting the cave and waited for an answer.

Derka's response took a serious tone. "I know that, sir. But, if you can get a ship that will put us in orbit, I can make it work."

Winner nodded. He had an uneasy feeling about Derka's assessment but had learned not to underestimate the young man.

"What about the message? How do we get it?"

"Any time the lab's closed," said Derka, "every kind of detection device you can imagine kicks in. And they're run off localized power sources so there's no way to shut them down. I tied the computer into that grid. All I need to do is install a line of sight tight beam antenna here at the cave, trigger my cell phone and the computer will key a server to send a message and we have the information."

Winner stood a look of determination on his face. "Okay. Let's do it."

* * * *

Just before eighteen hundred, Derka returned to the cave a big smile on his face.

Winner waited under a lamp, and used a large rock for a table decoding the message. Derka and Hulk waited a respectful few meters away; the rest of the forty or so people had already dispersed throughout the city.

Winner couldn't believe his eyes. He read the message aloud. "From: Dr. Leonid Vasiliv. To Winner White: Eyes Only.

"Mr. White, I have astounding news. You now have independent Faster Than Light (FTL) communication."

Winner ran his fingers through his hair, looked up into the black ceiling and slammed his fist in to his open palm. "Finally! This will make the difference." He didn't try to contain his enthusiasm. "Vasiliv has handed us what we need to beat Bartok."

Derka nodded. The current technology took almost three weeks to get a message to Earth. With Vasiliv's improvement, it would take less than six minutes.

Winner turned the decrypted message over to Derka. "You read it. He says you can build the devices."

Waiting while Derka scanned the papers, Winner noticed a man enter the cave, hurry to Hulk, and say something. His attention returned to the scientist.

Derka scanned the papers. He clenched both fists and thrust them out in front of him in a symbolic gesture, "I hope you've got that starship lined up. We're going to need it for more than getting away from here."

Winner knew why he wanted the ship but had no idea what prompted Derka's reaction. "Why?"

"Because, Mr. White, we don't have access to power generators capable of developing the energy required for this thing to work here on Saragosa. A starship will be needed to transmit FTL."

That didn't diminish Winner's enthusiasm. He could hardly contain himself. "So, we'll get a ship. We've eliminated the delay in sub-space communications. Damn!"

He brushed aside any thoughts about the commercial aspect. The first order of business was freeing Saragosa. The throb of his pulse matched his racing mind. This was the first news that could make a difference. Now he believed with confidence they'd find a way to defeat Bartok.

Hulk motioned Winner away from the group. "There's a pilot stranded in the city who has his own ship."

Winner's eyebrows shot up. "Let's get to him."

Hulk nodded. "We need to get out of here anyway so we've lined up a place in the city." He spent a few minutes filling them in on the tunnel complex that would become the resistance's headquarters.

"Right in the city?" Derka's voice seemed incredulous.

"Yep," answered Hulk. "It was the first permanent complex on the planet. Back then, it was cheaper and easier to build underground. They didn't have to bring as much building material with them. When the first people got here, they were developing hybrid plants, part of the terraforming and couldn't afford to let anything unwanted get into the ecosphere. So, the lab, living facilities, everything went underground. Tunnels run in a number of directions. We'll open alternate entries once we get situated."

Derka still looked puzzled. "I've lived here four years and I've never heard of these tunnels." He sounded almost chagrinned.

Hulk grinned at him.

Winner took it as a good sign. You never knew when the next opportunity to find a little humor might come. But it also meant the tunnels were not common knowledge.

Hulk stood, towering over everyone, especially the diminutive Derka, continued, "We're counting on Bartok not knowing either. His reinforcements will be landing before long. We will leave as soon as it gets dark."

CHAPTER SIX
Richard Hastings

Winner, Hulk and Derka waited at the forests edge for Melissa's recon patrol to report.

Finally, Winner's wrist com signaled dull green. It was a go for the first man to move out.

Five hundred meters of open area separated their cover from the city. Automatically controlled laser and flechette rifles guarded all the approaches.

Melissa and her squad shortly arrived at the spot they'd chosen to cross—less than two hundred meters from the controlled entry Bartok's troops used to come and go. Derka handed Melissa the laser rifle he'd altered to blind the sensor. She lay down on the ground and rested the barrel against a rock. She pulled her night vision goggles into place and took aim at the sensor. Slowly, she squeezed the trigger stud. There was no outward appearance of damage to judge her success; only the bright flash from the muzzle indicated anything at all had happened. If she'd blinded the sensor, no alarm would sound. If not . . . they waited. If no patrol saw the flash . . . they waited. Silence. It had worked.

"Wish me luck." Derka stood. No grin showed as he headed toward the city.

Single file, at fifty-meter intervals, they followed the young scientist onto the grass covered plain. Luna One's faint glow cast an eerie glow over the grassy field ahead of them. A faint wind stirred the air. At least it was from the city and wouldn't carry any telltale sounds they might make. Now only the open area now separated them and Saragosa City.

Winner shoved Hulk to get him started but the giant didn't move.

"You next Mr. White."

He had learned when Hulk called him Mr. that there was little chance of winning an argument. Winner crawled from behind the tree and started his trek across the open field. The Marine sent to neutralize the perimeter guard at a cairn not far away joined up behind Hulk. He pulled his hand across his throat and pointed in the direction he'd just come.

The Marines, one hundred meters apart formed a line. Each person would pass from one fighter to the next until they reached the relative safety of the first buildings.

They had crawled one hundred plus meters when a burst of laser fire erupted. Shouts came from the rubble ahead of them. Winner didn't trigger his wrist com, fearful it might betray their location. Besides, the shooting didn't seem directed at his group. He didn't know what set that first weapon off but it started a chain reaction.

The second he saw the flash Winner hugged the ground. In an instant, Hulk was beside him, the Marine crashed next to the giant. With all the commotion, Winner was certain they would come under fire.

Recognizing the danger of remaining in place, Winner's SEAL training took over. He jumped up and ordered, "Come on! On your feet! Run! Let's get the hell out of here." He pointed toward a concrete abutment at the edge of the first building. Fifty meters of open field lay between them and the wall. The distance would seem an eternity if they came under direct fire.

An enemy flechette rifle fired. It was too far away to do much harm but Winner was focused on its companion. The laser would take a few seconds to power up and that was all the time they had to gain cover. He pulled and shoved the other two men toward the rubble. The laser rifle would soon come to bear on them. Mentally, he timed it and yelled. "Get down."

The three dove over the small concrete wall as the blast grazed the top. Bits of flying concrete fragments burned his face. Shards of debris cut into his knees and elbows as he skidded on his stomach. Hulk and the Marine hugged the wall anticipating the next shot.

Winner didn't wait—the next discharge would be on target and would blast away the wall with a few shots. They had no chance if they stayed where they were. Quickly, he had urged them up and running to the edge of the building another five meters away. They closed the gap and cautiously continued deeper into the city. The aroma of decaying bodies and rotting garbage was as strong as ever. His memories of the three days he'd spent hiding from Bartok's soldiers were just as vivid.

Hulk moved silently as he guided them deeper into the city. The structures first built after they'd moved above ground eighty years before, had not fared well in the bombing. Made of local materials, they were no more than concrete and cinder block construction. The plasticrete structures built later were, for the most part, in better condition.

They covered three city blocks, checking every intersection before entering. Hulk changed direction and motioned them up another street. A man ran past, giving them no more than a casual glance apparently with sufficient problems of his own. The ongoing fireworks covered any sounds they made.

"Walk," ordered Winner between breaths.

They kept to the shadows, using the heaps of rubble to hide from roving patrols. At least the subdued light from Luna 2, just rising, worked to their advantage.

"In here." Hulk pushed Winner and the Marine between two buildings to a doorway, then through it. They stumbled over trash that littered the hallway.

The interior, even darker than the alley, left Winner grabbing for something solid to keep him off the debris-cluttered floor. His night goggles gave him just enough light to stay upright.

Quietly, they moved up the hallway and a short flight of stairs to a mid-balcony giving them an unobstructed view of the room.

"It's a bar," Winner quietly exclaimed, surprised a place like this was open, let alone doing a thriving business. A small fuel cell powered what light the room had. Only one bartender and waiter served the twenty or so people clustered at the bar and around a few tables.

Their entry had gone unnoticed. They didn't move. Winner didn't know these people and Hulk didn't signal any awareness on his part.

Hulk whispered, "We'll wait here."

"What for?"

"There'll be some visitors shortly, looking for us."

The Marine hand-signaled he was going to cover the alley doorway and crawled into the blackness.

Winner nodded but the man had already disappeared. He and Hulk sat, their backs to a brick wall. He pushed his goggles onto his forehead. The cold concrete floor offered little comfort.

The barroom door crashed open. Two soldiers burst into the building shouting. A brilliant light flooded the room. Winner and Hulk ducked below the parapet wall, armed their weapons and waited.

"Don't anyone move," the first soldier barked. One held a laser rifle on the group as the other played the strong light over each person. Seconds passed. Everyone remained still as ordered.

Singling out one man, a harsh order broke the silence, "You there! Come here!"

The small man, bathed in the bright light, slowly made his way across the room and stood before the soldiers. Winner saw no fear in his manner and motioned the Marine to stay put. The private held a position that commanded the room and alley doorway.

Bartok's soldier stuck his rifle barrel against the smallish man's chest and demanded, "Has anyone come in here in the last ten minutes?"

The little man shook his head. In full body armor, the soldiers dwarfed him.

"I asked you a question and I expect an answer." He again jabbed his rifle against the man.

The room was dead quiet. Then the distinct sound of a rifle being powered to its kill setting permeated the silence.

"Wait." A soft command came from the dark with a firmness that demanded attention. Winner watched as a tall older man walked into the glare of the soldier's light. His white hair, beard, rotund belly, round nose and high forehead gave him the appearance of an intellectual Santa. He stood at least a head taller than both soldiers and two heads taller than their victim.

"Perhaps I can help you, sir. I've been here for some time."

The soldier turned toward the distraction, his weapon aimed at the intruder that slowly approached from a dark corner. "What is it you wish to know?"

Winner turned to Hulk with a questioning look and lowered his voice. "Is that our man?"

Hulk nodded.

"Who in the hell are you?" the guard asked then ordered, "Move over here."

"I'm no one of importance," the tall man answered in a quiet soothing, reassuring voice. He made his way unthreateningly forward.

The soldier played the light over the man, flicking it over his face, then away.

The man's steel lined boot bottoms cracked against the cement floor as they moved to confront the soldier. No one in the bar so much as flinched. "Your name? And what are you doing here?"

"Hastings. Richard Hastings. My starship was on orbit for re-supply when the invasion started. I'm waiting approval to return to my ship." The calming voice continued, "You and your buddy are the only ones to come through that door since I arrived over an hour ago."

The soldier hesitated, unsure of himself. Then finally, with a slight shrug, he powered down his rifle. Without another word, turned, motioned to his comrade and left the bar.

At first, a hush continued over the patrons. Then they returned to their drinks as if nothing had happened. Winner sensed that if Bartok's soldiers harmed the small man they would have died on the spot.

Winner whispered to Hulk, "Get that man up here. We need to talk." Even in the dark, his eyes glistened with anticipation.

The big man moved quietly to the end of the alcove from which Hulk and Winner had observed the confrontation. Every eye in the room turned toward Hrndullka as he stepped into the dim light.

He slowly extended his hand to Hastings, "Thank you. I'm Vladislov Hrndullka."

The two large men faced each other. Finally, Hastings said, "Your presence here is a threat to these men." Again, the quiet voice wasn't challenging.

"I don't know how you know that, but let's leave. Someone wants to meet you. Will you come?"

"Certainly." Hastings nodded.

Winner followed the Marine from the balcony to the doorway of the alcove and then waited for the two men.

The Marine, night goggles in place, peered into the alley. He motioned all clear and slipped into the darkness. The three men followed.

Winner guided them into an alcove off the alley, stepped in front of Hastings and introduced himself.

Hastings nodded. A slight smile touched his face. "A thousand or so of Bartok's men are looking for you."

"I've noticed," Winner responded with a grunt.

There was no humor in his voice but his answer brought a large grin from Hastings.

Winner, despite his best efforts to be stern, found himself yielding to this man's likeability.

He relaxed. "Mr. Hastings, our situation is desperate. I must get off Saragosa. It is urgent that I find my fleet if we are to have any chance at all of defeating Bartok. I need your spaceship."

CHAPTER SEVEN
The start back

Hastings hesitated at Winner's bluntness. "I see. My employers may have something to say about your using the ship. They normally do not involve themselves in local issues."

"Local?" Winner questioned. "They could be next if someone doesn't stop Bartok. Who do you work for?"

Hastings nodded but seemed indifferent. "Actually, I had already decided to offer you my services. I will admit I didn't expect my ship to be involved." He took a deep breath. "The group I work for has no interest in the outcome. My involvement is my own choice but my employers are aware of my decision."

"Cryptic but fair enough," answered Winner. "And you still haven't told me who you work for."

Mr. White, may I speak alone with you?" The manner of Hastings question offered no threat.

"Anything you have to say can be said here and now." Winner was pissed at the suggestion and wasn't about to offend Hulk by letting Hastings cut him out of the conversation.

"I mean no offense to Mr. Hrndullka or the Marine, but I must speak to you alone."

"It's all right Mr. White," Hulk motioned the private to a lookout position and followed up the alley.

The 'Mister' Hulk offered ended any debate. Winner stripped off his night goggles, wishing Hastings could better see the hardness in his face.

"What is it Hastings? What is it that's so gawdamned secret?"

"I work for the Tri-Lateral Commission. In fact, I'm their only employee."

Winner could not have been more stunned if hit by a bludgeon.

He didn't insult Hastings by suggesting he'd never heard of the group, reputable by some standards, nefarious by others.

He stared hard at the man through the darkness. The Commission was three men, self-appointed, whose only concern was money, or more correctly, capital—the formation and movement of capital. Officially, the organization didn't exist, had no legal status and no moral claim to any position. Yet these three men, acting together, controlled enough wealth to influence monetary policy throughout the galaxy. And they did.

Winner stood silent for a moment. "Well, I'm at a loss for words. Maybe there's something proper to say at a time like this but I don't know what it would be."

Hastings gave a small chuckle, "If it isn't too rude of me to make a suggestion, how about, 'thank you and we're glad to have you with us'."

Winner grinned slapped the man on the shoulder. "I couldn't have said it better. Welcome aboard."

"Thank you. And I think we can work something out on the ship."

Winner moved with a determined step. He could not have been more pleased. Richard Hastings was the man he needed. "It must be my day. Let's get to our people."

They caught up with Hulk.

The Marine cautiously led the way, his laser rifle set to kill.

Moving single file, Hulk trailed him with Winner and Hastings behind. They had covered the first city block when the big man signaled them down.

They buried themselves in a mound of trash. A squad of soldiers ran up the street giving the alley no more than a casual glance. The Marine waited until the footsteps died and then motioned them to follow, crawling along the concrete alley.

Hulk signaled them into a slow jog.

"Care to bring me up to speed?" asked Hastings. "Why now? Why did Bartok pick this time to attack Saragosa? And what are you going to do about it?"

Winner ignored Hastings question and asked his own. "How does the commission feel about democracy on Saragosa? Do they think I'm wrong?"

Winner figured Hastings already knew that the other conglomerates had tried to stop him or expressed their dislike. Maybe they also knew that his own board of directors opposed it.

Hastings said nothing.

"I've received every kind of threat you can imagine attempting to force me to abandon the plan. Creditors threatened to pull their financial support if anything went wrong. And it has gone wrong in spades." He ached inside for the men and women still trapped in the city.

The four continued trotting along the dirty alleyway, their clothes saturated with putrid water. Winner noted that Hastings ran without effort, no shallow breathing, and no struggle to keep up.

The city storm and sanitary sewers barely flowed, the stench rising in the streets.

Hastings managed a grin. "Mr. White, you don't give a damn what the Commission thinks. And the Commission wouldn't have it any other way. It could care less what form of government is in place. What we, excuse me, they want is stability. Lacking that, they simply want to do business."

Winner suspected Hastings knew a great deal more than most people about WMC's business. Not that it mattered. Not that he could do anything about it, or wanted to at that moment. Right now, he didn't give a shit. His only concerns were Bartok and getting off the planet.

Unsure why he felt agitated, Winner eyed this newcomer in the dim light. He couldn't shake the feeling that there was more to Hastings being on Saragosa than just happening to be in the neighborhood when the war started. He didn't seem to be the type to get caught somewhere by accident. Everything he did appeared measured, calculated.

Crouched as they continued through alleys, Hastings quietly started a recitation. "WMC claimed Saragosa Prime, a sterile, barren water planet in the

Galon Sector of the Vega System, ninety years ago, about ten years after deep space travel became possible. I'm not sure how long it took your scientists to make it habitable—"

"Ten years," Winner answered. "And another five years before mining started."

They waited as the Marine checked ahead.

Hulk motioned to speed up.

They couldn't outrun the backed up sewers, soaked clothes and the unmistakable stench of death, but Winner had to hope they could outrun any pursuit.

Hastings continued. "The failure of the United Nations caused concern. Contrary to some people's wishes, the Commission knows there must be government and the rule of law. Again, we just don't care what form the government takes. We weren't worried about which corporations got there first or claimed the most territory. We didn't and don't want a major war to sort it all out."

Winner wanted to ask who we amounted to but knew he'd get no answer.

"Believe it or not, Mr. White, may I call you Winner?" Hastings didn't wait for an answer. "The Commission encourages competition. We even encouraged the isolated enclaves established by smaller companies and religious groups.

"While individual companies, some owned by Commission members, made money from the two major wars, we prefer matters be settled at the business and political level, not militarily. We supported the establishment of the Federation of Aligned Worlds."

Winner said, "It was the conglomerates only acquiescence to outside authority. And that was only because the wars became too costly."

"Perhaps," Hastings admitted. "The issue of a popularly elected government on Saragosa didn't preclude intervention. The Federation just didn't have enough clout to make any difference and left you standing alone. And that's assuming they wanted to help.

"The Tri-Lateral Commission works behind the scenes. The Commission limits its intercessions to the effects of the money on the three T's; territory, trade and travel."

But, what else was there where business was concerned?

"Totally benign!" quipped Winner. He didn't expect any support from the Commission though territory was the primary issue at stake.

"Ha." Hastings laughed. "I see you understand."

They stopped at Hulk's signal.

"Let's move," Winner said responding as Hulk motioned all clear from the street crossing.

At a fast trot, they continued down the alley, still several blocks from the tunnels. Winner decided to give Hastings some of his thoughts since he'd decided to involve the man. Hastings matched him stride for stride and his breathing wasn't laboring. The man was in remarkable shape.

"Neither Nimitz Crossing nor Minns Station by themselves are strategically important," Winner said. "But, together with Saragosa Prime, they offer control of the Galon Sector; in addition, they are the key or at least gateway, to the Vega System."

"And the key to a lot of money to be made," Hastings interjected.

"There is a lot of money waiting for someone in this system."

"Bartok knew this and would have invaded Saragosa no matter what. That was never in doubt. The democracy move was of no consequence. Your acquisition of Cellus IV may have accelerated his schedule, but Bartok wanted Saragosa. Your being here just added a personal edge to the invasion."

Winner grimaced. Hastings had just confirmed his earlier guess.

"We agree with your board of directors," Hastings said. "You did hock the company to buy Cellus IV. But, the Commission believes it was a good move on your part."

"Although it didn't do us any good."

"Bartok was smart enough to see Cellus IV's strategic importance," Hastings said. "He knew what would happen when it became part of the defense grid for the sector. He had to stop the integration of Cellus IV. And the best way to do that it was to take the real prize, Saragosa Prime."

Winner asked, "How long have you had your eye on us?"

It was Hastings turn to ignore Winners question. "It's now up to you to do the same thing. Retake Saragosa."

"Don't act so damned smug." Winner felt irritated that he was so transparent.

"When you make it out of the mess, correction, if you make it out of this mess, you'll be stronger for it." Hastings's voice dropped almost to a whisper. "In fact, as we see it, you'll be in a position to become the fourth richest man in the universe and well on the way to be the next person to fill a vacancy on the Commission."

An involuntary breath escaped Winner. He'd never given the Tri-Lateral Commission a minute's thought. Now, he knew why Hastings had come to Saragosa Prime.

With long strides, the four men covered the last fifty meters to the building hiding the tunnels. Fortunately, Bartok's scattered troops were nowhere in sight.

Quickly, they entered the ravaged building, stopping at the massive center column that supported what remained of the cantilevered roof. The shear size and bulk of the column had helped it withstand the aerial assaults and the ravage of years. The rest of the building, that part above ground, lay in ruins.

The Marine remained on watch as Hulk crept to a bas-relief on the column and pressed keys disguised in the markings.

A hidden door opened from the center of the column itself.

Within seconds, they headed down the stairs, bound for the labyrinth of tunnels below. The entryway quickly closed behind them.

One hundred meters down, they entered a large well-lit room. The white-painted monolithic concrete walls and ceiling enclosed an area large enough for

37

fifty people. Several rooms dotted the sides—tunnels led off to other areas of the complex.

Moving to a makeshift conference room, Winner introduced Melissa and Derka. He motioned everyone to sit down. "Glad to see we all made it. What happened up there?"

"They weren't shooting at us. We never engaged them," responded Melissa. "You did the right thing heading in another direction. Otherwise, you would have walked right into a column of soldiers."

Winner leaned forward and said to Hastings, "Derka has a plan for getting us off the planet and out of this star system. But it requires a spaceship."

With a huge grin he turned to Derka. "And now I have one. Compliments of Mr. Hastings."

Hastings said, "When I joined your group, all that I have, all that I am, came with the commitment. The ship is yours." Offhandedly, he added, "I have become rather attached to it and would like to have it back when this is all over. And in good working order. I do have some traveling yet to do."

Winner eyed him. The man gave up his spaceship rather easily. He kept his counsel, hardly containing the excitement of getting a spaceship.

Derka matched Hastings smile. "What's it called and tell me something about it—speed and range."

Pride evident, Hastings announced, "Topsail. Has a crew of six captained by Harlow van Gelden." As an aside he said, "Father's Dutch, mother's English. Excellent crew, holds thirty passengers or a good chunk of freight, can dock a shuttle through an external lock, capable of hyper, hull maximum Eta Band, artificial gravity. Only armament, hand weapons and some small laser cannons. No energy weapons. Six months flight in Alpha band, two weeks in Eta. And she has minimal cloaking capability."

"Good lord!" exclaimed Derka. "Who do you work for? That's one hell of a ship."

Hastings ignored the question. "When I came dirt-side, I brought skin suits, they're on the shuttle. If I can retrieve them, they'll be your cover to get to Topsail."

Winner looked at his wrist chronometer; "Three A.M. local. Do you feel up to getting the suits now? Bartok's reinforcements are going to arrive soon and that means movement becomes more difficult."

Derka nodded. "Yes. I'm ready."

CHAPTER EIGHT
The escape

"Recovering those skin suits is our first priority," Winner announced.

Hastings nodded.

"Someone should go with you. Someone who knows the way to the space port and has credentials from our new masters."

From his seat one of the posiform chairs, the small scientist bounded up. "I'm ready. It'll work if Masten hasn't put the troops on alert for me."

"If all goes well, we'll be back in two hours," Hastings said.

"The rest of us can get some food and sleep," Winner ordered. "It may be a while before we get another chance for either."

Two hours later, Derka and Hastings reappeared.

"We got the suits," Derka reported. "No problems from Masten's people. The bad news is Bartok's reinforcement fleet is on orbit. Twenty-two more ships to deal with. Troops are landing now. The word is forty-five hundred soldiers will be dirt-side with heavy equipment by noon. Fonso Carrel and Kirk Filbright have joined Bartok. Their ships are part of the fleet."

Hulk came down the tunnel, entered the largely empty room and headed directly for Winner. "There's no word on your mother or Daker Smithe. The word would have been out if they were captured or dead. I feel certain they're on the run."

Winner thanked Hulk. "Maybe." He brushed aside any further thoughts, glancing around at the group, and then taking a deep breath. With a smile he said, "Derka, Hastings and I will go to Topsail."

He looked at Hulk, "You're going to be on your own until I can round up an attack force and return. It may be a few months or more." That almost made him sick. He'd do whatever he could to trim down the time.

Hulk stuck out his hand, "God speed Winner White. We'll be here when you return."

Derka said, "I'll have to go up later. I need to be at the lab to make sure my plan works."

"And Masten?" Winner asked. "What's he going to do about your absence?"

Derka looked thoughtfully. "Masten has a habit of coming to the lab late in the morning. If you can time your operation so that it's done before he gets there, I should be able to slip away unnoticed. I'll join you afterward. When's the next shuttle leaving?"

Winner had misgivings about Derka's recklessness. He cast a waiting glance at Hastings.

Hastings answered, "Anytime you're ready."

"Okay." Derka turned to Hastings, "When you get to Topsail, have your communications people send this signal to Bartok's lead ship." He handed him a data chip.

"That would be Vengeance Two?"

Derka nodded. "That signal is a deception and tells them their telemetry has a problem with navigation and communications. I'll hack their computer from the lab to make it look like a hardware problem. Their diagnostics will tell them to change the Hyper Crystal Assembly. Normally, procedures require they change the transceiver and Phase Shifter, like they're a set. I'll be in the lab to makes sure they get the ones I've altered."

"It's a start," Winner said. "And things will get better. I promise. We will win this fight. Saragosa will be free." He knew things would get a lot worse before they got better.

He hesitated. "Mr. Hastings, when you return to the city, you can be of great assistance to Mr. Hrndullka. You are a neutral, as far a Bartok knows. Keep that status—it should be most useful to our Governor General. He will need someone who can infiltrate Bartok's organization or at least have some access to it. This will place your life in great peril. If you're discovered, Bartok will not hesitate to kill you." He never mentioned the Tri-Lateral Commission.

Hastings nodded. "I'm looking forward to working with Mr. Hrndullka and the people of Saragosa." There was no pompousness in his demeanor.

Winner thanked the two leaders. "We need to leave now and get to Topsail before Bartok tightens ground control. Melissa, assign your three marines to Hulk. You'll come with me."

"I've got only three extra skin suits," Hastings said. "So, that would solve another problem."

Winner, Derka and Melissa followed Hastings to an anteroom. Winner and Melissa spent the next few minutes getting into their equipment. With their re-breathers, the skin suits could keep a person alive for about twenty-four hours if caught outside a ship.

A dressed Winner White emerged first.

Hastings said. "The helmets are on Topsail. Winner, you'll need something for a disguise,"

"I'll be out in a minute," said Melissa. "I have something that should do the job."

They waited.

Three minutes later, an angry frustrated Melissa complained, "I need some help. I'm sweaty from wearing the body armor and I can't get this fucking, tight fitting son-of-a-bitchin' thing on."

The men stifled laughs, thankful she couldn't see them.

Derka grabbed his ribs as she banged against supply cans and anything else in her way. "Shit! Will one of you gentlemen get in here and help me?"

They stood looking at each other. It was a dammed good thing Melissa couldn't see their plastered grins.

Derka stepped into the room to help as Melissa again cursed all of them. In a few minutes, she walked out dressed in her blue spacesuit and to a duo of smiles.

Derka bowed as he walked out, with the biggest grin of all. The tight fitting suit left little to the imagination and they all knew she had nothing on underneath. Without her body-armor, Melissa was very shapely.

"The first one who says anything gets the shit knocked out of him." She turned to Winner and added, "Sir."

He gave a mock bow and quelled a grin. After a moment of quiet, he cleared his throat. In a most serious tone, he said, "Mr. Hastings, would you please see us to the spaceport?"

There was a round of handshaking.

Winner walked up the stairs leading to the exit. He stopped, waited for Hastings and Melissa to catch up. The topside scanner had yet to signal the area clear.

Hulk made his way past the other two and handed him a letter.

"It's for my wife. She was visiting Earth when this started."

Left unsaid was, "If I don't make it."

Winner took the envelope, placed it inside his skin suit and said, "I'll keep it for now, but you can deliver your own message when this is all over." He motioned Melissa and Hastings to continue.

Hulk disappeared down the stairway.

Winner was disgusted with himself. He'd never given a thought to Hulk's family and had shown the same callousness to all the people in the room. That was a gross oversight on his part. The fact that he'd been a SEAL and test pilot longer than CEO cut him no slack. He'd have to remember to ask Hastings if he had family.

Still, his job was to retake Saragosa and success would demand its price. There would be casualties.

They waited at the top of the stairway until the scanner signaled all clear. Then, Winner turned the door release. He, Hastings and Melissa headed into the dark.

* * * *

The space drone, named Carmaneer after Winner's mother's maiden name, sat on ten thousand square kilometers east of the city. As spaceports went, it wasn't very large.

That should work to our benefit, Winner thought. It would add to the congestion and confusion as Bartok's reinforcements made landfall.

Night would come in thirty minutes—a gray overcast sky was beginning to show. They had two hours to walk to the shuttle launch pad, but evading the ground troops, not finding the space drone, was the number one problem.

They stopped in a bombed out storefront and watched the street. What few civilians were out made sure they stayed clear of any soldiers. The troops always got the right-of-way.

"Here." Melissa handed Winner a tube. "Rub some of this on your face. When it dries, wipe off all the excess. It'll change your complexion."

Winner dipped into the canister rubbed his face neck, ears and hands. The stuff felt like grease.

41

As they neared the city center, the littered debris increased in the streets. Winner noticed that people who moved with authority went unmolested. Even so, he decided to stay in the shadows and not invite questions. As they moved through the destroyed city, it became apparent the soldiers' had changed their tactics. Troops formed barricades, with sentries at every intersection, facing outward to form a protective corridor.

"Bartok must be either on the ground or about to land," Winner said.

"Yeah," Melissa answered. "These guys are security types. Uniforms are different, black with white chest band. The first ones on the ground had a gray band." She turned to Winner and in the dim light asked, "If we see the bastard, do we take him out?"

The question had lurked in the back of his mind. If he and Bartok died today, who won? Bartok? He knew Melissa didn't have a weapon but he also knew some soldier would die giving up his rifle.

"No," he answered. "Too much at risk. If we attempt and miss, we gain nothing. If we kill him and die in the process, Saragosa still loses. Our time will come." *Assuming we can pull this off* went unsaid.

Dressed in space skin suits, they didn't seem out of place in the area near the port. Spacers commonly went up in skin suits. With several companies involved in the occupation, every conceivable uniform style was in view from soldiers, maintenance personnel to freight handlers to spacers.

Evading the soldiers, they finally gained the edge of the city and the spacedrome.

Daylight came quietly. Grey clouds signaled the beginnings of the storm season.

Winner glanced at his hands, dyed a sick brown color.

He looked at Melissa in the gathering darkness.

She shrugged. "Shoe polish. All I had."

Winner wanted to laugh but didn't. At least she could think on her feet.

"It will take over an hour to reach the shuttle launch site," Hastings announced. "We'll be going against Bartok's strength—control."

"Bartok's need for absolute control is also his weakness," Winner shot back. "Let's see if we can exploit it. No one in his organization dares make a decision. Let's keep moving. Don't cause any stir. These people don't want to bring Bartok any kind of problem."

Before them, low-silhouetted buildings dotted the landscape. Bartok's assault shuttles continued to land and take off from the pads nearest the city.

Hastings led the group eastward, avoiding confrontation. Without arms and open to view, they seemingly posed no threat and continued unchallenged.

"There it is," announced Hastings, nodding toward the blue-gray shuttle. "All we've got to do is get aboard that ship and take off."

Winner's pulse quickened when he saw movement to the north. "Guards! Shit! Any suggestions?" Their goal was still a quarter klick away. Fortunately, the guards seemed only casually interested.

"I'll handle them," said Hastings. "At least I have credentials to show. Maybe it will be enough."

Winner and Melissa stopped ten paces short of the guards and let Hastings continue forward.

Mindful some of the men were no more than hired killers; Hastings paused, saluted and announced, "Gentlemen, I am Richard Hastings. Here are my papers. I need to get to my vessel. I believe I have the proper clearance." He was careful not to make it sound like an order.

The guard took the papers, "Why the skin suits?" asked one.

In the voice that could soothe a savage beast, Hastings answered, "Standard fare, you know. Can't beat them. Won't stain, don't sweat, hard to tear them, tougher than hell. And the way you guys ripped this place, every little bit helps."

That brought a smirk from the sentry along with a nod.

Winner realized a major part of Hastings persona was his believability. And to these soldiers, he was simply telling the truth.

The guards seemed riveted to Hastings and paid little attention to Winner and Melissa, much to everyone's relief. A doff of the guard's hand signaled them aboard the launch.

The three entered the small vessel. Hastings took the seat nearest the cockpit.

Winner noticed the missing shoulder patches when the pilot turned toward them and gave the pre-launch instructions. The man had been a WMC shuttle pilot.

"We still need launch control approval and slotting to take off," the pilot reported. "Since we're only going into near planet orbit, we shouldn't have too long a wait. Although, military shuttles have priority."

Ten minutes later, they were entering orbit. The pilot's motion caught Winner's eye.

He unfastened his safety gear, grabbed a handrail and guided himself the short weightless distance to the cockpit. He followed the pilot's point along with the man's silent admonishment to say nothing.

Silhouetted against the black of space, Vengeance Two orbited.

The ship was bigger than Winner had thought but much smaller than Galactic Star. Still, Winner was impressed with the sleek lines of Bartok's command ship.

The pilot reached out and touched Winner's hand. Silently his lips formed, "Good luck."

Only then did Winner realize this was the same pilot who had brought him to the planet only a few weeks earlier.

"Stand-by. We'll attach to Topsails port-side docking clamp in one minute," the pilot said.

Sixty seconds later, the dull thud as the clamps locked rang like a bell through the launch. A red light turned green, signaling an airtight seal between the two ships. The metallic and steel seals clanged and hissed as the hatch opened. Hastings stepped through into Topsail. "Party of three, Permission to come aboard."

"Permission granted. Welcome aboard Topsail, Mr. Hastings."

Winner reached for a handhold. Topsail followed the usual custom of turning off the artificial gravity when a ship without the capability came alongside.

Since Topsail had been commissioned four years earlier, Harlow van Gelden had served as her only pilot. A small man and impeccably dressed, the graying captain immediately placed everyone at ease. Turning to Winner and Melissa he said, "Mr. White, Lt. Graves, welcome aboard Topsail."

Hastings spoke to Winner, "Mr. White, I formally transfer command of Topsail to you."

CHAPTER NINE
The escape

"Thank you." Winner turned to face Captain van Gelden. "Sir, it is your choice to continue in command of Topsail or to return dirt-side with Mr. Hastings."

The entire bridge crew's attention was riveted on the two men.

"I will be pleased to serve as captain at your pleasure Mr. White." Van Gelden accepted the extended hand.

The captain, a head shorter than Winner and thirty pounds lighter, dark brown hair, cherubic nose and reddish cheeks, gray eyes, sported a dark, grayish, purplish blue blazer cuffed with gold braid and white trousers with a razor crease.

As Hastings prepared to return to Saragosa, Winner remembered his earlier self-admonition. "Mr. Hastings? Do you have family?"

"Yes." His voice took a velvet edge, yet strong. "A wife and son on Earth. I would appreciate it if you'd tell them I'm fine."

The two shook hands. "I shall do so, sir," Winner promised. "And I will tell them of your commitment to the people of Saragosa."

With a nod, Hastings entered the shuttle.

A crewman secured the hatch. The all clear sounded. The pressure seal gasped and the shuttle moved away and gravity returned to Topsail.

Winner watched the small craft break orbit and point toward the planet. His jaw clenched and his eyes narrowed to slits. "Captain, when I tell you, send this signal, narrow band to Vengeance only." He handed him the data chip Derka had prepared.

Without hesitation, Van Gelden asked, "And what am I sending?"

Winner smiled. The man wasn't about to place his crew in danger without knowing why. "It's a prepared signal that will set in motion events that will, I'm assured by Mr. Derka, our resident scientist, ensure our escape. He'll join us shortly after the signal has been sent."

The truth was, only Derka knew the odds of his ruse working. Winner suspected it had as great a chance at failure as success.

There was no expression on van Gelden's face as their eyes met for a moment but Winner was certain the captain knew he was about to place his ship and crew at risk.

He turned to the sitting astrogator and issued the order. Then he continued toward the hatch that separated the rest of the ship.

"You must want to clean up." With a smile, he glanced at the shoe polish still adorning Winner's face. "I'll show you to your quarters."

Winner entered the cabin just behind the bridge and sat on the bunk. Neither he nor Melissa had slept for two days.

* * * *

Right on schedule, the intercom awakened him. Winner awoke quickly, a habit he'd developed during SEAL training that had stayed with him. He glanced at his wrist chromo, zero four hundred.

Moments later, he stepped through the hatch. "Admiral on the bridge," a voice to his right said.

Winner quickly put a stop to that. Protocol had its place but sounding off every time he entered was not necessary on this small vessel.

Within seconds, Captain Van Gelden stepped on the bridge. Winner smiled and said, "Captain, it is zero four hundred and five. Please initiate the transmission to Vengeance."

With that done, the hardest part began—waiting.

"Mr. White, Mr. Derka's shuttle has left the planet—ten minutes to dock."

Winner sat on the edge of the bunk. He still wore his skin suit and brown shoe polish. Someone had laid out civilian clothes across the bunk.

Topsail wasn't large as deep space ships went, but it did have everything long voyages required. The enameled titanium room had all the amenities, shower, toilet, desk, two posiform chairs and a coffeepot.

He stripped off the skin suit and headed for the sonic shower. The deck, finished with a blue matte texture, felt soft and cool to his feet. A few minutes later, he stepped from the air dryer and put on the civilian jumpsuit. A look in the mirror revealed a scrubbed red face, at last sans the shoe polish.

He felt the gentle nudge of Derka's shuttle as it attached to Topsail, then the lightness as artificial gravity switched off.

Winner opened the hatch from his quarters, grabbed a handhold and pulled himself along the passageway.

Melissa, in civilian clothes, was already at the docking bay.

Tongue in cheek he asked, "Regulation?"

She laughed, "It was either this or the skin suit. That's my entire wardrobe."

Using the overhead rails, they hand-walked the few meters to the port side-docking bay and greeted the emerging scientist. With gravity reinstated, Derka ducked into his quarters to change from his skinsuit. "Want to help?" he joked, turning to Melissa.

A sly smile touched her lips.

* * * *

Minutes later, Derka, dressed in a blue jumpsuit, headed for the electronic lab.

The six-man crew included two electronics types whom van Gelden immediately assigned to help him assemble the FTL transmitter. The young scientist's grin at the thought of what he was about to build left no room for doubt about how he felt. It would be a long night for all three.

Winner, Melissa and van Gelden came and went from the wardroom drinking more coffee than needed.

Twenty hours later, Derka slumped into a chair. Dark circles made his black eyes seem like bottomless holes. "It's done. But, there's no way to test it. We'll have to wait until we leave orbit. The energy expended when transmitting is so huge even the crudest detection system would pick it up. And at close range, it'll fry anything that gets in the way."

"Suggestions?" asked Winner.

Derka brushed bushy his jet-black hair back over his head, stretched out his legs, crossed his feet and said; "We wait."

"For?" asked Winner.

"Before I left dirt-side, I sent the jimmied hyper crystal unit to Vengeance Two. It will take some time for them to install and calibrate it. Once that's done, we can leave."

"Derka, you have a phenomenal capacity to understate the obvious. Why do I have the feeling our leaving may be anything but ordinary?"

Phalen Derka gazed out into space, anticipation lacing his voice. "You're right Mr. White. A number of events have to occur and in precisely the right order or it's our skin."

Winner, with persuading humor said, "Bring us up to speed."

From past behavior, Winner knew Derka would not play up their chances. If anything, the bright young scientist masked his concerns with indifference. All a ruse—I'll bet he's scarred shitless. Too many things could go wrong; all the clichés are pounding hell out of this young man. Every fear he could dream is visiting him. Our lives, the success of retaking Saragosa is down to efforts he initiated but can no longer control or influence.

Winner, along with everyone else, waited.

Derka looked from Winner to Melissa, then to van Gelden. The moment seemed to weigh heavily. His voice was almost a whisper. "It will take a few more hours for Vengeance to do everything that's needed. We have to de-orbit and leave during that window. Vengeance will see that something's wrong. I'm counting on this delay giving us enough time to get out-system."

He turned to the captain. "Get us in as close as possible to Vengeance. The emission signature they'll transmit will be too weak for the other ships to pick up. But we have to respond to their signal. Only they won't know it's us. That's when we turn tail and slowly run like hell. We need about one hundred thousand kilometers from our present location. Anyone paying attention will eventually see we're changing orbits. We don't want to alert them any earlier than necessary."

"The worst of all, waiting." Winner stood, stretched, and looked at his wrist chronometer. "It's fourteen hundred. Let's get a bite to eat, some rest and then into our skin suits. Be back here and ready by seventeen hundred standard.

* * * *

Winner followed his own advice but was back on the bridge with the captain within the hour. "My compliments to you and your crew. The ship is a beauty."

"Thank you." van Gelden nodded, obviously pleased with the praise. He continued pulsing the steering thrusters, holding a course that would take them close to Vengeance without causing undo alarm. At best, it was a guess on his part where that boundary was. If Vengeance's crew were on their toes, a challenge would come.

They were close enough that visual flight rules applied. Winner watched the unfolding scene out of the forward port, standing to one side to give van

Gelden an unobstructed view. "Any suggestions or instructions?" asked the captain.

Winner turned. "Captain van Gelden, this is your ship. If I don't like the job you're doing, I can fire you. But I will not overrule you."

The captain nodded his acknowledgement.

The number of spacecraft on orbit around Saragosa added congestion and helped van Gelden maneuver quite close to Vengeance before they were noticed.

Five thousand meters out, the com blared. "Approaching ship hold position and identify yourself," the order terse, unyielding.

Van Gelden tripped the thrusters, stopped the ship and opened a com link; "This is the corvette Topsail. We are changing orbit to accommodate one of your frigates that needed our assigned slot."

"State your destination."

Van Gelden keyed the final position he needed to make good their escape. It was a gamble. If Vengeance suspected anything...

Derka handed the seated astrogator a data chip, and watched the display.

A weak interrogation signal appeared.

"Send the validation now." Derka's order carried a sense of urgency belying his calm demeanor.

The minutes ticked away. "Proceed. Remain on current heading. Do not approach any closer to Vengeance."

Van Gelden double keyed the com link.

"Whew. Close, but it worked."

A sense of relief swept the bridge.

"We're not out of it yet," Winner said.

Two hours later, maintaining course and speed, Topsail was five hundred thousand klicks from Bartok's fleet and just where it wanted to be. Maneuvering to place as many ships between them and Vengeance as possible, van Gelden prepared to engage the drive. "In one hour, we'll be in hyperspace."

"Where are the personnel slings for entering hyper-drive?" Winner asked.

Van Gelden smiled, "We've got a few surprises too. We don't need them. Gravity field generators keep everything inside where it belongs. Only the engine and cargo areas are isolated. State of the art. We may be the only ship with a system like this."

Winner turned to Derka. "With this, our fighters would have an advantage beyond anything in space. No one could maneuver with them. They'd be untouchable."

Derka nodded. "I'd love a good look at the equipment." He looked at van Gelden.

"Be my guest."

Derka clapped his hands in anticipation.

The intercom erupted, "Hyper drive generators engaged—hyperspace in eight minutes."

"Which direction, Mr. White? Our present course is on a direct line with Earth."

"Fine. Earth heading is just what we need," Winner responded. "Take us out far enough that we can safely make our first FTL transmission to Earth and then we'll find Galactic Star."

CHAPTER TEN
Topsail

Van Gelden settled into the captain's chair.

As Winner left the bridge the captain commented, "I'll maintain this course for five hours standard, and then come out to send your message."

Derka headed for the laboratory, Melissa following.

Winner noticed Derka and Melissa both paid a great deal of attention to what the other was doing.

He smiled and considered Derka's brains versus Melissa's muscle. It was easy to see why Derka was attracted to the woman. Even though their personalities were complete opposites, a relationship might work.

Five hours later, Winner took his chair on the bridge and handed van Gelden the coded message.

The captain kept his gaze fixed on the plot display. "There's an asteroid group close by. I want to use them for shielding when we can make the FTL transmission. We're still under way at three tenths c."

Winner touched the intercom. "Mr. Derka, how long will it take for a message to reach Earth?"

"The people who developed this technology could tell you," Derka replied, "but I won't know until we send the message. Or I should say until we get a response. I do have instruments rigged to give us a good approximation."

"Join us on the bridge when you're ready to transmit," Winner ordered.

"Aye, sir, in a few minutes."

Van Gelden maneuvered Topsail in position to transmit undetected by Bartok's fleet while the young scientist climbed through the hatch. Melissa joined them a few minutes later.

"Mr. Derka, operating command is yours to make the first FTL transmission," van Gelden said.

"Mr. White?" Derka looked his way expectantly.

Winner handed the young scientist the data disc he'd prepared earlier. "Remember gentlemen," Winner said solemnly, "Earth doesn't know Saragosa has been invaded. They don't know we're on the run. The last they heard we were holding the first election for a constitutional government. My message gives them the barest of details. Primarily, it asks for the location of Galactic Star."

"It'll come as one hell of a shock," said Derka. A smile crossed the young man's face as he considered his role as the first to transmit FTL from space. "I hope we don't blow a fuse."

It was a figure of speech; Topsail, like everything that used electrical energy, was equipped with multiple divergent heat sinks to handle a power overload.

"Captain, it might be best if you shut down all non-essential systems. This transmission is going to use an enormous amount of energy." Derka added, "Especially if I've screwed up on the calculations."

"I doubt that." Van Gelden issued instructions. "It's done."

Derka keyed the computer and sent the message.

A noticeable change occurred on the power console display, a clear indication of a power drain.

Pensively he said, "Earth. Normal transmission speeds, the speed of light, takes twelve weeks round trip. Hyperwave cuts that to three weeks each way. Now we wait to see what this gadget does for us."

Winner could only hope that his headquarters knew the precise location of Galactic Star. Logistically, Earth was beyond immediate help to Saragosa. It would take at least three months for any kind of transport to travel from Earth to Saragosa. Even if anyone on Earth wanted to help.

The four retired to the galley where the cook, who doubled as their med-tech, had prepared a light meal. No one could sleep.

Winner spent the time preparing a detail account of Saragosa's fall for White headquarters. He included detailed instructions on what they should do to prepare for any retaliation during his absence. He had no doubt Simone Anacrode would take an aggressive approach to local security. She would have to move quickly to assure White's creditors that the corporation had the financial and military resources to retake Saragosa. She'd have to pull in every favor to do it. Hers might be the hardest task of all.

He hoped some of the other conglomerates would recognize the threat Bartok represented. Some of them must have ships and probably troops within a few light years of White's location. But even if they could help, would they? The ship's captains would have to act on their own. Without FTL transmitters, they couldn't get approval from Earth in time to be of any use.

Three hours eighteen minutes later, the elated van Gelden gave the astrogator, who doubled as hyperwave communications operator, the coordinates of Galactic Star—just received from Earth.

* * * *

Two days later, the astrogator announced, "I have contact with Galactic Star."

Winner's pulse quickened. He turned to see Derka make a fist and thrust it skyward in elation.

"How long until rendezvous?" Winner pulled back from his thoughts of Hulk Hrndullka and the people of Saragosa.

"Ten hours standard. We'll have visual in nine hours. You can carry on some communication at this distance."

"Thank you," Winner responded. "Captain, would you join me in my cabin? I want to go over some things prior to docking. I'm looking forward to your meeting Captain Ashcroft."

"Mr. White," Derka spoke, "Would you mind if I transmitted the FTL engineering data to Star? They could get a device assembled before we get there. Assuming there's someone on board who can handle it."

"Go ahead."

Captain van Gelden ordered initial contact with Star and Derka transmitted the FTL data that would allow the big cruiser to build the required transmitter. Star responded FTL less than five hours later.

Derka looked surprised. "That took talent. They've got some very good people on that ship."

With the newly installed equipment in place, they were able to pinpoint the location of the battle cruiser, cutting hours off the normal time required for approach.

Topsail dropped out of hyperspace within five hundred thousand klicks of the cruiser. Van Gelden stated his thoughts aloud. "That will leave us plenty of time to shed the necessary delta v.

He gave little notice to Winner, Phalen and Melissa stepping onto the bridge.

Three hours later the captain pointed. "Mr. White, Galactic Star."

Winner stood in front of the seat he'd taken earlier and looked out the forward view port. Derka stood behind him. She was still over three thousand kilometers away, barely detectable to the eye—no more than a white dot silhouetted against the black star-studded sky.

Van Gelden walked from the astrogator plot screen and stood beside Winner. "We'll dock in thirty two minutes."

Winner had been through these sideboards dozens of times. He knew the three thousand tourists on board would be expecting full military honors. While the ceremonies were not his cup of tea, he said, "Let's get it over with." They were now at war and a show of force never hurt.

Star notified Topsail it would fly the CIC's flag when he came aboard. As the flagship of White fleet, a role scheduled three years earlier when partially converted from a heavy cruiser to a tourist ship, it would become the command center for the upcoming battle.

First things first. Three thousand passengers who paid to be tourists, not Marines, were onboard. Winner had to find some way to get them off and back to Earth safely and quickly.

Galactic Star's crew and passengers had known of the loss of Saragosa Prime less than a day.

He remembered the first time he prepared for a fight. The giant ship and crew had never seen combat. No one had any real appreciation for how she'd do. Would some unknown design flaw cut short their hopes? There would be a certain amount of anxiety among the crew. Were they ready? At heart, though, the Star was a warship and Winner suspected the crew had the same sense of pride he felt. Only he knew it would take more than pride.

Van Gelden ordered Topsail's gravity generators shut down, minimizing any interference with Star's artificial gravity field. The clamps secured Topsail and Winner felt the pull of gravity return as the corvette settled. As Topsail was only slightly higher but considerable wider and longer than a Marine attack shuttle, it had plenty of room in the huge landing bay.

Winner watched the external bay doors close, allowing the inner doors to open to the rest of the hanger. He waited as the shuttle positioned for passenger debarking, the honor guard lined up along the gangway.

"Incoming com from Galactic Star, Mr. White."

He listened to the message and laughed. Star wanted to bring a uniform on board for him to wear. Only then did he realize he was still in his jumpsuit. "Captain, hail them. I'll wear what I've got on." They'd have to take him as he was.

Van Gelden did have an admiral's ball cap he handed Winner, gold braid fixed to the visor.

Winner, Phalen, Melissa and the Topsail crew, watched as the honor guard marched up the gangway. Applause and cheers broke from the crowd. Winner stepped through Topsail's open hatch onto the gangway of Galactic Star. "Permission to come aboard."

"Permission granted. Welcome aboard Mr. White," Captain Ashcroft responded.

Winner returned the salute and handshake.

"I stand to your command." Ashcroft reintroduced his XO, Commander Davenport and the officer of the deck. He cleared his throat and quietly said, "Colonel Abduhl al Cadifh sent word he would not attend."

Winner did not look at Ashcroft, acutely aware Cadifh's snub, while an embarrassment, was directed at him and not the Captain.

Winner tugged at his admiral's ball cap then stepped onto Galactic Star. He stood next to Captain Ashcroft, Derka, Melissa and van Gelden lining up behind them. The anthem played over the ships speakers and the 'bosun' piped him aboard. Al Cadifh's spot at head of the Marine detachment was vacant.

The bay erupted with yells from the tourists lining the catwalk above the hanger deck. Not bound by tradition, they clapped and cheered 'beat the bastard' and 'give'em' hell.'

Winner's lips pressed tightly and he formed his fingers into a 'V' sign.

"I see they know about the invasion."

"Yes, Sir," Ashcroft replied. "And, when I told them they would transfer to other ships so Star could do its job, most cheered."

Galactic Star was the first deep space heavy cruiser commissioned by WMC. The giant starship was the most powerful ever launched by a single conglomerate. Although two conglomerates had battleships in space, their technology was considerably older and less effective. Star drive and weapons development somewhat paralleled the early computer age. Scientist churned out innovations faster than the engineers and factories could incorporate them.

But I don't know how a crew could withstand it." Derka no more than finished saying it when he jumped, turned to van Gelden and exclaimed, "Your artificial gravity generators. That's how you can access the Theta band." It almost sounded like an accusation.

Van Gelden laughed.

Derka continued, "Mr. White, if we could make that system work on Star, the speed would increase by a factor of two. Hull strength becomes the limiting concern."

"Formidable," van Gelden said, looking at Star. "Awesome destructive power."

Winner nodded. "Yes and we'll need every bit of it. Mr. Derka, make it your project to adapt Topsail's grav system to this cruiser."

Derka grinned back his acknowledgement, the order completely to his liking.

Knowing that underneath a coat of paint lay a ship of the line, a battle cruiser, the most destructive warship in space, Winner could feel his adrenaline pumping. That power thrilled him. It could destroy a planet from space with its energy weapons. And she'd be with him at Saragosa.

Bartok had twenty-two battle types, the largest, Vengeance, but he had nothing as powerful.

Still, one ship, no matter how powerful, couldn't defeat Bartok's entire fleet. Winner had to find a way to overcome his enemy's advantage.

Winner had converted Galactic Star to civilian use, his first order after becoming CEO. That was three years ago. Six years earlier, his father had ordered the construction of Star—a product of his intuition.

"Jane's Book of Space Ships says Galactic Star is the fastest passenger ship in the galaxy," Derka offered. Her hull could withstand much higher levels than the passengers could tolerate. Few deep space ships had the luxury of a battle cruiser's hyperwave drive. Most were physically smaller by half or more, and since the difference usually went to engines, the result was exponential. Galactic Star was three times faster than any passenger competitor. The drive added not only speed but also an abundance of inexpensive energy to power passenger luxuries available on no other liner. If this first cruise was any indication, she'd never space without full booking. The reserve engine power also allowed Galactic Star to retain all of her original armament. Some ammunition stores had given way to passenger's linens and towels, but the Star had retained enough to be effective.

First, though, Winner had to deal with Colonel al Cadifh.

CHAPTER ELEVEN
Galactic Star

Al Cadifh would come around. This was the fight the colonel had trained all his adult life for and he would trade his front seat in hell to be in it.

The order of things would be different now that Winner was aboard and he would let Ashcroft set the pace. The captain ruled the ship as captains had for over three thousand years. Obedience was the first order. The captain's word was law and final.

Winner reflected on Ashcroft's résumé. Graduated third from the Command Space Academy in a class of three hundred. Led the battle for Minns Station that brought it under White control. Distinguished himself defeating a superior force from Nimitz Crossing that ultimately led to its capture as well. Appointed Governor General of both locations. Winner hadn't forgotten that Ashcroft personally led the assault to free his wounded father, Michael White.

The ceremonies concluded, the captain led Winner through the Marine guard to a crew-only passageway. Paying passengers followed the civilian stewards off the catwalks. The Marine honor guard withdrew to the crew-only side of the ship.

As they continued toward the hatch, Winner said, "Captain, you set the protocols. Whatever you decide is fine with me. Use your own judgment." He recognized that certain disciplines helped maintain order on such a vessel. Years of seafaring and space flight had set most standards.

"Thank you, sir," Ashcroft said. "The crew considers it an honor and privilege to have you aboard. It's traditional, so, we'll fly your flag."

Ashcroft's command voice left no room for doubt. About the same height and build as Winner, his voice carried the weight twenty years of giving orders. His brown eyes showed the same intensity.

Galactic Star had made the transition to civilian use. However, Winner couldn't help but notice that little had changed in the crew's habits. They remained military. Behind the crew-only doors, it hadn't changed at all—The Star was a ship of the line.

"Your trip to Saragosa was your first time aboard?" asked Ashcroft.

"Captain, that trip was the first time I'd seen Star."

Lord, he was proud of this ship and sensed the crew was also. He stopped for a moment to take in the surroundings. "This bay could handle at least ten shuttles at once," Winner remarked. The area was relatively quiet considering the number of people and activity as crew and passengers alike prepared for hyperspace.

"Three bays, each ninety meters wide, one hundred deep and a clear span of thirty meters," Ashcroft's arm swept the cavern. The catwalk, minutes before, holding excited tourists, ran the entire perimeter except through the door opening, with cranes suspended overhead at least ten meters high. Passageways opened along the catwalk leading to where Winner had no idea. In time, he would become familiar with the big ship. Now he could just be amazed.

As he watched, crewmen moved through the ship. The paint that three years earlier gave way to assorted pastels on bulkheads, walls to the passengers, was in-turn being replaced by navy gray and yellow caution paints. The Captain was wasting no time returning the ship to battle readiness.

"You're right. Ten civilian or six armored Marine shuttles," a new voice remarked.

Both men turned to see Colonel al Cadifh exit the bay through another hatch. The marine commandant had attended the ceremonies, just not at the head of his command. Neither said anything.

They made their way through the restricted opening and walked into a different world. Doors swished open and they stepped into the gravlift that quickly deposited them near the operations room, six decks above. Navy grey dominated the area along with the multiple color schemes identifying every conduit or pipe. No acoustical tiles hid the stacks of plumbing and electrical systems that ran along the overhead. Black and yellow-striped handholds dotted the bulkheads—clear evidence that at some time it would be without its artificial gravity.

Winner held his silence. He wanted nothing to delay the Captain from getting under way.

"Your quarters are next to mine, just behind the bridge," Ashcroft said. "Lieutenant Graves, Mr. Derka and Captain van Gelden have billets in the officer's area." He gestured up one passageway. "This way."

The Marine guard preceded them quietly clearing the way.

When they reached his cabin, Winner stopped short, startled.

A Marine in traditional dress blues, a stun pistol side arm strapped at her waist, rendered a hand salute. Her right shoulder sported the gold braid of the CIC's aide.

Winner returned the salute.

He knew a fight was coming—this Marine had Melissa's spot. More than that, this was an obvious breech of protocol and etiquette. Standards require a commissioned officer as his aide-de-camp and she would never serve as a guard.

"Sir. Corporal Marie Sampson," her soprano voice was quiet but firm.

"As you were, Corporal."

She returned to parade rest.

Al Cadifh was obviously pushing for a fight. He'd get one.

"What are your orders and who assigned you?"

Corporal Sampson snapped to attention. "Colonel al Cadifh, Sir. I am to be both your aide and orderly."

"Thank you. Carry on." He gave no outward appearance, but he knew all hell was about to break loose in Marine country. Someone had screwed up by the numbers and he had no doubt it was intentional. He didn't know the precise details governing these selections, but he was sure it wasn't the prerogative of the Marine commandant to make such an appointment without consulting the boss. Hell, even prudence made that obvious. The look he threw at Ashcroft didn't hide his irritation. But he also knew Ashcroft would conveniently not know how the matter was resolved. This was a Marine problem.

Sampson opened the hatch and moved aside, allowing Winner to step into his cabin.

Ashcroft followed. "Lieutenant Graves automatically came under the command of Colonel al Cadifh when she came aboard Galactic Star," Ashcroft said. "I suspect the Colonel used that as his authority."

Winner nodded.

He looked around taking it all in. The cabin was big enough to double as a living room. Beyond that, he could see a bedroom and a small mess area off to the right side. The bulkheads were barren, cold, no portholes, but it more than met his needs.

Ashcroft broke the silence. "I trust you're satisfied with the accommodations."

"They're satisfactory. How did you come up with this so quickly?"

"Usually this area serves as break room for the bridge crew. That function has been temporarily moved to the mess hall across the passageway."

"And in the few hours you had to prepare for my arrival you managed to convert," he said gesturing with his hand, "to this."

"Yes, sir." There was no hesitation.

"It stays only if you assure me no personnel have been indisposed as a result of the change."

That brought a laugh from Ashcroft. "Mr. White you have my word on that. I also might point out if I said anything else the crew would probably mutiny. As of a few minutes ago, Galactic Star carries your flag. We are now the envy of the fleet. Rest assured, this crew would not tolerate being denied the status that they personally derive from such an honor."

Winner accepted the remarks although his thoughts were of al Cadifh. The differing responses from the crew and the Colonel meant the Marine had some personal problem with Winner—probably with Winner's move from SEAL commander to CEO of WMC. He damned sure didn't want the problem but he'd deal with it. The warrior in him said if he needed to, he would kick some ass. The CEO in him reminded him he needed al Cadifh and hoped there was some way to handle this without further rupture.

Ashcroft interrupted his thoughts. "At your convenience, there will be a reception to present my command staff to you. In the meantime, I'll be on the bridge, Mr. White." He rose to leave.

"Fine. But, just a minute, close the hatch please." Winner assumed a casual stance until Ashcroft complied with his request. "I know when we're outside this room a certain standard must be maintained. However, when we're alone, I'm Winner and you're Fenn—unless you prefer another name."

"Works for me," Ashcroft came back with his easy and ready smile, but it still sounded like an order.

"Another matter. At the reception, I plan to reinstate you as Admiral and give you overall command of our naval forces. I will draft the plan of battle for the assault on Saragosa. Your official office will be Admiral-of-the-fleet. Get me the names of everyone affected by this. I assume you will recommend your XO for Captain and so on. Com me your list. Once I've approved it, you can notify your people."

"Thank you, Mr. White…Winner," a beaming Ashcroft responded.

"Now, Colonel al Cadifh. What's his problem?"

"I don't know, sir. He sent an aide just before your arrival telling me he had voluntarily absented himself."

Winner nodded. He walked into the bedroom as Ashcroft left for the bridge.

Someone had been very busy. A full range of uniforms hung in the closet. He rummaged through, found the khaki slacks, shirt and brown shoes that were standard officer fare and changed out of the jump suit.

He moved to the hatch, opened it. "Corporal, summon Colonel al Cadifh. Have him report here in person, at his earliest convenience."

CHAPTER TWELVE
Establishing command

Winner looked around at the cabin's bulkheads. They were almost as barren as what he had to bring to the fight. Just three thousand Marines scattered all over the universe remained under his command. Then there was the Federation of Aligned Planets, but it offered a token police force that stayed only in friendly places and was kept intentionally weak so it would be no threat to any of the six conglomerates.

Two hours later the hatch buzzer sounded and Winner laid down the status reports he been studying. Staying seated he ordered the computer to open the hatch.

A khaki-clad Marine stepped into the cabin. A deep resonating sound boomed, "Colonel al Cadifh, Commander, First Marine Brigade, Lancers." His voice bounced off the bulkheads; the ebony face looked as if it had never issued a smile.

The colonel came to attention directly in front of the seated CIC. Piercing eyes stared at some imaginary spot. He seemed chiseled from a two-meter obsidian block, his desert lineage hovered like a specter. The blackness of his eyes blocked any effort to see inside.

Winner didn't doubt he faced a resolute man, but, just by showing up, al Cadifh had already lost the first round.

Colonel Abduhl Mohammed Sarif al Cadifh, born into an ancient Berber tribe in North Africa, stood silent.

Winner let him stand for a moment.

He wondered if the man focused on what he saw as duty or something sinister. Actually, he wanted to tear into the man. It was a struggle for his CIC persona to maintain control and assert itself. This was the combativeness and natural competitiveness in him.

At eighteen, al Cadifh had enlisted in the North African Counter-Insurgency Command, part of the now-defunct United Nations. His battle skills and mental agility quickly brought him to the attention of his leaders. Sent to the command school for formal education, he graduated at the top of his class. When given the choice of returning to North Africa or Officer Candidate School, he chose OCS. Second in his class, he came to White's Marines where he quickly scaled the ranks to colonel.

Al Cadifh's responsibility included the portion of space outward from Sol to the Galon sector. To counteract an increase in piracy, his troops boarded Galactic Star, or any other outbound tourist or merchant ship just before it entered hyperspace from Sol's orbit.

Winner hid his anger as he stood. "At ease colonel." He extended his hand. "Glad to have you aboard. We need to get better acquainted. Please be seated."

Al Cadifh ignored the hand and remained standing.

Winner had to remind himself the retaking of Saragosa was the real issue. He couldn't let personal insult interfere with the objective. Yet, he had to establish who was in command. Allowing al Cadifh to ignore orders was simply out of the question. Al Cadifh would lead the ground assault regardless of his personal thoughts about Winner White. There wasn't anyone else with the experience to do it—at least not within a dozen parsecs.

Winner put an edge to his voice and motioned toward a chair. "Sit down, Colonel. That's an order."

The Colonel sat.

Winner had won the second round. He pulled a form chair directly in front of the Marine. Still standing he said, "We can make this easy or just as tough as you want."

He waited.

The Colonel didn't finch, still at rigid attention. But he had taken the chair. There was no doubt the absent honors when Topsail docked was intentional. Winner decided not to make an issue of it. Often times, you could tell by the sir what kind of Marine you were dealing with. The absence of it said a lot as well. Al Cadifh's record showed career and Marine embedded beyond any attempt by him to change it—not that he wanted to.

Realizing it was going to take some effort to break through to this guy, Winner sat. "We need to discuss a few things: first, the mission, possible troop strength and later tactics."

The Colonel sat unmoving. Winner couldn't tell if he was waiting for him to continue or for an order to talk.

"What's wrong Colonel? Do you have a problem with that? Why do I have the distinct feeling you're withholding something?"

"Do I have permission to speak freely, sir?" al Cadifh used sir for the first time.

"Of course. Gaudamit man, that's all I've wanted since you came in here."

"Mr. White," the colonel didn't hesitate, "As a Marine I don't like taking combat orders from a junior officer, SEAL of not. You got where you are by birth—someone handed you your rank. I don't see that it gives you the credentials to lead a fighting force. I want my people to have the best chance to come out alive and this command structure doesn't give us that."

"In your opinion." Winner leaned back from Cadifh, rocked his chair on its back legs. He wasn't about to let this man intimidate him. "Colonel, you haven't been told what the command structure is to be."

"You have my resignation if you want it."

That was the break Winner had sought. Al Cadifh didn't want out. He probably held a legitimate concern for his troops. But the real problem was his personal nose was bent out of place and getting in the way of his Marine nose. A long time ago Winner's father had told him he'd face the issue of being born to the manor, everything handed to him. He knew how to deal with this.

Winner thought over what he wanted to say. It was so clear in his mind. Fuck you Colonel. If you think for one goddammed minute, I'm going to let you intimidate me, you couldn't be more wrong. You will follow my orders or face a firing squad. And don't give me that shit about a Marine having to take orders from an inferior. What you really mean is you think you're too damned good to take orders from me.

But he needed the man's experience and leadership skills. The Marines would follow al Cadifh unfailingly. Having thought through his instinctual reaction, Winner felt better. Still, this man had to be willing to take orders and from him. As much as he needed him, al Cadifh had to submit or go.

"Colonel, you have a decision to make."

"I can stay or resign. If I resign, I'm under-house arrest until the war is over."

"You know the rules. I can't have a reluctant or recalcitrant commander. If you stay, it has to be without any reservations. You must accept civilian authority."

He smiled. "I sign the fucking checks. And, Colonel, I earned every military commission I ever had, just like I did my test pilot rating. Yes, I became CEO because of my birth. I can't help that and I don't apologize. I don't deny that who I am may influence some people, but if you think I'm going to crawl in some hole and hide because you resent me, then maybe you're not the man for the job. Frankly, I'm surprised you've put your career on the line by saying so. The fact that you're here is all that's saving your self-righteous ass."

Winner hadn't overstated it either. It took a lot of balls to confront him as he had. Al Cadifh was the kind of man he'd want next to him in a foxhole.

"If I stay?"

"We put this aside. If, after we're through at Saragosa, you want to pick it up again, you're free to do so."

Al Cadifh remained seated. He hadn't moved anything but his jaw since entering and taking the chair. Winner couldn't even see him breathe, he never got excited and spoke his mind.

Winner waited what seemed a long time. In reality, it was less than a minute, and then he pushed.

"Well, what will it be?" He moved his chair in front of the Colonel, feet spread, arms at his sides, relaxed, waiting.

Al Cadifh moved ever so slightly for the first time. "I would like to command the troops," he said. "I will follow your orders."

"Good." Winner continued, "I've reinstated Mister Ashcroft to flag command as Admiral of the Fleet and Chief of Military Operations. Your orders will come from him."

With that, al Cadifh clearly relaxed. "It would seem I was premature with my concerns. I have no problem following Captain . . . Admiral Ashcroft."

"Understand," said Winner, "Civilian rule is the order here. Not military."

"Yes, Sir. I accept that. May I ask the nature of our assignment?" Still, some tension tinged the question.

It was bullshit and Winner knew it. Al Cadifh was going to make him spell it out. "Ten days ago, standard, Zed Bartok's forces invaded Saragosa Prime and overran it. We're going to take it back. You're going to lead the invasion.

"At this point, I can't tell you how many people have died. We have no military organization remaining on Saragosa and damned little organized presence of any kind. Success or failure is entirely in our hands."

He waited for some response.

Al Cadifh, unyielding, seemed as hard, cold and barren as the steel bulkheads. He remained motionless. No expression came from his face or eyes.

Finally, Winner continued, "How many men do you have?"

"Aboard Galactic Star, one hundred Marines; mostly light combat armament. The 1st and 3rd battalions, nine hundred fully armed Marines are on two troop transport ships, the Adaval and Zachary. We are equipped to make a space-borne assault and sustain ourselves dirt-side for two to three weeks." His voice echoed around the room.

"One thousand against Bartok's four thousand. And we don't have three months to wait for more transports to arrive from Earth. Maybe five hundred security personnel from Nimitz Crossing are available to us. Plus what ever we can line up and arm on Saragosa. If we can get munitions to them, we should be able to pick as many as we want, but they're not trained combat fighters. We do have some allies who may help with troops or ships if they have any in the Galon Sector."

Winner walked to the small galley, poured himself a cup of coffee. He gestured the carafe toward al Cadifh and got no reaction so he set it on the only table. "I don't know when we'll hear from Saragosa. It's hit and miss at best. We do need all the information we can lay our hands on."

For the first time, the colonel seemed interested. "If I could suggest," he said his voice firm, "we can rendezvous with Zachary and Adaval, put the tourists on those two ships and bring my Marines aboard Star."

"Makes sense. Work it out with Admiral Ashcroft." Winner stifled a grin. It was exactly what Winner was thinking. And al Cadifh had called them his Marines.

The colonel added, "For what it's worth, ninety tourist have enlisted."

That brought a welcome grin to Winner's face but al Cadifh showed no emotion.

"Can you train them in time to do any good?"

"Not for fighting. But there's plenty of non-combat work. We'll make good use of them."

Winner leaned forward in the chair. "We're at least three weeks away from our attack. Maybe longer. I imagine tactical projections may change a number of times as we gather additional resources and information. You'll get everything we have on Saragosa—maps, whatever we can lay our hands on. In the meantime, we're getting everything we can on Bartok—his strengths and weaknesses." Winner tried to project a casual attitude, wanting to get a similar response.

Al Cadifh asked, "Is there anyone on the planet I can talk to?"

"Vladislov Hrndullka, Governor General. His people call him Hulk." Winner stressed the Hulk hoping al Cadifh might realize Winner didn't interfere in how a leader handled his people. "Radio contact is difficult—we have to listen all the time. Hulk will transmit when he can. What people we have there are operating under the most severe conditions. Anyone drawing attention courts instant death. Street executions are routine. Everything our people accomplish comes at great risk and all too often at a greater price."

"What about Colonel Ziron?"

"Did you know him?"

"He served under my command on a number of occasions."

"The colonel was captured and executed. A squad he'd pulled together defended the government office building. Two hundred soldiers attacked against his six. He took seventy of the enemy with him. Bartok's men were not kind. They hung him upside down from the front gate, stripped and shot him. His sacrifice bought me and a few others the time we needed to escape. Bartok's troops made a vid chip and circulated it."

Winner thought al Cadifh had looked hard-bitten when he first entered the cabin. Like obsidian, he recalled. Now, a resolute killer stared back at him. He looked into the man's eyes and saw the soul of Abduhl al Cadifh. If the colonel had his way, someone would pay dearly for Ziron's humiliation. Although they'd not resolved their personal differences, the situation was improving. And he was glad the man was on their side.

"Thank you," was all the colonel said. He hadn't moved so much as a hair since sitting.

Winner broke the strange silence that permeated the room. "I'm having an informal officers' call to present the rank and command changes. Mr. Davenport will be promoted to Captain and command Galactic Star. You should plan to attend. Admiral Ashcroft will be responsible for prosecuting the war and getting additional resources. I will assist him in that.

"Also, I'm forming a war council, consisting of the Admiral, the XO, Captain van Gelden, Phalen Derka, you and me. We'll meet each morning at ten hundred here in my quarters."

Winner decided to wash the rest of the dirty linen. "We have another matter to resolve—my orderly." He didn't give al Cadifh a chance to respond. "First, I don't want one. Secondly, as things stand, Lieutenant Graves will suffer unnecessary embarrassment with Corporal Sampson taking her place. If I replace Sampson, she'll be the one embarrassed. You've put me in an uncomfortable position."

Al Cadifh remained transfixed.

"Well? Are you going to sit there like a fettered goat?" Winner had delivered the Berbers' strongest challenge that didn't require a fight response.

Then the colonel moved as if someone had thumped him between the eyes. "WMC policy requires you to have an aide, for security primarily. Marine regulations state your rank rates an orderly. I combined the two jobs. Marine regulations clearly state I acted within my authority."

Winner doubted this had anything to do with regulations. There was more to it.

"Have you talked with, Melissa—Lieutenant Graves?"

"Yes. She's a Marine. She'll do as ordered unless—"

Winner didn't let al Cadifh finish. "Colonel, I don't like the situation at all. You need to find some way to remove this stigma from Lieutenant Graves."

Al Cadifh had returned to his riveted position. Winner noticed a bead of sweat on his brow.

"Is there something you want to tell me?"

"Yes, Sir. The two Marines are settling it as we speak."

Winner's head whipped up. "Fighting?"

Al Cadifh nodded.

Winner pushed back a moan. "Colonel, a commissioned officer fighting an enlisted person. What a fucking mess! That's a court-martial offense for both of them."

"Only if we pursue it. And besides, it wouldn't be the first time an enlisted and officer fought."

He suspected al Cadifh was referring to fights Winner had while a Marine— there were more than a few.

Al Cadifh's back seemed to become even more rigid. "I'm not supposed to know about it and certainly you aren't either. There will be a volunteer as your aide/orderly and that will be the winner." The bead of perspiration continued its trek, now down to his chin.

Winner, now standing, rolled forward on his toes, "What do you suggest, Colonel?"

With the question, his ebony exterior seemed to relax somewhat. "With your permission, sir, no fight is occurring unless we notice it."

It was too late to stop it and Winner had a strong feeling Melissa would win. Her Farside combat training almost assured that. "Okay, I'll see you after the fight," he stopped, "after the volunteer is known. This conversation never took place."

Winner was sure an audible sigh escaped the colonel's lips and the stony glaze that had permeated the Marine's face relaxed. He stood, "Yes, sir. Thank you. With your permission."

"Colonel, if there's anything I can do or provide you to help win this war, don't hesitate to ask."

"Thank you, sir."

Al Cadifh saluted, opened the hatch and disappeared into the passageway.

Winner returned the salute and said "Semper fi, Marine," before it closed.

He wondered if he'd done the right thing.

CHAPTER THIRTEEN
Know your friends

Winner was satisfied the colonel would follow orders. The battle for Saragosa was one fight the Marine wouldn't miss. Still, he hoped he and his troop commander could get along. At least for the time being, they were on the same side.

The com sounded. Davenport's voice shoved the thirty minutes with al Cadifh into the background. "We'll enter hyperspace at zero two hundred."

Winner hit the button. "I'll be awake."

"It's your stomach," retaliated the captain. The change of command had gone without a hitch.

At zero nine hundred, a knock sounded on Winner's door. He laid aside the orders-of-the-day, "Yes?"

"Colonel al Cadifh, sir, with your Aide-de-Camp." No emotion emerged from the colonel's chiseled face as he motioned toward the hatch.

Melissa step through the opening, dressed out in full Marine blues, gold braid circling her right shoulder. Her presence said she had won the fight. Her smirk told him it was a walk.

Coming to full attention, she saluted. "Lieutenant Melissa Graves reporting for duty as ordered, sir."

Colonel al-Cadifh excused himself and left the cabin.

Winner acknowledged Melissa with a nod. "Lieutenant, welcome aboard. Colonel al Cadifh couldn't have picked better. He's to be commended."

Normally, a CIC would rate a full Space Corps Captain as aide, but there were none on board other than Davenport. This really worked out the best for everyone. Winner was comfortable with her anyhow.

He stood and walked to the where the Melissa stood at attention. He clasped his hands behind his back. "Where did you get that shiner?"

She grinned again. "With your permission, sir, I'd rather not say."

Winner responded, "On one condition, tell me what does the other guy looks like."

"See for yourself, sir." Melissa opened the hatch and said, "Meet the Marine detached as your armed security. She will lead a squad of six who will see to your personal safety. Post, Marine."

Ducking down to clear the hatch and visor cap in place, Winner couldn't see the Marine's face. "Sir." She struggled to speak through puffed lips—her eyes didn't look good, both black. "Corporal Marie Sampson reporting for duty, sir."

Winner ignored the obvious and asked, "Whose idea was this?"

"Mine, sir." Melissa answered matter-of-factly. "Just doing my job as aide."

"You know Marine," he stepped close to Melissa again but kept his voice loud enough for Sampson to hear, "One of these days you're not going to have regulations, policy or whatever you quote with regularity to fall back on and I'm going to kick your butt."

"Yes, sir," she said stifling a grin. "If that's all, sir, by your leave."

"Dismissed," Winner said.

As Melissa cleared the hatch she looked back, the grin spread across her face, "Just let me know when you want to try, sir."

* * * *

Shortly before zero two hundred, Winner strapped himself into the web harness next to his bunk.

"Thirty seconds to hyperspace insertion," a voice calmly announced over the intercom.

Most people would be in bed. Nausea was much less a problem if you were asleep.

Winner grabbed the handhold directly in front of him and concentrated on it as the whine of the hyper drive reached the selected speed. He didn't close his eyes. He wanted to experience the full sensation of entering hyperspace on a ship the size of Star.

Captain Davenport's voice came back on the intercom. "In ten hours we re-enter normal space to check our position. It takes the astrogator about fifteen minutes to verify coordinates, make course corrections, and then jump back into hyperspace. Contact with the troop transports Adaval and Zachary in fourteen standard days."

Winner keyed the switch off and went to sleep, satisfied that the day had gone very well.

The routine quickly settled in to a ten-hour cycle. Winner gave Melissa the small medical packet sickbay issued to deal with space sickness and jet lag.

"I'll give it to Derka," the lieutenant said.

The rendezvous with the two troop transports, getting the passengers out of harm's way and Marines aboard was the priority.

On the third day, Winner joined the passengers and crew in ship wide safety drills to cover emergencies that might arise. Without enough escape pods to handle all the passengers, most of the effort went into damage control and how to avoid being a casualty.

Each passenger received a vac-skin suit, backpack and helmet or an assignment to an escape pod. If there was a fight and a hull breach with loss of atmosphere, the passengers at least stood some chance of surviving. Remarkably, the tourists seemed eager to experience the combat preparations, although in reality, the danger was so remote as to be negligible. Most understood Star would avoid a fight while they were aboard but the slim chance added excitement among them and morale remained high.

All messages were now preceded with the 'boson's' whistle, adding another level of proof that Star was again a ship of the line.

Winner waited for the piping to conclude. "Now hear this; The Captain will now address ships company and passengers."

Davenport's voice came over the intercom, "Secure from safety drill. Congratulations on successfully completing the safety drills. You'd all make good spacers." The com went silent.

Winner spent his spare time, and there was plenty of that, learning his way around the ship. Melissa led him down a maintenance ladder to the Marines training gym one deck below the main hanger. Cargo nets slung along the bulkheads held the material previously stored on the deck, opening a good-sized area.

Casually, she said, "Sir, I thought if you wanted to get a little Farside rehash in, we could do it here."

A grin passed Winner's face quickly replaced with a serious glare. "Good idea Lieutenant." He paused, "This isn't an effort to prove you can kick my butt is it? If it is, you've made your first serious mistake." That brought no answer.

"You can change in there." She pointed to a men's room. "There are sweats for you."

One hour later, the session ended. He and Melissa both nursed muscles that had been bent, twisted and generally abused. The guard took his station at the cabin hatch.

Winner stopped part way through the opening. A Marine stood in the middle of the room at attention.

"Who are you?"

"Sergeant David Overstreet, sir. I'm your orderly."

Fresh khakis lay at the foot of Winner's bed along with toilet articles.

Winner finished his entry through the hatch and stood looking at the Marine, not sure of what to make of all this attention. Was someone trying to make him look pompous? "Thank you Sergeant. That will be all. Dismissed."

Overstreet saluted and left without a word.

As was her custom, Melissa briefly discussed the next day's activities—neither had mentioned the workout.

"Who assigned him?" He pointed toward the departed orderly.

"I did. As your aide, I've been given total responsibility to see to your security and well-being."

"Don't you think you're overdoing it?" His fisted hands jammed to his hips.

"No, sir. Regulations clearly state what honors and staff you're to be provided and what you're not to have. I'm just implementing company/Marine policy and protocol."

"Remind me to give you a hard time over this."

"Yes, sir." Her tone suggested she was not particularly amused with his response.

Winner closed the hatch after his aide had completed her chores, stripped and entered the shower. He stretched; his tired muscles indicated tomorrow they'd be sore. A few minutes later, he emerged from the ionized warm air dryer, put on the clothes laid out, brushed his hair, headed for the bridge mess hall and coffee. He opened the hatch and the Marine on duty snapped to attention. "As you were," he said and entered the passageway.

"Good morning, sir," Derka said long lanky strides carrying him up the passageway. "Good timing," he added. "I've got someone I want you to meet."

Winner nodded and motioned him ahead. He trailed him into the mess hall, stopped at the coffee urn. Derka waited as he filled his cup. Cup in hand, Winner followed the young scientist toward a table in the corner, the guard a step behind.

Absolutely the most gorgeous woman he'd ever seen was seated ahead of them. He couldn't imagine Phalen working with someone that attractive and not saying something. Must be Melissa's influence. Winner hoped she was their destination.

She was.

The woman was young—early thirties he guessed.

She turned toward him, her smile captivating, sparkling blue eyes and jet-black hair adding to the allure.

Phalen stopped next to her and said, "Dr. Celia Markham, the boss, Winner White."

Winner watched in surprise as her cream-colored skin drained ashen. Her smile faded into a grimace. The lines of laughter that touched the corners of her eyes vanished.

"Oh." Then Celia stood, turned, and left without another word.

Phalen looked pallid. He stammered, "I—Mr. White I don't know what happened," he blurted. It wasn't unusual to see Phalen without words where women were concerned but this went far beyond the ordinary.

Winner stood looking after the woman. "It's obvious she doesn't want anything to do with me." Trying to make the best of a difficult situation he asked, "Why did you want me to meet her? Is she special to you?" He motioned Phalen to a chair.

The young man groped for a seat, clearly flustered and hurt.

Winner's guard retreated further from the conversation.

Winner took a sip of his coffee as Admiral Ashcroft walked up. "She sure stormed off. Problem?"

"It would seem so," answered Winner. "Won't you join us?" he motioned the Admiral to a chair.

"Derka introduced us and that was all it took. I got a look that would chill nitrogen." He didn't mention that she was the most gorgeous creature he'd seen.

"That bad? Who is she?" Ashcroft asked.

Winner turned to Derka. At that moment, the man didn't look like a scientist. Winner couldn't tell if his friend's reaction came from anger or embarrassment and he didn't push the young man.

"She worked with me on reverse engineering Topsail's artificial gravity device. Also, she was instrumental in assembling the FTL transmitter for Galactic Star. Brilliant mind."

Derka shook his head. "I'm sorry Mr. White. I don't know what happened. I don't know why she acted that way. "I don't—"

"Forget it," Winner admonished. "You're not responsible for her. If you can find out why I upset her, maybe I can set it right."

"Yes, sir," Derka distantly responded. "Thank you." He excused himself and left the mess hall.

Ashcroft changed the subject. "Mr. White, any time you want to come to the bridge feel free to do so. Captain Davenport has prepared a chair for you."

"Thanks. I'd like that. And I'll make it a point to stay out from under foot."

Leaning close Ashcroft said, "We've got a problem you should know about. Let's step into my cabin."

CHAPTER FOURTEEN
Tragedy continues

Ashcroft's cabin bulkheads were well appointed with certificates and awards, but mostly pictures of his Marine son. This was also his office—about what Winner had expected since it had been Fenn's home for the last four years. One was a citation issued by the defunct United Nations citing him for saving lives in a daring space rescue. Four soft-backed chairs sat in front of the large wooden desk and belied Ashcroft's penchant for conformity. The Admiral's excused his aide and poured coffee, then took a chair, ignoring his desk seat and invited Winner to another.

Ashcroft sipped his brew, then said, "I need to bring you up to speed. Someone on board tried to copy the FTL specs we received from Earth. We're looking into it but doubt we stand much of a chance to find who's responsible. Security's doing a person-by-person analysis of every passenger, crewmember and Marine. It's a precaution, just in case the priority-ticketing people missed something."

Winner listened without comment.

"We detected a tight beam transmission just after the attempt—a burst message from a rogue transmitter somewhere on board. We don't know what it contained or the exact destination coordinates although we're reasonably sure it was somewhere on Saragosa Prime. We've expanded our search to include the transmitter. And of course, we'll make every effort to not intrude unnecessarily on anyone's privacy."

"It's your ship, Fenn. And Davenport's," Winner added.

"The investigation started before we entered hyperspace."

"Do you expect trouble?"

"No one in their right mind will attack us. But we're ready in any case, at least with some of our laser and energy weapons," Ashcroft answered. "The passengers don't know but we've taken extra precautions to ensure their safety."

He paused for a minute and Winner waited.

"We'll be dropping out of hyperspace in four hours and I'd like for you to be on the bridge. I've got something to show you."

Winner welcomed the invitation. "This will be my first time on a cruiser's bridge. With your permission, I'd like to familiarize myself with bridge procedures."

He'd made it a point to stay away until invited leaving no doubt the Admiral had complete control.

"The crew would like that," Ashcroft responded.

"Do you need to move my quarters to accommodate Davenport's new job?" Winner asked.

"Captain Davenport has decided nothing's to change."

Neither man said anything as they leisurely finished their coffee. It was the first quiet time they'd shared.

Winner departed soon after, even more satisfied the ship was in competent hands.

* * * *

At fifteen hundred hours, Winner walked onto the bridge and instantly spotted the chair the crew had prepared for him. Ashcroft and Davenport were already busy at the astroplot.

"CIC on the bridge," the watch barked.

Winner took his seat between the two entry hatches, a high backed well-padded armchair with CIC emblazoned on the back.

Set to the rear of the bridge on admiral's land, it offered a clear view of the video plot-screens, both long and short range tactical, communications and navigation stations. Ashcroft's chair was immediately to his right and Davenport's centered on the bridge to the right.

A small two square-meter reinforced clearplast viewport to the front of the bridge that gave most of the bridge crew a small but unrestricted view ahead. A row of portholes dotted each the side of the vessel, their blast shields in the raised position. The OD's console, directly in front of the XO, displayed on command any information concerning the ship's condition.

Immediately to the XO's right, a recessed alcove housed the astrogator with central computer command and control, in reality, the pilot. Powerful synaptic computers executed his commands. Forward and to the XO's left was the weapons station, manned for the first time in three years.

The astrogator's area, set in an alcove, bathed in red light. The rest of the bridge was saturated with a subdued indirect white.

The communications officer sat next to the astrogator and had access to the plot screen along with the OD. An auxiliary engineering station remained unmanned.

Three hatches entered on the bridge. One led directly to Ashcroft's quarters. Marine guards flanked the two hatches that gave access to the rest of the ship. There was ample room for the bridge crew to move around unimpeded. It wasn't spacious, but big enough for each crewmember to work in relative comfort.

Winner watched the crew's quiet efficiency for over an hour. His sense of pride, never far distant where Galactic Star was concerned, swelled.

"Can your stomach cope with standing as we come out of hyperspace?" asked Ashcroft.

"I believe so." Winner had purposely delayed eating—it gave any prolonged nausea less to work with. He likened it to eating after your worst drunk

"Good. I've something to show you. When the OD tells you, join us at the astroplot display."

A few minutes later, the OD nodded and Winner joined them. He maintained a steady grip on the support stanchion as Star emerged from hyperspace. The world twisted and turned around him. Returning to normal space felt harder than entering hyperspace. But it only seemed that way. Some people got over it quicker than others. Winner, with the fortitude that made him an excellent test pilot, was one of the more fortunate. His queasiness dissipated quickly.

Davenport pointed at the plot. "See that"?

"See what?" Winner asked. "I don't know what I'm looking for."

"Of course," answered Ashcroft. "Just the reaction our visitor hoped for. People have a way of seeing what they're used to seeing. We've got a tag-along."

"Replay the re-entry," Davenport quietly ordered. He placed his finger on the plot board.

Winner leaned over as the data displayed. A faint light came on the screen among the hundreds of blips already displayed, then disappeared.

"That's it?" Winner asked.

"Yes," answered Ashcroft. "We've got the best man in the fleet on the console," he tapped the crewman on the shoulder. "Good work. Damned good work, Weims."

"We've been watching this bogie for two days. He alternates coming out of hyperspace seconds before we do and then seconds after. He stays about half a million klicks ahead, or behind and about the same off to starboard. He never shows up in the same place twice. It's taken us this long, two days, to get a passive fix on him. Like clockwork, he's been there every ten hours."

"Passive? He doesn't know we've spotted him?" Winner asked.

"No," responded Ashcroft.

"Why the blip?" asked Winner.

"Probably takes a few microseconds for him to shut down systems with detectable radiations," the operator answered.

"Incoming message for Mr. White," the communications officer said. Then added, "It's a tight beam burst transmission."

The OD added, "Sir, you can take it here with or without the headphones or I can pipe it to your quarters."

"In my quarters," Winner responded and headed for the hatch.

As he stepped through the bridge hatchway, the Marine sentry called, "CIC off the bridge."

Winner walked the thirty meters, entered his quarters, and ordered the computer to play the message.

"Winner?" Strain laced Vladislov Hrndullka's voice.

Winner girded himself for more bad news.

The vidcom continued voice only. "This message will be short and without video to minimize detection. This transmitter is all we've been able to get our hands on, and only hope you receive it. We know Galactic Star is your destination. We just don't know where the ship is."

"Winner," Hulks voice seemed strained and tired, "Marine Lance Corporal Damon Ashcroft was killed shortly after you left. He died defending some civilians who had taken refuge in a cellar. They'd hidden their children there and returned to feed them. All of them died. It's my understanding his father commands Galactic Star. I thought you needed to know." A weary sigh crossed space.

"Bartok controls the cities, mines and processing plants. We have the countryside although all bridges and Saragosa Road are his. He has limited numbers of troops and the countryside may be more than the invaders can handle. We'll make sure it is. We've managed to secure some weapons and with a little luck, we'll get more. Sorry to report no further information on Daker Smithe. Will transmit as circumstances permit. Contact frequency as we agreed. Transmit any time. We'll be listening. God speed. Hulk."

Winner dropped like a rock into a chair and replayed the message. Lord, he felt bad about Fenn's son. The mention of Daker Smithe meant they still hadn't found his mother. But then, neither had Bartok.

He had to tell Fenn immediately. He stared back at the logo on the screen, banged his fist on the chair arm. The company had become too lax in maintaining an honest guard for its people and it was his responsibility. A lot of good people were dying. He hoped those deaths weren't in vain. It was up to him and no one else, to make sure they weren't.

He'd been with Daker when word came of the diplomat's son's death in the battle for Nimitz Crossing. And now he'd learned of Fenn's son.

Winner ordered the vidcom off. He stood, hesitated, then walked to the hatch, unlatched it, slowly stepped into the passageway. He motioned the Marine guard to stand easy as he snapped to. From where he stood in the passageway, Fenn was visible leaning over the astroplot, his back to the entry hatch, continuing to surveil the bogie spaceship. Winner couldn't delay telling him. He hated this and he could only promise more losses.

Winner approached the bridge, held up his hand as the Marine started to announce his entry. Ashcroft turned at the slight disturbance. Winner motioned him from the bridge, retreated to his cabin and held the hatch open for the Admiral, then closed it behind him.

There's no good way to do this. Winner wanted to heave. He looked into the eyes of the man who had become his friend.

"Fenn, I just got a message from Vladislov Hrndullka… Your son has been killed."

In that split second, Winner saw another life slip away. The one Fenn Ashcroft and his son had planned together. He had known of their plans to explore a little of the universe together. His son's enlistment was up in ten months and Ashcroft had already requested leave starting the next day.

Winner watched the color drain from his friend's face.

"How did it happen?" Years of having to deliver the news to others offered no solace—Ashcroft's voice broke with the question.

Winner played back the tape from Hulk and stood silent.

Ashcroft said, "The people in that cellar didn't stand a chance." His shoulders heaved, a mild sob escaped in a whisper.

"His mother?" Winner asked.

"We're divorced, twenty-two years. She couldn't accept the time apart. I'll prepare a message for transmission to her."

Winner knew there was little he could do for the man now and said nothing. He watched as Ashcroft stepped to the intercom and keyed the bridge.

"Captain Davenport, I'll be in my quarters."

Ashcroft turned back to Winner. "I'd appreciate it if you kept this between us."

"As you wish," was all he could say.

The admiral opened the hatch, the Marine guard snapped to attention as the Ashcroft entered the passageway.

"Wait admiral. I'm sorry to bother you. But what's happening on Saragosa Prime, attempts to intercept messages, and our being tailed is more than coincidence. We need to capture that bogie. How can we do it?"

Winner wasn't lying about the problem. He also understood the need to keep Ashcroft busy.

The admiral's tired voice answered, "Give me a few moments. I'll join you in your cabin." His shoulders gave a slight shudder as he continued up the passageway.

Winner tried to put the pain and anguish he'd seen in Ashcroft's face out of his mind, but it hung like a heavy veil. His thoughts moved to the bogie that had been tailing them. This would smell in a vacuum, he thought.

CHAPTER FIFTEEN
The bogey

After a few minutes, Winner answered the buzz. "Come."

Admiral Ashcroft, face pallid and drawn, followed by Captain Davenport, came through the port. One other uniform trailed. "Mr. White, Flight Commander Zen."

Winner extended his hand to the smallish Asian man. "My pleasure. Please be seated gentlemen," Winner motioned then to the chairs.

Zen looked uncomfortable. He kept looking at Ashcroft.

Winner suspected the commander had picked up on the Admiral's strained behavior.

Winner said, "Admiral, it's conceivable that the problems on Saragosa Prime, attempts to intercept messages and our being tracked in deep space are unrelated but we can't take that chance. How can we capture that ship? I want to interrogate the pilot and get a look at what he's piloting."

Ashcroft took a deep breath, "We carry forty star fighters, Gorman class. Part of the conversion that we quietly held onto."

"Tell us how you'd do it."

Ashcroft seemed to warm to the task. Some of the distance that his voice carried disappeared, "When we come out of hyper drive, we never know if the craft will precede us by a second or two or if follow us by that same time. Both options have to be covered."

Ashcroft looked at Davenport and asked, "How many star fighters can we launch?"

Davenport stepped to the intercom, keyed engineering and waited for the response.

They all heard the clipped answer; Thirty. We're gettin' ready for the fight at Saragosa. The rest'll be out of maintenance in five or six hours. We can delay startin' the others.'

Davenport released the key, turned to Zen.

"I think we can do it with two. Hold the others in ready reserve, sir." the pilot said.

Davenport continued, "The bogie pilot is good. His ability to time his entry and exit of hyperspace is every bit as good as ours, down to counting one or two seconds. Of course, good navigation requires that we dropped out of hyperspace at a precise interval and we've set that at ten hours. Makes us very predictable."

"What keeps the bogie from going into hyperspace when we confront him?" Winner asked.

Zen responded, "Our fighters don't have hyper drive capability but we can paint him with a laser. He'll get the message when we lock onto him with our energy weapons. It takes him about ten minutes to complete the hyper drive engagement—time enough for us to reach and take him in tow."

Winner wanted to say Star's exit and entry into hyperspace was too predictable but knew it added to passenger comfort. As a warship, they'd vary the entry and exit times. But then Ashcroft knew that.

Zen continued, "The threat we offer will be too great. Even though it's three or four times the size of a star fighter, that small ship doesn't stand a chance against our weapons in normal space. He won't have time to engage his drive so he can't jump. And he can't outrun the fighters."

"How long until we can launch?" Winner asked." And if you need a pilot, I can fly your star fighter."

Commander Zen looked at him with surprise.

Winner smiled. "Commander, you took delivery of the first Gorman star fighter. At Star Base Ten."

"Yes, Sir. How did you know?"

"I was there. In fact, I was one of the test pilots who put that starship through its paces. I'm fully rated in that fighter."

"Well," A big grin crossed Zen's face. "What are we waiting for?"

Ashcroft didn't move. "My approval which you don't have and I'm not inclined to grant."

Winner didn't want to push the Admiral. He'd already told Ashcroft he would not interfere in the running of the ship, that the Admiral had final authority. Clearly his volunteering presented a problem. He wasn't about to pull rank—doing so would destroy Ashcroft's authority. He'd unnecessarily placed both men in awkward situation. But he did want to go and in his mind, the decision seemed obvious—he was the best man for the job.

Cautiously, Winner said, "This isn't going to be a shooting match."

"How do you know?" Ashcroft gravely asked. "Remember, your safety is paramount."

What Winner wanted to say was Bullshit! WMC is much more than me. It's thousands of dedicated people.

Ashcroft stood and faced Winner, "And you have no heir. Your death would leave no one to rally our forces. The financial vultures would move in. This would be over and Bartok takes by force and default what he wants."

Winner looked hard at the Admiral. "How do you know that?"

Ashcroft blushed bringing some color back to his face, "Bess," was all he said.

A grin crossed Winner's face. Bess Granger, his personal secretary at White Corporate offices, had served his father when he was chairman. "Well, she's right."

Ashcroft released a weary sigh and finally said, "Permission denied. We have very capable pilots to do the job."

Winner tried not to show his disappointment and irritation. The decision was final. He would protest no more.

"Back to the question. When do we launch?" Ashcroft asked.

"Twenty minutes," Davenport reported.

Admiral Ashcroft said, "I don't want that ship to get away. Why wait? Let's do it."

Winner clapped his hands.

* * * *

As the takeoff time neared, Zen approached Winner at the launch platform. "This decision weighs heavily on the Admiral." Almost as an aside he added, "Although, I think there's more bothering him."

Winner wanted to tell the commander about Ashcroft's son dying at Saragosa. Instead, he kept his word and said nothing.

He wished Zen luck and returned to the bridge to watch the intercept along with the bridge crew.

Prior to launch, the Captain ordered the bogie search parameters downloaded from the cruisers central computer into the star fighters. Star's main computer controlled the launch.

Zen's fighter launched two seconds before Galactic Star came out of hyper drive but remained inside the launch bay and the graviton envelope for the two seconds. Once launched, Zen would take a course to block the bogey ahead of their entry. The second fighter would attack one hundred eighty degrees opposite to cover a drop behind the cruiser. They'd have the spaceship between them.

The search program ran at launch in less than a second after leaving the bay. The dogging spaceship had dropped out two seconds early so Zen had the first crack at it. He locked on the bogey.

Both fighters converged.

Winner, along with Ashcroft, watched the events unfold on the view screen, the pilot's voices provided details.

"I've got him," the commander called. He'd set the computer to cut off the thruster after a one-tenth second burst, then two-blocked his throttle to set the program running and headed for the zone. With such a burst, if the engine didn't cut off at the right time, Zen would shoot out into space and chances of capturing the bogie would not be good.

The kick from his engine drove him further into the cockpit seat. The one-quarter "c" engine burst would still take him five minutes to get there, slow down and turn around. However, the capture was over by the time the second ship arrived. In less than ten minutes, Zen maneuvered his ship into grasping position and completed the capture, then headed for Galactic Star. Surprise was total. The bogie never had time to take evasive action—his only retaliation was a short tight beam transmission.

The pilots' chatter filled the bridge. The crew watched the capture on the plot screen and short-range scanners.

Then silence. The electronic beeps and squeaks stopped. For a split second, quiet settled over the bridge only to be shattered by static noise. The vidscreen submerged in an electronic criss-cross with patterns that mirrored snow. The screen was useless.

"What happened"? Winner and Ashcroft spoke simultaneously.

"Captain," exclaimed the plot controller. "I've lost the signal to the fighters. I've lost all signal capability. We're as blind as a mole and as deaf as a snake!"

CHAPTER SIXTEEN
Tribulations Continue

Winner stepped aside toward the rear of the bridge. Ashcroft and Davenport moved to the plot board. The screen looked like a snowstorm. "And no audio," said the astroplot operator.

Davenport barked, "Systems, report." He immediately headed for the vacant engineering station. The XO's fingers flew over the console, but nothing changed.

With an angry snort, he hit the override button and initiated the diagnostics program.

Exasperated, the plot operator said, "I'm sorry captain. I can't get anything. The controls don't respond. They're working but we're getting no signal or feedback."

Winner joined Ashcroft and Davenport at the plot board and waited. They'd done what they could, little as it was. It would take a few seconds for the diagnostic check.

The plot operator raced to the engineering console, frantically gouged at icons and tripped switches trying to bring life to the display. "Something's overridden the command structure," he exclaimed his voice raised showing stress.

"Or someone," Winner quietly said. "But who?"

"Some auxiliary communication systems are coming on line," the engineer said.

"Bridge. This is the Hanger Bay One security watch." A calm slow easy voice called over the intercom, a marked contrast to the excitement surrounding them.

The OD responded, "Bridge here. Go ahead."

"Have you authorized a launch? The hanger bay has decompressed. Hanger and outer bay doors are opening."

Davenport ordered, "No! Override the launch!"

After a few seconds, they listened to the dreaded report, "Sorry, Sir. The controls are not responding. Topsail has launched."

In disgust, Davenport turned to Winner and Ashcroft. "Topsail launched."

Davenport looked at Admiral. "Sir, I don't believe you've done me a favor by giving me this command."

Ashcroft just looked off into space. Winner was satisfied the Ashcroft found humor in Davenport's comment.

Ashcroft ordered, "See if you can locate Captain van Gelden."

They waited. "He's not responding to the ship wide hail or the intercom," the OD said.

"Crew alert," the Captain ordered." No threat existed on the long-range scan before we captured the bogie. I believe there's no imminent danger of attack. There's not sufficient threat for general quarters."

Winner silently agreed since general quarters would involve the passengers as well.

"When will the fighters be able to pursue?" Davenport asked.

"Don't bother. It's futile," Winner said. "Our fighters couldn't keep up with Topsail if they launched at the same time. I doubt there's anything around that could match her speed. And if van Gelden is at the helm, I'm sure of it."

Davenport grimaced. He accepted a key from al Cadifh that the Marine detachment had taken up internal threat positions.

Ashcroft nodded.

Winner smiled to himself. These men kept their wits, even while under great pressure.

As he left the bridge for his quarters, Winner said, "The War Council will convene in my quarters at fifteen thirty. Bring what information you have about these problems and be prepared to offer recommendations. I want to know who was onboard Topsail and the interrogation results of the bogie pilot or anything else that can help us."

* * * *

Twenty minutes later, the intercom squawked, 'Two fighters and one bogie docked and secured.'

Winner, Ashcroft and the Captain were already in hanger bay two waiting their return.

"Good job," the Captain offered to Zen and the other pilot.

Al Cadifh entered the hanger with a squad of Marines and took the captured pilot into custody.

Winner stopped the colonel before he could move the prisoner to the brig.

He walked up to the pilot, a smallish man with more the look of an accountant than a space pilot. "Do we treat you as a prisoner of war, pirate, spy or what?"

Dressed in civilian clothes, the bogie pilot offered no bluster but quietly gave both his name and registration of his ship.

Winner had no reason to doubt either. "Prisoner of war," he decided.

Ashcroft retreated to the catwalk.

Captain Davenport ordered al Cadifh to take the prisoner to the brig and question him.

"Admiral," Winner said, "I want your best engineering people to go over this spaceship. Mister Derka is to direct the effort."

Ashcroft nodded and walked away without any further word.

Zen looked at Winner. "Something's wrong. Something's eating on the Admiral."

Winner looked after the departing man and said nothing. He'd made plans to have dinner with Zen and the other crew pilots that evening and decided to extend the invitation to his staff. He'd do what he could to keep Ashcroft occupied.

Returning to his cabin Winner took a shower. Drying, he stepped across the room and answered the buzzing intercom.

"Yes."

"Colonel al-Cadifh, sir. The admiral has asked me to interrogate the prisoner. Is there anything in particular I'm looking for?"

Winner told al-Cadifh what he wanted to know and added, "Colonel, have you been advised of the meeting at fifteen thirty?"

"Yes sir." The reply gave no indication if he planned to attend.

Winner stepped through the opening and crossed the passageway for lunch, the guard closing the hatch behind him.

Thirty minutes later, he returned, walked to the intercom and played the taped message. "Sir," al-Cadifh's face filled the screen. Winner remained standing awaiting the message. "Admiral Ashcroft asked me to report the results of our interrogation. The pilot works for Zed Bartok. We believe there is no further threat in the area. A detailed report will be ready for the War Council."

Winner couldn't ask how much or what kind of persuasion they'd used. He really didn't want to know.

The big Marine was the first to arrive for the Council session and quietly took his seat as the others arrived.

Winner convened the meeting satisfied the insubordination problem was behind him. Everybody made use of the fresh coffee Melissa placed before them, then she took a bulkhead seat.

"Gentlemen," Winner began. "The retaking of Saragosa Prime will be brutal. Everything we've seen of Bartok demonstrates his ruthlessness. I do not believe Bartok has run out his string of surprises. Starting now, we put the enemy on the defensive and keep him there. He'll have to fight on two fronts, against Hrndullka on the surface, and against us and our people en route from Nimitz Crossing.

"The taking of Topsail had to be nothing more than someone taking advantage of an exceptional opportunity. Bartok couldn't have anticipated Topsail being on board and someone escaping with it. Still, he caught us off guard with the invasion—I won't underestimate him again. "Winner left unsaid the sloppiness he and Hrndullka had observed in the actual invasion.

"Bartok's assets are limited. I believe he's gathered most, maybe all, of the forces available to him. That is a weakness. And we will find more. Bartok has and will continue to make mistakes. It's up to us to have our plan well enough in hand to take advantage of what opportunities we can find, not to mention those we create for ourselves."

Winner sat back in the chair, his mind traced over the events of the day. "Mr. Davenport, what have you got for us?"

The Captain started his report; "Everything I have is preliminary. I've sent hyperwave messages to the Adaval and Zachary listing the munitions we want to take on when we meet in a few days. Those include matter/anti-matter long-range missiles and short-range energy munitions. We should be close to full armament when we arrive at Saragosa Prime. Also, Mr. Derka sent a hyperwave message to each ship detailing the assembly of an FTL transceiver. Within two or three days, we'll be able to communicate FTL with them."

The Captain leaned forward and punched the portable security computer in front of him on the walnut table.

Angry and embarrassed Davenport continued. "Celia Markham gained access to Topsail using the identification she was issued to help Mr. Derka analyze Topsail's anti-grav installation. Using that authority, she enlisted dissidents she'd met on Star to join her as crewmembers aboard the corvette. Together they stole and escaped with the ship. Security cameras show she entered the ship with Captain van Gelden at gunpoint. I would like for Mr. Derka to pick it up here."

Quiet surrounded the table.

The ashen Derka slumped slightly in his chair. He turned first to Winner. "Mr. White, I can't tell you how miserable I feel. Most of what's happen with Celia Markham is my doing. I trusted her." Derka sucked in a breath and continued.

"She had volunteered to help build the FTL transmitters before we arrived, so I invited her to assist in the inspection of Topsail's anti-grav system. I told her how we'd fooled Bartok's Vengeance in orbit at Saragosa. She used that information to blind Galactic Star, added a few twists of her own to launch Topsail and escape. I thought I was talking to a trusted employee and professional colleague. All the time I was giving her information to use against us."

"What can you tell us about her?" questioned Winner.

Derka answered, "Excellent scientific mind. And in every respect, a graceful caring woman. Class. At least I thought so until this. She had me completely fooled."

Winner gave an acknowledging nod, "Did you find out why she hates me?"

"Yes, sir," Derka responded, his features drawn.

You could feel the anticipation, as each man in the room waited for the scientist to continue.

"She said you murdered her father."

CHAPTER SEVENTEEN
Celia's Escape

Celia Markham walked onto the bridge. "Topsail—a marvelous ship you have, captain. Truly remarkable." Her casual manner belied the strength of this woman. She no longer carried a sidearm.

Van Gelden thanked her, showing no animosity or rancor.

She noticed her jump suit did little to keep the captain from watching her walk across the bridge to the navigation console.

"Did any fighters launched from Galactic Star?" she asked.

"No. I would imagine they're busy taking care of the ship that was tailing them," he answered.

Celia retreated from the front of the bridge and stood before the captain as if anticipating his question.

"Is it necessary for a guard to be with me at all times?" Van Gelden remained seated.

"You must forgive my suspicious nature. You were under the command of Winner White. Doesn't that deserve some consideration?"

Celia returned to the navigation console and looked at the heading and destination coordinates. "You could easily have changed them and the guard would never have known."

Van Gelden answered, "I gave you my word I would follow your orders unless the ship and crew are in jeopardy. And then I would advise you of the appropriate corrective action."

"Again, captain, forgive me. That all sounds too good to be true. I hope you don't think me cynical." Celia's look wasn't stern, but of someone not easily fooled.

Van Gelden offered no response, his hands clasped in front of his face, formed a contemplative steeple.

"What is our ETA at Saragosa?" Celia asked.

Van Gelden leaned over the navigation console, his hands remaining steepled. "Fourteen hours to landfall. Thirteen hours until we drop out of hyper drive. Thirty minutes to dump delta v."

"Excellent."

"What are our instructions for entering Saragosa space? I don't want to get vaporized before we reach orbit."

Celia gave him a *you needn't ask* look. "I'll give you instructions once we've entered normal space."

Van Gelden acknowledged her non-response with a halfhearted salute. "May I ask what's going on?"

"What would you like to know?"

"Just what I asked." It wasn't a challenge and it sounded casual. "Why did you and Mr. Derka meet with White on Galactic Star?"

"Mr. Derka didn't tell me it was White. And we didn't meet, as such. I didn't recognize him when he came into the mess hall with Derka. Believe me, if I had known it was Winner White, I wouldn't have been there. As soon as I recognized him, I walked out."

Van Gelden didn't let up; "You work for WMC. You've stolen their ship and running to Bartok."

Her voice sounded like a whip. "Winner White killed my father."

"But joining Bartok? Why?" His voice seemed incredulous.

Either he didn't hear what she'd just said or didn't believe it. Yet, Celia found herself wanting to tell van Gelden. He had that quality that elicited trust. "A little over four years ago, I was notified my father had been lost in hyperspace, two months out of Earth orbit. He was chief scientist of ocean biology for WMC. Their research focused on Saragosa's oceans for the last ten years." Pensively, Celia stood next to the bulkhead arms folded across her chest.

"Why was your father killed?"

She looked down at van Gelden, blackness seemed to cover her face as she continued, "Dad had left Saragosa Prime for return to Earth after completing his work. En route, the ship disappeared. WMC claimed there was no trace of the ship or people. I tried to get information from White. For four years, all I got was bits and pieces. They'd give me hope with some news then tear it away. Ships lost in hyperspace are rarely recovered but I couldn't get over the feeling WMC was giving me the run-around, giving me something just to placate me.

"About six months ago, a man contacted me at my home. He had information that Winner White was not only responsible for the disappearance, but had planned and carried out the assassination. Bartok had proof. Everyone on board killed and the ship destroyed in normal space. There was evidence it wasn't in hyperspace when communication was lost. Fifty people including a crew of six, all dead. Murdered! And for what? To keep something secret? Something so terrible or catastrophic Winner White didn't want it known? No. He did it for something so commercially viable, the secret could be worth many fortunes.

"My informants said father's work had the oceans of Saragosa ready for cultivation. White couldn't afford for that to become public for his own reasons, probably financial. Handled correctly, it means a great deal of money to White, Inc—in the long run, more than the mines on Saragosa.

Van Gelden nodded, letting her continue without attacking or agreeing with her story.

"White must have decided," Celia continued, "that the announcement that planet's oceans could sustain aquatic life was too important to just release to the press. They wanted to maximize the gain from potential investors.

"The caller gave me additional information. Put together with what little I'd been able to gather from White Lab, the caller persuaded me he was telling the truth. There was enough evidence to convince me Winner White was lying about the ship, my father—all of it."

Celia sat next to the Captain and exhaled a deep sigh. It seemed to help, to remove a burden. The darkness lifted from her face.

"The messenger put me in contact with another of Bartok's people on Earth." Celia quietly continued, "I was able to check him out and he seemed reputable, if bankers can be called reputable. He told me if I wanted to do something about my father's death just to sit tight until Zed Bartok got in touch with me."

Van Gelden attentively listened. Only Celia's voice and the hum of the hyper drive penetrated the silence.

"I checked on Bartok. Aggressive, domineering, prone to strong tactics to get what he wants—violence. His companies participated in three wars. All of this could fit everyone of the top six conglomerates—including WMC.

"Four months ago, I got a message from Bartok telling me to meet him on Namaycush. I took the next available space flight. En route, I learned he'd invaded Saragosa. Obviously, the plan was moving forward. He's there now and when you came alone with this nice spaceship, it was an opportunity that got me what I wanted."

"You'll have to forgive me," van Gelden said, "if I seem a little cynical. I find your story a little strange—frankly, unbelievable. A man like Winner White doesn't go around killing people. People like White, his father and those before him, make their money from the efforts of other people. And if he wanted your father dead, he'd have someone else do it."

Celia stood, feet apart, angry scowls lined her face, the darkness returned. "I'm joining Bartok to see that White doesn't win the battle for Saragosa. That he gets everything he deserves."

"White or Bartok?" van Gelden asked.

"Don't be impudent." Celia offered a steady gaze at the Captain; her fists balled up, and then eased as she sensed something more in van Gelden's comment.

The captain leaned forward in his seat, elbows on knees, "Many people on Saragosa have died because of Bartok. Many more will die. He's not an easy man."

She turned and faced van Gelden and said, "I regret that and wish it wasn't so. Maybe my being here can help put a stop to the killing. I do have a few secrets to entice Bartok to listen."

"Ms. Markham, you're an intelligent woman. But more importantly to Bartok, you're a woman. The fact that you're a most attractive woman is going to make it all the more difficult for you."

"I've had to handle tough Romeo's before," Celia answered.

"Not like this man. Your secrets don't mean a damned thing to him. You will submit to him or he'll kill you. And if he doesn't, you'll wish you were dead."

It was the first time Celia had heard anything but a mild, polite manner from van Gelden. She decided a cautious approach to Bartok might be in order. But she still had her suspicions of van Gelden's motives.

"Why should I believe you?"

"Without some proof, you shouldn't."

"Stalemate! What do you suggest?" she asked, again taking a seat beside van Gelden.

"These people that escaped with you," he said gesturing toward the crew, "Do you have their loyalty?"

"Considering they just betrayed their employer?" She leaned back in her chair, paused, "They're here for their own reasons. All I did was recruit malcontents. I can't say they're my people."

Van Gelden said. "Okay, at least you're not fooling yourself. You need to get some sort of protection. Bodyguards. They can't stop Bartok, but at least you'll have someone to watch your backside." He smiled as he said it.

She sat looking at van Gelden. "I'll take that as a compliment. But there isn't anyone on the ship or Saragosa that I could enlist for protection."

"Problem. But what I expected."

"Captain, if you have a plan to offer, I would appreciate hearing it."

Van Gelden leaned further forward in his chair. "You have the approach vectors and docking coordinates for us at Saragosa. And Bartok knows you're about to arrive. Correct?"

"Yes."

"Let's go in hot. About, twice the speed they've assigned us. We'll bypass the deep orbit phase and head straight for the docking coordinates."

"That may get us shot." Celia raised her eyebrows.

"I don't think so," he responded.

"You understand if my butt gets shot, so does yours."

Van Gelden stood, stretched, looked at Celia and said, "What a shame if that happened."

"Captain, I'm not the least bit sure about you. I think you can be trusted only so far. Bartok isn't the only one I need to watch. You'd better behave." She mockingly waggled a finger at him. Celia found she wanted to trust him. But she'd keep an eye on him.

* * * *

Thirteen standard hours later Topsail dropped out of hyperspace and maneuvered to dump delta v.

"Okay, we got past the deep orbit. What now?" she asked.

"We've got their transmission frequencies. During my first trip, here three weeks ago, I made it a point to get Security's frequency. We'll be able to hear everything they say to Approach Control and anyone else when we enter the control area—all of their private transmissions.

"Now, I want you to get on the horn and make sure they understand who you are and where you're headed."

Celia followed van Gelden's broadcast instructions, and then sat down to wait. It didn't take long.

Approach Control hailed the ship. "Topsail. Your present course and speed will not, I repeat, will not achieve your assigned orbit."

Van Gelden motioned her not to respond.

"Topsail, this is Approach Control. Acknowledge! That is an order."

Hesitantly, Celia again accepted van Gelden's admonishment and ignored the hail. A worried look crossed her face.

The speakers carried the message again, "Topsail. Correct your speed and direction to the designated coordinates. This is you last warning."

Celia raised an eyebrow and looked again at van Gelden.

It got her a smile and a wagging finger saying no.

It didn't take long. Van Gelden blew a low sigh of relief. The secure frequency came alive after the warning to Topsail. Security shot back on what it believed to be a guarded and scrambled frequency, "Better leave that ship alone. It's got Bartok's new broad on board. He won't like it if you split her tail with a missile before he does. And that includes shooting it up just for not following your little rules." A harsh laugh followed.

Celia angrily punched off the reception.

Van Gelden said, "The real world."

"Okay," Celia acknowledged with a shrug. "Maybe you're right. But it doesn't change my reason for being here." She'd not take any unnecessary chances with Bartok—perhaps there were two personas—the real one and the image painted by a PR group.

Van Gelden made a hand gesture and nodded his head as if he'd say no more.

"What about me?" he asked. "I'm as good as dead."

"You're a non-combatant," she answered, her voice expressed concern. "You shouldn't be in any danger. You were ordered to take White and his people away from Saragosa, and I brought you back at gunpoint."

The Captain's look seemed to doubt her. "And if you're wrong?"

She looked at van Gelden. "I think I know you well enough to know you have something in mind. What is it?"

"Let me make one transmission. The owner of this ship is on Saragosa. If he hears my message, perhaps he can be of some help. Maybe."

"Is he allied with Bartok?"

"No, neutral."

Why did she believe him? They were running out of time and options. All of a sudden, why was she having doubts… "Send it!"

Van Gelden keyed the console.

"You had the message set up." It was a statement. "How do I know you haven't already sent it?"

"You don't. But I didn't."

Celia watched van Gelden skillfully maneuver the spaceship to the mooring dock. Within ten minutes, the entire crew was aboard the launch and headed dirt-side.

Twenty minutes later, they landed at the terminal.

A soldier opened the launch hatch. He didn't look a day over eighteen. His black uniform with a white bandolier was immaculate and speech correct. "Ms. Markham. There's an air car standing by for you."

At least he has manners, she thought. Probably hadn't been in the military long enough to learn otherwise.

Without waiting, the soldier placed van Gelden under arrest.

The Captain didn't seem surprised. He did look at Celia. "See? I didn't just come in on the last load of dirt."

The remaining crewmembers boarded ground transportation.

"What are the charges," van Gelden tried to keep his voice at a level pitch.

The soldier placed the Captain in wrist and leg restraints then urged him from the terminal without responding.

Celia pursued van Gelden's question, "What are the charges?"

The young soldier looked at her, "Ma'am, we're only following orders."

She slightly raised her hand. "What are your orders?" The firmness in her question caused the young man to stop. It seemed an eternity before the answer came.

"We're to execute him—now."

Celia's stomach turned. My god, what have I gotten this man into? Had everything van Gelden said been true? Was everyone surrounding Bartok a butcher?

Stunned, she called on all her strength. "Where did you get your orders?"

"Colonel Masten, Ma'am."

"I was assured by Mr. Bartok anyone traveling with me would be welcome." She was bluffing. No, she was lying. She hadn't talked to Bartok but she had to try something, somehow delay, somehow keep this man alive.

Quietly using her command voice but subduing it, she ordered, "Don't do anything. I'll contact Mr. Bartok to have this corrected." Celia gave the soldier a cordial smile and added, "We can't have you shooting people who have Mr. Bartok's approval to come here, now can we? Without waiting for an answer she continued, "I'll have this cleared up shortly.

"Since I'm going to see Mr. Bartok now, Captain van Gelden can travel in the air car with me."

The soldier firmly responded, "No Ma'am. I'll wait with the execution, but the prisoner stays with me."

Celia had come to Saragosa to kill a man, now she had one to save.

CHAPTER EIGHTEEN
The rally begins

The words still rang in his ears, 'You murdered her father' as quiet descended over Winner's cabin. As a group, the War Council waited for a response. He searched his mind, "Was Celia's father's last name also Markham?"

"Yes. Jules Markham," responded Derka.

"When and where was this supposed to have taken place?" Winner, relaxed, was determined not to show any emotion.

"She didn't say," Derka answered. "All I found out was that he headed the Saragosa Prime's ocean biology research. She wouldn't discuss it further."

Winner made eye contact with each member of the council. "Gentlemen, I have no knowledge of any Markham before meeting Celia Markham. And certainly, I didn't murder anyone. Without more to go on there's nothing I can add."

The vidcom buzzed. The group relaxed and seemed to welcome the interruption.

Winner answered and Simone Anacrode's face filled the screen.

Winner punched in the access codes to the secure channel.

'Hello Winner.'

Even at this distance, it still took four hours for FTL messages to pass between Earth and Galactic Star.

"Good timing," Winner said. "We can listen to Simone's message together. I talked with her yesterday." He keyed the screen.

"It was encouraging to hear good things are happening. We've had some success and a few setbacks since we last talked."

Simone Anacrode as WMC's CEO, was one of the few corporate executives who commanded respect both in corporate circles and with many governments. In an era that saw the United Nations fail and the creation of toothless Federation of Aligned Worlds, Simone had been a major contributing figure to inter-world stability. Until she refused the offer, she was a leading contender to head the Federation.

The square jaw framed her jet-black hair and piercing blue eyes giving the correct impression that she was no one to fool with.

"The good part first. Last night two thousand of our Marines spaced, some for rendezvous with Galactic Star, the rest to join up with troops from Nimitz Crossing headed for Saragosa Prime. The troops are coming from several of our holdings so until you can get them all together, it may be a little confusing. I know they're scattered all over space but it's the best I can do.

"Those coming from Earth won't get there in time for to help retake Saragosa but can be relief troops. We're transmitting the detail on the troop arrival on another frequency as I speak."

The troops and transports Winner certainly could use and he needed fighting spaceships as well. The fleet was short fighters, destroyers and cruisers. He doubted it included any heavy cruisers. Those ships of the line formed too large an investment for most companies. Usually, destroyers and fighters provided guard cover.

Simone continued. "We had some offers of help, and some of the support includes troops from corporations friendly or who want to see Bartok taken down. It looks like you'll have to use your influence on a few of our more reluctant business friends. If we get everything that's pledged, it would mean about twenty-five hundred additional troops with transports. I've taken it upon myself to provide the companies helping us with the new FTL transceiver design. They have your general frequencies so you should be hearing from them shortly."

Not a problem thought Winner. Simone had no way of knowing Bartok gained FTL communications compliments of Topsail. In days, everyone in the known universe would have FTL com capability. So much for making money on the scientific breakthrough of the century. He was confident his engineers had patented the proprietary ideas. No time to worry about that now.

His attention returned to Simone. "The help offers we've firmed up are appreciated but if the rest come through, your force will be substantially stronger. With what the corporation is sending, along with al Cadifh's Marines and what you can mobilize on Saragosa, you can get rid of the son-of-a-bitch once and for all."

Winner smiled at Simone's demeanor and that brought assorted nods and grins of approval from everyone in the room. He would kill the bastard for the misery, pain and loss he caused many of WMC's employees. Winner had always considered his father had been killed fairly in the course of battle and held no animosity, only the loss.

She went on. "Now for the bad part. I'm having some trouble getting the money people behind us. They're trying to use our need for war credits as leverage. They want concessions, from stock options to positions on our board of directors. I've tried to contact your mother but now understand she's missing. I'll wait for your input before I go any further with the creditors.

"Most of our suppliers are running scared. The banks are telling them to withhold credit. In fact, they're being told to get cash with our orders. They're afraid they'll lose everything if WMC doesn't survive this war and bellies up. Of course, the banks are pushing the scare tactics. The banks accelerated all warrants and bonds. A number of small lenders have reluctantly followed the banker's lead."

Winner scrunched down in his seat. He understood how they must feel.

A small struggling company had little or no chance of influencing let alone controlling what was happening to them and was completely vulnerable. Every son-of-bitch and his brother who sees an opportunity to make some quick money is laying claim, even against the small companies that don't have the resources to fight. They were easy picking. Their day of reckoning would come after he took care of Bartok.

Simone added, "So far, we've been able to get around most of claims."

Without waiting, she launched into the big news.

"Winner, the board agrees with you on taking Bartok's assets. That includes hitting Namaycush at the same time you retake Saragosa. Damned right! Take everything he's got! Reparations, if you will, for the death and devastation he's caused on Saragosa, not to mention the loss of revenue from mining exports. We'll have tremendous death benefits to pay caused by Bartok. Let it come out of his holdings.

"We've gone along with your suggestion to publicly make Bartok believe he's dealt us a knock-out blow until you tell us to change our tune—although it's hurt our stock price.

"We took quite a hit when the news first appeared. Since then, there's been a rebound. We've been able to capitalize on our reputation to help hold things together. Our PR group is gaining a head of steam.

"Bartok's creditors are hedging their bets. Publicly they're saying if Bartok loses, they'll take his assets to settle the debt. But then, our creditors are saying the same thing about WMC. If we lose, and most think we will, they'll take over the corporation. Banks and commercial paper houses hold virtually every asset Bartok's got. He's in hock to the hilt. Even at that, once you kill the bastard, I figure we're his number one creditor. We have first claim because of his invasion of Saragosa. Our lawyers confirm this. They assure me we do have rights of recovery in the eyes of the Federation of Aligned Worlds and the Universal Court. And of course, if we are the occupying army, it's ours to lose.

"Every corporation in the universe will move against whatever assets Bartok has once it's obvious he's lost. We might as well make the best of it and be there first. We're preparing for a takeover.

"About Fonso Carrel, owner of Granger, Inc. and Kirk Filbright, of Filbright, Inc., the info we have is that they will soon return to their home bases. The word is Carrel told Bartok he'd done his bit, paid his debt.

"Filbright's hatred of you was almost enough for him to stay. But, from what we've been able to pick up, he's sure you'll try to retake Saragosa and doesn't want to be around when that happens. He did leave a substantial number of his troop on the ground. Everyone knows he's a coward at heart and this only confirms it. Bartok's boasted he's got everything nailed down and doesn't need them anymore."

Simone smiled. Winner knew that smile and it meant trouble for Bartok.

"If Carrel and Filbright are part of the spoils, let me know. Simone out."

Her image faded from the vidcom.

"That, Gentlemen," Winner slammed his fist into his hand, "is what we mean by the big fight." He turned to the group, a determined look on his face.

"Great news," Derka said.

Winner was pleased. Even though they'd not regained an inch of soil, his attitude reflected nothing but total confidence, a determination that wouldn't be denied. He might lose, but he'd never admit that possibility.

"A coordinated attack on Saragosa and Namaycush should provide Bartok with more than he can handle. He can't fight a war on two fronts. He's spread too thin. And our being in control of Bartok's holdings means anyone wanting a piece has to take us on. I don't believe there'll be any fighting after we capture Saragosa and Namaycush."

Ashcroft asked, "What about Granger and Filbright?"

Winner's response was immediate and emphatic. "They were in on the invasion—they go down with Bartok! They don't own any planets or asteroids, so we take anything they own in an outlying area and we'll sue for their terrestrial assets."

The meeting turned to the immediate problem, the assaults on both Saragosa and Namaycush.

"Admiral," Winner said gesturing with his hand. "It's your command." That decision wasn't made lightly since neither Ashcroft nor al Cadifh had been to Saragosa or Namaycush.

He watched al Cadifh out of the corner of his eye. The Colonel eased back into his chair.

Ashcroft said, "Colonel Hornblower will prepare the attack on Namaycush. The Order of Battle will be authorized approximately two weeks before the assault of Saragosa. The goal is both to take the planet and to cause Bartok to transfer some of the forces currently at Saragosa to the other theater. Hornblower will put together assets from Minns, Nimitz Crossing and Cellus IV. The attack will clearly demonstrate the capture of Namaycush as our objective.

"Now, the battle plan for Saragosa." Ashcroft pushed back from the table, stood, and ordered the computer to display the orbital hologram of Saragosa Prime.

"Mr. White, you and Mr. Derka have spent time on Saragosa, so please chime in anytime you wish. In fact, Mr. Derka, why don't you tell us about Saragosa?"

Using a laser pointer, Derka directed their attention to the hologram. "All of the landmass above sea level is concentrated at the equator. Even with the two moons and two suns, tectonically Saragosa is minimally alive, its activity primarily confined to under-ocean tremors caused by huge tides. No volcanic activity.

"The landmass essentially forms a belt around the girth of Saragosa, the equator. In some places, the land covers large areas. At spots it sinks below the ocean surface, creating islands. One four-lane highway runs the circumference, slightly over twenty thousand kilometers, with bridges connecting the islands to the main landmasses. That is the Saragosa Road. It's more generally used than Prime when off-worlders refer to the planet. The capital, Saragosa City, serves as the buckle, cinching it all together. The land varies in width from nothing to over fifteen hundred kilometers at Saragosa City. The terrain changes from seashore to plains to mountains. The higher elevations are very rugged but don't extend above the tree line."

Looking at Winner he added, "Lot's of good hiding places up there."

Winner reflected on how effectively Hrndullka could use the area. He could only wonder about his missing mother and Daker Smithe.

Derka turned off the laser pointer and continued. "Tidal action scours the shores and ocean beds releasing high ph minerals such as sulfur and salts. Distillation works only for drinking and processing water for industrial use. It does stink up the air a little. And during a storm, a lot."

Winner barely heard Derka. Perhaps the information Markham was carrying had gotten him killed. Still, if Bartok had planned all along to take Saragosa because of its potential to develop a fishing trade, then killing Markham made no sense. Was it a mistake? The specter of Jules Markham, a man he'd never even known, would not leave his mind.

He tore his attentions back to the description of Saragosa.

Ashcroft instructed the computer to show the suns, moons and the effect of the tides.

Derka added, "With two small, not too bright suns and two small moons, Saragosa has to deal with extraordinary tide conditions. Seawalls are a common sight, many over fifty meters high."

Looking at al Cadifh he said, "We have detailed topography."

The Admiral instructed, "Computer; Saragosa, Flora and Fauna display."

Every holo was easily recognized. Animals, trees and grasses originating on earth had changed little.

Winner glanced around the room at the other council members; their attention riveted to the display. "The computer has a good database on Saragosa. Access it any time you want."

Ashcroft continued, "Colonel al Cadifh will direct the ground force. Until he can link up with Hrndullka, my command will coordinate the resistance's actions. Captain Davenport will conduct the space fight. Battle plans will be coordinated with my command staff. Mr. Derka will assume responsibility for all intelligence, people and equipment. And that includes the forty-five hundred troops en route from Earth and friends."

He turned to Winner. "Abduhl needs a little more time before presenting his preliminary assault plan." He then yielded the floor.

It was the first time anyone on the council had referred to al Cadifh by his given name. Winner liked all the signs from the first meeting. The question of Jules Markham's death was still with them. He would find out what happened.

"Okay, gentlemen," he said. "You'll have the security access codes shortly for the information Simone mentioned Earth is transmitting. We'll meet again in two days."

The men filed out. He said to Melissa, "Be prepared to help any member in any way possible. Without a doubt we are going to win this fight and in a big way!" Without a doubt? He wasn't all that sure. A lot of people had to come through. A lot of ifs had to be satisfied.

He turned his attention to Saragosa, the taking of Bartok's empire and the need to keep his own creditors in line. He saw the problems as one in the same. He keyed the vidcom and prepared a message for home. "Simone, the creditor problem. No stock, no board positions and when we take Bartok's businesses, planets and the rest, WMC will not honor any debt against Bartok. Refer everyone who presents a legitimate financial claim not linked to Bartok's armament cost for warring with Saragosa to one of the banks holding Bartok assets. No exceptions."

Incentive is all the creditors are going to get, nothing more Winner resolved.

"Simone, emphasize the following—those who assist WMC in this moment of great need and peril will benefit in the spoils. Don't change a word of that last statement. I want it to sound pious."

"And just so it's said, WMC picks up all the cost of any loaned troops. We supply all weapons and munitions, pay all costs associated with the troops used in the war. And for the troops on loan, they keep whatever they've been issued once this is settled. Simone, make sure our lawyers have this thing legally covered." He ordered the message sent and keyed off the vidcom.

Melissa stepped back from the computer and handed him a data chip. "Here are the access codes for the rest of Ms. Anacrode's data transmission. This molecular computer is phenomenal. It's as if it senses what you want. I was hardly through entering my request and I had the access code."

"You're probably right. Derka says it's the most advanced AI programming and the latest in bio-molecular circuitry."

He punched the code into the vidcom. The screen filled with the data. "I see what Simone meant when she said I may have to help round up troops. From these locations—I wonder."

He punched the intercom. "Mr. Derka, Is it possible to install an artificial gravity system like Topsails on the captured corvette?"

"Theoretically possible, yes. I need to check with engineering to make sure the hull will take the strain and that we have the necessary materials. Give me a little time."

Shortly later, Derka called. "Yes we can do it. It'll take about six days. And while we're at it, we'll put an FTL transceiver on board."

"Do it!" Winner ordered. He switched off the intercom.

"Going somewhere?" Melissa asked.

"I'm going to do a little recruiting," Winner anticipated her next question.

"Six days. That ought to be just about right to get my people ready."

"For what?" he asked. He was sure of what was coming.

Melissa, calmly, without defiance, minimizing any argumentative attitude quietly said, "Understand we're going with you. Five other Marines and me. Your security detail. Where you go, we go."

Winner grinned. "Nope. But there's little for you to do around here and it will give me a chance to train your squad in some space techniques. You know, combat, rescue, how to operate a ship. They won't be all that professional when we get back, but better than when we left."

"Okay, Let's do it." She said with a grin of her own.

"Besides, you can relieve me at the helm. Kill some of the monotony." Flying in space had that major drawback. It could be boring as hell and usually was.

For the next six days, the detailed planning moved forward. Everyone involved more than did their job in preparing for the battles ahead. Winner felt a great satisfaction with the eagerness the people showed. Melissa trained her squad for corvette bridge duty. Commander Zen augmented her efforts by showing them how an enemy might attack and what little they could do to defend themselves on an unarmed corvette.

With the artificial gravity system installed and the installation and flight test complete, Zen stepped from the corvette. " Ready to go. Mr. White, you can travel at max, to the top of the theta band. No sickness. You feel nothing! And the hull can take it without any problem. I wish I could make the trip with you. This corvette is a pleasure to fly. We've copied the cloaking device and artificial gravity generators to install on our fighters."

Winner liked the excitement Zen showed. Good pilot reaction.

Derka leaned near Winner to whisper, "Our calculations show the ship can reach the Upsilon band. The hull can take the stress."

Winner raised his eyebrows in amazement. "That means time to Saragosa from our present location is only two standard days. And only one week from Saragosa to Earth. Are there any kickers?"

"May be. We really don't know how severe."

"Problem?" Winner replied.

Derka shoved his hands in his pockets. "Anything I've never dealt with is a problem until I have information on its response or performance. There's instrumentation aboard to collect data. It won't take long to figure it out once you get under way—that is if you take it to Upsilon"

Winner asked, "Does Commander Zen know about this?"

"No, sir," said Derka. "I felt if no one knew just how fast this ship could travel, it would add that much to your safety."

Winner wasn't keen on keeping secrets from his people. Zen had just completed a test flight and test pilots needed to know everything there was about the ship they were flying. Sometimes it meant the difference between life and death. He didn't want to let it pass. Yet, there was nothing to be gained by creating a scene in front of the hanger crew.

"Mr. Derka, after we leave, take Zen to dinner and tell him." It was enough said. The young scientist got the message.

* * * *

"Name?" called Zen from the catwalk where he'd retreated. "What's the ships name? You can't leave until we know what to call you." Everyone knew it was one pilot talking to another and not a commander talking to his CIC.

"Legere," said Winner. Stillness fell over the hanger deck. He turned around, surveyed the gathered few and saw their questioning look. WSS LEGERE! I like that."

The quiet continued.

"What's the significance?" asked Derka.

"I'm going on a recruiting mission and *Legere* in old Latin means 'to gather'. In French it means to gather for war."

CHAPTER NINETEEN
The hearts and minds

"I don't care," Bartok said. "That scum isn't well armed or led. You should be able to stop their raids. You have one week to get it done or I'll make a change. Do what you have to." He flipped off the transmitter switch and turned to Captain Blain.

His mood still angry, he said, "Get my launch ready. I'm going dirt-side."

A nod from the Captain sent his aide scurrying to the console keying the necessary instructions. Bartok's six-member entourage scrambled aboard the small ship with their volatile leader.

Bartok had expected a quick victory at Saragosa. That he got. And he wanted quick subjugation of the people. That he hadn't gotten. A resistance group had operated with impunity and he intended to stop it. Whatever it took.

Since arriving in Saragosa orbit, he spent as much time on Vengeance as possible. He hadn't felt the pleasure he expected once the planet was his. He couldn't explain the irritation that hounded him. The invasion had gone mostly as planned. There had been mistakes. But since there wasn't much initial enemy opposition, it really didn't matter. Maybe that is what's bothering me.

No, it was simpler than that. He hadn't killed Winner White and the resistance that had formed. Despite his protests, he'd learned that the partisans, the so-called Freedom Fighters, had somehow secured competent leadership. Freedom fighters, if he heard one of his men using that name, he'd kill him.

He had to defeat the rebels quickly. Saragosa would be the seat and crown of his empire. It had to become a financial asset rather than a drain on his resources. With it, he'd take his rightful place in the top six conglomerates and get the Galon Sector access points, Nimitz Crossing, Cellus IV and Minns Station under his control. Then everyone would have him to reckon with. He had only to finish the subjugation of Saragosa and its people and the other prizes would fall.

Captain Blain approached Bartok as the giant moved toward the planet-bound launch. "White captured the corvette but we now know the location of White's cruiser. Do you want to launch the missile sleds at Galactic Star?"

"What chance do they have of hitting their target? From this range?"

Blain declared, "They will hit Galactic Star unless shot out of space which isn't likely. We'll launch the platform carrier from here. By the time it reaches terminal velocity, its speed will be three times that of Star.

"Approximately one million klicks from White's cruiser, the sled's propulsion will shut down. It will continue, passively, toward Star. Once within range, the sled will release three neutron energy missiles. The weapon's drives are passive. The only energy signature they emit is for course corrections to maintain an electronic lock on Galactic Star's emissions. The target won't be able to pick up the course change signals. The missiles will have no trouble intercepting the cruiser."

"Launch," Bartok ordered.

Bartok brooded as he took his seat on the shuttle. His people had learned to recognize that mood, avoiding him whenever possible at almost any cost.

The pilots' commands and transmissions with ground control drummed distantly in the back of his mind. He hardly noticed when the steward came to his seat.

"Sir, you can disembark now. Your air car is at the terminal… The media are waiting."

"Media?" he roared. "Why in the hell haven't they been kicked off the planet?"

The steward stepped back, fear etched his young face. Shakily he said, "I think, sir, these are off-planet newsies. They were here to cover the elections."

Bartok wasn't pleased at a press office at the terminal but it would make it easier to control the reporters' movements. And it might help him control the information that left Saragosa. Once they'd served his purpose, he'd send them packing.

Bartok waved the steward away and stepped in front of a mirror next to the head. His all-white uniform sparkled. He adjusted his visor cap. The gold brocade glistened and he touched the bold crease in his trouser legs.

Satisfied with his appearance, he signaled the hatch open. He wasn't in any mood to meet the media, but he needed them to offset any bad publicity following the capture of Saragosa. Right now, Celia Markham was waiting for him. His host at the hotel had raved of her beauty. Bartok's blood raced. She was just a part of what was due him.

He stepped through the hatch onto the ramp.

"Mr. Bartok," one reporter called.

Bartok didn't recognize the man but waved to him and hurried through the terminal. The persistent reporter continued, "Why aren't we allowed outside the press office. I understand there's a lot of unrest across the city and also that you're about to execute a neutral without a trial."

Bartok turned to one of his followers. "Handle this guy!"

He used his public smile to hide the contempt for the press boiling inside. Long strides carried him quickly through the terminal to the waiting air car.

* * * *

People scurried around the tunnels. It was clear from the chaos of defeat, a sense of possible was emerging. Some of these people may not see the end of this horror, but they seemed resolved to do their part.

Hulk Hrndullka shook Richard Hastings's hand, glad to have the man's assistance. Hulk wanted to place him where his persuasive skills and talent for gathering information could be utilized to there fullest. Hastings suggested he manage the Hotel Crest in Saragosa City. The former manager had died in the initial bombing of the city, creating a legitimate opportunity to get Hulk's man in place.

Richard Hastings had asked for and got the blessing of the Tri-Lateral Commission to intervene on Saragosa—without their official endorsement.

In fact, no one could ever know of the connection with him. With his resignation as point man for the Commission, he accepted all the provisos for silence and moved with inspired dedication to help the people of the beleaguered planet.

Putting Hastings in now might raise a few questions, but it was worth the risk. The resistance desperately needed a spy close to Bartok. In such a position, Hastings could provide that and hopefully be invaluable. Still, Hulk intended to manage the risks.

"How do you plan to carry this off?" Hulk demanded. "Most of the hotel staff is still there. We can't infiltrate you or many of our people without raising suspicion."

"Do it brazenly and nobody asks questions," Hastings asserted. "I'm simply going into the hotel office and tell the staff I'm there to replace their fallen leader. In all the confusion, nobody will ask for any kind of verification and wouldn't know who to ask if they decided otherwise.

"I will convince Bartok I'm sympathetic and willing to follow his orders. And as manager of the hotel I'll be in a position to keep him convinced."

Two days after turning his ship over to Winner, Hastings was ensconced as manager of Hotel Crest. In the confusion following the invasion, Hastings's take-over, as he predicted, had gone unchallenged.

During the invasion, the hotel had lost six staff members. Hastings asked for and got six trustworthy fighters from Hulk to make up the difference, simultaneously giving himself a support base and convincing the remainder of the staff that he was a can-do manager. He assigned two fighters to each work shift so he'd have people in place day or night. He coached them on how to recruit others to help the resistance—risky but necessary.

Now, weeks later, the preparation was ready to pay off. Bartok had demanded a suite in the hotel.

Hastings walked from his second story office in the hotel, his consigliore, Arthur Petry, at his side.

In long strides, he covered the distance to the employees' mag lift, his aides' shoes hammering on the bare plasticrete as his short legs struggled to keep him abreast.

"Are we ready for Mr. Bartok's arrival?" Hastings asked. He would have to wait for his answer at least until they reach the main lobby, two floors below, The mag lift platform was large enough for only one person at a time. In the few days' he'd been there, Hastings quiet professional approach removed any doubts the hotel staff may have harbored toward him. In his eyes, they were professionals and he treated them as such. Scuttlebutt had already reached the hotel staff of how Bartok treated those around him. Many of the workers and professionals were ready to accept Hastings as a buffer from Bartok's temper. Evidence of this response was found in the meals the chef prepared for their boss. He patted his stomach—either he had to stop eating or start exercising, neither his first choice.

"Yes sir," the consigliore answered. "However, I do have a message from Ms. Markham. She wants to see Mr. Bartok in his office as soon as he arrives."

They stepped through the porter's door onto the plush carpet adjacent to the guest entry. There they would await the momentary arrival of Bartok.

Hastings pursed his lips and nodded his head. "Any mention of what she wants?"

"No sir. She just said it was imperative that she see him immediately."

Hastings had no idea what Celia Markham wanted but he understood her goals. He wanted Bartok alone for a few minutes as well. The news of Captain van Gelden's scheduled execution had reached him courtesy of Hulk's spy at the space terminal. He had to find some way of saving his friend and former employee from Masten's execution order.

Sitting on a hillside, surrounded by palm trees, the large sweeping drive to the hotel entrance provided a panoramic view of Saragosa City. Surface traffic was more common than air cars, which had to land some distance from the canopy covering the walkway to the lobby. Though, since the invasion, traffic other than military was a rarity.

Bartok's air car settled at the center of the sweeping circular entry. He wasted no time emerging.

Hastings walked down the steps, strode across the fifty meters to the landing pad. The big man did make an impressive figure. He couldn't be overlooked. Hastings stepped forward. "Mr. Bartok, Welcome. I'm Richard Hastings, your host at Hotel Crest."

Bartok's look was non-committal. Hastings understood the man seldom made rash decisions where his executives were concerned.

Hastings continued, "Your rooms are ready. Your security people have completed their inspection. You can go up at your pleasure."

Bartok removed his white, gold brocaded gloves and tapped Hastings on the shoulder with them, "I understand you worked for Winner White."

Hastings showed no emotion. "That is incorrect." And let it go at that. He wasn't about to challenge Bartok's authority at their first meeting. "Since you own Hotel Crest, you're the only person on Saragosa that I've worked for." That was the truth, although it was a stretch. Nothing existed on Saragosa, or anywhere else for that matter, to tie him to Winner White.

Hastings continued, "I've only been on the planet two weeks. This job came open when the manager was killed during the initial assault. I had no other commitment and thought my experience could help."

Bartok started to repeat his tap to Hastings shoulder with his gloves but stopped in mid air, as Hastings unflinchingly returned his gaze. Bartok lowered the gloves and asked, "Is Celia Markham here?"

Hastings knew she was but looked to the consigliore and got a yes nod. It meant she was being notified of Bartok's arrival as they spoke.

The consigliore said, "She's asked to see you immediately, sir. Said it was urgent." The shorter man almost bowed as he spoke.

Bartok slapped his gloves against his trouser legs, "Lead on." A smile crossed his face. He had anticipated this moment for over four months since learning Celia Markham was coming to join him. To Bartok, the why behind her coming could only mean one thing.

Hastings cleared his throat, "In your office?"

Bartok wheeled toward Hastings. Rage crossed his face, but the manager stood his ground.

"Goddammit!" Bartok regained his composure realizing they were still outside and in full public view.

Sternly, he looked at Hastings and ordered, "Take me to her rooms now."

"As you wish, sir. This way." Hastings stepped aside and motioned Bartok into the hotel foyer. Bartok's white uniform might have public appeal in Bartok's thinking, but the man clearly was a strain for those around him. Fear was resident in the eyes of the entire entourage.

Carpet muffled the storm crossing to the guests' main elevator. Bartok, Hastings and the consigliore all stepped into the lift. The clear monofilament door shut and they moved upward.

Hastings stepped first into the tenth floor anteroom facing Celia Markham's suite.

Bartok stormed past him, without knocking, opened the large double doors and stopped dead in his tracks.

Celia Markham, in all her beauty, blocked entry just with her presence three meters past the doorway. As impenetrable as a steel barrier, she walked forward, her hands lightly clasped in front at her waist. The dark blue business suite spoke all business and it didn't take binoculars to see that she meant it. "Mr. Bartok, I'm Celia Markham." She didn't offer her hand.

"Everyone out!" Bartok ordered. He seemed somewhere between embarrassed and confused. Two things were evident, he was pissed and his hormones were overworked. Bartok looked like a kid on his first date-rape.

"They can stay," Celia countered. "This won't take long."

Bartok almost choked on his rage.

Hastings stepped out of the line of fire, alarmed that Celia chose to be so confrontational. He had no way of knowing how van Gelden had prepared her for meeting Bartok. The cool, maybe cold image she projected showed strength and perhaps courage—maybe a foolish display but courage none-the-less. And Bartok had to deal with her.

Hastings, knowing Bartok's determination to win, felt this face-off was still up for grabs and knew Bartok would not quit. Yet, just by standing up to him and in public, Celia Markham may have won this first battle.

After a long pause, Bartok took a step back. Without raising his voice said, "Celia, I'm Zed Bartok. You've no idea how pleased I am to have you join us. It's a major victory."

"Thank you," she responded.

"I understand you wanted to see me. The consigliore said it was urgent."

Celia hadn't moved other than to slightly cock her head. "Yes, One of your officers, a Colonel Masten has ordered the execution of the pilot who brought me here."

Hastings choked back a gasp—Celia Markham was about to plead for van Gelden's life. Considering she'd started by alienating Bartok, he feared she might have made a tactical blunder—with Van Gelden's life at stake.

However, if she could pull it off, it meant he didn't risk exposure trying to save his friend's life.

"Yes. Van Gelden, I believe is his name. So, what's he to you?" Bartok seemed totally incapable of understanding that someone would ask for another human's life to be spared. "He's an enemy," Bartok continued. "Your captain is responsible for Winner White's escape from Saragosa. Colonel Masten knows the penalty and acted accordingly."

"I thought you made your own decisions." Celia seemed intent on antagonizing the big man.

Hastings stifled another choke. He didn't like the way the conversation was going.

"I do." Surprisingly, Bartok didn't sound defensive, "And in this case, I agree, so the decision stands. Van Gelden will be executed."

Celia remained unruffled. "Without van Gelden, I would not be here. He piloted his spaceship and never gave me any trouble. He always acted as gentleman." She stressed the gentleman. That was a message for Bartok. Subliminally, it had all the subtlety of a sledgehammer.

Hastings waited for Bartok's anger to erupt. The big man was obviously confused and didn't know how to handle this woman.

The giant slapped his gloves against his trouser leg, something of a habit with him. It most likely signaled growing anger or at the least, impatience.

Bartok stared at Celia as if weighing the benefits of appeasing this black-eyed beauty or forgetting about getting her into bed.

Hastings wished she'd used just a few womanly wiles on the giant. A little swing of her hips would go a long way in getting her way with him. As it now stood, two hard heads were butting for all they were worth.

Hastings feared Bartok would win this one at van Gelden's expense. He'd have to make his own effort to save his friend.

Celia weighed in. "Mr. Bartok."

"Zed. Please," Bartok offered.

She smiled and continued. "If we are to get along and trade information, help each other, let it start now." She wouldn't give an inch.

"I'll think about it." Bartok abruptly turned and left the room. At the door he stopped and wheeled to Celia. "You need a reminder. I run my operation. I don't like people challenging my authority."

"Give me this and you'll have my complete obedience."

Hastings could have sworn her lips moved in the slightest pout. Whatever happened, whatever she did, he knew Celia Markham had won.

Bartok turned to an aide, "Get Colonel Masten on the com. Tell him to hold off on van Gelden's execution but keep him under guard."

Hastings was amazed, stunned more like it that the question of who owned the ship never came up. There in the hallway, van Gelden's life came closer to being his own—at least for the moment.

Bartok said as he turned down the hallway toward the elevator, "Dinner at eight bells. In my room. Fifth floor."

Celia nodded.

Bartok's spirits seemed to lift. His walk sure did.

Hastings strode to the doorway unsure why the lady would place herself in what could be harm's way by having dinner alone with Bartok. "Ms. Markham, I'm Richard Hastings, hotel manager. If I can be of service, please don't hesitate to call."

"Thank you," she answered, the mannered calm of Hastings voice bringing a smile from her.

Hastings turned to follow Bartok. He hesitated a moment not wanting to seem eager or reluctant to either watching party—a maneuver he'd honed in his years as front man for the Tri-Lateral Commission. He'd need every bit of tact, diplomacy, verbal and body language, to weave his way through this minefield.

CHAPTER TWENTY
Hastings

Perplexed by Celia Markham, Richard Hastings returned to his second floor office. Certain the offices were bugged, he keyed the com and issued instructions to prepare Bartok's rooms and dinner menu. That done, he headed for the kitchen and lunch.

The staff watched as the chef approached him. They would follow his lead by watching where he sat Hastings. To the delight of both the chef and his staff, their new manager ate in the chef's corner.

After enjoying a wonderful lunch and complimenting the chef de cuisine, Hastings retired to his suite. He'd decided to stay in or near the hotel as long as Bartok was in residence. He was probably the only one who could or would stand up to the man. Well, there was Ms. Markham and Colonel Masten—he recalled. Masten seemed to have a great deal of influence with Bartok. On first hearing about the Colonel, he'd assumed the man commanded Bartok's army but that proved incorrect. Hastings had yet to figure out the role this man played in Bartok's scheme. He'd have to meet Masten and make his own judgment.

Hastings stopped in front of the room telecom. Accessing his personal database, he brought up the detailed plans of the hotel. Again, the telecom asked him for his special access code. He selected the three-D view of the hotel.

All the building's hidden passages and doorways came into view. It looked like a rat maze.

He sat in the large overstuffed chair and placed his feet on the leather hassock. His initial inspection of the rooms had turned up no bugs but his efforts were those of a tyro. Still, they would have to do for now. Heavy drapes covered the windows and doors to the balcony. The short piled rug, typical of hotels, did run a pleasing multi-patterned light blue.

He returned his attention to the video and the secret passageways. He started at the basement, viewed every route, where it went and what secrets it offered for entering or leaving the hotel. His people remained in charge of the hotel security for the moment, but he had to delete this information before Bartok learned of it. Bartok had ordered the installation of security cameras and audio pickups throughout the building, but that process was still underway and not yet operational. Hastings felt safe for the moment, yet, he knew to remain cautious.

Two hours later, he lay on the couch and slept. After less than an hour, the gentle vibration of his wrist com awakened him.

"Hastings here," he sleepily answered. He looked at his watch, three-thirty.

"Hastings here," he repeated.

Faintly he heard, "Hallway."

Hastings got off the sofa and went to the foyer door and opened it.

"Oh shit! Arnold." He knelt beside the unconscious bleeding consigliore.

He keyed his communicator. "Emergency! Get help up here. Medical and security. On the double! Alert the hospital we've got a major emergency."

He set about stopping his assistant's external bleeding, mostly cuts and abrasions. The swelling in Petry's abdomen meant internal hemorrhaging. Hastings feared the worst.

Within minutes, medical help arrived to assist Hastings with Petry's injuries. Years of self-sufficiency in space had prepared Hastings for most emergencies so there was little for the medics to do but move the consigliore to the hospital. Hastings followed in his ground car.

Located fewer than three blocks from the hotel, the hospital boasted an excellent staff and state of the art equipment. Bartok's assault had strained both to their limits. A semblance of order had replaced the chaos that had been the staff's daily routine after the invasion.

The emergency room doctor confirmed Petry had been unconscious for some time. Hastings thought back to the message from his wrist com, now knowing his consigliore hadn't called him. Who had? What brought Petry to the fifth floor? Why, was the man beaten? He had no answers.

The ER people worked feverishly to stop Petry's internal bleeding and reset broken bones. Three hours passed before he was wheeled to a recovery room. The consigliore's wounds were severe and would have been fatal if not taken care of.

The injuries were probably the result of kicks, fists, and clubs the doctor explained. There wasn't a knife, laser or gunshot wound on him. "But, whoever did this knew how to give a beating. It looks profession all the way. He's lucky to be alive."

Someone had wanted him out of the way.

Hastings left word that the hospital should contact him immediately when Petry gained consciousness or if his conditioned worsened. He returned to the hotel and immediately went to the security office. The new security camera and audio system was complete and activated and Bartok's people were now in control.

With Bartok's security personnel watching his every move, he tapped into the newly activated cameras and audio pickup replays to learn what he could about Petry's beating.

The security people questioned his review of the camera data but did nothing to stop him. Unfortunately, the surveillance equipment offered no help. Whoever had beaten Petry, or at least those that dumped him outside Hastings door, knew exactly when the new security systems were to be activated. But why Petry? He was no threat to anyone.

Abandoning the security system, Hastings walked down the corridor toward his room, his steps muffled by the thick carpet. He stopped abruptly when he reached his room. The door stood open a few centimeters. Someone was either in his room or had been there. Cautiously, he pushed the wooden door fully open.

"Come in Mr. Hastings. I'm Colonel Masten."

Hastings entered the room and looked around. Seeing no one else, he addressed the seated colonel. "What are you doing here?"

Masten stood. "I'm here to offer my services. I understand your consigliore met with some misfortune. I have brought a replacement." Gold shoulder epaulets glistened atop Masten's immaculate white uniform.

Hastings saw a shadow at the door. He watched a man enter and wondered how he'd missed seeing him in the hallway. Amazingly, the man looked more the part of a consigliore than the thug Hastings expected. He then focused his attention on Masten.

"You're well informed. I do appreciate your concern for the continued good operation of the hotel, but I will find my own help." He now knew who was responsible for Arnold Petry's beating.

Masten responded, "I am well informed."

There was hardness in this man and an eerie detachment. Hastings was certain the distance wasn't from reality. If anything, this man took practicality to the extreme. He had a reputation for seldom leaving survivors and never witnesses.

He listened as Masten continued, "Mr. Anthony, Ravel Anthony, is your new consigliore. You have no say in the matter."

Hastings took one step toward Masten and stopped as the Colonel's hand moved to his side. "Does Mr. Bartok know about this?"

Masten's hand dropped from the laser pistol. With a chilling coldness, he said, "Bartok appointed me to oversee all security and scientific matters on Saragosa. And this doesn't require his approval. And sure as hell not yours." The colonel exuded a malevolent calmness that Hastings took as a warning.

"I see," Hastings retorted. "Mr. Bartok has such confidence in you that he doesn't need to be kept advised of your actions."

"We are now your masters." Masten seemed to enjoy that. He turned to Anthony and said, "If Mr. Hastings doesn't cooperate, kill him."

Masten strode from the room gently closing the door behind him.

Masters, my ass Hastings thought. These people are going down! Hard! He had to warn Hrndullka and his own people before one of them tried to contact him. Exposure meant certain death.

He turned toward his new consigliore. "Do you have your own sleeping quarters or are you going to spend the night watching me?"

Anthony didn't answer the question but said. "Don't leave your rooms without letting me know."

Hastings needed to get away from the man. Obviously, his only purpose for being there was to keep track of him. Running the hotel was secondary.

"Mr. Anthony, if you are to be of any help in this hotel, we must operate in concert but independently. You do have hotel experience?"

"Yes."

"Then, as consigliore, you know there is a great deal to be done in preparation for tomorrow. It happens everyday, preparing for tomorrow. You need to be about it."

Anthony moved toward the door, then stopped and turned slowly. "Remember what I said. I want to know where you are at all times. Anything less than that and I'll kill you as Colonel Masten ordered."

Hastings watched Anthony close the door, and then stepped to the intercom. Suspecting all of his calls as well as movements were under scrutiny, he addressed the vidcom.

"Security office." Shortly, the screen revealed a dour face at the central station, the replacement undoubtedly reporting to Anthony or more likely Masten.

"Sorry," Hastings keyed off Security. "Kitchen," he ordered the vidcom. Security reappeared on the screen. The woman didn't seem surprised to be addressing him again.

"Mr. Hastings, all intercom and vidcom transmissions now go through security."

He keyed off the vidcom. He had to get word to Hulk. But how?

He tapped his wrist communicator. What had been a dour face now turned stern—the same woman. She attempted a smile. He shut it off. Most likely, every attempt he made was relayed to Anthony and maybe Masten. But, that didn't alarm him. In fact, he expected it. Bartok was consolidating his hold over Saragosa. These people ruled with fear and intimidation. Obedience was a condition gained by expediency—expediency or death.

He sat in the large overstuffed chair, thinking and scanning the room. Three surveillance cameras now dotted the walls. Casually, he arose from the chair. Cautiously, he strode through each room, mentally noting the movement and range of each camera; the bathroom didn't escape the electronic eavesdropping. He retreated to the main room and then to the sliding doors leading to the balcony, then back into the room. Seeing no camera on the balcony, he made his decision.

Slowly, he walked to the desk situated under the vidcom, his arms folded across his chest, seemingly in deep thought. With his back to the camera, he extracted a piece of paper and closed the desk drawer. Again, he headed for the balcony. On the way he picked up the pipe he occasionally smoked. Hastings stepped into the open air, eased a scriber from his coat pocket.

Shielding his actions from the room camera, he scribbled a warning note to Hulk and a message for Rap to delete the computer program showing the hidden passages. Then he tightly folded the paper and cupped it in his hand. He returned the scriber to his coat pocket and retraced his steps into the room. At the vidcom he spoke. "Maintenance Department."

True to her word, the stern faced security woman appeared. She said nothing apparently waiting on him to speak.

"I need someone from maintenance up here," he said.

"What for?" she asked.

Hastings added a scowl to his face, "Are you qualified to judge whether or not a maintenance problem exists?" Before she could answer, he said. "Get maintenance up here." and keyed off the screen.

He waited. The maintenance man assigned to this shift was one of Hulk's men—unless security had changed his assignments.

After what seemed an eternity, he answered the door com and breathed a silent sigh of relief recognizing Rap Sheets.

He led the man to the balcony doors, and showed him an upturned carpet edge—clearly a safety hazard. Quick repair brought the man a thank you and handshake passing the note for Hulk.

So much for high tech he thought. Now, to his plan.

Rap left Hastings's second floor rooms and dashed for the gravlift, its door closing as he slid past. It was going up but that didn't matter that much—it would come down. He reached into his tool kit and punched a small black box deactivating the gravlift security system. Only then did he unfold and read the note.

CHAPTER TWENTY ONE
Seeds of doubt

The seeds of doubt Captain van Gelden had planted in her mind had grown, especially after she'd met Bartok. Celia desperately needed hard evidence that Winner White really had killed her father. She also needed to do more to get Captain van Gelden out of harms' way. She would have preferred to dine alone but Bartok had insisted she join him.

Well, she could use the opportunity to pursue her goals.

She looked at her image in the mirror. The full-length, from neck to floor, sleeveless black gown suited her. A pearl choker matched silver crusted ear pearls, and pearl-covered handbag. A black fine-lace shoulder wrap completed the ensemble—all compliments of Bartok.

She would have preferred a suit for the dinner, but hadn't escaped Galactic Star with any of her wardrobe or personal items. The only clothing she'd brought with her was her blue jump suit. There'd been no time or opportunity to shop in Saragosa City. But she doubted that the war had left many shops open.

She checked the lock on her door after leaving, and then headed for the gravlift and Bartok's fifth floor room.

When she arrived, Celia pulled the black lace wrap over her shoulders and exposed arms and knocked gently.

Both doors swung wide. Behind them, Bartok smiled and gave a slight bow.

"How exquisite! Absolutely beautiful!" he exclaimed. "Please come in." He'd changed into a white tropical suit forgoing the coat and tie. Short sleeves exposed his powerful arms.

Celia acknowledged him cordially, walked into the room and handed Bartok her wrap. She would give her best effort to get along.

She continued past Bartok to the large window overlooking the darkened city. Off in the distance, the brightly lighted space drone continued to receive soldiers and supplies. None of the rooms in the Crest were plush by galactic standards, but they were generous in size. She glanced toward the darkened corner where Bartok had set the dinner table, a lounge and bar nearby. Glowing candles reflected from the glass walls made the area look much larger than it was.

"I hope they're no hard feelings over our discussion this afternoon," she started the conversation. "It's important to me that Captain van Gelden not be killed for bringing me here. I have no taste for murderers. That is, after all, what has brought me to Saragosa."

Bartok kept quiet. He moved to the bar, held up a bottle of wine, "82," he said.

Celia nodded. She returned to the bar and took a stool, Bartok still on the opposite side. "From White's private cellar or did you bring it?"

"From what I can tell, neither. Hotel stock."

"Too bad," she said.

"Come," Bartok said. "Join me." He motioned to the lounge.

Celia moved to the couch and sat, Bartok next to her. She kept to the edge of the cushion, a comfortable distance from her huge host.

She said, "This is the first time we've had to talk about Winner White. I've seen electronic copies, but I'd like to see the hard evidence he killed my father. Was there an independent investigation? I need to see those results."

"Later. We need to get to know each other. Especially now that we're working together." Bartok stretched out his hand and placed it on her shoulder.

Celia moved from under his touch. "Mr. Bartok. I'm here to find out how and why my father died and to punish Winner White for his actions. Until I'm satisfied on that account, everything will have to wait. I said you'd have my obedience but there are limits to even that." She knew this would anger Bartok but van Gelden had warned her the man was immune to what anyone else wanted or said, especially if it was a woman. At first, she had doubted van Gelden's assessment of Bartok—not any more.

Celia could see Bartok was struggling to keep control. He wasn't accustomed to anyone, particularly not a woman, thwarting him.

"If you insist." Bartok slammed the wineglass on the table in front of them holding the hors d'oeuvres, breaking the stem. Tossing aside the shards, he stalked to the bar, poured himself a shot of bourbon and downed it before walking back to the table. "If we are to get along, I expect a totally different attitude from you. I'll tell you about Winner White and it won't take me long. But when that's over, I expect things to be different!"

Celia didn't move or say a word.

Bartok was furious. It wasn't in his character to tolerate being ignored, yet Celia was ignoring his tirade.

She reached over the finger food tray and selected a choice pâté.

Bartok rejoined her on the off-white leather covered lounge and tried a smile—it had all the character of a snarled grimace.

"Four years ago," he said, "White was working at Gorman. Three months before he returned to Earth, he disappeared, dropped out of sight. Faked records to make it look like he was still at the test base on Dema-Alpha One. But, he wasn't. My people have evidence he was seen in the area where your father's ship disappeared. He was there. He did it. He tried to hide it." Bartok stopped and leaned back against the pillow of the Lounge.

"How does that tie White to murder? Your spy showed me correspondence, flight data. Where is that? And what about motive? Did my father know something White didn't want disclosed? What you're giving me makes no sense. My father worked with other people, not in a vacuum. Other people had to know about his work on Saragosa.

"So far, White just needs to supply some answers to his whereabouts." Celia hadn't heard anything of value. At least anything that brought her closer to knowing what happened to her father.

Bartok moved to the edge of the lounge, resting his elbows lightly on his knees; he turned to face Celia, their legs almost touched. She saw him look at the closeness of their bodies and sensed his frustration turning to rage.

She stood abruptly and walked to the sliding doors. Opening them, she stepped onto the balcony. She welcomed the gentle breeze as it brushed her face and the relief it brought from Bartok's stifling closeness.

She looked out over the darkened city. Few lights showed. The city was still without electrical power, the fusion generators remained off line at Bartok's orders.

Light on his feet for such a big man, he followed her to the balcony rail.

"Mr. Bartok. I need proof. I need to be sure of what I'm doing before I kill Winner White or I'm no better than he is."

He held open his arms. "Later. Tomorrow I'll make our complete files available to you and you'll be convinced. In the meantime, let's enjoy the evening." His hands, larger than any she'd ever seen, seemed to blot out the light as they spread to engulf her.

Before Bartok knew what was happening, Celia pulled up her arm and threw her entire weight into his wrist, then ducked under and away from his embrace.

"I'm not up to this. I need to go back to my room. Could we put this dinner off until tomorrow?" She had no intentions of returning, but she needed him to think otherwise. Could it be that there simply wasn't any real information on the disappearance? Although she and her father were both successful scientists, they'd never learned to trust people in power. Like most researchers, their people skills needed honing. Well, even a rough sharpening would be an asset. Maybe that distrust had blinded her to the truth. She needed time to think—to sort out her feelings.

She left the balcony and continued toward the door.

Bartok blocked her exit. He spun to grab her, then reeled back when he saw he was faced with a laser pen gun capable of inflicting a severe wound, even death in the right hands.

Bartok quickly overcame the initial surprise, scowled and said, "How did you get that past security?"

She sensed she may have the advantage and pressed it.

"I am a scientist and we do have our ways—and I know how to use this," Celia said in a whisper. In that instant, she doubted everything Bartok's people had said about her father's death. Everything they'd showed her could be forged —or could have pointed the finger of guilt at the wrong man.

Maybe she'd believed along what she wanted to and it played into Bartok's plans. Maybe she'd misjudged the investigators at WMC. Maybe she'd condemned Winner White unnecessarily. She wasn't ready to concede that but she recalled White's investigation officer had offered her access to what information they had. She'd reviewed it. It was no help and she assumed it had been cleansed. Maybe no one knew what happened. It was becoming obvious Bartok either didn't or was lying.

She stopped. The blackness she'd felt earlier when thinking of her father's death and Winner White returned. Only this time, something told her the right target was before her. She wanted to say, "If you ever touch me again, I'll kill you!" But she held her temper and her tongue.

Bartok tried to step in front of the double doors, his face red with anger.

She beat him there, adding to his rage. Quickly, she opened the door and stepped into the hallway. It took all of her will not to look back—but Bartok would see that as weakness and would surely pounce.

The sound of breaking glass and cursing echoed through the opening. The guard outside the door moved a step further into the hallway as if to distance himself from the rage.

Celia bypassed the gravlift and punched the button for the elevator. She stepped past the opening door, not waiting for it to fully retract, and then noticed the other rider.

"I'm going up."

She acknowledged with a stiff nod, still shaken from her encounter. Apparently, the man sensed her nervousness or anger. She didn't know which it was herself.

"Those are Bartok's rooms. You must be the woman we've heard so much about," he said.

She spun on her heel and faced the man. Her anger not yet satiated, she lashed out, "I don't know what you heard, but I'm not his woman. I came here to find out who killed my father. That's the only reason!"

The man feigned a recoil from her verbal blast but she was sure it was just an act. He didn't seem to be easily cowed.

Why had she told this man—a total stranger? She had to settle down. She had to control her emotions.

"Is it?" The man quietly asked. "The word's out you're here to kill Winner White because he killed your father."

"How do you know that?" she asked.

He shrugged. "Lady, from what I just heard, Bartok's mad at you. That means all his people are mad at you. And I don't think you'll find many people among Winner White's supporters who'll welcome you with open arms. I'd say you have a lot of problems."

She'd been so sure just days before.

"Would you mind pointing that thing somewhere else?" He motioned with his finger.

The laser pen gun was pointed at the man's head. Despite her mistake, he smiled. It helped her relax a little.

"Sorry. I'd forgotten about it," she responded returning it to her handbag.

"Did you threaten Bartok with that?" he pointed to the laser.

"Yes."

"Lady, do what you want, but I think you'd better get the hell out of here. From what I've seen of Bartok, you're in worse trouble than I thought."

"I can take care of—"

"You believe Winner White killed your father?"

111

Only then did she notice the surveillance camera. She placed her hand over her mouth. The look in her eyes questioning if she'd said something she'd regret.

"It's okay. I neutralized both the video and audio when I got on the elevator; delayed feedback on a looping circuit does the trick. It keeps showing the last frame it was seeing when I click this little gadget." He pulled a small black box from his tool case. "No one can hear or see us. I'm the maintenance man here. I helped install these things."

She found it easy to believe him. "Bartok's people convinced me that White killed my father. And I've not seen nor heard anything to change that." She wasn't the least bit sure she did still believe it. What she'd just heard from Bartok sounded too bogus to be believed.

Her lift companion leaned against the wall. "Winner White may have done what you say, but I doubt it. That isn't the man I think I know."

"You know him?" She didn't tell him of her brief encounter with Winner on Galactic Star.

"Yes. He was giving this planet to us. He was on Saragosa Prime setting up our first democratic elections when the attack came. We were about to pick our own political leaders. He barely escaped after the attack.

"And he will be back with a vengeance. And there will be more ass kicking than you can believe. Bartok's a dead man, he just doesn't know it." Almost aside he added, "And so is the butcher Masten."

"So you know Masten." It wasn't a question. "All I want is the truth. I want to know how and why my father died."

Cautiously, the man said, "Maybe I can help you."

The lift stopped on the tenth floor. "We need to get off here. This is the top floor and the elevator goes back down immediately," the man said.

They stepped into the hallway. He reached into his toolkit, and she heard a click reactivating the elevator surveillance systems.

He held his finger in front of his lips.

Once in the hallway, he motioned her to one of the few spots not covered by a camera.

"Like I said, maybe I can help," he whispered.

Celia asked, "Did you put cameras in my rooms?"

He cleared his throat and said, "Yes Ma'am. All the rooms." He raised an eyebrow. Anticipating her next question he went on, "Yes, that one too."

A smirk of disgust crossed Celia's face. She looked off in the distance and asked, "What do you need of me?"

"We have to leave here. And there's no returning. At least for you."

Startled, her voice a menacing whisper she said, "Why should I believe you? For all I know, you're just another minion of Bartok's. You just claim you disconnected the security cameras. And no one tried to stop you? Not a likely story."

"Have it your way lady. But I thought you'd like to know that an effort to free van Gelden is under way as we speak."

She spun to face him. In that instant, she knew this man was telling the truth.

Celia stared at the man for a long moment. "You know, I want to believe you. Captain van Gelden is guilty of following orders. No more. It would mean a great deal to me to know he's free.

"Do you have a name?" she asked.

"Donald Sheets. My friends call me Rap."

That brought a laugh. "Been arrested, huh?"

"Just once," he whispered with a grin.

"Are you with the resistance?"

Rap didn't answer immediately. The friendly face hardened, "My family and many of my friends died in the attack. Which side do you think I should be on? Which side would you be on?"

She let out a deep sigh, "I understand. We better be gone before Bartok changes his mind and comes calling." Celia suspected he would think over their confrontation and still come to her room. He didn't give up easily.

Celia could understand Rap's feelings. At least his path was clearer than hers. If she stayed, she'd have to face Bartok again and she may not be twice lucky. Bartok wasn't interested in what new scientific information she could provide. To him, she was just another woman. Someone to have, or to take.

But where could she learn the truth? That was really all she wanted. Bartok's story wasn't believable. And it may be because he knew the truth. Rap still hadn't told her he was part of the resistance.

For what it's worth, she thought, I've heard Bartok's story. Maybe it's time to hear White's.

"Okay Rap, what happens next?" she asked.

His manner changed. His look became grave. "We go to your room first. Act normal, do what ever you'd normally do. I'll shut off the cameras and audio stuff." He reached into his toolkit and extracted the small control box.

"You get out of that dress and into something you can travel in—in not very nice places. Pack what personal stuff you absolutely need. Not too much. We have to move quickly."

Celia led Rap the last twenty meters to her room, opened the door and entered.

Rap trailed behind her. He went from room to room shutting down the surveillance system then turned out the lights.

In the dark, Celia pulled her jump suit from the closet. In minutes, she was dressed.

"I'm ready," she whispered. Of that, she wasn't the least bit certain. Her world was changing faster than she wanted. Most of her life, decisions had been well ordered, thought out and as deliberate as possible, seldom hurried. Scientists were trained from day one that being thorough was more important than speed—it served them well in research. Now it seemed she had only her gut to go on.

Rap led her to a paneled wall in the closet. He felt out two spots and pushed.

The wall opened.

He returned to each room, reactivating the surveillance equipment.

Celia waited at the opening. The closet was the last to receive the treatment.

He motioned her quickly through the cutout into a dark passageway and then followed.

As he closed the panel, Rap punched the activator for the closet surveillance and sealed the opening, then pulled out a light cell. "Whispers only. We have to go all the way to the basement—ten floors."

Squeezing in the narrow passage, he handed her a cap to cover her hair. "This place is full of wall tunnels and things that crawl. It's like an old medieval castle. Hastings told me to wipe them from the computer but the security people control the database. If Bartok's security people find it, most likely we won't get out alive."

She stuffed her hair under the cap. Rap looked at the result and gave a slight grin accompanied by a little wave of his hand as if to say looks great.

She smirked back. After all, it wasn't a fashion show.

Rap brought out a phased laser pistol. They maintained a quick pace; paused only to listen for any sound that may have signaled their discovery. Celia didn't mind the narrow corridor or the musty smell. The walkway appeared abandoned for years. Pipes and conduit crowded much of it. Their steps created small cloud of dust, and each foot of progress dragged her body through the countless cobwebs crisscrossing the passages.

They stopped at a wooden ladder and then Rap started down.

She followed. A creaking rung brought fear of discovery and stopped their descent until they dared hope they hadn't betrayed themselves. She heard the occasional muffled blast of a vehicle launch from the space drone and guessed they were near an outside wall.

At the fifth level the descent ladder stopped.

She followed Rap along another narrow passageway toward what she guessed was the rear of the building.

He leaned close to her, pointed to an enclosure. "Gravlift," he whispered. Rap shined the light at the decking that served as the walk platform around the lift.

Foot prints.

He knelt beside the marks, inspecting them. He whispered to Celia, "Combat boots. No way to tell if the tracks are recent. No way to tell if it's Bartok's men."

He was lying. Prior to the invasion, boots like those had never been on Saragosa.

He shoved his phased laser pistol into his tool kit and armed it, using the container to stifle the noise. They move lower into the building.

Ten minutes later, they were in the basement. The passageway ended in the equipment room tool closet.

Rap listened for any noised that didn't fit the normal hum of the machinery. Hearing nothing, slowly he opened the door and peered into the room.

Large fuel cells that provided the hotel's electrical power dominated the area around them and gave good cover to the storm sewer that would lead them away from the Crest Hotel.

Opening a utility cover, they climbed down a steel ladder to the underground storm sewer. Rap struggled to replace the heavy cover, his body bent under the weight. Celia climbed the narrow ladder and together they slid the cover in place.

He dropped to the sewer floor and helped her down, "Thanks," he said. "We've a ways to go yet."

They crossed the knee-deep water to the sewer wall, stepped up on a walkway that ran the length of the tunnel. At least the water is only inches deep up here Celia thought. She put her hand over her nose trying to stave off the reeking odor that dominated the rancid air.

Almost apologetically, Rap said, "The sanitation plants were badly damaged during the orbital bombardment. The storm sewers normally can handle the overflow, but with all the trash and other derbies from the devastation, they're overloaded. And most of the city was built before each building had its own waste disposal."

She couldn't tell how far they trotted but figured about two kilometers. Her lungs were burning. She guessed it was the running, although the stench was hardly bearable.

Rap stopped, "I'm sorry Ms. Markham, I have to blindfold you. Until we know for sure whose side you're on, we can't take a chance on you giving away our position."

Celia held out her hands as if to say, "What can I do?"

Rap gently put the blindfold in place, then led her some distance. Finally, he steered her to an iron ladder.

She climbed the twenty or so rungs out of the storm sewer and gulped at the fresh air. Celia slowly turned in the cool breeze as if using its freshness to rid her of the sewer smell. It dawned on her they hadn't removed the heavy iron cover. Others were there.

She heard a voice say, "This way."

She stopped.

"It's okay," Rap said. "They're friends."

It had been some time since she'd hear anyone called a friend. It was most likely the resistance group that Rap was taking her to even though he'd never said so.

Someone guided her to a ground car. Minutes later they stopped. A hand helped her to the pavement and they descended a flight of stairs to a landing then again down stairs—over sixty steps she counted in total, the blindfold still in place.

She heard voices in the background. Someone told Rap he had to return to the hotel and help Hastings escape.

Celia jolted hearing Hastings's name. Damn she thought. He's part of the Resistance too. Doubt crowded her mind. I might have been better off staying at the hotel, she thought. Rap was probably right, there was going to be some serious ass kicking before long. It might be hers right along with Bartok's. But then, a lot could happen. This fight wasn't over. Bartok still held the advantage, with superior numbers in men and firepower on the ground and in space. Maybe Bartok was a dead man and maybe he wasn't. She was neutral in the fight between White and Bartok. Bartok's evidence might be suspect, but that didn't mean Winner White hadn't killed her father. Her purpose remained unchanged.

She stood quietly and alone for a few moments. Then someone approached.

A deep rumbling voice spoke, "Remove the blindfold."

As her eyes adjusted, she saw a man even taller than Bartok in front of her.

"Ms. Markham, I'm Vladislov Hrndullka."

CHAPTER TWENTY TWO
The forces gather

Admiral Ashcroft stood next to the newly appointed CAG—Commander Zen.

Together, they watched Legere, with Winner at the controls, launch from the side bay. A spirited maintenance crew had completed changes to accommodate a total of five Marines, satisfying Company policy requirement that Winner travel with adequate security.

"Commander," Ashcroft said, "One objective of Mr. White's trip is to obtain deep space fighters. I have no idea how successful he'll be. You'll need to form an air group and be prepared to hanger all the fighters we can hold in our shuttle bay. Be optimistic. He's a resourceful man."

"Aye, Sir." Zen had often mentioned he'd like a full shuttle bay. He seemed eager to put his ideas to work.

Following the launch, Ashcroft returned to the main bridge. Captain Davenport bent over the display awaiting telemetry confirming Legere's course. He stood at Ashcroft's entry. "Why is Mr. White personally going to the Galon Sector? With the power at his disposal, corporate power, why doesn't he apply his muscle and get what he needs?"

Ashcroft answered, "For Mr. White, it's much simpler than that. If you're asking someone to die for you, look him in the eye when you do it." The admiral left for his quarters, the boson called "Admiral off the bridge."

* * * *

Winner had been first to board the ship. His spirits were high. Finally, he was doing something positive toward getting rid of Bartok. His recruiting mission would give him time to think through the battle plan. One man could fly and navigate Legere through its central control system. It did offer separate navigation and communication stations. He would use those to train Melissa and her squad on space navigation and piloting. You never knew when it might come in handy. For the first time in a while, he was alone with his own kind of people, fighters—warriors. He could let his hair down, at least a little. He knew the problems of a mixed group isolated and away from base. Although this was different, he was still CIC.

Winner stepped around the small bridge as he had during the conversion and he continued to marvel at the layout. Excellent. Despite being small, Legere's bridge was exceptionally well designed. It gave the feeling of room, probably from the ease with which anyone could move. Bartok had an excellent reputation for spaceship design and Legere showed it.

Movement around the ship was important considering seven people taxed its usable space. With no up or down in zero gravity you could use all the inside of the spaceship, something lost in the luxury of artificial gravity.

Winner's quarters, just off the bridge, were small but adequate. A bunk, desk that included a vidcom with computer terminal and a sonic bath and a head would be his home for the next ten days. What few clothes he'd brought were stored above the bunk.

Melissa had the quarters next to his and the two shared the head. A few meters aft of her cabin, behind the bulkhead in the cargo storage, her squad rigged hammocks. A small head and galley fronted the engine room.

He greeted Melissa with a smile as she stepped through the bridge hatchway. "Welcome aboard lieutenant. How much do you ground pounder's know about space flight?"

"Only what you airdales let us know. In other words, not much, sir," she responded and added a snappy salute.

Winner returned the honorific, noticed she'd turned to the Marine entering behind her, and winked as she said it. The remaining squad members filed onto the bridge.

"Actually, only that it's get sick time, going in and out of hyperspace."

"Lieutenant, won't happen on Legere. At least not from entering or leaving hyperspace. Maybe too much booze, of which there'd better not be any on board. But that's all."

Melissa stood at attention facing him. "Your orders, sir."

"Assign each member of your squad a duty station. They'll all learn something about flying a spaceship over the next few days. Report to your duty station. By the time this flight is over, you'll be an experienced spacer." Some of the jobs were make-do but Winner knew how boring space flight could be. It would give them all something to do, including him.

"Lieutenant, as Officer of the Deck, you are responsible for navigation and the actual flying of the ship."

"Do you really think I'm ready for that?" she asked.

"No," he bluntly answered. He walked around the bridge checking each station. "I'll be watching every move you make."

Melissa blew a sigh of relief.

He grinned.

She sat at the astroplot. "Course, Sir?"

"We'll use Galactic Star as base reference Lieutenant." He pointed out the various references she'd need to watch and what each meant. "Plug our destination into the computer." He pointed to the screen.

Melissa raised her hand like a student.

Winner grimaced. "Lieutenant Graves, it isn't necessary to raise your hand. What do you want?"

"How? And where are we going? And what icons do I punch?"

The little girl in her touched Winner. He laughed and gave the command authorization. "Computer, primary override. Set origination. Maintain all references from Right Ascension zero, Declination zero." Keeping the levity of the moment, he added, "Wasn't that easy? Nothing to it."

Melissa watched the numbers appear on the plot screen: Ten hours twenty eight minutes forty-four seconds, RA plus twenty degrees twelve minutes thirty-five seconds, DEC.

"That's where we're going," he said. "Hit that key. That locks in Star's location so we'll be able to find her when we return."

Winner said, "Computer, display coordinates for Zinter asteroid cluster in the Galon sector and enter as our destination."

They all listened to the computer, "Course eighty-eight degrees fourteen minutes RA plus eighteen degrees four minutes eight seconds DEC."

Winner continued, "Computer, calculate duration of flight; Power settings, Alpha through Zeta, one hour steps, course verification at step ten."

The computer answered immediately, "ETA to Zinter asteroid cluster, twenty five hours, nine minutes, standard—time deficit unknown."

Winner thoughtfully rubbed his chin. "Even the computer's unsure of how the higher ranges of hyperwave will affect time."

He turned to the job at hand, "We've a lot of space to cover in the next ten days."

Melissa responded, "Aye, sir. Course set. Ready to sequence on your command."

Winner took his seat at the front of the small bridge. Most spaceships had the manual controls at the rear of the bridge. Legere's fronted it like most space fighters. He liked the view and position the station provided.

He pushed aside the manual control panel. "Engage main drive engines; engage artificial grav. When we reach three tenths c, sound the alarm and engage hyper drive generators. We'll see what this machine can do, a little at a time."

As a test pilot, he'd had this much speed available but only in research craft. Trying something new brought back memories of Gorman Industries test facility and a sometime raucous past. It also brought back the pained last three months and the pure hell that would never go away. He nursed the moment, held it close. It was a time in his life he would never forget.

Winner felt a slight change in gravity as the generators engaged. The whine of the main drive engines increased although it wasn't bothersome—noise cancellation equipment modulated the vibrations transmitted through the hull. Winner wanted to hear the noises of a ship. It helped him get the pulse of the beast. Sometimes you could detect problems before they got life threatening if you understood your vessel and sound was one of the ways it communicated with you, if you listened.

Legere's acceleration was at a steady rate and hardly noticeable thanks to the artificial gravity. It wouldn't take long to reach hyperspace entry speed.

Winner said, "A number of small companies operate mines in the asteroid belt. We've already been in contact with them. Melissa, see if you can raise anyone on a tight beam FTL transmission before we enter hyperspace. Let them know we're on our way. Give our ETA."

"Aye, sir," answered Melissa. She issued instructions to the corporal operating the com link.

White's FTL technology had spread across space with every passing ship. During the previous six days, they'd communicated with over twenty other stations as more and more locations installed the new technology.

He wasn't making any money on the discovery his labs had developed, but the faster communication greatly helped him gather the forces he desperately needed for the assault on Saragosa. Sometimes, things have a way of working out, he thought.

One hour later, Melissa sounded the alarm and engaged the hyper drive.

Winner monitored Legere's progress as the sleek ship reached speeds that would have been impossible only days before. As in his flight test days, he carefully learned the capabilities now at his command. Derka said the hull could handle Upsilon, almost five hundred times the speed of light. But he wasn't ready for that. He'd take it a step at a time.

Once underway, he set up watches of four on and eight off for the squad. He and Melissa would stand twelve on and twelve off. She took the first watch and Winner stayed on the bridge to instruct her.

"Lieutenant," he asked. "How much do you know about Legere?"

"Just the little I've learned from Phalen. He said the hull was made of the strongest hull material known." She pondered a minute, and with a staccato delivery said, "It's a hybrid—beta-carbon—nitride covering a titanium-tungsten-mag hull."

"Very good. And speed?"

With Bartok having the hull technology Winner wondered what other surprises waited them at Saragosa.

"Phalen said the ship would go faster than you'd take it."

"Give the man a cigar," Winner said.

Melissa smiled.

"Maybe I haven't been keeping you busy enough," Winner teased. "It seems you've spent a lot of time with Mr. Derka. Not keeping him from his work I hope."

"Depends on how work is defined." She clearly enjoyed the verbal joust.

"I think I'm losing this." Winner threw up his hands in mock surrender.

Hours later, Melissa headed for her cabin. She'd stayed at her station for fourteen hours, anxious to learn everything she could.

* * * *

Twelve hours after that, Winner stood and stretched as Melissa entered the bridge for her watch, "The computer's running the ship. If anything needs attention, it will tell you. Any questions?" Without waiting for an answer, he stifled a yawn, "I'm going to get some sleep."

Seven hours later, Winner re-appeared on the bridge. Melissa looked at the plot chronometer.

"Yeah, I'm early. Thought I would make a stab at furthering your education."

"Please, spare me the shame." She pressed the back of her hand to her forehead.

"Some appreciation I get for the sacrifices I make." He jammed his hands into his pockets. "Let's continue your instruction."

Winner pulled his shoulders back and assumed a posture as if gazing off into space. "We've got enough time on this leg to reach upsilon but let's hold it at zeta. We need to digest the collected information before going any faster. Not that I want to right now. We have to slow to achieve orbit or convoy with another vessel or asteroid. Then, of course, we still have to drop out of hyperspace and verify our heading and position. And just as importantly, verify time. Speed doesn't help much if we get lost."

Winner swung his control panel back into place. After a few minutes of working, he turned his chair around to face Melissa and pointing to the plot board. "Enter this. It's the rest of our flight plan. It'll take us to another five or mining companies. They're the last companies out here large enough to be of help to us."

The complete flight plan would take them to ten possible sources of help— the Zinter asteroid cluster held five of them, companies that might be able to give military assistance. That complete, he returned to his plan to recapture Saragosa.

Almost two hours passed before Winner ordered the drop out of hyperspace. With the artificial-grav unit, Legere didn't suffer the long delay usually experienced leaving hyperspace above the alpha level nor did it have to dump excessive delta v.

"Melissa, I want to tight beam this message to Galactic Star, code and scramble it."

She looked questioningly at him.

"I want to know if Nimitz Crossing and Minns Station are still under White's control. Also if they now have FTL communication capability."

Within minutes, they had their answer—Bartok hadn't yet attacked Nimitz Crossing, Minns Station or Cellus IV. Apparently, he still had his hands full at Saragosa Prime and didn't have reserves to commit to an assault against the outlying locations. Bartok's resource crunch would only get worse when he learned Namaycush was under attack.

As each piece of information came in about Saragosa, Winner's confidence grew. Bartok hadn't completely subjugated the planet. He had to be draining resources not easily replaced. So far, they had no word of reinforcements heading his way. Winner wondered why Fonso Carren and Kirk Filbright had dropped out of the daily reports. White's forces would be consolidating both Marines and material, getting stronger while Bartok gradually lost momentum. Still, Winner would not delay the invasion—first, he assumed Bartok could find some means of gaining reinforcements. Second, he wouldn't leave the people of Saragosa under the butcher's control longer than he needed to.

"Tight-beam a command response signal to all three remaining outposts," he ordered. The command response signal required that only the senior command person respond. Winner would check any protocols they received to verify if those responses were valid.

In less than an hour, a coded and scrambled message came from Nimitz Crossing, Colonel Mordichi Hornblower, senior Marine officer, commanding. Winner sent Hornblower his orders:

"Colonel Hornblower following is your authority to organize and lead an expeditionary force to capture Namaycush. Use all available assets you have under your command at Minns, Nimitz Crossing and Cellus IV. The attack must clearly demonstrate the capture of Namaycush as your objective, nothing less. Time is of the essence. The attack force is to leave ASAP. Approximately one million klicks from Namaycush is the asteroid cluster, Marmadies. Enter the cluster, hide and await my command to attack. Good luck."

Melissa keyed Winner's Commander-In-Chief command signal to verify the transmission's legitimacy, then sent the same message to Admiral Ashcroft.

As the senior combat officer in the area, Hornblower would lead the diversion. The fact that he was the only senior officer in the area didn't bother Winner.

He hoped the Colonel lived up to his name—the attack needed to make a lot of noise. It had to divert a substantial amount of Bartok's Saragosa force to the defense of his home world. Winner suspected Fonso Carren and Kirk Filbright were on their way to attack Nimitz Crossing and Cellus IV. Hornblower's spoiling attack would divert them and hopefully, a number of the spacecraft surrounding Saragosa would re-deploy to defend Namaycush.

None of Hornblower's ships possessed sufficient hull strength for anti-grav generators. Alpha level hyperspace would be their maximum speed. To help hide their approach, the movement would be circular. After two days travel in deep space, the raiders would be able to keep the Marmadie asteroids between them and Namaycush. The transit time to Namaycush's quadrant was seven standard days. With no fighter escort, they would be exposed and vulnerable if discovered, but now everything was a gamble. The risks were great but necessary.

Almost thirteen hours later, Legere dropped out of hyperspace and asteroid Z-3 appeared on the plot board. The closest star was a little under three hundred million klicks away. What little sunlight reached this area reflected eerily from the thousands of asteroids. Fortunately, this group of space rocks had a stable orbit, slowly moving under gravitational influence its distant sun.

Winner issued the command he would repeat at least half a dozen times on this mission. "Lieutenant, standard spacewalk orbit."

CHAPTER TWENTY THREE
Recruiting

Winner stood at the front of the bridge and watched as the void swallowed the dark asteroid. Legere raced to a safe distance before entering hyperspace, twelve days of very successful recruiting completed.

Like diamonds scattered over a black velvet carpet, the panorama of stars spread before him.

Usually inspired by what he thought of as the drama of space, now his mind was a parsec away, anticipating the invasion of Namaycush.

Hiding among the asteroids would be tricky for Hornblower's invasion fleet. Damned risky as a matter of fact. The flight crews will have to be at their best. Danger from collision with speeding asteroids was greater than from enemy fire. The Marmadie asteroids were not as orderly as those in the Zinter belt.

Winner took his seat and said, "Lieutenant, Juice it up. Let's go home. We've had a good recruiting trip. Transmit our ETA to Star." The mission had been more productive than Winner had thought possible—unfortunately, it hadn't been more than he'd hoped for or more than what he needed.

With an air of pride, he told the Marines, "You people have shown progress as a flight crew." They all got a lot of hands-on training done. The crew wasn't green anymore—either from inexperience or space sickness. They were molding into a competent flight crew. More importantly, they'd become a team and that would carry over in any encounter they would face.

Melissa responded, "Aye, sir. Galactic Star next stop. And thank you." She punched the controls to send both Legere and the message on their way.

In almost the same breath she said, "Sir, a message from Galactic Star."

"Let's hear it, Lieutenant."

Captain Davenport's stern taut voice came over the com. "Legere, we are under missile attack. Admiral Ashcroft is dead. Have sustained damage to the ship. Hull momentarily breached, venting contained. No passengers injured; origin of attack unknown. Fighters launched to provide cover. Under way at available speed for rendezvous with Adaval and Zachary. Arrival in ten hours. Davenport."

Before the message finished, Winner was on his feet. Through gritted teeth he ordered, "Lieutenant, I relieve you. I have the helm!"

Melissa responded instantly, "I stand relieved." Hands folded in her lap she grimly watched him activate his console.

His taking command had nothing to do with Melissa's competence—in that instant, he needed to take action, to do something. What he had in mind, he couldn't assign to anyone other than himself. His frustration had grown as he'd continued to take casualties without being able to deliver a blow to his enemy.

"Computer, increase speed one band every hour to Upsilon level."

For the first time, a space ship would travel five hundred times the speed of light—they would travel as no human ever had. He added, "Computer, monitor and report any anomaly."

Returning to his command console seat Winner asked, "Computer, at Upsilon speed, ETA to Galactic Star?"

Immediately the answer came, 'Thirty-six point eight hours, standard; time debt unknown'.

Never again, he thought. He had to lead the fight for Saragosa. He'd not been raised in one of the most powerful families in the universe to stand by as others died. He would kill that sorry bastard Bartok himself. Winner looked toward Star. The stars didn't seem as bright as they had before.

CHAPTER TWENTY FOUR
The fight begins

Winner headed Legere toward Galactic Star, the staged speed increases, his test pilot experience and the instruments his sole guides. If at any time something didn't track, he would cut their speed. His anger had not replaced reason. It added to his cunning and determination. Those who knew him would recognize his mood—he had become his most dangerous.

On the approach to Galactic Star, he viewed the damaged cruiser; his thoughts more on Admiral Ashcroft. He was the last of his name. Only friends remained to mourn him.

One missile had hit the big cruiser head-on, detonating against the deflector shield that fronted Saragosa. Most of the explosion had dissipated into the nothingness of space. A second missile hit aft of the bridge, at the boundary layer between the forward and number one side panel shields. As fate dictated, that had been Ashcroft's quarters. Shields were breached, the Admiral lost, vented to space.

Legere lined up on Galactic Star's rear docking bay and landed.

Winner stepped to the deck. Melissa and her security squad followed. In the background, he heard the boson's shout: 'Flag is aboard.'

A grave Davenport saluted him. He started to speak and Winner waved him silent.

In the short time he'd had to check Davenport's record, he'd found the man had no actual combat experience but had studied the strategies of every major war and of the exceptional use of armed force—and had written on both subjects. Winner was pleased to see the man was also an advocate of the principles of Cincinnatus, agreeing with the Roman general's concept of civilian authority rather than the military governing conquered lands. He believed the military's job was to wage or prevent war, not govern. In fact, that was what had originally attracted him to Ashcroft.

"Captain, Let's be clear on this. You are not responsible for Admiral Ashcroft's death." While hindsight might argue fighters should have been deployed for cover from the start, Winner couldn't afford a diminished captain leading the fleet. There was plenty of blame to go around for mistakes already made and those to come. There hadn't been a war fought that went completely according to plan and he didn't expect this one to be different. The chaos of battle, the fears and weaknesses of men, created mistakes. Winner started forward.

Davenport remained rigid, strain clearly showing on his face, and said, "Sir, there's more."

The Captain's words were like a hammer. Winner braced himself, sensing only bad news was to follow.

"Colonel al Cadifh has been in contact with Hrndullka. Bartok has ordered fifty civilians shot for each attack on his troops or any buildings or other equipment; one hundred people executed for each soldier killed. Al Cadifh has advised Hulk to stand down and wait for our assault. We also know Bartok has

Kenneth E. Ingle

ordered Fonso Carrel and Kirk Filbright to reinforce his troops and squadrons. Transmissions from both men's planets indicate they're doing just that."

Winner's anger soared. Through clenched teeth, he ordered, "Get under way for rendezvous with Adaval and Zachary, all possible speed."

He had to get the three thousand passengers off Galactic Star. All the forces he could muster were now coming together, yet he still couldn't act. Repairs were still under way and it would be at least ten hours before completion. In the meantime, people were dying—people he was totally responsible for.

He pushed aside thoughts of his last three months on Dema-Alpha One— memories triggered by this news. Bartok was more than enough to fight now. He didn't need to fight himself.

"We'll mourn our dead when the war was over." And that would include many more, of that he was sure.

"Sir? Hyperspace?" Davenport asked.

It was a legitimate question. Entering hyperspace meant recall of the fighters. The ship would again be unprotected. Winner was about to make the same command decision that had taken Ashcroft's life.

"Yes," he ordered.

Long deliberate strides took him through the hanger deck to the gravlift. He looked up at the civilians gathered along the catwalk; their silent looks monitored his every step and both trepidation and fear showed in their faces.

Winner could understand their doubts. They'd seen the ship attacked by an unseen and unknown killer and the Admiral-of-the-Fleet lost.

Winner asked, "How are the passengers taking this?"

"They're glad you're safely back," Davenport answered.

Winner turned to Melissa, "Inform the War Council I want a meeting at twenty hundred. In my quarters."

"Aye, Aye," she responded.

"If I may, sir," Davenport interjected, "A battle command and control center has been established just forward of the ship's Command and Control and aft of the bridge."

* * * *

A grim Winner White, dressed in his field khakis sporting his new CIC collar bars, five stars in a circle around one star, worked the deep space transmitter as he waited for his staff to enter the room. "Simone, send me all the information you can find on Jules Markham, from the day we first heard about him. Include all the information turned up in the investigation of his death. Also, send all info on Celia Markham from the day we hired her. ASAP."

No one spoke as they entered and found their places. The deteriorating conditions at Saragosa cast a shadow over the room.

"Please be seated, gentlemen, Melissa."

Davenport, Derka and al Cadifh sat at the table, Melissa took a seat next to the main hatch and near the computer console. Winner remained standing.

126

From the new center, Winner could coordinate all aspects of the battle. Everything he would need for command and control was in place. While Galactic Star was self sufficient, its resources were not unlimited, yet Derka had worked his electronic wizardry. He pulled a small box from his pocket, flicked a switch on its side and said, "It's an electronic and holo neutralizer. Just in case someone's trying to screw up my handywork."

Winner welcomed Derka's words. The man had a way of easing a taut atmosphere; and it worked here in the council room. Smiles appeared on every face—except for al Cadifh's.

Derka went on, "Admiral Ashcroft ordered the room equipped for command use shortly after you left on the recruiting mission. We've gathered every technology available to assist you in leading this fight."

Winner looked at the ramrod stiff al Cadifh as the giant spoke. "With the admiral's death, we assumed you would wish to command. I think I speak for all of us, we are ready to follow your lead." As quietly as the man spoke, his voice seemed to bore into the bulkheads.

Winner hadn't thought about their clash over the orderly since the two soldiers had resolved their differences. He felt no hesitation at taking al Cadifh at his word.

"Thank you gentlemen. Fenn Ashcroft was a fine officer. He was also my friend. I shall miss him." He wanted to say more but didn't. He would honor his friend after the battle. There would be others to eulogize. Too many.

Winner looked into the eyes of each member.

"Gentlemen, I need your most honest judgment. I'm sure you always give your best, but now I need something different, something more. I need your gut feel, taking into consideration, Namaycush, Hornblower's attack, Carrel, Filbright reinforcements and the main assault. Am I moving too quickly? Am I placing everything at risk by not waiting until we can build an overwhelming force?"

For a number of minutes no one spoke.

Derka stood, turned to face the group. An almost eerie presence permeated the room.

Looking first at each member, Derka directed his attention to Winner. "Mr. White, I have something to say. Take this in the spirit in which it's given. We are one. Some of us were born on Saragosa. It is our home. Bartok is killing our families, friends and destroying all that we know as home. I say we attack now!"

Winner solemnly nodded his head and said, "Of course, Phalen."

In quick succession, the group agreed. "Set the battle plan in motion," they said to a man.

Winner nodded again. "So be it. We are committed to the destruction of Zed Bartok and to freeing Saragosa Prime. I see Admiral Ashcroft had decided to call this operation Freedom's Dagger. If there's no objection, we'll keep the name."

Nobody objected.

He took his seat at the table. "The situation on Saragosa has grown desperate. Bartok is slaughtering people for defending themselves and he has reinforcements on the way. We will be out-gunned and out-manned but we shall win!"

Winner asked, "Has Colonel Hornblower reported? Has he reached the Marmadie asteroids?"

"Yes, Sir," answered Derka. "He arrived on station two days ago—he believes undetected." Besides the recruiting results, it was the only good news they'd had.

"Fonso Carrel and Kirk Filbright. What about them?" Winner probably knew more about those two than did anyone else in the room. He'd locked horns with both during the previous three years.

He answered his own question; "Carrel is a threat because of what he can bring to the fight, if he chooses. He doesn't like Bartok and if freed of the financial control, would stay out of the fight—but in for a penny, in for a pound. The man will fight. Filbright, by nature is a coward. No more than a lackey to Bartok. Carrel has a personal dislike for WMC that dates back to problems he had with my father. His fleet is bigger than Bartok's but there's no way he'll commit it all to the battle for Saragosa."

"That agrees with the transmissions we've been monitoring," Derka said. "Carrel is leaving a substantial part of his fleet and Marines to protect his home world. Bartok raised hell with him but Carrel held his ground. Filbright is sending everything he has, which isn't much. Three ships. Two fighters and one cargo carrier. Both fleets are due to arrive at Saragosa in eight or nine days."

Winner said, "When Hornblower attacks Namaycush, Bartok will turn Carrel and Filbright around to handle that threat. This means, no addition in his forces at Saragosa. Any suggestions?" Winner knew what had to happen.

He listened with satisfaction as al Cadifh spoke. "I suggest we immediately order the few forces left on Minns, Nimitz Crossing and Cellus IV to attack Carrel's and Filbright's reinforcing fleets. They may be no more than a gnat pissing off a bull elephant, but Bartok won't know that immediately. It should give Hornblower an undisputed first strike at Namaycush. Do that right on the heels of the Minns attack and it might panic Bartok, cause him to send reinforcements to help his home world."

"Thank you Colonel. I agree," Winner said.

He asked, "Mr. Derka, what's our inventory of troops and ships available for the fight?" If he had access to all the warships White owned, he could overwhelm Bartok in hours, maybe minutes. But those ships were scattered all over the universe and in many cases, almost as needed where they were. Space was a dangerous place. Most were months away from being any help. But delay was a two edged sword. It gave Bartok time to reinforce his Saragosa position and many more civilians would die at the butcher's hand.

Derka keyed the computer. An overhead projector displayed the results as Derka listed them: "fighters, one hundred twenty-nine; destroyers, eighteen; tankers/troop carriers, fourteen; Assault landing craft, twelve; one heavy cruiser and one corvette; four thousand fleet Marines; Hrndullka's two thousand guerillas in place." With admiration, Derka noted that two destroyers had joined them compliments of a lady Winner had dated a few times back on earth.

To Winners chagrin, a note from the lady accompanied the ships, the image sealed with a kiss.

Melissa blurted, "Wow. That must have been some date."

Winner spun toward the lieutenant.

The red faced, embarrassed Marine added, "Sorry, Sir. My apologies to everyone."

He turned his chair to face the grins of his staff, knowing it was best to say nothing.

"It's not the numbers we'd like to have, but that's our fighting force." His cruiser was worth a dozen destroyers and fighters if it could be brought to bear properly. Davenport was untested in a major battle but he was the best the fleet had to offer now that Ashcroft was gone. One thing was certain; they couldn't afford to waste any combat assets. A battle of attrition meant certain defeat.

"And Bartok's combat strength?" Winner asked.

Derka responded, "Computer, display list of Bartok's forces at Saragosa Prime."

Derka named them: "fighters, 80; Destroyers, 35; cargo/troop carriers, 100; assault craft, 40; frigate, 1; troops, 25,000. He also has the two energy cannons dirt-side we installed over a year ago. Hulk reported twenty thousand enemy troops already on the ground. I classed his destroyer Vengeance as a frigate. It has the speed and armament—just lacks the size."

Al Cadifh broke the silence. "Bartok did not come to fight a space battle. He's equipped only for a surprise ground assault."

Winner picked it up there. "We have the edge in any space match up. But it's close enough to call even. Whoever has the best tactics and deployment will win that fight. On the ground, the enemy has a major advantage. The energy cannons, superior troop numbers and already entrenched position gives Bartok superiority where it counts." He kept his voice calm and level even though he didn't like the looks of things. Hrndullka's fighters, while willing, wouldn't bring much to the fight.

Winner studied the numbers. "Hrndullka needs combat supplies, guns ammunition and medicines. Nimitz Crossing, Minns and Cellus IV have one thousand troops after manning for the Namaycush strike. Their fighters, destroyer escorts and transports are all we have to attack Carrel and Filbright."

If Bartok split his forces between Namaycush and Saragosa the numbers still didn't evened out. An invading force usually required a minimum of a two-to-one majority to succeed and preferably five to one; Winner faced just the opposite. Bartok still had the advantage of superior numbers.

Melissa intervened, "Sir, a message coming in from one of our fighters. Computer display message." All eyes focused on the screen. 'Have visual contact with missile platform. Emissions track indicates point of origin, Saragosa Prime. Orders?'

"Where is the fighter?" asked Winner.

Melissa punched at the console. "Three million klicks out."

Davenport said, "With your permission."

Winner responded with a smile meant to reassure Davenport. "It's your ship."

The Captain ordered, "Change the activation frequency and hang a short range warning buoy on it. All fighters return to Galactic Star."

Winner said, "Gentlemen, all of this means nothing if we don't solve the problems of supplying Hulk and attacking Bartok's forces, both in space and dirt-side."

He looked at al Cadifh, motioned with his hand the Marine had the floor and sat.

Al Cadifh cleared his throat—it sounded like a lion's roar. "Captain Davenport came up with an idea that I like for getting initial supplies to Hulk. With your permission, I'll ask him to present it."

Winner looked to Davenport. Maybe the man was everything Ashcroft said he was. "Your turn, Captain."

Davenport leaned one elbow on the table and called for the space plot.

A three-D view of the Galon region appeared as a hologram. Davenport pulled out an old fashioned telescoping pointer. It couldn't reach all of the holo so he used the laser pointer.

"This will be our location after rendezvous with Adaval and Zachary." He shifted the pointer. "And here's Saragosa Prime. In hyperdrive, it's a four-day trip, standard time. Our problem is twofold. First, we have to be within one million klicks of the planet to launch the supply craft. Second we must do it without attracting too much attention. Notice, I said too much attention. We're not going to be able to get by with this plan without Bartok knowing something's going on. So, we'll let him know but only what we want. One of the destroyers on loan to us, the Sizemore, will approach Saragosa space giving as big a signature as possible. Bartok won't recognize it but he'll know it isn't one of ours. We expect to be turned away. In fact, we're counting on it. As Sizemore drops out of hyperspace, it will eject the supply launch toward Saragosa. The launch will coast the rest of the way to Saragosa, using short undetectable thruster bursts to keep on course, shed delta v and land. The launch is rigged to be stealthy.

Once it's ejected the supply launch, Sizemore will turn about, seeming to leave the area. Four hours after the launch is on the ground, the fleet will attack. When our attack opens a hole through Bartok's fleet, the Marines go dirt-side."

Winner pressed his hand to his head. "Those poor bastards in the supply run are going to be space sick. Shit. I'm glad I won't be on that launch." He'd ridden one of those forced assaults and knew how miserable the Marines and crew would feel. He suspected al Cadifh had suffered through more than one also.

Anticipating the reaction Davenport said, "They'll have time to get over any space sickness."

Winner detected a little amusement at how casually the Captain dismissed the concern. It wasn't uncommon for Marines and space forces to rib each other over the maneuver.

Davenport continued, "If we get lucky, Bartok won't turn Sizemore away until much later. If so, the launch will be ejected at a lower speed, may even get down to three tenths c."

"The colonel said, "It looks like the best bet for supplying Hrndullka."

Winner stood, "Makes sense. Tell Hulk to prepare his people as if they had the equipment they needed. Get them as ready as he can. We don't have the luxury of time or resources so when we begin the assault from space, we'll send more transports to the surface with as much armament for him as we can.

"Now, the assault on Saragosa. What do you have to offer?" Winner stood before them ready to give his ideas if they had nothing to present.

All eyes in the room turned toward Davenport. He didn't waver. "Obviously, there are many possibilities available to us. We believe we'll be fighting from a diminished but improving position."

Winner felt Davenport's choice of words appropriate. They clearly indicated the man wasn't overstating what he was bringing to the battle.

The captain continued. "Computer, project a holo of the estimated positions of Bartok's space forces around Saragosa." Dots of light appeared, Saragosa in the background as a large blue-green ball. "We can attack in a number of ways. We can take him head on in a battle of attrition, which we can't win. We can split our forces, into two groups, which is extremely risky. If one group is beaten, the other will be blown out of space."

"Sir, an incoming priority message for Mr. White from Mr. Hrndullka," Melissa said as she read the computer screen.

"Let's hear it," said Winner. Hulk still used audio only, to burst messages. It was harder to detect. "Daker Smithe and his wife were captured today," the guerilla leader reported. "Condition and location unknown. Will advise."

Winner closed his eyes. Everyone in the room knew his mother was with Daker. By naming her as his wife, Daker hoped to keep her identity from Bartok and his people. Winner wondered how long that subterfuge would last.

"Back to business," Winner said. It tore at him, but he couldn't let it seem his mother was more important than anyone else.

Davenport said, "Sorry Mr. White."

Winner nodded and the Captain continued, "While it's risky, I plan on splitting the fleet." He keyed the computer to run a simulation and added his own description. "You can see for yourselves. Mr. Derka has managed to configure seven fighters with anti-grav systems. Those ships will leave the fleet, and attack from ninety degrees off our port. They'll go in first. With their AG, they'll be able to out-accelerate and out-maneuver any fighters Bartok launches. Once these fighters penetrate the outer defenses, Bartok's fighters should retreat to protect the fleet. In their favor, it also shrinks the perimeter they have to protect. In any case, one half of our remaining fighters will follow, attacking targets of opportunity. The main fleet will attack along the main access with the rest of the fighters."

Winner had no doubt his pilots were infinitely better than Bartok's and one-on-one dogfights were just fine with him.

"Galactic Star, with the destroyers and fighters screening, will strike at the center of Bartok's fleet. Star's energy cannons have a greater range and more destructive power than anything we've seen in the enemy fleet. We should be able to open a hole through them. That divides them into three groups. Once divided, we can take them out one at a time. Star will focus on Bartok's destroyers. Our destroyers will provide cover and diversion for our fighters, then isolate the tankers and cargo vessels once we've broken through. When done with that, they will join up with Star and help where needed. If any enemy ship offers to surrender, we give–them one minute to jettison their fuel. If they take any longer, we'll kill them. All available runabouts will pickup survivors, ours or theirs."

Any ship that left a battle without picking up spaced survivors would have been condemned in any port.

"Marines will wait behind the fleet and follow us to the surface."

Winner watched Davenport intently. The captain had obviously spent many hours considering the alternatives, looking for any edge he could find. He remained seated giving them time to digest Davenport's plan and reach their own assessment.

"Comments, questions Gentlemen?" Winner asked after several minutes of silence.

For the next thirty minutes, questions were posed and answers given. Quiet finally settled over the group.

"Colonel, that brings us to your Marines and their assault," Winner said.

Al Cadifh, ramrod straight, keyed his console.

All eyes in the room turned to the warrior as he cleared his throat, stood and walked to the center of the display area. "Gentlemen, I won't try to blow any smoke. This is what every Marine envisions, what he trains for every minute of his career. And it isn't a matter of heroics. As one great general said, 'heroes usually die becoming heroes.' I don't want any heroes. Let the other bastard die. We want victory. And we aim to have it. Nothing less."

Winner savored the sense of pride he'd felt a few times before and it always felt good. A look around the table showed he wasn't the only one.

Al Cadifh continued, "With the reinforcements Mr. White secured, we can do our job. We will retake Saragosa!"

What went unmentioned was Winner's vow to kill Bartok.

The colonel wasn't delivering bravado—he was just a Marine doing his job.

Al Cadifh resumed, "The spaceport will serve as primary landing site. Bartok has a large contingent of troops located there. With Galactic Star targeting anything that moves, we believe those enemy troops will not show themselves until we're on the ground. That gives us a foothold. It's up to us to keep it and widen it to a secured landing area. Our main concern was how to get arms to Hrndullka. Captain Davenport has already detailed that. Once the assault starts, we have to get a lot of Marines and material on the ground quickly. Enough to give Hulk's people a chance against Bartok's heavily armed troops until we can create a coordinated offense. In addition, we want liaison people on the ground to help in these efforts." Al Cadifh sat down.

Every word positive, no doubts, no hesitation—here's what we're going to do and how it will be done. Winner couldn't have been more pleased.

Derka asked to lead the liaison mission. His efforts were totally dependent on the success of al Cadifh's troops.

The Colonel stood at the table. "Bartok doesn't have a command and control center we can take out. So, our first objective will be the space drone. Once secured, it will become our base of operation. The one major problem is that it's totally exposed. There's no terrain to help in its defense. This fact will make it possible for us to take the spaceport, but it works against us in trying to hold it. We would like to have Galactic Star in close orbit to take out any high powered or long range weapons."

Davenport nodded. "Just tell us what you want. We'll deliver."

Al Cadifh concluded his presentation. "After that gentleman, it will be hand to hand, street by street combat. Just what Marines are good at." He sat.

As Winner stood, al Cadifh's last statement stayed with him—a lot of those Marines would die. "Thank you colonel. Computer off.

"Gentlemen, I don't need to tell you a lot of things have to happen just right for this to work. And we all know few plans seldom work completely in the chaos of battle. All of you need to develop contingency plans." Winner instructed the group to get their staffs together and work out a precise timetable for implementing each phase of the attack for the war council's approval. "When do we rendezvous with the transports? He asked.

"Two hours," Davenport responded.

"We'll transfer the passengers to Adaval and Zachary, then meet in twelve hours to approve the Order of Battle."

Winner stood before the group. "I do have one other matter—I've decided to change the name of the Galactic Star to Deliverance."

"I like it," said Davenport. The rest of the council agreed.

"If there's nothing else, you're dismissed."

Winner watched the room empty. He sat heavily in the chair, his head in his hands. The plan seemed good—particularly given the limited war resources they had.

"Uh, sir?" He was startled at Melissa's voice.

"I thought you'd gone with the others."

"Mr. White, I'm sorry to hear about your mother. I wanted you to know all of us are behind you. What you were doing, the free elections on Saragosa, you didn't have to do that. We wouldn't want anyone else leading us to war."

Winner thanked her. Many brave people were going to die. Had he done all he could to warrant that trust? He wondered.

CHAPTER TWENTY FIVE
Vladislov Hrndullka

In his hotel room, out of view of the ever-prying cameras, Richard Hastings read the note, crumpled it and quickly chewed the incriminating information. From his inside coat pocket, he tore a piece from the hotel's daily schedule and jotted his response.

He stepped into the hallway, took the gravlift to the basement and made his way to the maintenance shop. The office was empty, all the workers out on calls. Carefully folding his message, he slid the note into a crevice behind the wainscot covering the office walls. He could only hope, without any sure knowledge, that the note would be retrieved in time to help.

Two days had passed since Bartok had ordered Captain Harlow van Gelden's execution. Only the relationship Bartok hoped for with Celia had kept the Captain alive this long—now it sealed his fate; her pleas for the captain's life fueled Bartok's retribution.

Every effort Hastings made to free his friend had failed. His course was clear. He had to free the Dutchman before morning, the scheduled time of the execution—alone if necessary. Hastings could wait only a few hours before acting.

If someone was to contact him, he had to be accessible, out in the open, not cooped up where the surveillance cameras or any of the other eavesdropping gadgets could watch or listen to everyone entering his room or talking to him. Hastings gathered up an inspection report, left his office and started touring the hotel—ostensibly looking for problems; it was his excuse for being on the move.

Word did come. Standing off the main lobby, Hastings saw Rap place his hand behind the false façade that fronted the dining area. That's where he would find the message.

Hastings walked at a brisk pace past the façade and in one flowing natural move snatched the message from its hiding place. He then returned to his room and retreated to the far end of the balcony beyond the range of the camera.

Unfolding the note, he read its message.

He would have help in rescuing his friend.

Told where and when to meet his accomplice, he would stay in his quarters until it was time to leave. He made a leisurely pass through his rooms disregarding the cameras.

* * * *

Hastings casually walked through the lobby making no effort to disguise his movement—his jogging clothes and running shoes clearly indicated his intentions. In anticipation of just this kind of opportunity, Hastings had undertaken daily runs in and around the hotel grounds.

He entered the bar, repeating the daily ritual, casually acknowledged the bartender, then waiters and passed through the rear door into a storage room that led to a frequently used loading dock. Most sentries had become accustomed to his evening runs and seldom bothered him. He eschewed his ground car and jogged along in the dimly lit street leading from the hotel. Debris left over from the initial raid on Saragosa City still littered the streets.

He stayed to the shadows covering a little over two thousand meters on the main thoroughfare until he turned up an alley. There, he stopped and rapped lightly on a door.

A mask-covered head beckoned him in.

Hastings followed his guide along the dark hallway to where another man waited. In the darkness, he was unable to see any part of his informant.

From the blackness the voice said, "You have to move quickly if you want to save van Gelden. He's to be executed this morning."

Hastings had no idea of the identities of his guide or informant. That was as it had to be. Capture by Bartok or Masten meant a certain but not always quick death. If your contact was unknown, even torture with the brain scanner at the laboratory wouldn't give Bartok or Masten compromising information. Not that it kept them from using it.

Hastings asked, "Where are they holding him? What do we need to do to get him out?"

"First of all, it isn't we. You're going to do this. Personally, I don't think you'll get out alive let alone save your friend."

The messenger went on, "He's still at the spaceport, the ops building, in one of the rooms reserved as an overnight cell. During the third shift, there's only one soldier on duty."

"Why just one guard?" asked Hastings.

"Roving patrols. And they are a little short handed," was the answer. "There must be at least a dozen air car patrols. Two men in each."

The informant continued, "You'll have to kill the sentry but that's the way it is. It won't be hard to get your man out of the building once the guard's out of the way. Off the spaceport is another matter. But, it ain't going to be easy to get to the guard. Every man out there knows what happens if things don't go right. So, if you have bright ideas about knocking the guard out, forget it. You ain't doing him no favor by conking him. Even if you get that close. Remember, if the prisoner gets away, Masten will kill the guard."

Hastings tried to get what information he could from the shadowy talker. He agreed it wasn't going to be easy. "When do the day guards come on duty?"

Hastings got no answer. The messenger was gone. He and his guide were alone.

Seconds later, following the man's lead, Hastings was at the top of a ladder climbed down through an opening. Cautiously, he scaled the ladder and stepped into the darkness. There he felt his way along a wall, alone. His guide had left him.

No smell or sound gave him any clues to help know where he was. Ten steps from the ladder, he jerked back. Told someone would meet him, the touch still came as a surprise.

"Shit! You scared the hell out of me!" he whispered not knowing who he was talking to or if what he'd touched was even a person. He waited.

As if someone had read his mind a voice asked, "The third shift's on duty, why not do it?"

For the second time in as few a minutes, Hastings responded, "Gaudamn! You scared the hell out of me. Who are you? And yes. Let's get van Gelden out now!"

"You didn't think I'd let your pilot die without trying to save him did you?" the voice whispered.

Hastings breathed a sigh of relief, his heart racing, "Hulk! Lord! Am I ever glad you're here."

The big man wasn't particularly glad to be there. Given his choice he'd be at the mine working or maybe on vacation. He'd never been a violent man and didn't relish being head of the resistance. But, it just seemed to happen. All his life he'd been taught not to use his size against someone smaller. He had grown up being the gentle giant. Nicknames didn't mean much and the Hulk moniker hadn't bothered him when the miners tagged it on. Born and educated on Saragosa, Hulk, on earth, might well have been a superstar in professional football. He never complained about not having the opportunity, but then he seldom complained. Growing up, he'd let others glory in the limelight, often letting them take credit for his deeds. Once the invasion started, Hulk found he had a temper far beyond what came in kid fights and competitive sports. When those near and dear to him were harmed, someone paid.

"Follow me," the giant said.

The two men left the darkened hallway, returning to the tunnels below. Shortly afterward, the stale moist air of the storm sewer told them where they were.

Hastings ran, trailing the big man in the dim, and sometimes absent, light for an eternity—at least his lungs told him it had been that long. Hulk finally climbed a ladder to the surface, the moonless night hiding their movement from a seemingly private thoroughfare. He motioned Hastings to crawl behind him.

A few meters farther, the giant entered another building. Once inside, Hulk pulled Hastings to his feet and from somewhere produced a parcel, "Here, get dressed."

Hastings quickly donned the suit he'd pulled from the package as Hulk stripped off his coveralls.

Hastings said, "Uh, okay, but we're just going to walk around and do all these wondrous things including free van Gelden and no one's going to stop us. Right?"

"Yes, Doctor. I'm going to administer last rites and you're going to make sure he's in good health. We don't want to execute a man sick in soul or body. Now do we?"

"Hulk, you're something else. You never cease to amaze me."

"Please, sir, I'm Father Dugan and you'll address me accordingly." He assumed an air of piety, and rather well according to all, but coming from the big man that was something to see. It looked like an elephant doing Shakespeare.

They made their way down the nearby stairs to the city garage.

Hrndullka said, "We'll get an air car to the spaceport."

Hastings didn't say anything. He marveled at how the big man moved so quickly.

Hrndullka found the car at the far end. He and Hastings settled in and using the thrusters exited the garage. Halfway across the space drone, Hastings slowed the air car. "Looks like trouble." He pointed to the night vision view-screen installed in the instrument panel.

"Keep going," Hulk ordered. "We're expected. Just don't act suspicious!"

The patrol air car pulled in front and signaled them to stop.

Hastings cut the power. The car settled to the ground as he opened the canopy.

Hulk said, "Keep your hands where they can see them at all times."

Hulk had their papers out before the guards reached the car. One walked to the opening the other took a position at the rear, weapons ready.

The guard casually scanned the documents. "Padre, we don't like killing innocent people. I don't envy you having to give this guy his last rites. I had guard duty inside last night and talked to him. Seems he was just in the wrong place at the wrong time."

"I would gladly trade places with you," Hulk said to the soldier.

He held up one finger, signaling Hulk to wait as he turned his attention to his helmet earpiece. "Seems we've got a little drunken disturbance at the hangers. Go on." He returned the papers.

Hastings blew a sigh of relief as the patrol car sped off. Almost as quickly, he ordered the computer to continue toward the spaceport terminal.

"Nothing to it," Hulk said.

Bullshit, Hastings thought.

Hulk added, "The disturbance will last ten minutes. That's all the time we've got to get in, get van Gelden, get out, and get back to the sewers."

A few seconds later, hulk ordered, "Stop at the front of the spaceport, on the circular driveway. There's nothing to hide us—we'll be exposed. Walk into the spaceport as causally as possible. If you've got a laser pistol on you, leave it here."

Hastings left his sidearm, stowing it under the seat. Hulk didn't have to be there to rescue van Gelden. He could have sent any number of people. If fact, Hastings thought, that would have been the smart thing to do. He'd have to talk to Hulk about that if they got out of this.

Dim lights surrounded the main building as they approached. Apparently, no space travelers were expected—the area was deserted. The building took on an ominous appearance. Only one story protruded above ground, maintaining the low silhouette the space drone required. Now, even the darkness ceased to be their protector.

The two men neared the spaceport entrance. Hastings presented his ID card to the automatic scanner and Hulk inserted his. Hastings held his breath. His card had been valid just an hour earlier at the hotel so he didn't anticipate a problem—unless the overly efficient security guard decided his run was taking too long. Hulk's card was a different matter entirely. Hastings expected alarms to go off as the machine read what he was sure was a fake holo-encoded card.

Hastings tried to appear unconcerned when the door opened. He did breathe a silent sigh of relief. It was a good thing nothing around had monitored his heartbeat.

Hulk approached a guard protected by a bulletproof plasti-screen.

The sentry showed no sign of alarm as the two approached. Apparently he'd been told a priest would come to see the prisoner. He stood and challenged the two men when they neared his screen, accepting the papers Hulk handed him through the slot.

"This is Mr. Hastings, from the hotel. He's the closest thing we have to a doctor available to us. He'll monitor the prisoner's life signs. Mr. Bartok didn't want to take a real doctor away from the troops."

The guard nodded. "Come this way."

The hidden lock buzzed and the side door opened.

The three walked down a narrow dimly lit hall to a windowless back room. Van Gelden, sitting on his bunk, the only furnishings in the room, ankles clasped in chains, made no effort to hide his surprise at seeing Hastings. Hrndullka he'd never seen before and thought him a priest.

Hastings shook van Gelden's hand. "Harlow, this is Father Dugan."

The pained look on the pilot's face said it all. Van Gelden heavily sat down on the cot, a look of resignation covered his face.

Hastings didn't like putting his friend through this wringer, but they had to play this out until they knew this guard was subdued and he knew for certain no other soldiers had been notified.

Satisfied everything seemed to be as it should, the guard said, "I'll leave you now."

Hulk turned to him. "Turns out we're leaving and you're staying."

The guard quizzically looked at the big man—then reality set in and he tried to draw his laser side arm.

Hulk grabbed and disarmed the man without effort, being almost twice the size of his adversary.

Despite what the informant said, Hastings knew Hulk wouldn't kill the guard unless necessary.

Hulk asked, "Where are the keys to the ankle chains?"

When an answer didn't come, he violently shook the man.

"In the desk." The frightened guard quickly surrendered the information.

"Wait," said van Gelden. "I've watched them open those drawers. There's a sequence to follow to open the desk or you'll trip an alarm."

The look Hulk gave the sentry made the man cower.

Hastings retrieved the keys.

Van Gelden rubbed his ankles and quietly said, "Thank you. Both of you."

The matter of the guard was quite different.

"Are you going to kill me?" asked the soldier.

"No," answered Hulk.

"Then take me with you as your prisoner. If you leave me here, Colonel Masten will kill me. I'll help you in any way I can. Just take me with you."

The fear in his eyes touched Hastings. Hulk seemed unmoved.

Hastings spoke, "I say he goes with us."

Hulk picked the man up, dangling his feet almost half a meter off the ground and pulled them face-to-face. "Do you have any idea what I'll do to you if you bring harm to any of my people?"

"I'll do what ever you want. Just don't leave me here. I don't care about Bartok." The fright in the guard's voice was pathetic, more than Hastings wanted to hear.

Hastings remarked, "Being a sinner in your parish must be tough."

Hrndullka chuckled, then turned his attention to the prisoner. Within minutes, he'd bound the soldier's hands, gagged him, inserted makeshift earplugs and blindfolded their willing captive.

As quickly as they'd come, they were gone. Van Gelden had escaped his executioner.

Retracing their route, they were soon in the sewers.

Instead of going to the underground headquarters in the city, Hulk led them to the hills bordering on the north. At times, trees and dense underbrush eased their escape—at others they hindered their movement.

They traveled for almost three hours at a hard pace. The elevation got higher with each step. The rocky terrain made surveillance impossible except from the air or orbit. To neutralize both possibilities, the men wore a shroud that blocked any return signal. They finally entered a cave only minutes ahead of daylight.

"Welcome to your new home," Hulk said to Hastings and van Gelden. "You do need a home don't you?" he asked. "That is unless you want to return to the hotel."

"Some priest you make. All I ask for is sanctuary, to be among friends and what do I get? A dirt floor to sleep on, meals to match the floor, cold and a gun. Where did I go wrong?"

Hrndullka said, "Look at the bright side. How long has it been since you had the run of a mountain retreat?"

Hastings threw up his hands, "How could I have been so parsimonious?"

Hulk asked, "What the hell does parsimonious mean?'

Van Gelden shook his head. He didn't know.

"Stingy, selfish," answered Hastings, then added, all levity gone from his voice, "You shouldn't have exposed yourself that way. You should have sent someone else to help in this man's rescue. It was totally unnecessary."

Hulk turned the prisoner over to a guard and rejoined Hastings and van Gelden.

"How can I thank you?" the pilot asked. "I'm willing to do whatever I can to help you and your people."

Hrndullka said, "Good. I don't know where we'll use you yet, but use you we will." He slapped van Gelden on the back almost knocking the smaller man down. He completely ignored Hastings admonishment.

CHAPTER TWENTY SIX
Richard Hastings

Hulk turned and walked from the area, Hastings hurrying to catch him.

Hastings felt a gentle breeze moving through the giant cavern held constant at twenty-two degrees C by giant scrubbers. The nearby sea got any unwanted foreign particles. Most of the caverns were natural formations so little structure was required to support the high ceiling.

Old hydrogen fuel cells resurrected from storage now generated energy for all their power requirements, relying on the sea for the necessary hydrogen. The only emission, water, was completely usable and the system gave off no radiation; detection was all but impossible.

"I don't want to stay cooped up in this cave. Surely there must be some place I can be of service."

Hulk laughed. "I don't mean to be rude, but what can you do?"

Since Hastings had taken on running the hotel, Hulk had left all contact up to Rap. He had never found the time to get to know the man.

Hastings thought a minute. "You've kept Bartok's forces busy running around the planet chasing your people. I can organize and coordinate. How much better could your efforts be if you had someone to help you with command and control? I could gather, collate information and make it more usable for you. And I can handle a gun."

Hulk wanted the man's help. Hastings might not know the art of war but he hadn't either when command fell to him. He had found you learn quickly in this business or not at all. He thought for a minute, "Yes, I believe you could help us. I've given some thought to an operations type—you can do both, operations and command and control."

Hulk extended his hand, which Hastings gladly accepted.

"Welcome aboard commander." Hulk motioned his new addition along and continued to walk through the long cavern, deeper into the well-lighted mountain hideout.

"The major problem we face is that Bartok has ordered the execution of civilians for any offensive actions we take. A second problem is that he's captured Daker Smithe and Mr. White's mother, Zena. To the best of our knowledge, Bartok doesn't know her identity—yet. Daker passed her off as his wife. Third, we're low on supplies."

"Quite a full plate of problems," Hastings commented. "What actions have you been able to take so far?"

"Colonel al-Cadifh has asked us to stand down until his forces arrive." Pensively, Hulk added, "I think Mr. White is about to invade Saragosa."

"He's moving much quicker than I'd thought possible," Hastings said.

Hulk rubbed the day-old growth on his face. "I hope not overly quickly."

The big man knew it took time to gather a force. He'd learned the consequences of fighting with too small an army, not to mention lack of adequate firepower. And training it, that was another matter. And unlike Winner, Hulk didn't have the problem of building a space force. Winner still had to get through Bartok's orbital shield. Nothing could happen dirt-side unless the space shield could be defeated. "But it can't come too soon for us." They were running out of everything. Medical supplies were close to non-existent and ammunition was dangerously low. Al-Cadifh's stand down order was almost unnecessary. Hulk's volunteer army was close to having nothing to fight with.

Before he could continue, a courier approached and handed Hulk a note. "From Deliverance, sir." The big man read the message and passed the pad to Hastings, "Celia Markham is being transferred from the tunnels under the city to this location. Care to join me? I plan to interrogate her further."

"Delighted," Hastings answered. "What have you learned so far?"

Hulk grunted, "Not much. She's been in lock-up most of the time. In fact, all the time. I've been busy trying to stay one jump ahead of Bartok."

He stood silent for a moment then said; "We've checked her out as best we could. The Lab computers here had a brief file on her. After WMC Labs hired Celia, they found they had a real treasure on their hands. She was identified as a 'comer', has tremendous potential. During her first years at WMC, there was talk that she could someday be director of the labs."

"No doubt," said Hastings. "What she went through to steal Topsail from under the noses of the crew of Galactic Star, umm, Deliverance, says a great deal about her capabilities."

Hulk added, "Things kinda went sour when her father disappeared returning from a field trip to Saragosa. He'd been working on the ocean fertility problem for WMC and said he'd found something significant. Bartok says that's why WMC, or more specifically, Winner White, had her father killed, his ship destroyed while it was in hyperspace."

Hastings asked, "Do you think WMC's responsible for Jules Markham's death?"

"I doubt it. White's tough, but he's no killer. Bartok say's he killed him but there's some evidence he's lying."

"Any suggestions?" Hastings asked.

"Yeah," Hulk answered, there was a distance to his response. "We've stopped our raids. We'll focus all of our efforts on freeing any of our people in Bartok's prisons. That includes Mr. White's mother and Mr. Smithe."

Hulk led the way to what appeared to be a conference room, a few chairs and a table the only adornments. He and Hastings sat at the small table to await Celia Markham's arrival.

They waited in silence. Hulk's patient manner added a calm that Hastings admired. The big man had a reputation for keeping his own council and it stayed intact.

Shortly, the door opened and Celia Markham entered. The guard backed out, leaving them alone.

Both men stood and greeted her. She accepted the offered chair.

For a few seconds, no one spoke and no one moved. It seemed a sizing up period although Celia couldn't imagine why. They'd met before.

Hulk opened the meeting, "I regret your confinement but there was little other choice."

Celia suspected her imprisonment was more a matter of convenience to Hrndullka than anything else. "Your people were always polite and courteous. I lacked little other than my freedom. Something even Mr. Bartok didn't deny me."

Hulk ignored her retort. "You've met Mr. Hastings."

She nodded to Hastings. "Circumstances weren't too different then than they are now I believe, except your masters seemed to have changed."

Hastings smiled. "No ma'am. They haven't. I'm just being more forthright about whom I chose to keep company and council with. My loyalties have always been with the WMC and the people of Saragosa."

"Unfortunately," Hulk said, "detaining you was necessary. Your flight from the hotel and Bartok says nothing about loyalties, particularly since you stole Topsail from Galactic Star." He hadn't adjusted to Deliverance and made no mention of the name change. "You placed Captain van Gelden's life in jeopardy."

Celia shot back, "That wasn't my intention. I told Bartok van Gelden was my prisoner."

Hulk didn't respond but continued, "We cannot risk you disclosing our location or any information you may have gained, by accident or on purpose."

"Understandable," Celia remarked. "That's the reason you had me blindfolded, plugged my ears and then moved to wherever we now are."

Hulk shrugged as if to say you know how it is. "Ms. Markham. When we talked some days ago, you stated the only reason you had for being here was to find out who killed your father." He folded his huge hands and placed them on the table. "I would like to put this behind us. I want to help you resolve this now if possible or at the least as quickly as can reasonable be done."

"Why?" Celia asked.

"Just having to tie up resources to guard you is reason enough. But then, I have my doubts about Winner or Michael White murdering anyone, let alone your father."

"Oh." Celia showed mock surprise. "I suppose they are above such a dreadful act."

"I don't know, but I do have information perhaps you've not seen."

She kept her manner distant but listened. They just might have something new.

"Ma'am," Hulk said. "Many of my people have died, some are still dying and more are yet to die. While I sympathize with your loss, your father's death has commanded more of my time than it's worth. No matter what we find, the past is out of our reach."

She held his gaze as he continued. "What I hope is that we can work together the future."

"I'm willing," she said. "What do you propose?"

His small chair squealed under his enormous weight as he punched his wristcom. "Bring in the computer terminal."

A guard entered the conference room, placed the machine in front of Hulk and disappeared back the way he came.

With a few strokes, the screen displayed rows of data. Hulk took another chair and moved it beside his. "Ms. Markham, if you could join me here, I think what I have to show you will be most meaningful."

Celia wasted no time. They had traded verbal jabs but that didn't matter now. Sometimes a moment arrives where a difference can be made and deep inside she sensed this was one of them. She moved to the other side of the table and took the offered seat, her eyes focused on the small screen.

Hulk continued, "Obviously, you remember the date your father's disappearance was reported."

"Yes, I do," she answered.

"That was during the time the records showed Winner White to be on Dema-Alpha One working as a test pilot for Gorman Space. But a very thorough investigation shows someone altered the records. There is sufficient evidence to say he really wasn't on the planet. He was gone. No one knows for sure where and certainly not why."

Celia backed away from the screen. She felt her fears were vindicated. "You just proved Bartok was right! Then how can you defend..."

"You haven't seen it all."

Hulk's large fingers, almost like battering rams, sought out their intended targets with surprising delicacy.

The screen blinked and new information filled it.

Hulk pointed to a particular line.

Celia gasped. "His mother was gone from earth at the same time. Do you know why?"

Hulk responded with a softness that had been absent from his earlier words. "Not for certain. But I suspect it's more than coincidence. We think she was with Winner and most likely his father. There are only two people who know, Winner and Zena White."

She asked, "Didn't I hear she was captured by Bartok?" Actually, what she'd heard was Daker and his wife was captured. The rest was a guess.

Hulk looked down at her, "For someone who's supposed to be out of circulation, Ms. Markham, you're remarkably well informed."

"Well, you know how gossip travels." The truth would have set Hrndullka off so she decided to say no more. The guards were very willing to talk to her on matters they thought not critical or confidential. To her captors, it was whiling away time. But to her, it was information.

Hulk didn't acknowledge or deny what she'd said.

"Why are you telling me this?" Without waiting for an answer, she added, "I've got it. If I don't go along with whatever you want, I'll be staying here and your secret's safe. On the other hand, if I do as you ask, then you trust me not to divulge anything like this location or troop strength."

"That's the general idea." Hulk went on, "Most importantly, Daker needs our help. You can be sure Winner's deeply concerned for him and his Mother. His first commitment is to the people of Saragosa."

Celia paused a moment reflecting on Hulk's comment. That must mean the invasion is not far off she thought. She needed time to think this out. What would White's invasion mean to her?

"As long as I'm your prisoner, this information brings neither of us relief." She was convinced Hrndullka was about to drop a bomb.

Hulk pushed back from the table, glanced at Hastings. "We think you could help us free Daker Smithe."

The curtain clouding Hulk's face seemed to open, anticipation replaced it.

The look on Hastings face showed he was as surprised as Celia was.

She wasn't sure why, but she didn't sense any trick or subterfuge on Hulk's part. "How?"

Hulk stretched his huge arms in front of his chest as if seeking to pull in the right words. "We don't know where Bartok's holding Daker. We want you to get the information for us."

Celia's expression didn't change. She said, "That means going back to the hotel, facing Bartok again."

Hulk remained silent then said, "You may be our only hope. Over the last few days, we've not been able to find anyone willing to talk. To tell us where the two are being held."

"So, you're looking for some pillow talk?"

"That's not the issue. The information is."

"For you it isn't." By now, Celia realized he would do whatever necessary to protect the lives of his people. And she wasn't one of his people—of that, she was certain. Yet, in a strange way, she admired the man.

She asked, "Then what happens?"

"We get them out."

"And you're not going to tell me how you plan do this. Never mind. I think I already know." she added shaking his response off with the wave of her hand. "If I don't know what's going to happen, I can't tip them off."

Hulk nodded.

"Then how do I get out? If you pull this off while I'm at the hotel, I'm as good as dead. Is that part of the plan?" Is this a high stakes chess match—my life for Zena White and Smithe? She doubted that it was Hulk's intention, but that was certainly one of the possible outcomes. A little reassurance seemed in order.

She looked at Hastings. His astonishment at the conversation seemed to equal hers.

She watched Hulk rub his hands, then brush at imaginary flecks on the tabletop. Inwardly, Celia smiled. Leaders, good maybe great in this man's case, can have fidget moments. It was apparent that he'd said all he was going to. It was up to her. He'd not threatened her or suggested dire happenings if she didn't help.

"We need two plans for your escape. The second one in case we can't get you out."

"In other words, I'm on my own."

Hastings quickly interjected, "Not entirely. We still have people in the hotel."

Celia knew she didn't have the luxury of time to make a reasoned decision. She decided to take what seemed the best course. If White's invasion failed, and she hadn't returned to Bartok, the odds of her getting off the planet alive were virtually nil. If the invasion succeeded, she'd have the advantage of helping to free White's mother. Or at worst, trying to help her escape. Maybe she could make the best of a tough situation.

"Rap Steele," said Celia with a smile. "He told me to let him know if I ever needed help."

Hulk asked, "Does that meant you'll do it?"

Celia answered, "Yes." And wondered why. Maybe it was because something inside told her she could trust both men. So far, they'd kept their word, done what they said they would.

As they rose to leave, Hrndullka said, "By the way, Mr. Hastings and I rescued Captain van Gelden a few hours ago."

The relief almost overwhelmed her. With tears in her eyes she said, "Thank you." And found it hard to recall when she'd meant it more.

CHAPTER TWENTY SEVEN
Celia Markham

Dawn crept over the horizon as Celia Markham directed the driver to the Hotel Crest. Clear morning air was a relief from the heat and stench the two suns would bring by afternoon. She could only hope Bartok bought her story.

The car stopped in front of the long stairway. She stepped to the blue cobalt colored stone pavement polished by years of use.

Take a deep breath and relax she told herself. She clutched a small valise to her chest. Everything she could pack to help her escape was in the small bag.

With Hulk's help, she'd gotten some everyday dresses to wear when it came time to leave the hotel. Dressed in a high neck, two piece dress someone had found in one a bombed out businesses, she made her way up the steps.

The guard was in blues with gold piping and white ammo belt, his dress a clear indication Bartok was in residence. The absence of body armor signaled control was being established. The sentry didn't recognize her as he stepped in her path and said, "Miss, I'll need to see your identification."

Celia, projecting quiet self-assurance, which she didn't feel, said, "Sorry soldier. I don't have any. Just call Mr. Bartok. Tell him Celia Markham is checking in."

The mention of Bartok's name had the anticipated effect. The soldier froze for a moment. By the time he regained his senses Celia was past him.

Few people were in the lobby and that included workers.

Within minutes, she cleared the front desk and entered the gravlift, her fingerprints registered for the door key.

She waited for the lift doors to retract, stepped through the opening only to see Bartok standing in the space usually filled by the double doors to her room. His black trousers, white open collared shirt, no coat and street shoes showed he'd hastily dressed.

Hasty or not, he was very much awake. A guard stood nearby laser pistol holstered at his side.

"I should have you shot," he barked. He turned and order the guard standing just inside the door, "You, outside."

Scowling at Celia he said, "Just who in the hell do you think you are coming in here like you owned the place? Particularly after the shit you pulled." Bartok continued to block the doorway.

Celia held up her hand, "I know where Hrndullka's headquarters are. Now, do I get in my room or are we going to have this conversation in the hall?"

She'd decided before ever reaching the hotel not to back off with Bartok. He would interpret any withdrawal as weakness and drive even harder to repair the damage his ego suffered earlier when she'd threatened him and then left the hotel. It was a good thing because at that moment she realized just how much she loathed the man. Her skin crawled at the thought of him touching her.

Bartok ordered the surveillance cameras in her rooms shut down. He wasn't about to open this part of his private life to his hired snoops.

That taken care of, he stepped inside, clearing the doorway.

Celia entered the suite and immediately headed for the bedroom. "I'll be right back," she called.

The black gown worn the night she'd fled still lay on the bed where she'd discarded it. A few steps had her at the dresser and then to the closet. Quickly, opening the valise, she put the dress with the hanging garments. The rest she dropped to the floor and covered with the black gown she'd retrieved from the bed. She stepped before the mirror, brushed her hands through her jet-black hair and smoothed imaginary wrinkles from her clothes.

She reentered the large drawing room. Bartok was at the bar pouring a drink. "It's a little early for that isn't it?" she asked.

He ignored her remark, turned, leaned back against the rail and placed his elbows on the bar at the same time hooking his heal on the bottom rail, "You've got a lot of explaining to do. Where have you been for the last few days?"

"Locked up in a cell at the resistance's headquarters. And I know where they are." She strode casually across the room, and then stood near the closed windows leading to the balcony watching his reflection from the glass.

"You're going to tell me that and a lot more, like how'd you get out of here last week?" He stared hard at her. "Stop playing your fucking games with me."

Celia couldn't tell if his anger kept him from bellowing or if his primal fears of betrayal were ordering his behavior. Well, she wasn't a psychiatrist, she'd have to wait and see. Bartok was angry but maybe not beyond reason, she hoped. His first priority had to be Saragosa. He hadn't gotten where he was by being stupid. She'd been told Bartok believed most power came from the barrel of a gun. She was sure his glands ruled every other thought.

Celia had already decided to do everything she could to protect herself, both from Bartok's advances, which she knew would come shortly, and from White's pending invasion.

She turned from the balcony. "Mr. Bartok, what happens after White invades—and you defeat him of course?"

Bartok shot a sinister look at her. But in that brief glimpse, Celia saw the seeds of doubt flash across his face. Bartok had told her more with that look than words ever could—his denials meant nothing. She would use that. She knew the man was without any moral constraints. In fact, she could think of no redeeming qualities. She knew it had been a mistake to place her trust in him.

"Don't go stupid on me. We both know White doesn't have anything but the passenger ship in this area. Yeah, I know it used to be a cruiser," he waved his hand as if to rid himself of a demon, "but it was stripped and converted into a fancy space liner. I've seen all the bragging on it. If he waits until he can get men and material from all his holdings, it'll be too late. The banks and his other creditors will strip him. My lawyers are pushing that end of it as well. He can't come close to matching me in troops or arms. And I've got him beat in space almost two to one. Plus, I've got reserves coming from two of my pals."

Celia was even more convinced Bartok wasn't as sure of victory as he wanted everyone to believe. And pals? It was a stretch of the imagination for her to envision Bartok having a drinking party with pals.

He might have reserves coming, but she'd bet they weren't pals.

To unbalance him a little she said, "You haven't beaten a ragtag bunch of resistance fighters. And you outnumber them more than four to one in personnel and unbelievably in arms."

The look Bartok gave Celia would have cracked concrete and he said, "I've put Masten in charge of Saragosa City. His order to kill fifty civilians for every raid and one hundred for every one of my soldiers killed has put a stop to the aggression. I was too easy before. Now they are paying for it."

Almost indifferently, she said, "So you win. What happens to me? Am I free to leave or do I have to stay on Saragosa?"

She walked from the balcony door to a large overstuffed chair and sat down on the very edged, her legs curled back slightly under her.

He was clearly aggravated with her but in the short time she'd known him she'd learned his body language more often told the truth and his mouth lied. She shuddered to think she'd even considered siding with Bartok if the invasion failed.

"No, lady," There was a sneer in Bartok's voice. "You get to travel with me." He made no move from the front of the bar.

"That's an option we can consider. But I'm a scientist. I've trained all my life to be in research. I'm really not cut out to go planet hopping." The last thing Celia wanted was to be taken where she had no means of escape from Bartok. She was determined not to board a transport of any kind with the man.

"Cut the bullshit. Where're the renegades' headquarters?" Bartok pulled a laser pistol from his pocket and laid it on the bar.

"Shoot me and you'll never know."

"Probably, but I'll feel better than I have since you ran off." There was almost a chuckle in his voice.

Celia smiled. That she could believe. With her reaction, she watched Bartok relax. "Yes, I did treat you rather badly." And she wasn't about to apologize.

"A mind-probe could get the answers," Bartok continued.

"No need for that—I came here to tell you about it. The headquarters are in the tunnels under the old museum. I think it was one of the first buildings built in Saragosa City. It was abandoned for years then converted into a museum. Most old timers had forgotten about the caverns below and of course, those that came later never knew of their existence. It was just forgotten."

Almost yawning, Bartok asked, "And how do we get in?"

"Short of drilling, there's only one way. The center support column of the museum is the entry way to the caverns below and that's where the leaders are." Celia laid out the combination for entry.

Bartok tried to show indifference but he wasn't doing well. There could be little doubt he was pissed. They'd been operating their headquarters right under his nose. Right in the middle of his army. "How did you get this information and how did you get away?"

Celia reached in her dress pocket and pulled out a small hand-held computer. "I swiped this and put everything I could on it for you to get into the caverns. As for escaping, they were moving me and I was able to distract my guard. "It was almost the truth. What she didn't tell Bartok was that Hulk and his people entered the data. Celia was one of the last to leave the base, along with her guards. They were giving Bartok nothing. Celia guessed the location added little for the invasion. Having no strategic or tactical purpose, it made no sense to expend assets to defend it and the caves had no offensive use. The need to verify the information she'd given him would hopefully buy them some time.

Bartok took the computer. As if on signal, Colonel Masten stepped into the room.

Bartok handed the computer to the colonel, not a word passing between the two.

A sadistic grin permeated Masten's face as he looked from the computer to her.

A chill ran through Celia.

The killer left the room as silently as he entered.

Bartok looked at her, his chin lifted slightly. "Now we can get down to you and me, in my room."

"I'm starved," Celia said. She was sure facing Bartok would be easier on a full stomach.

Bartok lit up and said, "Let's have brunch in my room in thirty minutes."

"I'll be up in a few shortly. Freshen up a bit you know," Celia said.

* * * *

Rap Steel jumped onto the gravlift and rode it to the basement. He'd verified Celia's arrival and the two were meeting in her room. He monitored Masten's departure from the hotel and admitted to mixed emotions where Masten was concerned. He never felt sure whether he was better off when he could see the man or if he was out of sight. Either way, the killer was seldom out of mind. To him, the man reeked of death. Rap watched Bartok leave Celia's room then shut down the computer and returned to the gravlift.

Getting off on the fourth floor, he made his way to Celia's room showing his pass to the guard standing next to the door. Quickly, he gave a light knock on the oak molding.

Rap breathed a silent sigh when he saw the look of relief on Celia's face. He needed to talk to her. Hastings had only told him to expect her return and to contact her as soon as possible.

"Good morning Ms. Markham. It's good to have you back. I'm following up on the complaint about the security system. I need to inspect it and report back to my supervisor."

Celia looked at the guard. He didn't know there was no such report.

His nod gave the needed approval.

Rap stepped into Celia's suite and closed the door.

"Am I ever glad to see you," she said grabbing him around the neck with a huge hug.

"Well, that was nice," he said. "How did you get rid of Bartok?"

"Easy. Are all of you men so gullible?" she asked.

Rap returned the tease, "If you mean where women are concerned, yes."

"Simple. I mentioned I hadn't eaten today and was starved. Bartok took care of the rest offering brunch in his suite—in about ten minutes."

Rap checked the surveillance equipment as they spoke. It was his excuse for getting in.

Celia noticed his attention and said, "Bartok turned it off. I suppose it'll be coming back on."

Rap stepped to one of the spot he knew was out of the range of the cameras and waited. Shortly, his hand-held analyzer told him the system was functional. He pressed a few buttons and stepped back toward Celia.

"It's off again, for the moment. Are you sure you want to go to his rooms again? The last time, things got a little tense as I recall."

"As they will this time," she said with an air of indifference. "Look," she paused placing her hands to her face, "when I go into Bartok's room he'll cut off the cameras. I want you to come in through one of those secret tunnels of yours and inspect his quarters. Bedroom, office if there is one. You know, see if there's anything, maybe a computer, to tell us where Smithe and his wife are imprisoned. It's probably the only chance we'll get. I'll keep Bartok occupied in the main room.

"Rap," Celia continued, "I've got a feeling we are about to be invaded. All hell is going to break loose around here and I want to be gone! We simply don't have much time. Get in there and see what you can find. And let me know one way or the other. If you've found their location, I'll get up and leave. If not, I'll try another approach on Bartok. How can you let me know?"

"Just like that. You'll get up and leave or..." Rap left unsaid what would happen next. If she stayed, that was nothing she wanted to think about.

"That's my only plan. Now, how can you tell me if you've found the information we're looking for?"

Rap sat next to the computer stand. He ran his hands over his face, then through his hair. "If I find what we want, why don't I just walk into the room and shoot the bastard?"

"That would certainly alert me. It would also alert the guards outside. And then, genius, how do we get out and how do we get the information to our people?" She knew Rap was searching for an answer as he made light of a difficult situation. That she'd said our people pleased her.

Rap picked up on it and smiled.

Finally, he said, "Make sure to have brunch over near the balcony, looking out and preferably with Bartok's back to the opening. I can make the outside lights blink off and on. A series of short blinks means I got the information;

long dashes no. If Bartok's back is to the glass doors, and since it's daylight, he won't see the lights."

"Let's do it. If you discover Smithe's location, I'll find a reason to get out and go to my room. We'll leave the hotel just as we did before, through the tunnel and sewer."

"Done," said Rap and he left her room.

Celia startled herself. I'm actually getting a rush from this.

* * * *

Celia arrived at Bartok's door as the kitchen entourage emerged from the service gravlift. Two guards stood outside the door of his suite.

Bartok wasn't in sight as she entered with the chef, so she watched as the staff prepared the setting.

The bellhop moved a heavy table into place, Celia making sure it was near the balcony. Three waitresses and the chef fussed over the placement of each item. Silver utensils, silver napkin holders and silver candelabra ringed a vase of black orchids.

A few minutes later, Bartok entered the room. Celia stood and walked behind the bar. He followed, pouring champagne for both.

Keeping the bar between them, Celia accepted the glass. She then moved to the table as the maids finalized the setting.

Because she'd moved first, Celia was able to choose her chair and sat facing the balcony, forcing Bartok's back to the opening.

As he raised his glass suggesting a toast, his com light lit, indicating an urgent message.

Bartok strode the few meters back to the bar and spoke harshly into the device.

He stormed back to the table and slammed his fist on the table. "Empty? The goddamned place was empty?"

He wheeled to face her. "They let you escape! What did they think I'd do? Sit on my ass and wait a week before checking this information."

His anger was so intense, she moved her chair back from the table to prepare for the attack she felt would surely come.

"Maybe I should give you a few minutes to work through this. I'll wait in the hall." She stood and moved away from the delicious smelling food. As she neared the door, the balcony lights blinked quickly off and on.

Bartok didn't answer. In fact, Celia doubted he'd heard her. His orders into the com showed his mind was far from either food or romance.

Without another word, Celia stepped through the hallway door, nodded to the guards and without hesitation, entered the gravlift. It was time to get out of there.

Within minutes, she was in her room and Rap had the escape panel open.

"That didn't take long. How were you able to get the information so quickly?" she asked.

"Dumb luck," Rap said. "Bartok's computer was already on. It was in the first data file I accessed. I did open three more files to disguise what I was looking for."

He gestured at the opening. "This is getting to be a habit. We have to stop meeting this way."

Once inside the darkened hidden passageway, Rap stopped long enough to send a message that he had the information. She didn't know who he was transmitting to and Rap didn't wait for an answer. Now, all they needed was to get to the storm sewer and they were free of Bartok—hopefully for good.

She was ready for the long run they'd have to make. Ankle deep in water, they proceeded south through the sewer for over two kilometers. Less debris floated in the underground drain than had on their previous journey, the result of efforts over the last few days to clean the devastation from the city.

Rap stopped a few feet from a utility cover, the light through the drain holes casting a shadow across his face. He motioned her toward a ledge half a meter above the water and again motioned her to sit down. Soon another man joined them. Rap introduced him as Adrian.

"Earlier, I heard you say our people. Ma'am,"

"Celia, please."

He seemed to ignore her plea. "We're about to make a raid. I don't have time to hand you over to anyone else for safekeeping. I only have two choices and one of them is for you to accompany us."

Adrian, standing behind Rap to shield his actions, pulled a laser pistol from his coat pocket, something she was sure wasn't meant for her eyes. She felt cold with fear but said nothing.

Rap said, "Ma'am, I have to know what side you're on."

Celia's fear almost overwhelmed her. With Bartok, her fear had been mixed with anger. This time it bordered on stark terror. "You didn't say anything about Winner White."

"No ma'am. Even though I don't believe he had anything to do with your father's death, that's an argument between you and him. Even Mr. White would agree we're fighting for something a lot bigger."

Celia reached out to touch Rap, but he pulled back with Adrian remaining behind him.

She folded her hands and placed them in her lap.

Rap started talking again, almost as if he couldn't stop. Almost as if he kept talking all of this would go away. Finally, he slowed in his jabbering, his usual seriousness settled in and he said, "I got to tell you, if you in any way jeopardize our efforts to rid ourselves of Bartok and his bastards…"

Celia felt a stirring that couldn't be denied. It was something that she'd been feeling for some time and she was pleased with how easy her words spilled out. "I want to work with you and the rest of your group." Celia watched Rap's face, looking to see if it was the face of a colleague or executioner. "Do I need to pledge my life?"

He grinned and said, "You just did. Come on." He took her arm and helped her back into the water. "Let's go help someone. We're going to meet our people, free Zena White and Daker Smithe. I suspect you've known all along it was Zena White and not Daker's wife that Bartok captured. But, so be it."

As the three continued down the sewer she asked, "Couldn't do it yourself, huh?" She motioned toward Adrian.

"Nope. How do you shoot someone you've twice taken out of harms way?"

CHAPTER TWENTY EIGHT
The rescue

"You say she left with the maintenance man?"

Masten nodded. "His name's Steel. He's the only one missing. We've suspected him for the last few days. He must have known we were closing in."

"Why the hell would she come back if she intended to leave within a few minutes?

"He got into your computer while you and Markham were eating," Masten said. "He entered four files, apparently looking for military information. We don't know how much he got."

Bartok nodded. "Find him! Also, find Celia Markham." He took a long look at Masten. "Quickly! Kill them both!" There was a chilling finality hanging over his words.

Masten smiled.

* * * *

There wasn't time to hand Celia off to any one else, the flight from the hotel coming sooner than anticipated. She had to accompany Rap to free Daker and Zena.

Continuing south a number of kilometers through the sewer, Celia, Rap and Adrian climbed from the utility hole into the basement of a warehouse. Over the next ten minutes, six armed people, all in body armor and with combat field packs emerged from the shadows. Rap was the first to speak as he introduced himself, as did each member. Celia was surprised with introductions but then remembered her guards talking about anonymity. The people in the resistance seldom knew each other—it was added protection. She accepted a small backpack from a man in fatigues.

"Food, water and other gear," he said with a big smile.

Rap told them to sit down on the concrete floor. "Ms. White and Mr. Smithe are being held at an abandoned processing mill about seventy klicks west of Saragosa City." He pulled a map from his backpack and marked the spot. "The place is isolated, hard to get to, but that works for us as well. We've got to move before they take them to the city."

A man in the back spoke, "There are submersibles south of the city, about one hundred meters off shore in twenty meters of water—four of them. They're straight south of the sluiceway. Sapper crews hid them after they planted the offshore assault barriers. They'll be more than enough to get us to the old mill. There are wet suits in your packs."

Rap said, "It's almost noon. We'll assemble south of the mill and attack just after sundown. Each of you knows how to get there." Splitting the team into groups of two for the submersibles he asked, "Any questions?"

Getting none, Rap said, "See you at twenty-one hundred. Good luck!"

At an easy trot, Celia and Rap made their way to a small gully a few klicks south of Saragosa City and followed it toward the ocean.

Once well away from the city, Celia jogged beside Rap. "I'm hungry. I haven't eaten in almost twenty-four hours. Can we eat, even on the run?"

Rap waved toward a growth of mangroves; "We can stop here. We're at the sluice." They halted under the small outcrop and ate. "Once you're finished, we'll get into our wet suits. It's about one half klick to the shore and there's no cover until we get in the water."

No cover? Celia looked ahead to the only smooth area in sight. Crags made up the rest of the beach. She'd heard of Saragosa's monster tides and that much of its shoreline showed the rugged effect of the eroding waters driven by the planet's two moons.

Their timing couldn't have been better. An enemy patrol boat entered the small bay and passed within meters of the miniature subs hidden offshore at the bottom of the inlet. The mangroves growing in the shallows gave good coverage, hiding the base of the copse that shielded them.

Celia didn't let the boat's sudden appearance interrupt her meal. Twenty hours without food saw to that. As she waited for the patrol boat to leave, she rested in the slight shade, a welcome relief from the unrelenting suns.

Rap checked his wafer-thin chronometer. As the patrol boat vanished, he announced, "fourteen hundred."

Stowing the rest of the meal, he pulled out a wet suit and full body underwear. He sealed the backpack and asked, "Are you a good swimmer? I know it's a little late to be asking."

"I can stay up with the best."

"Good. We have to get to the sub. It's about one hundred meters straight south, on the bottom. Just stick close to me."

Celia dug out her wet suit and underwear. By then Rap pulled a plastic sleeve from his pack, "Salve, you'll need some of this." He handed the container to her. "Cover your entire body with this before you put on the underwear. Particularly your hands, face and feet. It keeps the sulfur in the water from blistering your skin.

Celia followed Rap's lead, pulled her goggles into place, and was in the water swimming at his heels, her street clothes stuffed into the backpack. He signaled to take a gulp of air and dove. She wasted no time, inhaled all the air she could and dived behind him.

Loaded with rifles, backpacks and ammo belts, they had no difficulty in staying submerged.

Even through the salve covering her exposed skin, Celia could feel the sulfur sting. Few signs of plant or animal life existed, only the hint of yellow and green from the mineral concentrations tainted the water. She wondered if her father had really found some way to resolve the problem of the poisons in the water. Still, mangroves grew in the shallow water, perhaps…

She didn't have time to finish the thought. Rap had reached the sub and extracted breathing helmets. She grabbed the mouthpiece, expelled her depleted air and pulled hard on the fresh supply. She didn't remember that air could taste sweet.

They mounted the saddles astride their small transport and Rap steered westerly toward the processing mill constantly on alert for the marauding patrol boat.

Six hours later, they crawled to the rendezvous. "How many guards?" Rap whispered as he gathered his helmet and night goggles.

"We count six," Adrian answered.

"Nine to six." "Just the numbers I like," Rap said.

Celia accepted a quick course on the use of the combination eyepieces. "Night vision, telescopic, laser detection and heat-sensitive, all wrapped into one," her helper whispered.

Following Rap's advice, she decided to stay in the wet suit until the fighting was over. "It's rugged and besides, in combat it looks more dignified than street clothes, especially a dress."

Even through the night goggles, Celia couldn't ignore the grin on his face. She accepted the laser pistol he offered.

Two of Rap's people had been observing the mill for over three hours. They reported no sentries inside with the captives. As this was the boonies, even for Saragosa, the guards were less than vigilant. The watches were four on and four off and the next change was due at twenty-two hundred. The off-duty soldiers camped on a knoll southwest of the mill; the two duty guards patrolled the parameter together.

The area leading from the shore to the mill was a gradual uphill slope although the mill itself was nestled in a small dale. The first settlers on Saragosa built the mill to use water runoff from the mountains to the north. It had outlived its usefulness over fifty years before.

Rap surveyed the landscape. As a boy, he'd played here enough times to remember every inch of the land, every place to hide. No trees, lots of gullies, a few large boulders scattered along the ground and the enemy had done nothing to fortify the area. They were on Rap's turf, which was why he had volunteered for this job.

He divided the group into four teams, three of two each would take on the guards. The fourth team consisted of himself, Celia, and another woman, Dotty Sanchez.

"We'll make a direct assault on the mill. It's our job to make sure no harm comes to Ms. White and Mr. Smithe," he cautioned both.

Celia had figured out their assignment required the least combat skill but was potentially the most dangerous, certainly to the hostages. Yet, she knew if it came down to a choice between the hostage living and their rescuers, the hostages would win out.

To make sure they gained entry, the attack group wouldn't stop to return fire during the assault. Rap made it known the enemy was better equipped than they were. The initial assault had to prevent the guards from communicating with their command. Anything less would mean failure of the rescue.

They would be exposed until they got inside the walls of the building. Their most important assets were surprise, running like hell and a little luck.

Rap made a final round talking with each group and then dispersed them.

Celia lay behind some rocks and surveyed the ground her team had to cover —two hundred meters and damned little to hide behind. The moons hadn't risen yet. The mill, while surrounded by rocks and crags sat atop a crest, totally exposed.

Rap winced as his wrist com sounded its message alert. He unsnapped his earplug and inserted it.

Even in the dim light, it was evident to Celia that something was happening.

The man stood ramrod still, almost as if transfixed. His hands made fists and his body shook. As Rap turned toward them, even through the night goggles, she saw tears well in his eyes and a monstrous grin splitting his face.

"The invasion has begun! Let's get these people rescued!"

With quiet determination, Rap sent out the order, "Now!"

On the dead run, Celia, Sanchez, and Rap headed for the mill. Any thoughts of the invasion had to be pushed aside.

They'd covered fifty meters, avoiding one known guard location, only to come face to face with a soldier. Celia shot first—years of skeet shooting paid off.

The soldier never got out of his administrative position nor uttered a sound.

Three minutes later, Rap and the two women burst through the door.

Celia scanned the area and headed for the first room off to her right.

Daker was on his feet, placing himself between Celia and Zena White.

"We're here to get you safely back to our people," Celia said. "Stay down, away from the window."

Crouched, she made her way to the two, now huddled on mattresses lying on the stone floor. "I'm Celia Markham. Come with me." Her calm but decisive voice had the necessary effect.

As Celia neared the door, Rap acknowledged Smithe and Ms. White. "I'm going outside to help." The sounds of a firefight reverberated from the walls— the assault wasn't going as well as he'd hoped.

Celia almost fell when Rap grasped her shoulders. "Get those people out of here. We'll catch up when this is over." He pulled the four in close to cope with the noise outside and gave them the location of Hrndulka's base.

Through her night vision goggles, Celia watched Rap leave. She told Sanchez to stay with Zena and Daker and moved to the second floor, positioning herself at a window to provide cover fire if possible.

She followed Rap's movement toward the fight. Enemy guards raked the area with automatic flechette weapons. It was impossible for any of Rap's people to move and the gunners would cut them to pieces if they stayed where they were. With some guards holding the guerillas in place, a single shooter had only to move a short distance, to a slightly higher location, and Rap and his people would be totally exposed.

Celia ran down the stairs. If the guards had summoned help, it could arrive soon. She had to get their wards out of the mill. She could only hope that the enemy would forget about these hostages. Regardless, Rap had told her to get Zena and Daker moving. She beckoned Sanchez into the hallway. "I've got to help our people."

She motioned toward the area south of the building. "Take Ms. White and Mr. Smithe out the north door. Keep a northeasterly course and put as much distance between us as possible. We'll catch up with you."

Rap wasn't going to like this but Celia couldn't leave the fighters when they needed her help.

Without a questioning word, Zena White and Daker Smithe left their prison behind, Sanchez leading them into the darkness. It was over fifty kilometers to the base and safety.

Celia crept back to where she'd killed the guard earlier, picking up his weapons—a flechette rifle and a laser pistol. She wished it were the other way around—at any distance, flechettes were indiscriminate in their killing. Taking his bandoleers, she retraced her trail to the mill, through the building and out the front entrance flanking the enemy.

Celia noiselessly crawled forward as fast as she could. Sulfur permeating the soil boiled up in her eyes. The intensity of the fighting increased. She winced as the yells of wounded and dying increased and knew both sides were taking casualties. Reaching a slight crest, she sighted the two guards. Their razor weapons raked the ground, tearing everything in their path to shreds.

Celia crawled to a position to keep her own people out of the line of fire from her flechette rifle, aimed and squeezed the trigger. Two quick bursts and both guards died. The only sounds reaching her were cries of the wounded.

She scanned the area, assuring herself no further threat existed. She called to the other partisans and got the required response. All seemed clear.

Cautiously, Celia pushed herself from the dirt and walked forward. She dropped to the ground next to Rap. He was dying, his body shredded by a direct hit from a bundle of razors.

She took his hand in hers and held it close. He opened his eyes and smiled for the last time. Celia wanted to scream but couldn't, to be sick but wouldn't. She laid her dead friend's hand on his chest and turned her attention to the living.

There was no way the wounded survivors could stand a fifty-kilometer march. She called the corporal over, "What's our count?"

Still, seemingly in a daze, she looked around, "Ours—three dead, three wounded and you, Sanchez and me. Theirs—five dead, one wounded."

Celia grabbed the corporal's shoulder. "Rap's dead. Are you up to leading this group?" Celia knew it wasn't her job but the corporal seemed in a daze.

"Ma'am, I just made corporal. If you'll take command it's all right with me."

Celia was ready. She didn't relish putting her life in the hands of an eighteen or nineteen year old. "Let's get the living into the mill, both sides." She looked around, selected a man with minor wounds, and said, "Make a sweep through the area Gather all med kits, ammunition, weapons, food, water, everything that can keep us alive and bring it to the mill. Hurry."

Once in the mill Celia said, "Corporal, you're in charge. The wounded can't be moved. See to it they are cared for. We'll send help as soon as we can, maybe two or three days. You have enough food and medical to last over a week, longer if you ration it. Sanchez and I will take Ms. White and Mr. Smithe out of danger. We'll be back for you."

Celia didn't know that at all but what else could she say to a kid she was leaving behind with little protection, wounded people and no doctor?

Celia gathered food, water, med kit and ammunition then set out to find Zena, Daker and Sanchez. Over the next three days, they'd need even more than luck.

She knew the group couldn't be far ahead. Zena White had to be in her sixties and Smithe at least that. The rugged mountains were not an easy climb. They probably hadn't gone much over a kilometer even with an hour's head start.

An hour later and four klicks into the hills, Celia finally caught the group.

She called to the trio; "I'll never underestimate you two again. You're doing better than two klicks an hour. Ready to rest?"

Daker looked at Zena—the look he got back would have shamed Edmund Hillary. "Nope," Daker said. "We keep going—got lots of ground to cover before we rest." He handed a water jug to Zena, then took a swig himself.

For the next hour, they continued to move higher into the mountains, the terrain increasingly difficult. Celia said, "Maybe you don't need to stop, but I do." She didn't want the bravado of Zena and Daker to get the best of them.

They settled behind some large boulders. "Take off your packs," she ordered.

Daker leaned toward Celia on his elbow and said, "We've heard about you. You're the White employee that came up here to kill Winner. Why?" His manner wasn't menacing, just matter of fact.

The two moons of Saragosa cast a silvery sheen over the land; rocky crags laid shadows around them. Celia could clearly see the faces of the three people that waited for her answer. Zena White's expression hadn't changed. Celia had seen that same look on her father's face, *Well, what have you got to say for yourself?* Right then, she didn't have anything useful to say.

Finally, Zena asked, "What is it that makes you think Winner is in any way responsible for your father's death? As I understand it, Mr. Markham was returning from Saragosa and his ship disappeared in hyperspace. It does happen occasionally, even with today's technology."

Celia didn't detect any malice in Ms. White's question and searched for an answer—an answer without her own pain that seemed to match the pain of this lady whose son she'd openly vowed to kill.

She thought for a few minutes then said, "My father was hired by WMC specifically to study the oceans of Saragosa, to find the answer to making them resourceful. It was his career. As a scientist, he also had the responsibility to say if it wasn't possible. The results could have a direct impact on White's financial future on the planet. White needed a positive analysis. The company had tried since colonizing the planet to make the oceans productive. Dad hadn't published his results when he left Saragosa for Earth. The general word was …"

"Rumor," Daker interjected.

Celia's only reaction to Daker's comment was to pause. "… was the oceans could be productive but White wasn't ready for public release of the information.

"Winner White was missing from his job at Gorman Space Corp. at the same time my father disappeared. There was an attempt, a very clever one I might add, to cover up his being away and it's never been explained. That and a few documents Bartok supplied, possibly forged documents, I now realize, formed the basis of Bartok's proof."

Zena White sat unmoved, erect. She placed her hands in her lap. Celia inwardly flinched at the unblinking gaze that descended upon her.

"Winner was with me," she quietly said.

Daker turned toward her, a small smile touching his lips.

Zena repeated, "Winner was with me, my husband, his wife and daughter."

Celia couldn't hide her startled look.

Zena continued, "You're surprised about Winner having a wife and child. Rightfully so. He was quite late in telling Michael and me."

Daker sat with his mouth agape.

Sanchez stopped and looked back as she moved outside the group to take up her watch.

The statement caught Celia off guard. Nothing she could have done would have prepared her for Zena's admission.

Winner's mother said to Celia, "You also failed to mention that Bartok was reported to have killed my husband. Nothing could be farther from the truth."

Zena brushed a tear away, took a deep breath, released it and continued, "Winner had married a year earlier. He didn't tell us until the grandchild was born. Made Michael furious. I was happy for Winner and immediately left for their home on Philomel. I had suspected something was happening although I had no idea what. Winner had become, um, distant in a way. I hadn't ruled out he'd met a woman that interested him. His com letters to us came less frequently. You may know Winner wasn't very keen on the corporate life. He really didn't want anything to do with running the company. That's why he spent so much time as a test pilot. I suspect he was afraid if we knew he'd married, we'd put more pressure on to change his mind. When the baby came, Winner's conscience wouldn't let him keep Michael and me away from our only grandchild. My husband sent a pinnace to return the three of us up to earth. Michael planned to join us sometime during the return trip. Winner stayed behind and was to come about a month later.

"We believe Bartok attacked—no…we know—Bartok's people attacked the pinnace thinking Michael was on board. But it was my daughter-in-law, the baby and I. By the time Michael got to the ship the attack was over, Winner's wife and baby were dead."

Zena took a deep breath—tears ran down her cheeks. "It was true Michael was dying. I think I was the only other one that knew for over a year except his doctor. We did tell Winner a few months earlier. I'm sure that affected his decision to return to earth with his wife and baby. My husband was wounded in the battle for Nimitz Crossing and later became ill while on an expedition to some damned planet." A quiet sob slipped passed her lips magnifying the loneliness in her voice. "There wasn't a cure. The disease didn't even have a name. He died shortly after Winner got there. My son and I quietly returned to Earth to put our lives back together."

She leaned toward Celia and said with a voice that conveyed inner strength, "You see young lady, my son had nothing to do with your father's disappearance. Before Winner got canned as CEO, I used a little of my clout to get elected chairwoman of WMC. That's how I got him the CIC office and kept him involved. Believe me, I knew what was going on."

There was a determined finality in her words and Celia dared not challenge them, not that she wanted to.

"Ms. White, I believe you. Can you forgive me?"

"For what? You've done nothing I wouldn't have done in the same circumstances. Now, let's get moving. Winner has a war to win and a bastard to get rid of. We just may be of some help."

Toward the close of the second day, Celia said, "We'll make camp here." They'd climbed over and around rocks all day long. She was tired. The others had to be.

She chose a small stand of trees growing from an outcrop of rocks. It gave good cover in case anyone was looking for them. The top of the crags made an excellent perch for watching the areas surrounding them. Their progress had slowed over the last kilometer.

Daker said, "The terrain changes to a plateau shortly. It will be much easier going." The group decided they would rest for four hours, then resume the march.

Celia was astounded at the pace Zena and Daker maintained. She climbed to the top of the outcrop and began her watch. Sanchez was already asleep. She adjusted her goggles to the changing light. The suns were setting and another hour would pass before the moons came up.

Two hours into her watch, Celia whispered for Sanchez to join her. "Look over there."

Sanchez looked to the southeast, where Celia pointed. She adjusted her goggles, changing from night to infrared two or three times before she spoke.

"Shit. Looks like the party's over. I make out three of them, soldiers. They don't seem to be in any hurry. That means they haven't spotted us."

"Come on," Celia ordered. Sanchez followed her off the rock. "Mr. Smithe, you know this terrain. How far to Hrndullka's base?"

Daker immediately answered, "About ten kilometers, maybe a little less."

Celia removed her helmet. "We've got trouble. Soldiers, and not ours. About a kilometer southeast." She turned to Zena and asked, "Can you travel?"

"Given the alternative, you bet."

Celia smiled at the answer. "Good. Mr. Smithe, you, Ms. White and Sanchez are to head for the resistance camp now." She turned to Sanchez and said, "Your job is to get them there safely. Whatever it takes."

"Yes ma'am. You can depend on it."

"Where you going?" asked Daker as Celia changed from the wet suit into her street clothes.

Celia grinned, "Just going to give them something to think about. Liven up their day—well, night anyway."

Daker started to protest but Celia cut him short, her voice blunt and curt. "This entire expedition was to free you two." Her voice softened. "A lot of good people died getting us this far." Celia traded rifles with Sanchez, opting for the laser and its greater accuracy.

Daker patted her on the shoulder. As she stood, Zena already putting on her backpack, gave her a kiss on the cheek. No words passed between them but Celia was grateful.

For the next twenty minutes, she watched her charges move toward Hrndullka's camp and safety. She reached for her rifle and headed east toward the soldiers but slightly north to parallel a small creek running along their path. She wanted to keep the squad from crossing her groups' trail. With heat sensors, the soldiers would pick it up without any trouble and the rescue would fail.

Celia reached the water well ahead of the soldiers. She stepped into the cold mountain runoff and continued toward them. She thought out her options. She'd lose in a gunfight. Three to one doesn't lend itself to a long life. She needed to keep the men from discovering there were others with her and to buy time for Sanchez to put as much distance between them as possible.

Celia quietly moved further down stream, her feet and legs beginning to feel the effects of the cold water. Thankfully, the cold fast stream kept the rock bottom clear of moss and other slippery growth.

She wanted to get behind the soldiers. Make them come back from the direction they were heading, away from the tracks her friends were leaving. Celia stopped behind a boulder sitting midstream and watched the three men pass not fifty meters away.

It was time. She laid her laser rifle on top of the boulder and started splashing, thrashing and sputtering like she was drowning and headed directly for the soldiers not ten meters from the water's edge.

"Well, well, well. Look at the pretty little fishy I just caught." The first soldier grabbed Celia by the blouse and hauled her onto shore. The other two roared their delight.

Without any hesitation, one soldier took off his coat and said, "This one's mine." Obviously, they'd done this before.

Celia rolled aside, avoiding the man's lunge. She pulled the laser pistol from its holster—the whine, as it charged, stopped the men in their tracks. "The next shot will make a capon out of you. And if I don't, Bartok will."

Invocation of Bartok's name did what she wanted. The men backed off.

CHAPTER TWENTY NINE
The invasion

Al-Cadifh and Derka arrived in the CAC room together, buried deep in discussion.

A good sign, Winner thought. The Berber had a reputation for using every asset he could lay his hands on. Anything to get an advantage in a fight. Winner never knew what Derka might conjure up and al-Cadifh was making the best of him.

Captain Davenport and Melissa arrived seconds later—she seemed to be bending his ear. Davenport leaned to his side straining to hear what she was saying.

Winner couldn't pick up on the words and the talk stopped when both realized he was watching. All of these people had put in long hours preparing for the invasion, yet they looked fresh and full spirited.

"What are you two conjuring up?" Over the last few weeks, Winner had observed Davenport and liked what he saw. A meticulous planner, Davenport left nothing to chance. His 'we will win' attitude was infectious.

Melissa glanced quickly at Davenport and got no reaction. She answered, "Nothing, sir. Just trying to cover every contingency."

Each took his seat around the table except Winner. He walked to the area set aside for holograph displays. "I have a taped message from Simone. I thought you might like to view it."

The group focused on the telecom as Simone Anacrode came into view. She was her usual self and didn't mince words. "Winner, you better win. Between the bankers and lawyers trying to carve off parts of WMC, we have a full plate. Only a victory will save this company. The Federation of Aligned Worlds isn't helping. They're waiting to see who wins. By the way, I called them cowards. After you win, you'll have that bunch to placate."

Aldofo Baranca appeared on the screen, angry and close to crowding Simone aside. Baranca was an appointed board member and more than used to speaking his mind. Winner had named him to make sure he didn't get a rubber stamp board of directors.

"We know the opposition this democracy idea of yours has stirred up—some call it a show on your part, a dangerous precedent. There are more influential people against than for it. But you can't let that son-of-a-bitch Bartok win."

The CEO reasserted herself, turned to Aldofo and thanked him. She seemed reluctant to sign off. "Well, Winner, I wish I were there to go into battle with you. But I'm not. The best I can do is wish you good luck and God speed."

Winner keyed off the view screen. "Perhaps I was wrong in declaring open elections for Saragosa. I don't happen to think so. Business thrives in a stable political environment. People do as well. I don't believe free selection of a government had anything to do with the invasion."

He paused. "Now to focus on what's ahead. You've prepared well. We know our limitations and the enemy's capabilities. Bartok has more ships, more troops and greater firepower. As you heard, we'll get no help from the Federation, not that we expected any.

"Yet I believe the advantage is ours. We pick the time and location of the initial attack. Perhaps more importantly, many of Bartok's soldiers are mercenaries. They're in this strictly for the money. If they realize their side is going to lose, they'll run. If they can't escape, they surrender.

"Colonel Hornblower attacked Fonso Carrel's and Kirk Filbright's fleets and Namaycush two days ago—these were all standard times. The first bit of luck came when WMC's forces hit Carrel's fleet before it cleared the Krighton System and immediately followed with the Namaycush attack. Carrel split his forces, not realizing it was the same people that had ambushed him. Bartok dispatched eight warships from Saragosa after receiving the news.

Winner keyed the projector—Saragosa and ten million kilometers of space surrounding it appeared in the holograph. He summed up events of the last few days. Then he added, "Day three, Sizemore started its run on Saragosa, that was twenty-three hours ago and she will drop out of hyperspace in thirteen hours, eject the troop and supply launch for Hrndullka and move back to join up with the battle group." What he didn't add was that for this to work, Bartok couldn't recognize Sizemore as part of Winner's attacking fleet.

He walked the length of the CAC room. "Our fleet will start movement toward Saragosa in fifteen hours. Thirty-eight hours from now, Deliverance and the fighters will initiate their attack."

Winner looked at the bulkhead chronometer over the display screen, "It's now zero nine thirty of day three. Captain Davenport, you will begin the attack at twenty-one hundred on day five. Once orbital superiority is established, Colonel al-Cadifh, launch your Marines. Hopefully that won't be a long wait. Questions?"

He got none.

"Then good luck gentlemen, Melissa."

* * * *

Responding to the com alert, Winner slipped into his skin suit and retrieved his helmet.

The door buzzer sounded. He said, "Enter. Ah, Melissa. I want to cover some things with you. Sit down." He motioned to a chair.

"This is the first time we've been in battle together and both of us should have some idea of what to expect from each other. What plans have you made?"

Melissa stood, drew herself up to her almost one hundred sixty-eight centimeters. "A full squad will accompany us at all times. Skin suits and body armor, helmets are the uniform of the day. Weapons include laser, hand and shoulder, flechette, hand and shoulder, two energy rifles, laser and concussion grenades, K-bar knives and full vision goggles. Backpacks are standard dirt-side."

"Sounds good to me, Lieutenant."

"Yes, sir. We're ready."

Turning to the insistent buzz, Winner leaned back in his chair and flipped the manual intercom switch, "Yes."

"Davenport here, Mr. White. Battle stations will sound in one minute."

"Thank you Captain." He flicked the switch off. "Well Melissa, are we ready? Better be." A smile came with the remark.

"A few days more might have helped some people but not enough to make a difference. Colonel al-Cadifh has his Marines ready. I know I wouldn't want to come up against them. His people are primed."

"Good." Winner smiled.

Melissa didn't move though Winner clearly thought the conversation was over.

"Anything else. Lieutenant?"

"Yes, sir. What about you, what are your plans? If you decide to go dirt-side are you going to try to ditch my squad?"

Over the few weeks they'd been together, Winner finally ended giving his guard the slip. He'd used up most of his tricks to elude them. "That's what you and Captain Davenport were talking about at the war council meeting."

Melissa's blush confirmed it.

Winner smiled "No Melissa. I'll behave." This woman had pledged her life for his if it came to that.

The claxon sounded. He clapped his hands as the intercom blared battle stations—a call that hadn't changed in over four hundred years. "Good luck, Lieutenant, let's go!"

He didn't feel like making bravado or macho statements when many brave people were about to die. Yet, he felt exhilaration just at the thought of putting an end to this terrible nightmare. And he admitted an adrenaline high.

He stepped from his quarters, Melissa a pace behind him and they headed for CAC. Crewmen in the passageway hurried to their battle stations.

Within seconds, Winner and Melissa were in CAC. Derka was already at his control console directing the crew. Ready reports were simultaneously flowing into the room and to Deliverance's bridge from the fleet.

They had the order. No radio, telemetry or tight beam transmissions to Saragosa, Hulk or the fleet until the actual invasion order, only short-range line of sight ship-to-ship communication. The last message to Hrndullka gave no clue the invasion was about to begin. Winner regretted not telling the man, but if Bartok were reading their messages, the invasion would fail.

Once the attack started, the first message to Hrndullka would be to keep his people out of the way until the Marines were on the ground. And above all, to keep civilians from any impromptu uprising.

"CAC, Bridge. Thirteen minutes until our main battle group engages the enemy's orbital fleet. Mr. White, would you care to join me on the bridge?" Davenport asked.

Winner grabbed his helmet and was out the hatch; Melissa scrambled to keep up.

The boson called CIC on the bridge as he and Melissa cleared the hatch.

Winner joined Davenport at the plot table, Melissa taking up a position at the rear of the bridge.

Davenport nodded a welcome. "Alpha squadron will lead the attack. Draw some attention. Beta squadron will attack fifteen minutes later. Both will hit ninety degrees off our port side and eight million klicks ahead of us," Davenport pointed to the screen, "and about two hundred thousand klicks before we enter the fray."

Winner studied the plot. Bartok's fleet was in a standard orbital defense. A weakness. His first worry had Bartok discovered their efforts and drawn them into a trap? But, Bartok always used a standard orbital defense. The use of mercenaries required standard tactics—something those fighters already knew. Without training, absolute chaos would result. The defensive alignment did have some advantage—it relied on brute strength instead of trying to gain a tactical edge placing the cruisers at the core surrounded by destroyers then fighters. Winner knew that if he couldn't gain some advantage the fight would go against them.

The outcome of the initial attack and maybe the entire battle depended on the four fighters equipped with anti-grav capability making up Alpha Squadron. Numbers meant little against these fighters. Unless Bartok had added the devices to his fighters, the anti-grav star fighters would tear his defending fleet apart. There was nothing to stop them except a lucky shot or another fighter with AG. The downside was less space for fuel and the added mass from the gravity generators cut the fighters' range and time in space dramatically. The fleet's best pilots manned the fighters. Winner had personally chosen these men and he had no doubts about their skills.

The danger was that Bartok could have matched them. After all, he'd had Topsail under his command for weeks. His scientists could have examined the ship or Celia could have told him of its capabilities—just as she'd told him of the faster than light communications.

Captain Davenport motioned the Boson' to hit the ship-wide com button and listened as the mates' calm voice said, "Attention on deck. Now hear this. The captain will address the fleet." Derka had rigged a narrow beam transmitter. The limited range would keep the messages from the enemy.

"This is Captain Davenport. We will engage the enemy in two minutes. Alpha Squadron will attack first followed by Beta. Deliverance and the rest of the fleet will engage the enemy in thirteen minutes. Once our fighters attacking the port side have accomplished their assignment, it's up to us to do our part. Our goal is to drive straight through the enemy's fleet and divide it. Sizemore and her battle group are on the starboard flank and fighters are on their way to support her.

"The balance of our star fighters will support the rest of the fleet and take targets of opportunity. Once we've penetrated their defenses, every ship has a wingman. Use it or you're on your own.

"Deliverance will take out the largest enemy ship, destroying their in-orbit energy weapon capability. We'll then take an orbital position to launch Colonel al-Cadifh and his Marines and continue on orbit in support of the ground troops.

"I know you have trained well and will do your job. Good shooting."

He keyed off the com and said to Winner, "We have the best helmsman I've ever cruised with. It's in the crew's hands."

Three-tenths c was the rated maximum thrust matter/anti-matter engines could develop, even in hyperwave ships but Davenport needed four tenths. Hull strength controlled how fast a spacecraft traveled. Deliverance had one of the strongest hulls in the known galaxy. Davenport flashed the message to engineering.

The response was immediate, "Four tenths c available for five standard minutes. Engineering control transferred to bridge."

He noticed Winner's glance. "It's standard procedure. When we operate outside normal perimeters, responsibility automatically goes to the bridge. Don't get caught with someone other than the captain deciding it might be too dangerous." He smiled. "If the captain screws up, no one else gets blamed." What he didn't say was if the matter/anti-matter engines overloaded, those to blame wouldn't be around—nor would anyone else within one hundred thousand kilometers.

Davenport said, "We'll drop out of hyperspace to watch the star fighters' initial attack. Deliverance will reenter hyperspace for three minutes. When we come out, we'll be shooting."

He returned his attention to the plot and said, "We'll be going straight through Bartok's fleet. The Alpha and Beta Squadron fighters should siphon off a part of the enemy fleet, and Bartok should be expecting us to enter at three tenths c. The time to retarget us at the higher speed works in our favor."

Winner said, "Let's hope they don't guess what we're doing and wait until we slow."

"We'll get one hell of a bloody nose if they do," Davenport responded.

"Alpha fighters have engaged the enemy!" The announcement crackled. "Beta squadron will engage shortly."

The first flight of fighters appeared on the screen. "Three down." Flares spotted the plot board. "Theirs," he said. "Looks like a destroyer getting in the mix."

"Captain Davenport, Derka here. That destroyer is the Hendrix. And initial data indicates that their fighters are not equipped with anti-grav."

Deliverance's data banks instantly produced the information to the bridge plot screen and relayed it to the fighters. The Hendrix's operating parameters made the outcome inevitable against those four fighters.

Both men watched the four tiny blips on the plot screen turn on the much larger but slower ship. Two fighters attacked from the rear disabling its engines; the other two took the more heavily gunned destroyer head on.

Try as they might, the larger ship could not bring its superior weapons to bear on the fighters. They maneuvered faster in three planes than the destroyer's guns could target. No matter which way the tin can tried to turn, it exposed itself to darting raids and pinpoint laser fire.

Winner envisioned a large predator animal harassed by smaller carnivores and losing.

Deliverance's communications officer keyed the fighter's inter-ship messages into the bridge speakers. Winner could visualize large gaps appearing where the destroyers gun ports had been, laid open by the tormentors. One by one, the smaller ships were taking the teeth out of their foe.

Two fighters broke off to renew their attack on the destroyer's fighter escorts. A second pass. The destroyer exploded, lighting up the battle display and taking a fighter with it. A crew of one thousand gone. Winner winced at the loss of lives.

"Beta Squadron engaging enemy," the plot-board spotter said then added, "Sizemore battle group has engaged to starboard."

Davenport leaned over and placed both hands on the plot. "Now we take losses. This is strictly pilot ability. I hate to pull the four anti-grav fighters but if we're to make a run down the throat of Bartok's guns, they have to join up with us."

Both men watched the fight unfold and listened to the reports.

In less than three minutes, six fighters were lost. The star fighter's ability to absorb damage was limited, nothing approaching a ship of the line. Many of Bartok's pilots were as good as White's. They dealt their share of death.

Davenport moved to the larger screen. "Engage their main fleet in three minutes..."

The helmsman's fingers raced across the controls to engage the engines. He secured himself to the seat in front of the giant plot screen, waited three minutes and signaled the tactical officer, "Drop out of hyperspace. You have control of the matter/anti-matter engines. Come out shooting."

They sat back to watch the battle.

Winner felt the first hit, somewhere aft on the ship. The constant hammering and brilliant flashes of their own guns masked some of the destruction inflicted on Deliverance. Damage and casualty reports streamed into the bridge tactical command center from the entire fleet. Deliverance hadn't yet suffered a hit that threatened the life of the ship. Stronger and much more resilient, she could take more punishment than older models.

TCC responded to every message. Sometimes, it was the wounded and dying reporting.

Davenport keyed the holo putting the entire battle up for the bridge crew to see. Despite being outnumbered more than two to one, their attack from three sides threw Bartok's fleet into chaos.

Winner watched the helmsman maneuver Deliverance as if it were part of him, vertical every bit as common as straight-ahead. He seemed to have a sixth sense of where to be and how to position the cruiser to make an enemy miss or give her gunners the best chance of making a kill.

Coming out of hyperspace at four-tenths c, Deliverance targeted and killed the first two ships it encountered. Two destroyers stayed fifteen thousand klicks to the rear to protect the big ship's engines; four ringed the launch bay doors but kept a healthy twenty thousand klicks distance. The four-anti-grav fighters seemed to be everywhere. When not killing someone, they disrupted any effort or maneuver attempted by the enemy.

Deliverance's gunners worked in sync with the helmsman, taking advantage of every opportunity his hectic path through Bartok's fleet presented. Winner watched as Deliverance's energy cannon hit one destroyer head on. The smaller ship seemed to stop in space then disappeared in a blue light, not even the usual space debris marking its passing—another thousand people died.

Sizemore's attack did what it was suppose to accomplish—cut off the one route Bartok's' fleet needed for regrouping. There simply wasn't any place to run and no place to hide.

Winner was thankful the launch bays hadn't taken any hits. It wouldn't take much of a shot to disrupt the troop launch. Fifteen dirt-side ships were crowded into room for ten. Sixteen hundred troops crawled over the machines —there was no space to walk around them.

He turned his attention to Saragosa as the communications officer signaled an incoming message.

Vladislov Hrndullka's face appeared on the screen. "Mr. White. It's dammed good to see you."

"Thank you," responded Winner. "What's happening dirt-side?" Winner keyed al-Cadifh into the conversation as he motioned Davenport to the screen.

Hrndullka rubbed his hands together almost in delight.

Winner realized this was the first time the man had any real hope of things changing on Saragosa.

"The launch from Sizemore landed. We have the Marines and supplies safely in our hands. We hid the launch in the mountains."

Hulk's manner changed. "You ordered us to stand down until the main Marine force arrived. We had to disobey that. As soon as you engaged their spaceships, Bartok ordered all civilians arrested. He executed anyone that so much as voiced a concern. We've had to fight back. Small bands of our people have attacked a number of Bartok's soldiers to free civilians. And we will continue to do so. "

"Of course," said Winner. He could hardly contain his anger that he couldn't do anything to help the people and that he couldn't risk telling Hrndullka of the impending invasion.

Knowing al-Cadifh was less than thirty minutes from landing on Saragosa did nothing to ease his pain and anger. All he could say is, "Do the best you can."

Winner wanted very much to let the man know they were on the way, that it would soon be over, the matter decided one way or the other. But even he couldn't be sure that the battle would end in Saragosa's favor. Bartok still commanded overwhelming firepower in space and on the ground.

Hrndullka continued, "I do have some good news. Daker showed up with your mother early this morning. Both are fine."

Winner breathed a silent sigh of relief. "Give Daker my thanks and tell mother to stay out of trouble."

Hulk laughed and continued, "They have some story to tell. Celia Markham played a large part in their escape."

It was the first time Winner had seen Hulk laugh. He shrugged his indifference, "Give her my thanks." He recalled his first encounter with her in the ship's mess hall. He had no idea what had changed her attitude or if it had changed. Right now, he just didn't want to give the time or energy to Celia Markham.

Hulk added, "I wish I could. She let herself be captured so your mother and Daker could escape."

Winner felt embarrassed and was glad he hadn't voiced his thoughts. "Well, it looks like we'll just have to save Celia Markham. It seems the least we can do." And he meant it. Winner felt an odd sensation toward the woman. The battle at hand took his mind in a different direction, but the thought lingered.

Hulk nodded his agreement.

Winner heard the distant dull thud more than felt anything, yet the damage claxons made known they'd taken a major hit.

"Looks like you've got your own problems."

Winner flicked the com switch and looked at Davenport. "How bad is it?"

"They're using high energy x-ray torpedoes with matter/anti-matter detonators," someone said. "This has to be the same kind of missile that killed Admiral Ashcroft. Probably fired from a tow sled."

Winner and Davenport listened as the XO reported, "The missile breached the outer hull, port side maintenance area. The entire section vented to space. The hatches and bulkheads are holding and the surviving maintenance crew is reinforcing the exposed surfaces."

Davenport said, "Our energy cannons can take out one or two missiles if they have time to target, but not if the sleds fire an entire salvo." Located just forward of the engine rooms, one on each side of the ship, the canons had limited pointing range. Most aiming required turning Deliverance. Only nine degrees of movement to a side was available to the gunners. That was more than enough to do its job at fifty thousand klicks. But less than thirty thousand meant the ship had to perform critical maneuvers to make the guns effective.

Davenport said, "Eight missiles from one of those things would take us out of action, probably kill us. So far, their shots have been no more than two at a time."

Missile sleds were virtually undetectable at the ranges they had to fight. They gave off no emissions until the missile fired and so far, all came from random locations. Some sleds used compressed air to launch the missiles from their housing, the weapon ignited after getting some distance from the platform. Then it was too late to take evasive action.

Davenport punched at the plot table keyboard, studied the display and said, "We lost thirty-two crewmen. We can't take many more hits and remain in the battle.

"The fight has our fleet bunched up. If there are more sleds out there they could wipe us out in a few seconds. The entire fleet. We have to find and destroy those missiles." Almost as an afterthought he ordered, "Have the fleet disperse, two hundred thousand klicks."

Winner had been silent, studying the holo Davenport had put up earlier. One area of space had been strangely inactive during the fight, almost as if the enemy had intentionally stayed away from it. And anyone shooting from that location had a clear path to the WMC fleet. "Captain, have your helmsman steer course 316 by 45 degrees ascension, relative. Order your energy cannon to widest spread possible, center on the coordinates with maximum fire until the failsafe takes the cannon off line."

Davenport didn't hesitate. Maximum power meant a major drain on the ships energy generation system. He motioned the 'boson to open the ship wide com, "Now hear this. This is the captain. We are going to maximum sustained power on one energy canon. All non-emergency systems are to shut down in one minute." He ordered the helmsman to the new heading.

Winner quietly ordered, "Fire when ready."

The space surrounding 316 degrees by 45 degrees turned into a living hell. Everything within six thousand kilometers on either side disappeared, within ten thousand klicks burned to uselessness and within twenty thousand it was damaged beyond fighting capability.

No one spoke for a few seconds—only the hum of equipment permeated the air. One shot destroyed the heart of Bartok's fleet including its command and control. Winner had found the nest of missile sleds Bartok was waiting to unleash.

The realization that the space fight was over finally sank in. The bridge crew let out a yell heard down the passageways.

Winner was sorry for the lost crewmen but they still had a battle to win. "How much longer until we know the outcome?"

Davenport smiled, "Those of the enemy who can, are running, the rest are surrendering. We have orbital supremacy. It will take a little time to mop up. We can launch the Marine's dirt-side on your command."

Winner could tell Davenport wasn't through. He smiled and said, "You're holding back."

Davenport offered his own smile, "Four ships were captured by boarding parties—completely intact. Another eleven capitulated outright, never fired a shot. Another dozen or so damaged ships will be added to the take before we're through."

"Our losses?" Winner asked.

Solemnly, Captain Davenport reported, "Sixteen fighters lost, no major ships out, extensive damage on most of the fleet. Eight hundred dead and as many wounded. We were very lucky, no hits on the assembled assault teams."

"Congratulations, Captain. My compliments to you and your fleet commanders and crews." Both men knew it wasn't over—but they'd survived the first round.

Davenport added, "Part of the thanks goes to the anti-grav system Mr. Derka installed on the four fighters. And of course, your deduction about the missile sleds location. They made the difference. And—I did study your analysis of the battle for Nimitz Crossing. You may have recognized the entry maneuvers we employed were very reminiscent of your father's strategy in the battle for that planet."

"It was your victory, Captain." Winner clapped Davenport on the back, then turned his attention to the Marines.

Winner keyed the com, "Colonel al-Cadifh, you may launch when ready."

174

CHAPTER THIRTY
The warriors

From the catwalk above the huge hanger bay, al-Cadifh spoke into his intercom, "Buddy up, everyone. Check your weapons. Battalion commanders, man your assault craft. Launch in twenty minutes."

Each launch carried a company of Marines led by a captain. Three companies formed a battalion with a major in charge. Considering both a battalion commander and himself on the same ship an unnecessary command risk, Al Cadifh assigned Major Henderson to the second assault vehicle.

Al-Cadifh focused on the upcoming battle, yet he remained totally aware of every movement around him. That awareness was part of what made him a formidable warrior. He ran every potential battle scene through his mind and what he would do to be victorious. He never allowed a losing thought—it was always how to win.

He turned to his second in command, Lt. Colonel Marshall Reasoner, a mustang. "Waiting is the hardest part. Everything you forgot to do pops into your mind. By the time we hit the dirt, I'll swear I didn't get shit done that I wanted or needed to. For twenty-two years I've always worried about the same thing when it's time to go to war."

Reasoner laughed. "Colonel, you say that every time we go into a fight. I've been with you off and on for twenty years and nothing's changed."

Al-Cadifh looked at his second. Almost the same age, Reasoner had worked his way up through the ranks, coming out of boot camp a private. He remembered the first time they'd met and wondered how or why someone so small would want to get into what he'd always considered a muscleman's line of work. But he'd learned, Reasoner's wiry and leather tough exterior had roots at his very core. One hundred fifty two centimeters tall and barely seventy-two kilograms, the hard work he'd put in on his father's farm on Omicron had physically prepared him.

Al-Cadifh's respect for his second was earned and well-placed. Reasoner had that sense of a fighter, whether in a brawl or on the battlefield, and the knack for surviving. Most of all, men willingly followed him—that the colonel admired above all else.

Only once had Reasoner talked about his earlier life. Six days after his second's seventeenth birthday, a violent earthquake had killed his parents turning the farm into a mass of jumbled dirt and rocks. A month later he'd joined White's Marines. After five years of service, he'd taken four years to roam the universe leading a vigilante group fighting pirates.

Michael White met him there and asked him to re-join White Mining Marines as a second lieutenant.

Al-Cadifh first met him two years later at Simpson's Star. Almost five years passed before their paths crossed a second time. Reasoner had been assigned to his command and promoted to captain. Saragosa was their third tour together and first since Reasoner had made light colonel. Only the best mustangs made it past major.

"You still throw that knife?" asked al-Cadifh. Talking helped calm his nerves. He marveled at how calm he felt. He fully understood that one day he wouldn't return from combat.

"At fifty feet, your ass is mine," Reasoner responded.

The colonel laughed. "When are you going to learn the metric system? You have to be the only Marine, maybe the only person, who uses feet and pounds."

"Learned it on Omicron—that's all they used. Worked there and it works for me now."

Al-Cadifh's casual attitude changed becoming somber. "We better get aboard. Good luck Marsh," he clasped his second's hand. "Semper Fi."

"Same to you, Sarif. Semper Fi."

Few men knew al-Cadifh's mother most often called him by that name, and even fewer were permitted to use it.

The colonel started toward the gravlift that would take him to the hanger deck, his mind already thinking ahead to the landing on Saragosa.

"Colonel. Sorry, I didn't mean to startle you." Winner stepped from the gravlift, Melissa and her squad a step behind.

"Mr. White." Al-Cadifh saluted but said no more.

"Walk with me please." Winner led al-Cadifh to the gravlift. The doors sighed open and they stepped in headed for the hanger deck leaving Melissa and her squad on the catwalk.

"Colonel, if you can take Bartok alive, do so. He should stand trial."

"Then face a firing squad," an unsmiling al-Cadifh said.

Winner grinned. He knew the law also and the only choices that a court had were a firing squad or hanging. "Don't jeopardize anyone trying to take him alive. Just, if given the choice, bring him back alive. Good luck." Winner shook the colonel's hand.

The colonel's black piercing eyes glistened and al-Cadifh said, "If possible, alive. And thank you sir."

He smiled and watched as the colonel poked his head in each of the fifteen assault launches offering words of encouragement and heard him say, "Let's go kill something."

Winner returned the offered salute before the Marine stepped into the lead launch.

Winner retreated to the gravlift and cleared the hanger bay as the claxon sounded for depressurization and venting to space. The launches would exit within minutes. Melissa and his guard met him as they headed for the bridge.

Winner stepped into CAC. Derka and Captain Davenport bent over the master plot. He asked, "What's going on? Why haven't we gone sub-light for the approach and launch?"

"Problem," Davenport said. "We just got a message from the resistance."

Winner waited at the hatchway.

Finally the captain said, "That energy cannon at the spaceport is the problem. Rather, the problem is that son-of-a-bitch—" Davenport stopped and composed himself. "We can't attack the cannon. Bartok's holding civilian prisoners in the same building. Deliverance can't take out the cannon without killing all the captives, which means the Marines can't land. It would be suicide."

Calmly, Winner asked, "What about another site? Mr. Derka, you know the terrain. What about the processing plant?"

The young scientist answered, "We're coming up on it now." He studied the plot, punching buttons to get readouts.

"Well, the bastard did what I'd do. There's an energy cannon there also. He's covered both sides of the planet. And we have to assume he's put civilians there also."

"Is Colonel al-Cadifh aware of this?" asked Winner.

"He knew about the installations at the spaceport. The relocating, he should have anticipated."

"And Bartok using civilians as a human shield—how do you prepare for that?"

Davenport answered, "Sir, he's piped into the com circuit."

"Range?" Winner asked. "And what's the intersect distance of the two cannons from the planet?"

Derka answered, "Two point nine million klicks, ninety degrees to the equator. He's got it covered. Everything else is zero. Effective range on those cannons is over six million klicks."

"And no way for us to get under or around this defense." Winner's stated what everyone knew.

"Not from space," Derka said.

Winner backed away from the console. "Captain Davenport, get Mr. Hrndullka on the com." He sat down awaiting the contact.

There was almost no wait.

"Hrndullka here. Go ahead."

"Winner White, Hulk. We've a major problem. The energy cannons at the spaceport and the processing plant are preventing us from landing Colonel al-Cadifh with his Marines. We need for you to take out one of those cannons, preferably the one at the space drone."

"Okay," Hulk casually answered. "Anything to get you people down here. We could use a little help." The grin on Hrndullka's face told enough. The invasion was ready and so was he. But he wasn't taking the assault on the cannon lightly. "You know about the civilians, Mr. White. Unfortunately, we can only take our chances where they're concerned. They may become casualties."

Winner nodded his awareness. "Keep us posted Hulk." He keyed off the com, and turned to the others. "Any recommendations for taking out the cannons?"

Derka said, "Destroy the deflectors built up around the base of the cannons. Without those everything on the ground within one hundred klicks will fry when they're fired. Even Bartok won't want that. It would take out the spaceport and Saragosa City."

"Without the shields," Winner said, "he'd have to re-deploy his troops and supplies before firing the cannon. By then, al-Cadifh's Marines will be on the ground. Pass this on to Hulk immediately."

Derka nodded, then spoke into the com.

Winner stood. "Captain Davenport, would you join me in my quarters?"

"Aye sir."

Winner motioned Melissa to remain outside in the passageway and closed the hatch behind the captain.

He sat down heavily in a chair and motioned the captain to a seat.

"What kind of chance do you give us?" Winner asked. He wanted constant input from his staff.

Davenport answered, "So far, we've managed to counter every move Bartok's made. I'd say the advantage is still ours if we get around this cannon problem. It won't be easy. Hulk will take casualties and probably lose some of the hostages."

"We've got to start thinking like our enemy."

"I considered the second energy cannon but when reports failed to materialize, I forgot about it. As far as putting the civilians around the cannon, I didn't think about it either. Yet, it doesn't surprise me. Bartok's tactic is ancient because it works. Fortunately, just because your enemy is bestial, doesn't mean we have to be to defeat him."

Winner nodded.

"As you said earlier," Davenport continued, "there'll be enough screw-ups to go around, on both sides. We just want to capitalize on Bartok's mistakes."

"Yeah, you're right. That will be all captain." He looked at Davenport and said, "You better get back to work. Somebody has to run this ship."

Davenport opened the hatch, inviting Melissa and Winner's orderly inside as he stepped into the passageway.

Winner stared at the bulkhead. Everything Davenport said made sense.

"Sir, is there anything I can get for you?" Overstreet asked. The young Marine looked sharp in his khakis.

Winner took a while to answer but them managed a smile, "No, sergeant. Thanks and you can return to your battle station." He took no noticed as the orderly left, his mind playing out the recent events and his force's response. What he really wanted was some time alone—time he wasn't going to get.

Melissa remained next to the hatch. "Mess call in ten minutes, Mr. White. Want me to bring you something?"

Winner answered, "No Melissa, I'll eat in the mess hall."

After a few more moments of thought, Winner returned to the bridge, Davenport acknowledging his boss with a smile before returning to the orbital display.

Winner punched up the overhead screen, "What's so interesting?"

Davenport said, "Mr. Derka worked up this display to illustrate the coverage those energy cannons give Bartok over Saragosa."

Winner looked at his chronometer. Less than an hour had passed since he'd ordered Hrndullka to take one of the cannons. It was unreasonable to think it would happen this quickly. It could take anywhere from one hour to a day to capture or put one of those guns out of commission once he got a strike force organized.

Winner stayed at the consol to wait out the results. Each minute seemed an eternity and the quiet on the bridge emphasized each minute.

Winner's head jerked to the overhead screen at the urgency in Captain Davenport's voice, "Mr. White, check the screen!"

He quickly stepped to the plot. Davenport was already pointing to a blip. "What is it?"

Derka was first to respond. "That's Topsail; it's launched from the space drone! Shit—it's on a heading toward the energy cannon. The pilot's going to put that thing right on top of the cannon!"

Winner asked controlling the alarm in his voice, "How do you know? Why isn't he going to just crash into the cannon and destroy it?"

Derka didn't look up from the plot but responded, "Topsail has matter/anti-matter sub-space engines in addition to the hyperspace generators. If those engines vent, for any reason, everything on the hemisphere will disappear."

Winner reacted immediately, "Colonel, are you wired in?"

"Yes sir." The voice boomed.

The sense of urgency in Winners voice galvanized the entire bridge crew, "Captain, how long will it take for the Marines to land?"

Davenport looked at the plot, "Over six hours from our present position. We can't launch from here. The Marines would never make it."

Winner quietly answered with a sense of urgency, "I have no intention of launching from here. Whoever is flying Topsail must know the enemy will do everything it can to get that ship out of the way.

"Colonel, get your people saddled up. We're going in."

Winner continued to issue orders determined to take advantage of this unexpected opportunity.

"Captain, head Deliverance toward Saragosa. I want us in a low orbit as soon as possible, no more than ninety-six kilometers. With any luck, the Marines should be on the ground within the hour. Use the main drive engines and get us there before Bartok recovers from this. The man is insane enough that he might destroy the planet rather than loose it and we can't give him the chance to figure that out. Topsail's pilot has given us the chance we needed. And it may be our only chance. Let's not let them down. And call Hulk. Order him to defend Topsail now with whatever forces he can muster."

Winner returned to his chair wishing he were on the ground and in a position to do something active to make the best of this dramatic change in their favor. He tried to imagine what Topsail looked like plopped down on cannon and could only smile. "It must be van Gelden at the controls. Payback time."

The Marines had to be on the ground before Bartok recovered. At most, Winner figured they had maybe an hour. It was a chance and only that but an effort that had to succeed.

He walked to the giant plot board and watched Deliverance's descent.

CHAPTER THIRTY ONE
The assault

Standing inside SGL-1, al-Cadifh keyed his com unit. "This is Graybar One. Listen up people. Get ready for a rough ride. If you have your harness tight, tighten it more. Deliverance will drop us at ninety six thousand meters. Stow any space type gear; you'll only need dirt-side equipment."

Al-Cadifh took his place at the front of the cabin just aft of the cockpit bulkhead and tightened the harness around his large frame. He counted the minutes until the huge bay doors opened. This was always the toughest time. Waiting wasn't his long suit.

For fifteen minutes, Deliverance handled the air turbulence, her mass more than adequate to the chore. Finally she signaled that they were close to launch.

Through the cockpit window, al-Cadifh watched the clamshell bay doors swing slowly aside.

Even inside the launch vehicle, the change in air pressure was noticeable as the high altitude atmosphere of Saragosa surrounded them. At that altitude, Deliverance was at risk—a risk she had taken to deliver the marines close to their target.

The overhead light glared red, then changed to amber.

The instant that light turned green, launch engines took over.

The takeoff was bumpy, al-Cadif's launch strained to stay upright. Behind him, trailed fourteen assault craft each loaded with one hundred Marines.

The violent turbulent descent to Saragosa Prime began.

* * * *

Small arms fire pelted al-Cadifh's landing vehicle as it neared the ground. At this distance, it was no more than a greeting, someone's way of letting them know a nasty welcoming committee waited below.

Long shadows of dawn bathed Saragosa City and the space drone. "Colonel, look." The pilot pointed through the forward view screen.

Al-Cadifh loosened his restraining harness and leaned forward into the cockpit. Topsail sat astride the cannon complex in what had been the space drone operations building.

"Gaudamn, I'd never believed it if I hadn't seen it with my own eyes." But it wasn't the space ship that concerned him. From half a klicks up, he saw troops gathering on both ends of the space drone. "But which were the friendly's?"

He keyed his com unit, "Mr. Hrndullka, what are your coordinates?"

Almost immediately, a location appeared on his vidscreen and on the pilots plot.

Al-Cadifh keyed his com again, "Colonel Reasoner, I'll take three companies and join Hrndullka on the west end. You and the remaining twelve companies establish a skirmish line three thousand meters to the east of the cannon." He keyed the coordinates. Reasoner saw the same information he did. He'd know what to do.

"Aye sir," the response crisp.

Al-Cadifh wasn't sure which he hated the most, the buffeting launch, or the hits they were taking from the ground. He'd never considered shooting someone out of the air very sporting, but he had to admit he'd shot a few. He wasn't too high on airdales.

He surveyed the spot where his group would put down on the city side of the space drone. He wanted to link up with the resistance fighters before engaging Bartok's ground forces. Confusion would reign supreme once they were on the ground and the fighting started. The last thing he wanted was Hulk's people caught between him and the enemy.

Al-Cadifh grabbed the overhead restraining bar as the ship cascaded to the side. The cabin filled with acrid smoke and fumes. "Pilot? How bad is the hit?" he yelled into the com.

He got no answer. Al-Cadifh popped the release on his shoulder seat harness, struggled to gain a handhold and some foot purchase toward the front and struggled past the bulkhead separating the cockpit and cabin.

The ship gyrated wildly.

He grabbed the back of the pilot's seat and pulled himself into the cockpit —to find the entire port side shot away, the cockpit open to the atmosphere. Both the pilot and co-pilot were dead, the launch in freefall.

Al-Cadifh yanked at the dead pilot's belt release and shoved the man through the gaping hole. There was no time to pull him to the cabin.

He snapped his harness to the wildly bucking seat and grabbed at the controls. A quick glance at the instrument panel brought an involuntary reaction the ground was way too near—he jerked back hard on the control yoke and two-blocked the throttles to the firewall.

Al-Cadifh threw up his left arm as the right front nose of the launch piled into the ground, showers of sparks filled the cockpit for an instant before it collapsed crushing everything between it and the cabin bulkhead. The vehicle cartwheeled across the concrete tarmac, shedding the main rear hatch, then breaking the fuselage at the cabin emergency side door and spilling its precious contents.

* * * *

"Cover me," Hulk yelled as he raced the four hundred meters toward the downed Launch.

At the fringe range of the enemy's small arms, an occasional flechette hit his body armor—the lasers only warmed his protection.

Halfway there, he glanced behind him and saw at least twenty of his people running, following him firing laser grenades and automatics as they laid down suppression fire.

Broken in half and lying on its side, the launch offered forth its dead and dying, spilling Marines across the tarmac. Body armor saved some fighters but in the sharp impact the suits became wedges of death for others.

Ahead of him, the remaining two launches skidded to a stop and discharged their human contents. Hulk reached what was left of the cockpit of the downed launch and called for medics—although it was obvious there was no need right there.

After a moment contemplating the ruins of the cockpit, Hulk ran among the downed Marines, signaling where a medic might help.

Soon resistance fighters and Marines from the two remaining launches surrounded the downed craft. Hulk heard orders barked from a distance and the group reformed into a half circle on the landing crafts south side, sending their own curtain of death toward the enemy.

"Who's in command?" Hulk yelled.

"Colonel al-Cadifh," came the answer.

"His second?"

"I'm Major Henderson. Lt. Colonel Reasoner is at the other end of the spaceport. Colonel al-Cadifh?"

"Dead," Hrndullka said. He introduced himself to the major. "I've got four hundred fighters here with orders to take the energy cannon before they get that space ship off."

Major Henderson tapped his wristcom, relayed to Lt. Colonel Reasoner Colonel al-Cadifh was dead, that only twenty Marines out of one hundred survived the crash, and that his group and the survivors had linked up with Hrndullka.

Reasoner ordered the emptied landing crafts back to Deliverance. There were still fifteen hundred Marines in space to put dirt-side.

* * * *

Standing on the bridge, his fists clenched against an unseen enemy, Winner listened to the battle com. He was sorry the colonel was gone—the man had been a fighter and his quick reactions to the enemy's movement would be missed. His thoughts turned to Vladislov Hrndullka and Lt. Colonel Reasoner.

Winner keyed the com to the Marines assembled in the armory waiting for the returning landing craft. He assured them Reasoner would lead them to victory. He motioned Melissa to his command chair, "Have Overstreet prepare my body armor."

"But sir." Everything about her protested.

Winner turned on her and in a level voice said, "Lieutenant Graves, you have your orders."

"Yes sir." She spun a sharp about face and left the bridge.

Davenport walked to the command chair, "You're not thinking of going dirt-side are you?"

"If need be." Winner didn't want a debate. The battle was engaged. Even with al-Cadifh's death, they had a chance of winning and he wasn't about to let it slip through his fingers. He didn't doubt the people on the ground but sometimes it took that something extra-ordinary. And if his being there could make a difference, he was ready.

* * * *

Major Henderson, a non-descript mustang, squatted beside Hrndullka using the downed launch as cover.

Shouting over the sound of small-arms fire peppering the hull, he said. "You know this building. What's the best way to attack it without hurting the civilians?"

"Will the Marines east of here be part of our assault?" Hrndullka asked.

"They have their own objectives. Fifteen hundred more troops will land within the hour. We may get some of them along with heavy armor and air-transport. But we have to secure this spaceport and quickly if they're not going to get shot out of the atmosphere. That means we have to take that cannon."

Hrndullka looked up at a commotion coming from east of his position and saw someone running toward them. Shortly, a body slammed into the space next to him.

"Lt. Colonel Reasoner." The scrawny officer stuck out his hand. "Glad to meet you."

Hulk's hand dwarfed the Marines but he could feel the steel in the wiry man's grip.

Reasoner smiled, "Yeah, I know. I'm not big enough to fart."

Hulk laughed and said, "Somehow, I just don't believe you." He slapped the Marine on the back almost knocking him off his haunches. "Sounds like you people are in a real scrap toward the east."

"These guys may be mercenaries," Reasoner said, "but they know how to fight. Right now, they've got no way off this planet except in a box. If they can't cut a deal, they will fight, hard and well."

"Your recommendations for assaulting the building?" Reasoner asked.

Hrndullka thought for a minute. "Based on what the major said, Marines should concentrate on rooting out the soldiers in and around the building. We estimate twenty to thirty inside armed with hand weapons and ten or so outside. My people will protect your left flank and rear. Once you've got the upper hand, we'll go after the captives." He pointed toward the building housing the energy cannon and ignored the spaceship, "From the corner, the western approach is blind. You need to attack there. Once you've engaged the enemy at close quarters, my people will attack from the northwest. That side is nearest the civilian prisoners. Beyond that, it'll just be a dog fight."

Reasoner scanned the areas Hrndullka pointed out. "At least we won't have to worry about field artillery. They won't shoot at their own cannon. It'll be a different story after we capture it and get that spaceship off." Looking at Topsail sitting astride the building, he slapped his leg and said, "Damnedest thing I've ever seen." He turned back toward Hulk and Henderson. "Do it."

Hulk hesitated then asked, "Why haven't we taken more ground fire from Bartok's soldiers? Topsail is out of their line of fire."

He got no answer. Reasoner had already set out to return to the main fight on the east-end of the spacedrome.

Hulk tapped his wrist com, "Mr. Hastings, I need an answer. Where is the enemy? We're getting small arms laser fire and some flechette but it's a token effort. Have you any signs of the enemy grouping for an attack?"

Hastings came on the com, "There's a group of them, about two thousand strong, southwest of the spacedrome—maybe two klicks. An additional thousand or so will join them in about an hour. Some squads are still rounding up civilians. I have no idea why they haven't launched an attack on your position."

Hulk nudged Major Henderson, taking his attention from the building they were about to assault, "What about us getting some fighter aircraft support?"

"Negative," answered Henderson. "Seems they've all got matter/anti-matter reactors. If one of them got hit, there wouldn't be anything to fight for let alone anyone left to fight."

Hulk said, "It's the same problem both sides have with Topsail. If the containment field is broken on the reactor, everything goes in a flash."

Henderson nodded and added, "Tell your people to be extra cautious where they shoot."

Hulk smiled, "This is home to these people. They've all got families here. It's a mistake they won't make."

Henderson added, "I'm assigning two Marines as liaison." He motioned toward two corporals, "Pascal and Onichi, Mr. Hulk Hrndullka."

Hulk, followed by the two Marines, crawled off toward his ragtag army. His people had no uniforms, but the supply launch had given them body armor and weapons equal to Bartok's—except artillery and aircraft.

A few minutes later, he joined the four hundred fighters assembled behind a concrete buttress wall on the west-end of the spacedrome.

Hulk stood before the group, clearly uncomfortable. "We're about to assault the operations building. Some of our friends, neighbors and maybe family are in there. Lives will be lost in the attack. Some of us will die in the assault and bringing the captives out. If anyone wants out before we attack, you're free to go. Nothing will be held against you."

He waited.

No one moved.

Finally, he spoke again. "The Marines will take on most of the enemy holding the building. We'll probably see many fewer guarding the prisoners. But the enemy is hardened, ruthless and well trained—we know that from many other encounters. We also have to cover about four hundred meters of open space just to get to the building.

"Earth is our ancestral birthplace, but Saragosa Prime is home. After Mr. White announced his plans to turn the planet over to constitutional democratic rule, some of you purchased your homes. White has a business interest in winning Saragosa back from Bartok, but it is our home we're fighting for. Let's free ourselves of this pestilence."

Hulk turned toward the targeted operations building. "Form up. We have to cover that open space," he made a sweeping gesture at the area before him, "to get to the building. It isn't going to be easy or neat."

A line of men and a few women came together at the buttress wall. What only a few people knew was that Hulk had approached certain ones, all men, and asked them to take the front ranks. They would most likely be the first casualties and they were the older members. It wasn't fair that they take more of the risk than others, but they all believed the future of Saragosa was in its young people. The less of it spilled the better.

Hrndullka unshouldered the laser rifle and took his place at the head of the column.

CHAPTER THIRTY TWO
The future of Saragosa Prime

"Too many people in the wrong places," Hulk said to no one in particular. "Not enough on the southern front. The Marine's battle force deployment is screwed up."

He heard a blast and signaled his people down.

Concrete shards splattered his body armor and heat from an aerial laser beam swept under his face shield. He keyed his wrist com. "They're coming. Check your weapons."

Shifting to command frequency, Hulk spoke calmly but with urgency. "Colonel Reasoner? Major Henderson? Somebody tell me what in the hell's going on. Where is the enemy? Is the ops building my responsibility?"

Reasoner's raspy voice crept from Hulk's com, "I've been hit." Then only battle noise came across the wristcom. A second voice said, "Colonel Reasoner's dead."

Hulk sat down behind the concrete parapet wall protecting his irregulars. He hardly noticed the cool relief it provided from the morning sun. "We've lost our entire command structure. What else can go wrong?"

* * * *

On Deliverance's bridge, Winner rubbed his forehead. Casualties had been heavy but no more than anticipated—but this was a critical moment. Individual Marines would fight bravely but they needed someone in command. "Com. Open a channel to Mr. Hrndullka and Major Henderson."

The second the channel opened, he spoke calmly. "This is Winner White. Major Henderson, you have Marine command responsibility. Who is senior on the eastern flank?"

Seconds passed before a voice replied, "That would be me—Major Daniels."

Winner ordered, "Major, you have responsibility for the eastern forces. Colonel Henderson has overall command responsibility."

Winner had no real idea if these were the people most qualified to lead, but he didn't have time to run psychological profiles.

Winner continued, "Colonel Henderson, reinforcements have left Deliverance and will land in thirty minutes. I suggest, in the meantime, you move four companies from the eastern front to your command.

"Mr. Hrndullka, you need to split your forces. Take a group to assault the ops building, secure it, and free the prisoners. Your remaining people are to protect the southern group's right flank until the reinforcements arrive from the east front and Deliverance. Once your replacements are in place, disengage your flanking people, move them north of the ops building and establish an escape route for the civilian captives. Henderson and Daniels will cover your assault."

Winner received the commanders' acknowledgements.

He stood for a minute at the plot board reviewing the battle scene. His troops retained the initiative and he wasn't going to lose it.

Winner asked, "Have we made contact with Topsail?"

"No sir," came the response from the com officer. "Its com systems are either down or offline."

Winner studied the display, repeating the events, trying to decipher what Bartok's forces were up to.

"Where's Bartok?" he asked.

"Last word had him at the processing complex," the com officer replied.

"In fact, most of his command structure is on the other side of the planet with him," Davenport added. "Along with Celia Markham."

At the mention of Celia's name, Winner glanced at the Captain. He'd not had much time, in fact any time, to think about her. But he felt a tinge of excitement at getting to know the lady who had saved his mothers life.

"It's turned into a chess game," he said. "Bartok makes a move with the captives. Van Gelden's move neutralizes one energy cannon, we invade." Winner hesitated a minute seemingly drawing on some laid-aside knowledge. "Except, now that Bartok's in the mines, he belongs to me."

Winner motioned to the Com officer and said, "Contact Colonel Henderson." A few seconds passed.

"Henderson."

"What's all the activity at the south end of the tarmac?"

"Tunnels." Henderson responded. "The enemy's putting everything into tunnels, equipment, ammunition, everything. Look's like they're moving underground."

Winner backed away from the plot. "Captain, we've got to get Topsail off the planet. Get your destroyers in as close as possible to provide cover for its escape."

"What—"

"That bastard plans to blow Topsail. He's on the other side of the planet; his army's protected underground and our troops are exposed on the tarmac. He's going to destroy Topsail and everything in this hemisphere."

"Aye sir." Davenport immediately dispatched the orders.

Derka stepped onto the bridge as the Captain completed his com to Sizemore and a sister ship. "If anyone's within two thousand meters when she lifts off, she'll cook them."

Winner frowned. "How'd van Gelden get the ship astraddle the ops building?"

"His anti-grav thrusters. But those won't help him launch."

Winner turned from the plot. "Get Mr. Hrndullka for me."

"Mr. White. Go ahead."

Winner took a deep breath. "I think we know what Bartok had in mind."

Amid Hulk's uncharacteristic cursing, Winner relayed what they believed Bartok planned. "That's the way I see it. Our timing screwed up his plan. We think his people inside the ops building were to set the explosives, retreat to the tunnels, then blow the bird rupturing the matter/anti-matter containment. We need to get the ship out of there and into orbit. I've sent destroyers into low orbit to provide cover but—you've got to take the building and get the people to the hills before Topsail can take off."

"Understood."

The silence said it. Whatever needed doing, Hulk would do. He always had.

"Captain Davenport," Winner said. "Mr. Hrndullka is remarkable. My respect for the man's talents has grown each day. And I had a high regard for him after our first meeting. Captain, I hope he will be the first president of Saragosa Prime."

"That would be great," Davenport said. "But with all due respect, we have a war to win first. It'll make his first few days in office much less eventful."

Winner laughed. "True. But I had something else in mind. Something more immediate."

Davenport stood at the plot table looking at Winner. "Provisional president?"

Winner grinned. "What do you think?"

Davenport crossed the bridge and shook Winner's hand. "I think it would give the people of Saragosa Prime the legitimacy they deserve. The very thing Bartok tried to deprive them of. And renewed hope if they need it."

And the needed break between military and civilian rule Winner thought. Although leading the partisans gave Hulk a military role of his own.

"Looks like the next move is ours," Winner said. "I'm going to go for a checkmate. Tell the hanger bay to have my launch ready to go dirt-side in three minutes." He motioned Melissa to follow as he headed for his cabin.

* * * *

"You people heard him. Nothing's changed. Let's get it done." Hulk breathed a deep sigh of relief thankful a firm hand was in control. He wasted no time implementing the orders.

The drainage curvature built into the tarmac kept the southern forces from view but Hulk could see the Marines begin their move from the east across the tarmac toward the southern flank.

Henderson's voice squawked the com. "Deliverance, we need orbital help. Put whatever you can on these coordinates."

The destroyers, already in low orbit to provide cover for Winner's landing and Topsail's takeoff, responded with devastating accuracy and effectiveness. Hulk watched the laser flash arc from the sky and rip through their targets. The surface curvature of the tarmac hid the intended victims.

"You're right on," Henderson said. "Hit them again."

A second light traced a path through the atmosphere; something exploded in a huge ball of fire—probably an ammo carrier. The air hissed and crackled, lightning shot out from the ray. In the charged air, Hulk instinctively ducked, then punched his wristcom, "Everyone make sure you're grounded." Getting electrocuted by your own laser discharge was a real possibility.

They didn't have long to wait. The air discharged the built up electricity with a spectacular display. Bolts of charged particles gave a short menacing performance that stood out against the double suns' morning rays.

Hulk keyed the other commanders and Winner. "Why aren't they making a bigger fight of it? They outnumber us three to one. Something isn't right."

He listened to reports from Daniels and Henderson and decided the invasion had caught the enemy off guard and totally unprepared.

Chaos works both sides of the street he thought. The orbital laser blasts had stirred some of the enemy to more aggressive action.

Henderson reported, "They're trying to close with us. I think they want to get in too close for the space ships to fire on them."

Moments later, he added, "Our reinforcements are landing. Mr. White, if Mr. Hrndullka is ready, he can attack the ops building."

From the launch headed dirt-side, Winner confirmed the attack order.

A hot wet wind blew over the tarmac. Dancing heat waves built across the vast concrete surface, making the moving troops shimmer like dark ghosts. The Marines were the major force to be dealt with and would be the focus of any attack. The enemy had the weaponry to stand off and pound Henderson with their mortars, yet it was trying to close on him.

Hulk didn't know what Daniel's battle scene was like but suspected it wasn't much different than what he was seeing. Hulk spread his people at the buttress walls bordering the tarmac edge flanking Henderson's west approach. It was the only barrier to hide behind. If Bartok's soldiers attacked, rather when they attacked, the walls wouldn't help. It would still be a slaughter. Two thousand trained soldiers against less than four hundred irregulars didn't take much figuring." If they were to die, they'd do it together.

One of the liaison Marines assigned to Hulk's command said, "Sir, Corporal Onichi. We've commed Colonel Henderson. He suggests Pascal and I take the remainder of your irregulars, how many is that?"

Three hundred fifty," Hulk answered.

Onichi continued, "And prepare the escape route to the north—into the hills."

Hulk thought the Marines too young to lead people into battle, until he looked into their eyes. Any doubts disappeared when he saw their dead-serious expressions.

He motioned his own lieutenants forward. "You'll be under the command of these two men."

Hulk asked, "Who's senior?"

"I am, "Onichi answered.

He doubted the man could be over nineteen. Hulk ordered, "Maintain an open com link with Colonel Henderson, me and Major Daniels at all times. Good luck."

He turned his attention to the operations building not sure, what he was going to do with fifty people. Too many, he thought. Fifty people assaulting that small building, all of them wanting to get right in the middle of the fight, would get a lot of people killed unnecessarily. Pointing to the nearest group he said, "You ten people cover the north exit. Wait for my signal then go after the captives.

"The rest of you follow me. We'll take the outside guards. Once the outer perimeter's secure, you," he selected another group of ten, "follow me. We go after those holding the building interior and civilians."

Hulk relayed his intentions to Colonel Henderson.

Henderson shot back, "Better hurry. It's almost hand-to-hand combat here. Only the laser fire from orbit is keeping them from overrunning our position. They're trying to outflank us. Keep yourselves between the enemy and Topsail. That spaceship is the only edge we've got."

"Remember what you're shooting at." Hulk repeated the admonishment often to his troops.

Hulk motioned the fifty men to spread out behind the concrete wall covering one hundred meters of the tarmac. With ten men moving north, the remaining forty moved on the run toward the building five hundred meters east.

The only things visible on the tarmac were the destroyed SGL where al-Cadifh along with eighty Marines died, the ops building and Hulk's fifty irregulars. The surviving SGL's had already left the planet, picked up the rest of the Marines and would land in less than thirty minutes.

Hulk again heard the familiar whump of a heavy flechette mortar, even Bartok's men were wary of the danger Topsail continued to present.

Topsail was both a blessing and a hazard. No one in their right mind would deliberately try to destroy it. That meant minimal offense. That was the blessing. The hazard—if someone did hit the spaceship and breach the matter/anti-matter containment...

Out on the tarmac, with little cover, Hulk continued a crouched hard run toward the building. Stay in the open and get wiped out, or take the perimeter guards head on in what appeared to be a suicide charge. Neither choice offered much hope.

Laser mortars flashed not twenty meters away, throwing shards of concrete, lethal as any blaster. The sound of flechette mortars continued.

"Incoming," someone yelled.

Hulk joined his comrades vainly trying to claw into the concrete—anything to avoid the terrible wounds the small knives inflicted on soft tissue and bone. The incoming flechette knives, mixed with needles and laser pulsed blasters, spread across the tarmac leaving death and destruction.

Hulk jabbed at his com button, "Medics. We need medics up here."

Soldiers with large red crosses emblazoned on their tunics moved from the protection of the buttress toward the downed fighters.

Within seconds of the explosion, he had the assault team up and running toward the building weapons, firing as they did.

Hulk glanced back over his shoulder, only twenty-seven followed—despite their body armor, the knives had found plenty of soft marks. A third of Hulk's force gone before they reached their objective.

Troops in the ops building directed mortar shots onto Hulk's position. So far, though, the enemy's fire from the ops building remained sporadic.

Hulk urged his fighters forward. "Only flechettes and lasers on stun. No blasters," he reminded them. Topsail loomed ever larger astraddle the building.

To the east, morning rays of daylight cast long shadows across the space drone. At sixteen degrees, the westerly ocean morning breeze stirred. A familiar scent wafted past Hulk. He looked to the west. Ominous clouds were building. A major storm was in the pot. He didn't remember the moon cycles and they hadn't had a satellite weather forecast since Bartok's invasion. But if the twin moons rose as the storm was building, Saragosa would be faced with tortuous weather including tidal waves of one hundred feet.

The ops building had to fall quickly. Time was against him getting the civilian prisoners to the hills and safety before the storm hit. Not to mention the need to get Topsail safely away.

The big man keyed Henderson. "If you can hold them off us for ten minutes, we'll take the building."

Now he had to make good on his commitment. Freeing the prisoners would be an affirmation to his people, their first real victory after weeks of suffering. My people, he thought, the people of Saragosa Prime.

Hulk saw a man move from the relative safety of the building to get a better shot. His flechette pistol severed the enemy's torso, the pungent smell of ozone from laser rays mingled with the sick sweet smell of death.

He motioned the remnants of his company into a flanking movement isolating and exposing two more guards. Both died instantly from laser bursts.

"Damn," Hulk shouted. "I said lasers on stun." That kind of disobedience needlessly gets people killed."

The two men next to him put shock grenades on the tips of their gun barrels. One died from a blaster before he could fire his weapon, Body armor didn't hinder a blaster at that range. The second man's shock grenade landed behind the barricade sheltering the remaining seven outer defenders. There was no place to hide—at close range, a shock grenade stripped flesh from bones. Two survivors surrendered.

Dispatching one man to guard the prisoners, Hulk motioned the remainder of his company forward to join him behind the strut of Topsail.

The Ops building was virtually without windows. Narrow slits near the ceiling line admitted light to some rooms. Others had no openings to the outside. The building's main entrance was on the east, with a northern rear entrance. He would attack the east entry—the north was already under fire from his detachment.

Hulk's attention was solely on the ops building. "Bring up the laser cutters. Let's open up the building front." The men he'd selected to follow him in the final assault moved forward. A sense of déjà vu crept over him. He and Richard Hastings had rescued Captain van Gelden from this very building the morning of his scheduled execution.

"What about the hostages?" someone asked.

"Most likely they're in the north wing. That's where I'd put them." Not only the fate of the prisoners concerned Hulk. He was nervous about the absence of fire from the building. He keyed Henderson. "Colonel, something isn't right. The people in the building should be shooting at us.

A movement caught his attention. "Hold on," he added. "Something's going on."

He stopped his group ten meters from the building. Being caught out in the open kept his mind off the intense, unrelenting sun.

A white rag flew from the building front. "Looks like they want to parley," Hulk said. "I'll talk to them."

Hulk positioned his six men, down from the ten he started with, for maximum protection in case this was a trap. "Hold your fire until I know what they're up to."

Along with the two of his people, he approached the building. Two soldiers emerged, a sergeant leading the way.

Hulk ordered, "Surrender your arms and the civilian prisoners. There's no need for you or my people to die."

"Maybe," said the sergeant. "But what happens to us if we do?"

Hulk pushed hard. "You'll be our prisoners and taken to a safe place. The war is over for you."

"Away from here? And quickly?" asked the soldier.

"Yes," Hulk answered. "Why quickly?"

He got no answer.

Using his left hand, the sergeant reached across his body and handed over his pistol. Well, I'll be damned, Hulk thought. They really are surrendering. He forced down an expression of surprise.

"Order your men to turn their arms over to the civilian prisoners and exit the building to the north," Hulk said. He motioned the two men with him into the building and the four watching to new positions at the entrance.

Hulk spoke into his open wrist com. "You've all been listening so you know what's happened. Attend to the civilians needs and then get them moving."

Henderson broke into the conversation. "The enemy's withdrawing."

Hulk could see the incoming fourteen SGL's. He didn't believe an enemy would withdraw in the face of an attack inferior in both number and armament.

He turned back to the captive sergeant. "Again, why? Quickly. What were your orders?"

The sergeant, not a big or belligerent man said, "To set explosives then vacate the building. Head for the south end of the spacedrome and get in the tunnels. All of us. When you people got on the ground, blow up the building and the space ship.

"The bare assed truth is you got here before we could make it to the tunnels. If anyone punched the button and we weren't below ground, well it's obvious isn't it."

"Sergeant, you stay with us. Your men leave with everyone else."

He ordered the civilians and captives on a forced march to the north, the security of the hills.

Hulk keyed Colonel Henderson, "Our original orders were to destroy the energy cannon deflector shield. Any changes?"

"Standby: Belay that order. Try not to damage anything. Command wants that cannon operational."

Winner's voice boomed over Hulk's wrist com. "Is the building secure? Have all explosives been removed?"

Hulk keyed his com button. "Yes. And I kept the non-com in charge here to make sure." He asked the sergeant, "What about your people in Saragosa City?"

Hulk knew the answer and fought to keep his temper. He wanted to see if the soldier would tell the truth.

"They were evacuated to the other side of the planet early this morning. Your invasion kept us from escaping to the tunnels and Bartok ordered us to blow the building. Kill us and you."

Hulk jammed his hand down on his hips, "Shit. This is crazy, beyond my comprehension."

Winner's voice sounded over the com, "I'm on my way in."

Hrndullka assigned people to provide armed cover for Winner's landing.

The Sizemore launch was a brute, as heavily armed as anything Hulk had ever seen. The cannon-festooned craft, making a hot landing—standard for a combat landing—skidded to a halt. The rear ramp hit the tarmac with a loud bang, Melissa and six heavily armed, body armored Marines established their own perimeter. They took no chances and no others person's word with the life of their commander. Winner, followed by Derka, stepped from the craft.

Henderson continued to call in suppressing fire from the orbiting destroyers. Hulk's wrist com played forward the Sizemore's commentary, "They're breaking. They're heading for the tunnels."

Within minutes, the three thousand Marines the WMC had on the surface controlled the entrances to the tunnels. Bartok's troops had little choice but to surrender. Their entire plan was to get underground and blow Topsail. When that collapsed, it was surrender or die. Mercenaries are quick to realize when they have lost the advantage.

Henderson commed in. "What do we do with the prisoners?"

Hulk thought for a moment—what was to be their haven was now their hell. "Keep them where they are. We've no better place to hold them."

Henderson accepted the surrender and ordered the captured officers to disarm their troops and make the best of the situation. They would be in the tunnels for some time as prisoners of war.

Colonel Henderson said, "Mr. Hrndullka, we'll take this operation from here on. I think your people need you."

"Yes, of course. We do have people still held captive and a certain valiant lady to find and rescue. He glanced at Winner as he said it. "We're going to free them."

Winner ordered Topsail manned and into orbit.

CHAPTER THIRTY THREE
The appeal to reason

Quiet filled the room. Henderson nodded, a grimace flicked across his face. He was the first to speak, "Mr. Hrndullka, I could use your help. Your knowledge of the processing area and the mines is better than anyone else's."

Winner had been there, he knew it wasn't going to be easy. People were going to die.

* * * *

Bartok stormed across the mine office, his rage unchecked. Someone had to be giving White information. But White couldn't get him now, no matter what traitors might linger in Bartok's organization.

Buried deep under the surface of Saragosa, the mines provided him with what he needed. A place that was virtually impregnable. A place his enemy couldn't reach him while he planned his retaliation. He had to find a way to defeat White. He punched his wristcom. "Masten, in my office, now."

He paced as he waited for the colonel's arrival. His thoughts jumped from the loss of his fleet to the surrender of Namaycush and to the humiliating defeat of his army with hardly a shot being fired. Now he was holed up like a rat. How had White been able to pull this off?

Masten appeared at the door, his anger clearly showing. He wasn't a common soldier and clearly resented Bartok's treatment. He stood at the entry, holding his position.

Bartok laughed. In a lowered, conciliatory voice he said, "Get your ass in here." He needed this man more than ever and couldn't afford to alienate him. He'd need to be very careful how he handled his volatile killer.

Masten walked into the room, followed Bartok's motion and took a chair at the long steel table.

Typical of most mining complexes, the office held few amenities. In the hours they'd had to prepare, Bartok's engineers had installed a telecom and holo. It dwarfed the coffee bar installed next to it. Huge exhaust fans whined as they worked to remove the odors of weeks of stagnated air.

Bartok stepped to the bar, poured himself a cup and said, "Care for any?"

Masten nodded.

Bartok handed over the mug. "What have you prepared in the way of defenses?"

Masten sipped at the cup. "You know we're not going to get out of here alive."

"Bullshit," said Bartok. "I've always found a way and I'll do it this time. This guy's been lucky. And it's time for that luck to turn my way."

"You never lacked for self confidence." Masten reached for the keyboard lying on the table and punched away. A holo of the mines and processing area appeared over the com center. He pointed out the coverage of the one remaining energy cannon. "If White exposes his fleet to the cannon, we're ready to take them out. So far, they've stayed on the other side of the planet. We still have a passive array on their side. It's unmanned so it might go undetected. We know the position of every vessel in orbit."

Knowing his fleet was gone, Bartok studied the display. "What about a ground assault?"

Masten switched images. "We've five hundred well-armed troops guarding the approaches to the energy cannon and the mines. We hold the high ground and have all approaches covered. We can hold off a ground attack indefinitely. Our perimeter forces are just inside the protection of the cannon blast shield. So, if White does come by ground or air, we can use the cannon to annihilate anyone or anything within a fifty kilometer radius."

Bartok slapped the table, its metallic ring echoed off the walls. "And we've got enough food and water to last us forever. We've got the time we need to either beat them or get away." He looked hard at Masten then grinned, "To fight another day."

"At least White isn't making any money as long as we hold the mines," Masten said.

"Let's go over the layout of the tunnels again."

Masten obeyed his leader and keyed the holo.

As they studied the mine schematic Masten asked, "What about the woman?"

"What about her?"

Masten questioned, "Any way we can use her as bait?"

Bartok thought a minute, "I don't see how. She came here to kill White. So, she escaped from us. We still caught her wandering the countryside. She'd obviously gotten lost and it was either surrender or try to live off the land. I have no use for her."

"You're naïve," Masten said. "The resistance helped her escape the hotel, that maintenance guy, Sheets."

Bartok rubbed his forehead and said, "I don't care. Take her. Do whatever you want with her. If you can work something, do it."

Silence settled over the two, each lost in his private thoughts as the hologram image of the processing area and mines rotated before them. Bartok stared into the image, looking for a way to gain the victory he had to have. His very soul demanded it.

* * * *

Winner and the command staff studied the holo of the processing area and mines. He motioned Henderson beside him. The deep rumble of the raging storm penetrated even the concrete walls of the hotel.

"Winds are over one hundred fifty kilometers," Hrndullka said. "And they may go higher."

Winner keyed Deliverance, "Captain Davenport. Have your weather people been monitoring this storm? Any predictions?"

"Yes to both questions, Mr. White. I just received the forecast and am sending to you now."

The group hovered around the display. Their discussion was low but studied.

"That low pressure area is the most intense I've ever seen," Hulk traced the outline of the storm center with his finger. "There'll be a lot of flooding."

"How long will it last?" Winner noticed the storm movement was almost nil.

Derka altered the projection. "Let's see if the forecast goes beyond today."

The new display showed Saragosa City taking the first hit, with the front then moving toward the west following the coastline. "In four to five days the storm will be over the mines with little loss of intensity," Winner said.

He turned to Derka and asked, "Can you raise Bartok on the com system" I think it's time he and I had a talk."

"If he's listening, I can get to him."

Winner stood in front of the vidscreen waiting for Bartok's image to appear.

Bartok blustered, shouting at the image before him. "Well, if it isn't the great Winner White. If you've called to gloat, it's premature. We're not done by a long shot." A hint of doubt emerged. "If not here and now, later."

Winner ignored the outburst. "This is your only opportunity to surrender. You have no way out of the mines. You may be able to resist for some time but eventually your resources will be gone. If you want to die there, so be it. But at least release your prisoners and let those people who want to give up, do so. There's no need for them to die in a lost cause."

Bartok's answered with a screamed, "Fuck you," and a fist to the cut-off.

The screen went blank.

"Try to get him on line again," Winner said.

After several minutes, Masten appeared in Bartok's place.

Winner marveled at the enigma that stood before him. Handsome by most standards, well educated with a doctorate in physics, immaculately dressed—but a bloodthirsty psychopath.

"Mr. White. If you want to deal with someone, it will be me. Mr. Bartok has advised me he will say no more to you until you're his prisoner, at which time he plans to kill you. In fact, he's asked me to participate. I look forward to the event."

"And if you lose?"

"Should we not gain a victory or escape, there's little chance I'll come out of this alive."

Winner shook his head, a wry grin on his face. "Colonel, I know of no place in the known galaxy you'll be able to hide, assuming you do get away. It is my intention to see that justice has its way with you. Even if I have to administer that justice."

Masten, threw his head high. "Ah, warrior to warrior. How could either of us wish for more?"

"Masten, you're no warrior. Just a butcher that fell in with someone who would let you fulfill your crazed obsessions."

Masten grinned.

"Tell your master," Winner said, "I have the man beside me who dug those mines. He knows every secret, every hidden entrance and exit—and they're not marked on any holo. We will be in your midst and there's nothing you can do to stop us."

Masten smirked, "We'll be waiting."

Winner punched off the holo as Hulk said, "There are no hidden entrances or exits to the mines."

Winner grinned and replied, "You know that, but they don't. I expect they'll pull people off the perimeter to protect their ass. That should help us a little since we do have to come in through the mine's front door."

Hulk shook. "I'm glad I'm on your side."

* * * *

For the next twenty-four hours, Winner monitored the storm's progress. Along with Colonel Henderson, he studied the prospects for getting into the mine. The slow-moving storm blessed them with the time they needed to investigate every possibility and formulate their best ideas.

"What I wouldn't give for a little help from orbit to take out that cannon before my Marines attack," Henderson said.

Winner agreed but he just couldn't justify risking a ship. The ground cannon had a split-second advantage and could shoot before a destroyer cleared the horizon and could bring its guns to bear. The first shooter won in this kind of situation.

"I understand you're one of the best at hand to hand combat."

Henderson shrugged.

Winner continued, "Let's go to the gym. There're a few moves I need to work on."

Melissa sent one of the male guards along with Winner. She agreed her duties went only so far and would observe. Derka joined her to watch the two.

The men didn't take long to change and were quickly engaged, testing each other.

Henderson picked himself off the mat, feigned a jab and parried a thrust from Winner—but Winner's thrust was a feint and Henderson's block was a mistake leaving his left knee exposed.

In one quick move, Winner kicked the sinning knee, sending Henderson to the canvas.

"I think I've been conned, sir. Three times on my butt is enough. I feel like a punching bag. I'm the one who needs practice."

Winner laughed and helped the Marine to his feet.

Melissa leaned against the wall her hand covered a smile while Derka seemed uninterested.

Henderson dried the sweat from the back of his neck and asked, "Have you figured out how we're going to get from here to the processing area without being detected?"

Winner sat down on a rolled up mat and motioned Henderson to sit beside him. "Bartok has a passive relay post on one of the mountains. We have to get past it undetected. Deliverance will orbit above the station to make it look like it's going to attempt an attack on the energy cannon. We're pinning our hopes on the array staying fixed on Deliverance. Using SGL's, we can cover the two thousand klicks in little over three hours. We'll follow the storm, stay on its perimeter until we reach the cannon and cave entrance. Floodwaters drain quickly in that rocky area. As the waters recede, we'll hide close to the mine entrance. When Bartok's soldiers deploy to the energy cannon perimeter, we knock out the cannon, take the cave entrance, Sizemore takes out Bartok's soldiers. The rest of our people mop up the outside while we retake the mines."

Both men knew this was the sanitized version. It wasn't going to be that easy.

CHAPTER THIRTY FOUR
The mines

Three shuttles skimmed the Saragosa Road's plasticrete surface. At almost five hundred KPH, they would reach the mines before the storm abated, with three hours to prepare their attack.

Winds swirled around the craft but offered little challenge to the heavy SGL's. Environmental filters kept out the pungent aroma of Saragosa's angry ocean. Each Marine wore a space suit and skin suit under their body armor. The helmet and suit maintained a controlled atmosphere. At the least, they'd be dry and breathe fresh air.

Winner worried the strap on the blaster rifle Melissa had issued him. "Lieutenant, get me a laser." He handed her the blaster.

Melissa laid aside her helmet, unfastened the lap harness and stepped to the arms locker next to the entry hatch and retrieved the weapon. She inserted a charged cartridge, handed it to him and returned to her seat without a word.

Winner noted her quiet attitude. Must be wound tight.

He thought to how the battle needed to play out. Generals paid attention to the Order of Battle—soldiers worried about staying alive.

If the energy cannon fired, everything was over. Bartok's passive antenna array Bartok pinpointed every vessel in space. But it suffered from two deficiencies. It couldn't tell which spaceship was most likely to attack and ground effect brought on by the storm's severe electrical discharge gave it a blind spot in the lower atmosphere. That's where the shuttle launches would hide, allowing them to get within a thousand meters or so of the mines and the cannon. The intense electrical storms rendered the mines area detectors useless. Once the storm abated, the advantage swung back to Bartok.

From the lead shuttle, Winner said, "We'll be in position before Bartok's soldiers redeploy." He lightly popped his fist on the pilot's shoulder and said, "Make sure the launches leave the area immediately. But don't go too far. Find someplace to hide."

"Yes, sir. You can count on us," the pilot responded.

They could take out the cannon once it was in sight. But that would alert Bartok and he'd most likely stay holed up. The mine doors were almost impenetrable. Better to wait until Bartok's troops returned to their original defensive positions—then the mine entrance would be open. After that, the plan was hand-to-hand combat—no strategy except a Marine, a rifle and a bayonet.

He sat back in his seat and looked at the chronometer on the bulkhead, two hours until touchdown.

"I'll stay tied into your communications grid," the pilot promised. "Just call. We'll be there."

Winner joined Melissa and her squad as they cleaned their rifles—again.

She looked up to him. "Sir, may I speak frankly?"

Winner grinned, "Don't you usually?" In body armor and with her helmet off, she looked like an overstuffed doll.

She didn't seem amused. "If we are to protect you, we need your cooperation. I'm asking that you give us a chance to do our job."

Winner looked into her eyes. He understood and accepted her concern. "What do you want me to do?"

"Let the two SGL's go in first. That puts two hundred Marines on the ground before you land. When we exit, my squad will form a circle around you. All you have to do is stay in the circle."

Melissa was right. As much as he wanted to lead the attack, it was the Colonel's job. He needed to let the Marines carry out their orders. "Okay, Melissa. We'll do it your way."

"One other thing, sir. Earlier at the ops building when you learned Bartok was holed up in the mines and later at the hotel when your staff was discussing the attack plan, you said Bartok was yours. Is there something about the mines the rest of us don't know?"

He looked at her, a slight smile touched the corners of her lips, "I'm going to have to keep an eye on you. You're just too damn perceptive. And yes, there is something not on the mine layouts and we're going to use it."

He paused for a moment. "I need something from you. Remember these soldiers are mercenaries. As long as they think no one can touch them, they are very nasty. Don't let them take you alive."

"I'm a Marine," Melissa answered. "You're not telling me anything I don't know."

He finished assembling his laser rifle having already cleaned and checked his side arm.

"Touchdown in one minute." The pilot's voice cut through the silence.

The launch settled on a ledge straddling a crevice. Water almost a meter deep gushed through the narrow slit.

"Best I can do, sir," said the pilot. "Nothing but rocks and crags around here."

Winner put his helmet on and signaled Melissa to move out. The Marines stepped through the rear hatch avoiding the rushing cold waist deep water. Rain splatter against their face shields reducing visibility to less than three meters. Gaps between sections of body armor brought home the power of wind-driven rain. The skin suits did little to ease the sting.

Melissa motioned a Marine to anchor a rope between the shuttle and a small rock outcrop above them. She grabbed the line and climbed to a ledge a few centimeters above the raging torrent. Standing against the 100 KPH wind was a challenge, walking against it almost impossible on the slick rocks. It would be another hour before the storm slackened.

The squad led the exit and the command followed. Only after all had safely disembarked did Melissa pull her K-bar knife, cut the shuttle free and watch it disappear into the driving rain.

A tap on Winner's wrist control brought low intensity light goggles into place. He spotted another group of Marines and motioned Melissa to establish a hard wire com link with him and another with Colonel Henderson.

Once in direct contact Winner said, "On your command, Colonel."

"Understood," Henderson responded.

* * * *

Forty-five minutes after landing, Melissa tapped Winner on the shoulder. "Winds are abating. Down to seventy."

"Colonel? You get that?" Winner asked.

"Yes, sir, we're tied in."

Henderson's people knew the routine—everyone down out of sight and stay that way.

The colonel tried to rub an itch on his nose and only smeared his faceplate. He laughed, mentally reviewing assignments thrashed out dozens of times. Alpha Company would take out the controls to the cannon. Charlie Company would go for the mine entrance. Sizemore was to engage the perimeter troops.

Amazed at how calm he was, Henderson leaned against the granite escarpment. The image of his wife and three sons touched his mind and he softly pushed them back.

Except for the space fight, bows and arrows could have handled most of this war, he thought. Technology wasn't the key here—Marines on the ground with rifles were. The truth never changes—if you want to take and hold ground, put grunts on it.

This wasn't his first time in combat but his first with overall tactical command. And the first time his Commander-in-Chief was a part of the attack force.

Usually, the command structure stayed intact, but this war hadn't followed any rules. Al Cadifh and Reasoner had died before either fired a shot. He smiled. *Maybe I ought to shoot first.* In any case, he'd remember to keep his head down.

"Winds down to forty KPH," his helmet earphones crackled. The rain abruptly stopped but the wind continued.

Less than a minute later, the first enemy troops emerged from the mine entrance and spread toward the perimeter.

Henderson signaled their emergence to Winner.

The Marines to Winner's left and right sighted their bazooka lasers on the hinges to the giant doors that sealed the mine entrance. A near miss wouldn't work. The shooters had to get it right—there wouldn't be a second shot. Once the massive doors closed, the kind of weapon that could open them would destroy most of the people inside and devastate everything outside within a two hundred kilometer radius.

Henderson waited until Bartok's guards reached the pre-defined deployment point and whispered, "now" into his com. He hand-motioned his own company forward.

They moved past the boulders abutting the concrete apron that fronted the doors. Water run-off no longer cascaded around them—the plasticrete apron spread it harmlessly across the flat surface.

All around him, the world exploded.

The time for silence had passed. Up and running, Colonel Henderson led Charlie Company toward the one hundred meters distant the mine entrance.

Off to his left the cannon control panel exploded in a shower of sparks.

Although they had to be surprised, Bartok's mercenaries reacted instantly, opening fire.

Flechette blades, blasters and laser fire cut through the company. All around Henderson, Marines fell, but he pressed the attack. Charlie would take the mine entrance or die on the wet plasticrete approach.

Alpha Company held its position, but had accomplished its primary mission. With the cannon disabled, they turned every available weapon on the enemy, providing cover fire. From far overhead, the fleet made its presence— precision laser fire devastated the enemies midst.

* * * *

Ahead of Winner, two Marines reached the entrance wall, firing flechettes toward the huge partially opened doors. Those deadly razors and needles ricocheted into the mine entryway.

Winner heard screams above the wind—the result of soft flesh meeting steel knives. Under cover of blasters, two squads rushed through the entrance.

They were in.

Winner keyed Alpha, "The perimeter? Status?"

The answer came as he ran to join Henderson at the mine entrance. "Alpha's got Bartok's outer perimeter forces isolated. Deliverance blasted hell out of the poor bastards. We have them sealed off. The shots that hit us at the mine entrance were all that the enemy got."

Winner motioned toward the opening but Melissa held up her hand signaling a halt.

Winner fought the urge to plunge ahead and waited as Melissa and another Marine crept past the massive door, rifles ready, and surveyed the inside. The fighting had moved a few hundred meters past the entrance. She signaled everyone move inside.

Someone asked, "Any idea how many more soldiers are holed up in here?"

"About two hundred," Henderson answered.

The mine floor sloped gently upward from the door, reducing the risk of floodwater entering. Ahead of them, offices, equipment, crew quarters and elevators to the lower levels filled most of the area.

Four hundred meters into the mine, the shaft split into two tunnels. Plaques above each elevator shaft proclaimed Odd and Even. Tunnels one, three, five, seven and nine ran off the Odd vertical shaft; Even accessed the rest. The tunnels split many times following veins of ore.

"Any prisoners yet?" Winner asked.

"About a dozen, sir," a sergeant answered.

He pushed open a nearby office door and said. "Bring the lowest ranking prisoner in here for interrogation."

The sergeant hesitated. Winner gave him a look that sent the battle-hardened veteran hustling after a prisoner.

Winner unlocked and removed his helmet. He pulled a chair to the middle of the floor. The room, normally used for rest breaks, contained a machine that provided him with a hot cup of coffee. He took Melissa aside and whispered to her as the prisoner entered the room.

None too gently, Melissa's squad searched the man. The prisoner appeared a grizzled veteran. No chevron's, he'd probably been busted more times than you could count.

"Want him in the chair?" Melissa asked through her com link.

Henderson appeared at the door. With the mine entry secured, a lull settled over the group. Fighting would start with renewed intensity once they moved into the shafts and tunnels.

"No," answered Winner, each word clipped. "The chair is for me."

Any who had learned anything about Winner White could see why he'd made it as a test plot and SEAL.

Following Winner's plan, a dozen people filtered into the room.

Winner casually walked to the chair and sat. Melissa stood at his shoulder, sidearm ready. Her armor and helmet hid her sex.

Winner glared at the prisoner. "Have you ever held higher rank?"

To his complete surprise the soldier shook his head. "No."

"Do you know who I am?"

"No."

"Do you know where the civilian captives are being held?"

The soldier didn't respond.

"I asked you a question."

Sweat trickled down the prisoner's brow.

Winner suppressed his grin. He had the man he wanted.

"I have no intention of sitting here waiting for an answer."

Melissa punched her wrist pad bringing on line the external speaker. "Sir. The war's over for this man. Let me have him."

His coffee cup in one hand, Winner opened the other in a gesture that said go ahead. He guessed the soldier had seen how Bartok treated prisoners. In fact, he was counting on it. One-on-one and without backup, most mercenaries avoided fights. They'd test this man.

The soldier's eyes widened, a grim smirch touching the corners of his lips.

Melissa holstered her laser pistol. Meticulously, she took off her helmet and body armor. The skin suit left little to the imagination—Melissa had curves in the right places and the right size.

Slowly, almost teasingly, she reached behind her head and removed the beret. The flaming red hair cascaded over her shoulders.

Then she drew her K-Bar knife and stepped between Winner and the prisoner. "Everyone out of the room."

Winner and Henderson stayed but the others left, some with reluctance, and concerned looks.

Abject fear filled the mercenary's eyes, his lips freezing in a plea. This man had served long enough to know the reputation of women who hired out as mercenaries, let alone those who'd gained rank. The soldier had no way of knowing the lady wasn't a mercenary. All he could see was the cold uncaring look on Melissa's face and the knife as she twirled it in her hand.

More sweat trickled down his brow, across his cheek.

Melissa touched the blade to the running sweat, scooping a small amount on the knife. She touched the razor sharp tip to her tongue creating a trickle of blood—which she spat in the man's face.

He seemed frozen in terror as her blood joined the sweat running from his face and soaking into his collar.

Without waiting, Melissa kicked his legs apart and slowly moved the knife into his crotch, razor-sharp blade up.

It was more than the soldier could take. His knees betrayed him with a slight sag. "They're in the bottom tunnel," he blurted.

"All of them?" asked Winner.

"Masten, Colonel Masten had some looker with him. He took her somewhere else. He didn't go with the others." A whine edged the soldier's answer.

"A looker?"

"Yeah, a woman."

Winner didn't react. "Bartok?"

"I don't know."

Winner stood, walked to the prisoner. "If you're lying, you'll wish you were never born."

"It's the truth. I'm just a fuckin' grunt. I told you what little I seen."

Winner hated to see a grown man cry. "Get him out of here."

He waited until the prisoner was through the door then turned to Melissa. "I don't know whether to give you an acting award or warn Derka."

Melissa removed a medication packet from her backpack, spread it over her the cut she'd inflicted on her tongue then snapped on her body armor. "As one great general said, 'It's only important that I know if it was an act'."

Winner bowed to her and said, "Enough of this Sara Long. We've got a job yet to do."

Melissa curtsied. "Who's Sara Long?"

Winner said, "A twenty-first century lady who killed over one hundred men with a knife. Some say she never died."

"Maybe someone's related to her," Melissa added.

"Most likely Masten." With a grin Winner added, "Just as long as it isn't you. Let's finish this."

CHAPTER THIRTY FIVE
The mines

Henderson stuck his head into the mine office. "My people will be ready in one hour."

Winner rested his hands on the back of a chair, leaned forward and acknowledged the Colonel's report. "This is where it all started. The very reason for our presence is in these mines."

He wasn't talking about Bartok. "It's just as well we put an end to this war here."

A deep rumble echoed through the labyrinth, "Bartok sealing off the tunnels," he said. "This planet is home to over one hundred twenty-five thousand people, many of them born here and have never seen Earth. These people are fighting for more than their livelihood. They were about to vote in their own government, rule their own lives."

Everyone understood—without the minerals secreted below, only the oceans would lay claim to this rock in space.

Winner reflected over the terrible hardships the people of Saragosa Prime had endured in conquering the planet. Many things taken for granted in polite society were luxuries here. The first, and often only, order of business now was survival. Winner fought back the weariness that crept over him. They'd all gone thirty hours without sleep but he wasn't going to be the first to slow. He refilled his coffee cup and motioned Henderson to join him and Melissa at a table.

The synthetic top rang when their cups clanged to the surface. "Polymorphous carbonate," Winner said. "Just sounds like metal. It's about all that lasts any time in this air.

The sound brought back memories he'd not had since accompanying his father here many years ago.

He turned to Henderson. "See what intel your people have gathered."

Henderson keyed his wristcom pad and barked the order.

"Colonel," Winner asked. "Why didn't Bartok give tactical command to Masten? They outnumbered and outgunned us. We've won every battle because of their mistakes."

Henderson shrugged. "Maybe his colonel rank isn't real. All talk. Anyhow, mistakes often determine the outcome of most battles. I look for the enemy's mistakes. It's harder to recover from your own screw-ups. Especially when the enemy exploits them."

"Perhaps," said Winner. "I've checked Masten's history. He's proven himself in combat. Bartok hired him from Fonso Carren over two years ago. He graduated from a military academy with honors, went on to get a doctorate in physics and then joined the mercenaries. His accomplishments in planning and executing a battle plan are first rate. He commanded a company at Brixen's star —that got him noticed. Later, he held overall command in the fight that led to the defeat of the United Nations forces at Mars Station. Although nothing's ever been proven, he's apparently been psychopathic since coming of age."

Winner stopped when two intelligence officers, Mutt and Jeff, he thought, entered and were introduced.

The Major, whom Winner would remember as Mutt, spoke. "Sir, the civilian prisoners are on level nine. Enemy troops hold every level except this one. Can't tell where Bartok is. From telecom traffic, it appears they've set up a command center on the fifth level."

"Why the fifth?" asked Henderson.

Mutt continued, "It's the newest and most self-sustaining—has its own environmental system. And they can seal it off from the main shaft. Its doors are similar to the main entry doors. Word is they have plenty of armament and enough food and water to hold out for months. If they want, they can hole up in there and blow the access routes to everything below. That would be the main shaft, equipment shaft and the stairs."

The officer seemed through with his report.

"Do you know where Celia Markham is?" Winner asked. She had sacrificed her freedom for his mother and Daker Smithe and now her life was in the hands of a madman. He couldn't let it end that way.

This time the second officer, Jeff, spoke. "Colonel Masten and three guards were reportedly seen leading her down the stairway. No one knows where they are."

Winner looked at the two officers. "Anything else?"

"No sir," they responded in unison.

Henderson spoke, "Thank you, gentlemen. That will be all." The two saluted and left the room.

Winner waited until the door closed and said, "Level five is where phosphorus and magnesium are mined."

Henderson looked at Melissa.

She shrugged questioningly.

"From Chem. 1," Henderson said, "I seem to remember bad things about both of those elements."

"As you should." Winner leaned his elbows on the table and folded his hands. "We've always had a problem with phosphine gas down there. Bartok could pipe the gas into the ventilation system and without space helmets and rebreathers, we'd all be dead in minutes. And if that isn't bad enough, both the phosphorus and magnesium are highly reactive. Phosphorus burns on contact with air and magnesium—if fired, it will burn until nothing's left of it. Some chemicals can slow the process, but even they give off toxic fumes."

Henderson leaned away from the table and punched his flashing wristcom.

"Alpha Company here sir," all three at the table heard. "What's left of Bartok's perimeter troops have surrendered. Most of Alpha Company is available to help in the tunnels."

"Good job, Major," Henderson said. "Use what troops you need to secure your prisoners and order the rest to report here." He punched the wristcom to standby.

Winner keyed Hulk. Waiting for the big man, he reflected over the complete confidence Henderson showed in his people and the commitment it inspired.

The screen popped alive.

"Mr. Hrndullka," Winner said. "I need your input. How do we deal with Phosphine gas? And is magnesium a problem?"

"Phosphine—wear protective clothing and rebreathers for starters," Hulk answered. "Once fired, magnesium can penetrate any organic or metallic substance, given enough time. As magnesium sulfate, it normally isn't a problem. In that state, the ignition temperature is four hundred degrees centigrade."

Hulk returned to the phosphine, "There are lockers located on every level that contain anything you may need against the gas. I'd suggest skin suits with helmets. Cover that with body armor and then use the suits from the lockers. Sensors located in the tunnels provide about a twenty twenty-second warning. That's the best you can expect."

"Bartok's holed up on level five," Winner said.

"Bad news. I suggest you circulate air from outside. It'll smell a little like rotten eggs but you can endure that. The exhaust fans can change the air in the mines every three minutes. Bartok can flood the mines with phosphine only one time. That is, if there's even any of the gas down there."

Melissa feigned holding her nose.

"Like it or not," Hunk continued, "the airborne sulfur is something of a lubricant—and therefore a retardant to phosphorus."

"Thank you," Winner said. "What's your situation?"

"Matters are progressing quite well here. If you need more troops or supplies, we can assist you immediately. I sent our best mining engineer to you. He should be arriving about now. "Oh yes, Richard Hastings and Captain van Gelden boarded Topsail and left orbit a few minutes ago. Hastings said to tell you he was looking forward to meeting with you again—very soon."

Winner thanked Hulk and signed off before turning back to Henderson. "Where can I pull up a holo of the mines?"

"We've set up a command center next door," Henderson answered. "It's got everything we should need."

Winner followed Henderson, Melissa at his side. Outside the door, the rest of her security people took up positions around them. To the other side of the giant cavern, Marine squad leaders were lining out their people, preparing for the tunnel assault.

"Sir," Melissa asked. "If phosphorus burns in air, how is it mined?"

"Drills are inserted from above. The drill bit and stem are submerged in water. Oil sits on top of the water and seals the whole operation. The slurry, oil and minerals are pumped up the hollow drill stem to storage tanks designed to hold the mixture."

"I'll stick to the Marines—simpler."

Winner smiled. He entered the command room. The engineer had arrived and was putting finishing touches to a transmitter installation. Projection screens lined the walls permitting display of the smallest detail for analysis. Cameras—normal, zero light and infrared, covered every square centimeter of the mines. Wall monitors projected the images.

Except level five. Cut off. Shunted to Bartok's command center, Winner suspected.

A holo projector sat at the west end of the room along with the communications equipment. Winner called the engineer to join him at the holo.

He punched up the mines and spent some time reviewing the layout.

"How many ways out of these tunnels?" he asked.

In a quiet unhurried voice, the engineer pointed to each object as he explained. "We refer to the two vertical shafts servicing the ore-producing tunnels as Odd and Even. The tunnels off Odd are one, three and so on. The two service shafts are identical and each contains two elevators—one for personnel, and the other for small equipment. Isolated in each shaft is a stairway that goes from top to bottom. The service shafts are offset ninety degrees to the large equipment shaft. The heavy equipment shaft has dozens of cranes, hoists and platforms scattered along its length. Air ducts, both intake and exhaust, there can be as many as a dozen in each tunnel; slurry pipes, one to a tunnel. That's it."

"No gravlifts?" Henderson asked.

"Nope. Too dangerous. Tools fall off belts too often, drop down the shaft. We had a man killed and over fifty injured so we took out both lifts."

Winner asked, "What's in those locations now?"

The man cleared his throat. "Well, if a person rigged some way to climb the shaft that would be another way out. Sorry."

Winner said, "Take your time. Is the holo complete? Is there anything else we need to be looking at? Old layouts, you know, drawings you had before this fancy holo?" He measured irritation into his voice. He wanted the engineer to know he had to be right. "Grab a cup of coffee and talk this thing through."

Winner leaned back in his chair, cup in hand and waited.

The engineer called someone on the telecom and spent a few minutes reviewing some files. Finally, he said, "Other than walking out the front door, that's it. The only other holes penetrating to all tunnels are for communications, water, electrical. And none of those shafts are over six inches in diameter. The slurry lines and air ducts go directly to the planet surface. Everything else originates and ends here on the administrative level."

Winner stood and thanked the men. His thoughts turned again to Celia, Markham and Masten. His mind was already exploring the corridors beneath them.

"Mr. Derka sent some communication gadgets for everyone," the engineer said. "Even the troops. Should allow you to stay in touch even deep underground."

Melissa was first to accept one of the small transceivers.

Henderson examined another. "It's an implant."

The engineer seemed happy for a subject other than his omission of the gravlift shafts. "Yes and there's a doctor standing by to inoculate everyone."

Henderson asked, "What are its operating limits?"

"About a thousand meters through this rock, and once inserted they're activated. They receive all the time and have voice-activated transmission. Only a wearer hears what's being received. A detector has to be within half a meter to pickup their presence."

Henderson authorized the injection, just behind each person's ear. A doctor and corpsman entered the room.

Winner's bodyguards searched the medical team. The CIC stood, arms ready, as he waited for his implant. Melissa, standing next to the doctor, selected the syringe and implant.

The doctor smiled. "Very thorough."

Melissa acknowledged the comment with a smile that didn't last a second. She grasped her laser pistol in her holster, charged the weapon, but kept both in place. No one in the room missed the whine; every eye was on her, then the doctor.

"Proceed, doctor," she said.

With the injection completed, the doctor headed for the door, visibly shaken. Winner glanced at Melissa, then spoke to Henderson. "Take Bartok alive if you can."

"Come on Lieutenant." He motioned to Melissa. "We have a lady to rescue."

CHAPTER THIRTY SIX
The tunnels

"Colonel Henderson, Lt. Graves, wait a moment. I want a few words alone with you," Winner said.

They waited as the room cleared. "How do we shut off these voice-activated transmitters?" he asked.

Henderson frowned. "Don't know. Just a moment." He stepped to the door and called the engineer back.

Winner followed the man's visual instructions placing his wristcom next to the implant and spoke. Nothing transmitted. "What about when we have our helmets on?" he asked.

"Keep your wristcom in contact with the helmet and you're okay. "

"Thank you," Winner said.

"That will be all." Henderson nodded to the man.

The engineer closed the door behind him.

Winner turned to his cohorts, his wristcom away from his neck, "Just in case Bartok or Masten can hear." He slammed his fist into his open hand and said, "I'm going to find Celia Markham and take out Bartok."

Henderson scratched his chin. "Yes sir. Care to tell us how you're going rescue the lady?"

Winner covered the implant. "Test shaft."

The two waited for their leader to continue.

He faced them, his excitement evident. "Ever hear of Winston White? He started all this. Came here, drilled test holes all over this planet looking for ores. All but three he plugged, and one of those he secretly sealed. That was twenty years before the commercial excavation started. The Odd and Even main access shafts are centered on two of those holes with the secret shaft in between. This shaft connects every tunnel, intersecting the door hinges on each level. That's how we're going to bypass the elevators and stairs to find Celia. Colonel, the test shafts are too small to move the troops you need for your assignment. But for finding the lady, it's a natural."

Melissa asked, "What are the chances that hole is still there and usable?"

"Should be pretty good. It was dug in solid rock."

"Why isn't this shaft on the holo's or old drawings?" Henderson asked.

Winner grinned. "The old man was sly like a fox. I suppose you could say he didn't trust anyone to keep his secret. He dug the main shafts at the exploratory holes and kept the rest of the information off the charts. Apparently, he wanted another way out. Didn't like the idea of only one door. So—"

The three walked from the office. Winner wished Henderson good hunting; the Colonel saluted and left to join his troops.

Winner led Melissa and her squad into the refuse room adjacent to the shafts.

He pulled his laser pistol from its holster adjusted it to the lowest setting. When the familiar whine ebbed, Winner aimed it along the wall baseline directly above where he estimated the massive hinges to be and fired.

One section of the wall vibrated, leaving a faint outline of a panel.

Winner released the trigger, jamming the gun into its holster. In the same motion, he pulled a laser knife from its sheath beneath his body armor and traced the mark.

A panel opened.

Winner coughed, placed his wrist next to his transmitter. "This one-hundred year-old air's a little stale, but it's breathable. There's a room like this on every level with an access panel. We're going down this shaft. We'll check each tunnel and find Ms. Markham. Any questions?"

Getting none he continued. "Sling your rifles, clip a lanyard to your pistols and flashlights. We don't want anything falling down the shaft. Keep quiet. Shaft walls carry sound." He put his helmet on and locked it in place.

Winner started toward the shaft but Melissa motioned she'd go first and pushed past him.

She was halfway into the shaft before Winner, wristcom covering the implant and broadcasting on the suit-to-suit transmitter asked, "How are you going to find the access panels, Lieutenant?"

She didn't answer.

Winner said, "I'll make you a deal. I'll go first, find the panels, open them and you go in."

Melissa slid out of the opening.

Feet first, Winner crawled into the short passageway.

His feet found the ladder and he started down with Melissa following close behind.

One at a time, her squad entered the shaft above her. Lined with more of the synthetic steel and only a meter in diameter, it extended to level nine. A fall meant a three thousand-meter drop and all of them welcomed the safety harnesses.

Three hundred meters in, Winner stopped at level one, inserted the laser knife, loosened the panel and moved down the ladder.

Cautiously, laser pistol in hand, Melissa opened the covering no more than a centimeter and peered past the huge hinge into the refuse room. Slowly she opened the panel, her eyes quickly scanned the area.

It was empty. She slid through the opening; Winner followed and motioned the remainder of the squad to wait in the shaft.

He moved to the door that accessed tunnel one. Carefully, he pulled down on the steel door's latch handle, gained an opening and peered into the tunnel.

A few seconds later, he closed the door. "Soldiers," he mouthed, motioning her toward the panel.

Inside the shaft, Melissa placed her wristcom against her helmet. "Aren't there going to be soldiers in all the tunnels? How are we going to know if Masten's there without going in?"

"Masten isn't working with a large contingent of soldiers. I'm betting when we find a tunnel without soldiers, that's where we'll find Masten and Celia."

Winner continued down the shaft to tunnel three. When Winner opened the door from the refuse room to the tunnel, only the noise from the exhaust fans rustled through the cavern.

"This is it." Winner knew every Marine in the mines was listening.

"Colonel Henderson, we've found them on level three. Put guards on the exhaust fan surface vents just in case someone tries to crawl up that way."

He doubted they would. Shutting down the exhaust fans would be obvious and crawling past them while they were running wasn't possible.

Henderson answered, "Yes sir. It's already done."

Winner motioned to Melissa.

She jerked open the metal door and dove into the hallway, her rifle fanning the front access.

The floor's non-skid surface stopped her effort to slide so she rolled toward the opposite side of the anteroom opening to the tunnel.

Two Marines followed, rifles covering left and right approaches.

Winner and the remaining three waited in the refuse room.

Nothing happened.

Rifles covering each other, the group entered the large room.

Offices crowded the area around the entry door—all empty.

Moving from room to room, Winner and the Marines set about clearing the tunnel. With no one behind, they didn't worry about securing the cleared areas. Winner didn't have the people to do it anyhow.

Melissa motioned a Marine forward past another corner.

A blaster caught him mid-stride and he died instantly. At short range, the Marine's body armor proved useless.

She yelled venting her hell at the enemy as she turned her laser toward the opening, melting everything attacked by the deadly ray.

"You might want to take that thing off high heat," Winner cautioned. Then he added, "Cover me."

He dropped to the floor, rolled hard to his right and laid down a continuous blast from his laser rifle.

Scrambling to his feet, running and firing from a crouch, he headed for a column fifteen meters away/ Melissa's squad laid down a withering curtain of fire, adding a brilliance that temporarily blinded everyone. He reached the pillar and dropped behind it before called to her, "Okay, Lieutenant, your turn. Everybody cover her."

He put down his laser and shouldered his flechette rifle, firing toward the tunnel opening as Melissa ran across the open corridor and dropped beside him.

Sparks flew and metal rang as the iridium-titanium steel needles ricocheted from or pierced whatever they hit.

A scream came from down the tunnel. He'd found flesh.

Winner flicked his wrist control and helmet goggles snapped over his eyes.

The shooter could be anywhere. He scanned overhead. The jumble of tubes, ducts, conduit and pipes generated every temperature on the scale and made a perfect hiding place. He was looking for anything that didn't belong in the mix but he. He found nothing.

"The shooter must be on the floor."

A noise rumbled down the tunnel. Winner turned toward it. "What's that?"

"Nothing like I've ever heard," Melissa answered.

The noise became a constant roar. Then it changed.

Sorting out the high pitched whine, Winner recognized the screech of an overloaded electric motor, but there was more. Finally it came to him—a linear accelerator. He still didn't know what it meant.

Abruptly the sound stopped, the silence jolting everyone.

Winner felt certain if the enemy soldiers planned to attack it would have happened when the noise was at its greatest.

"What was the Marine's name?" Winner asked.

"Untama," Melissa answered, "Corporal Unta Untama."

"Known him long?"

"Six weeks," she added.

"What was he like?"

"Sir, we've still got enemy soldiers out there trying to kill us," she protested.

"No, Melissa. If they were going to attack, they'd have done it when the noise level was at its highest. Mask their movements. What was Corporal Unta Untama like?"

Melissa slumped against the pilaster, her breath slowly seeping between pursed lips. "Good Marine. He never talked about his family. Wanted to learn to swim. From Central Africa. He'd never seen an ocean until he enlisted. The Navy SEALs were his idols. Wanted to join Strike Force One."

"Yes, he'd need to know how to swim if he wanted in that bunch."

Winner said no more about the young Marine. It wasn't his intent to slight the dead man's memory, but the living still needed attention. "Lieutenant. We need to convince the enemy to surrender. There's no need for anyone else to die."

Melissa's mouth dropped open. "Sir, Masten isn't going to surrender." She seemed mystified by Winner's taciturn behavior.

Winner pointed up the tunnel. "Looks like we won't have to convince them."

Celia Markham, still wearing the orange jumpsuit, waved a white flag. Behind her, three enemy soldiers, without weapons, hands in the air, walked down the tunnel toward them.

"Masten isn't here," Winner said. He had no idea what had happened back in the tunnel but suspected it was tied to the loud noise that pounded the area a few minutes earlier.

Celia was the first to speak. "Mr. White, I'm Celia Markham."

"Yes, we've met. Aboard Deliverance."

Celia nodded and a slight grimace touched her lips.

One of the soldiers, a sergeant, stepped forward, "We surrender."

Winner smiled and said, "Ms. Markham." He motioned to the soldiers, "There were four of you."

"Your flechette got one. We told him he'd never get past you."

Winner returned his attention to Celia, "Are you all right? Do you need medical attention?"

"No thank you. I'm really in pretty good shape."

Winner didn't say what he thought, but his wry smile and slight nod said enough.

A hint of a smile touched the corner of Celia's mouth as she met his gaze.

"Where's Masten?" he asked.

The sergeant raised his hands in an unknowing gesture. Celia's breath slipped out in an audible sigh. "You may find this hard to believe. Masten climbed into a capsule that was injected into the slurry pipeline. It was the last we saw of him."

"A pig," Winner said. He called Henderson. "Have you been listening?"

"Yes, sir. I just talked with my men on the surface. They found the pig. Masten made it past our guards. I'm afraid he killed the pilots of your SGL and escaped. Captain Davenport's trying to track the launch but doesn't hold much hope. It left orbit."

This confirmed that Masten was not an integral part of Bartok's forces. But why had he been here? Winner had learned enough about the man to know everything he did had a purpose.

Melissa's squad searched the soldiers, removing anything that could be used as a weapon. "Mr. White," she asked. "What in the hell is a pig?"

Winner absently smiled, picked up his flechette and laser rifles and slung them over his shoulders. "It's a capsule—some call it a slug. It can be sealed and injected into a pipeline. It moves between pumps, the slurry does all the work. Except in this case the accelerator assists since the movement is almost straight up. Centuries ago, pigs were used in pipelines to separate the contents in the line—and to move information, oil logs, that kind of data. What Masten did was very risky. If anything had gone wrong, he'd have boiled in that thing. Friction between the slurry, pump and pipeline keeps the temperature around one hundred twenty degrees centigrade." But nothing had gone went wrong. Instead, Masten had escaped.

Winner had no doubt that he'd hear from Masten again.

Melissa nodded.

Winner led the way to the front of the tunnel. "Let's get out of here." Arriving at the main door he said, "Let's take the elevator."

Melissa punched the buttons.

When the door opened, she stuck her head inside and announced it was clear before stepping aside to allow Winner and Celia to enter.

The explosion ripped away the tracks that guided and the elevator and held it secure.

With nothing to hold it, the steel box fell.

The blast knocked Melissa down and into the cavern, her squad sent tumbling like bowling pins.

Stunned by the blast, Winner groped for something solid, some way to avoid the open doors and certain death. Finally, they hit hard as the elevator jammed against the shaft walls, abruptly stopping its cascading descent.

One hundred fifty meters down, Winner and Celia lay unconscious at level five—Bartok's holdup.

"We found them in the blasted elevator," the soldier gloated. "Booby trapping the lift paid off."

The soldiers dumped Winner, his body armor ripped from him, skin suit stripped to the waist and Celia in her orange jumpsuit, onto the floor of the large cavern.

Bartok clapped his hands. "I knew it. This bastard's luck finally ran out. We've been delivered."

The huge man danced around the unconscious pair. He kicked the unconscious Winner, his unrelenting rage never ebbing. Spurred on by the soldier's laughter and Winner's blood, Bartok continued the beating.

One of the officers stepped forward. "Sir, we may need him to get off this planet. I'd suggest you not kill him now."

The big man paused, his foot ready to strike the mutilated enemy sprawled defenseless before him. With a visible effort, he settled his foot harmlessly to the steel floor. Rage momentarily left his face replaced by a puzzled expression as the need to survive struggled to pull him back to reality.

"Sir, do want me to tie them?" a soldier asked.

"Him," he pointing to Winner. "Put him in chains."

"And her?"

"In that room." Bartok pointed toward the rear of the large cavern. "I'll strip her."

Laughter echoed off the polished walls.

One soldier bent to gather Celia in his arms. Brushing the man aside, Bartok pulled a knife and with one stroke slit the orange jump suit covering her.

Another soldier grabbed the garment and jerked, exposing her breasts.

Bartok's insane hysteria, only momentarily held at bay, returned. He knelt beside Celia, grabbed the exposed ample mounds. His yell, not passionate or anticipatory but primal, echoed from the walls.

Celia stirred, flailing her arms to fend off the bruising hands.

Bartok slapped her viciously. "You bitch. You'll be sorry you turned me down. You fuckin' bitch, you betrayed me. When I get through with you—no no…" he was lost in a world beyond reality. "When every man gets through with you…" he stopped mid sentence again.

He'd lost it.

Bartok's rage caused the two solders to back away. "And the women too," he yelled, "get their turn. After me." His laugh bombarded the cavern.

Cradled in the soldier's arms, Celia thrust her arm over her body to deflect the groping.

Bartok's backhand smashed the side of her face. He raised his fist again but stopped when Celia's head swung away no longer aware of the coming blow. A trickle of blood ran from her nose and mouth.

Winner lay unconscious and bleeding on the floor.

"Lock them up. In separate rooms," a quieted Bartok ordered.

The tumbling elevator swam in Winner's dim awareness as consciousness slowly returned.

An eternity passed, the numbing roar of the blast ebbed.

Nudged by the guard, and roused to the edge of awareness by the cold steel floor, Winner opened his eyes.

His face and chest hurt. He tried to touch the pain—the chains rattled to the movement but the noise seemed far away and had nothing to do with him.

The guard prodded Winner's chest with his toe. "Better get used to it. Things aren't going to get any better."

Winner didn't answer. He tried to sit up. It was slow. Excruciating pain throbbed through his body. He puzzled with his bonds. He absently struggled with the chain that bound his feet and hands. He cast a vacant look at the guard who held the loose end. Winner paid vague attention when the door opened and another soldier entered with wrist cuffs.

Using the wall as a support and seated on the floor, Winner raised himself.

He heard the words but understanding eluded him, "Want these?"

The answer skipped before him.

"Yeah. Lock this chain to something…. One of those pipes." The guard pointed toward a cluster of piping against the wall.

Winner remembered the silence as the two left the room. He closed his eyes and leaned against the wall.

Slowly, lifting his hands, he traced his fingers over his face.

His bulbous swollen lips felt nothing, but his fingers told him the truth. He looked at his naked chest and for the first time realized the explosion hadn't torn off his body armor and skin suit. He was a prisoner.

CHAPTER THIRTY SEVEN
The will to win

Winner lay back down and let the cold steel floor soothe his pain; consciousness faded in and out.

From the mist, a woman's voice called.

Puzzled, he gazed around the room seeking the source.

He sat up, looked at his chains, pulled on them, failing to understand what they meant. His name sounded in his ear once again.

His mouth answered without his brain being involved at all. "Yes, I'm here."

"Thank god you're alive," Melissa said.

"Where are you?" Henderson demanded. "What's your situation?"

Reality jolted him into awareness and his mind grasped to hold it.

Winner tried a deep breath and felt the pain of cracked ribs. Through swollen lips he answered, "I'm chained in a room. I don't know where I am." His muddled thoughts poured out; "Celia's not here. What happened?"

"All we know is an explosion blew the elevator loose," Henderson answered. It dropped down the shaft and jammed at level five. You must be Bartok's prisoner. We're coming after you…. And Ms. Markham."

Thoughts of Celia stirred unusual feelings. "How and when?"

"We'll use the secret access and the elevator shaft. When we assault the tunnel, do what you can to stay out of the line of fire."

As he talked, Winner crawled two meters toward the corner pipe securing his chain. A little slack in the links made a weapon of his shackle.

"What about the prisoners on level nine?" He never got an answer.

The door banged opened.

Bartok, followed by at least thirty soldiers, stomped into the room.

His white uniform, brown with dirt and blood, added to the wild-eyed rage plastered on Bartok's face. The man was insane. Winner's bruises and aches needed no further explanation.

Bartok screamed at him. "Well, the big-shot piece of shit. How does it feel to be on the bottom for once?"

A soldier approached and asked, "Want me to unchain him Mr. Bartok?"

"Hell no." He shoved the soldier aside and stepped toward Winner.

The major who had pulled Bartok back from the edge earlier protested. "Sir, we still need him to get out of here and off this planet. What are you going to do?"

The major's determined voice made clear this was a soldier who meant business. His purpose, clearly stated and resolute, was to get out of this lost cause alive. Some of the soldiers quietly nodded their agreement—scowls and a few derisive remarks came from others. Bartok troops were restless and doubtful.

"What do you think I'm going to do?" Bartok raged. "I've got the great Winner White." He held up his hand to stop the scattered laughter, "I must correct myself." He drew himself up to his full considerable height. "I have the great Winner White the fourth."

After the troop's laughter ebbed, Bartok added, his voice close to choking on his words, "I'm goin' to kill him. Just like I did his father."

Although he was chained in the corner of the room, watching Bartok strut before the remnants of his army, Winner knew he couldn't wait for Henderson's Marines.

Bartok's major wanted was a way out and Winner was that instrument. The soldier wasn't a danger. Bartok, however, meant to kill him and Winner would be damned if he'd make it easy for the bastard.

The maddened leader stepped toward Winner, his giant hands hung limply at his sides.

"Bartok," the major yelled. "Goddammit stop. Without this man, there's no fucking way we're getting out of here alive."

The major waited quietly, but poised to act, as his point sank in. "Alive, we can bargain; kill him and we all die."

Bartok spun toward his new antagonist, clinched, his hands looked like sledgehammers.

Knowing every Marine within a thousand or so meters heard what he said Winner seized the moment. Struggling to speak through bloody and swollen lips he said, "You soldiers need to listen to the major. We can cut a deal to end this war. There's no way you're going to get out of this tunnel alive other than by negotiation."

Bartok exploded. "No. I'll kill him." Animal rage erupted in the giant.

Then he hesitated a moment—a moment too long.

He seemed lost, confused.

No one moved.

Bartok grabbed a nearby rifle by its barrel and swung as if it was no more than a twig.

In an instant, Winner came to his knees, pain from his cracked ribs shooting through his body. Coiled like a cobra, the chain locked firmly in his grip Winner watched and waited. One step closer and his tormentor would be near enough for him to strike.

Bartok took that step.

Winner swung the slack chain at Bartok's knees knocking him off balance. He sprung from his crouch, stepped behind the giant and looped the chain around the huge neck.

Ignoring his own pain, Winner ducked low, twisted, yanked and somersaulted his enemy backward.

The sickening sound of Bartok's head hitting the steel plate floor ended the fight. Bartok, his feet still in the air, quivered and died.

The room erupted in chaos.

Still chained to the pipe Winner moved further into the corner to see what the next seconds held.

Stray laser shots from Bartok's soldiers burned holes in walls and the ceiling as they argued with the mercenaries, the major shouting down calls for revenge.

A tunnel explosion shook the room. Henderson and his Marines were meters away.

Finally the major won his point—none of the soldiers wanted to die.

He walked to Winner. "We'll negotiate. Your release for our freedom and a way off this planet."

Even though Henderson now was in control of the tunnel, Winner was still a prisoner and the major controlled the moment. Any one of the soldiers in the room could kill him and not even the major could move fast or decisively enough to stop it. Winner had to admire the officer. In other circumstances, he would have made a good addition to his Marines. "Include Ms. Markham and the civilian prisoners and we can talk," Winner said.

"Agreed."

He waited as his chain was removed before demanding, "Where's Ms. Markham?" He tried to keep his voice calm but feared the worst.

Winner followed the major.

Henderson, his Marines securing the tunnel, joined them in the tunnels.

The major stopped about one hundred meters further into the cavern and pointed. "In there."

Winner opened the door and found Celia unconscious on the floor. Tenderly, he pulled the jumpsuit over her naked breasts.

Before he could rise, a medic appeared next to him. With a quickness that comes from working under battlefield conditions, the doctor broke a capsule of smelling salts and held it under her nose.

Slowly, she regained consciousness.

Winner smiled. "Other than a couple of black eyes, swollen lips and a few more bumps and bruises, you look pretty good."

The medic performed a quick check of Celia's vitals and reassured Winner the woman had suffered no permanent damage.

Winner sagged to the floor and gently cradled her in his arms. "You're going to be all right. It's all over."

* * * *

Winner strode from his room feeling great things lay ahead. A clean bill of health from his doctor helped. Three months after the war ended, Hrndullka and the people of Saragosa were ready to relegate to history the days of company ownership and invasion. Winner took pride in having completed what his ancestors had set out to accomplish.

He stepped off the hotel gravlift, strode the few steps to the door and pressed his palm against the register. As he waited, he ran his hands over the suit, checked his ascot, in-fashion on Saragosa, and generally fidgeted.

He hadn't felt this way for a long time. He was acting like a schoolboy and liked it. He stiffened as the door opened.

"Hi. Come in. Don't you look dapper?"

Winner just stood there.

Dressed in a black satin high-necked full length gown with a white pearl necklace, all made more lovely by creamy white skin, Celia looked even more beautiful than he remembered.

She stepped aside inviting him in. Her arms covered with long white gloves swept open, again an invitation.

Winner remained frozen.

"It's all right. In here, you're as safe as you want to be. Besides, it's time for the inauguration."

"Sorry," Winner said, entering the room. "I just hadn't remembered how truly beautiful you are."

"Thank you," Celia said. "How long has it been since we were last together? Two days? Your mother warned me to watch out once the doctor had given you a clean bill of health."

It had been a long time since Winner had felt emotions like the ones swirling through him. It exhilarated him and he didn't want to let go.

From the bar she asked, "Care for a glass of wine?"

He checked his chronometer and said, "Yes, we've got time." In fact, he'd timed his arrival in hopes something like this would happen. He marveled at how clever he was and how everything was going according to plan.

Winner accepted the Tiffany Favrile wineglass and held the goblet up in a toast, "To you."

He embraced her as their lips touched in a lingering kiss.

Celia rested her head on Winners chest—the smell of her hair; the closeness of her body stirred all of Winner's emotions.

"We're going to be late if we don't go. Now."

Winner hated to back away. "Maybe Hulk will understand if we're late—or don't show up at all."

Celia tilted her gaze to look up into Winner's eyes, "Behave. You started all this when you decided to make Saragosa Prime a republic. You know Hulk is being hailed as the George Washington of Saragosa don't you?"

"Yes," Winner answered. "And I couldn't be more proud. It really feels good to have been a part of this."

"Let's go," she urged.

Winner released her and set his glass the bar. "Lady." He smiled. "Whatever you say."

* * * *

Winner stepped to the podium, waving to the standing ovation from the crowd. The space drone tarmac suited the occasion well. The population had swollen to one hundred fifty thousand inhabitants and most were present to see and be a part of the founding of the Republic of Saragosa Prime and inauguration of Vladislov Hrndullka as their first president.

Winner held up his hand to quiet the crowd. He didn't want to dampen the enthusiasm, but rather to have his say and turn the party, and the planet over to Hulk.

"People of Saragosa Prime, you have spoken and spoken well. Some of you say I gave you independence. Not so my friends. I just gave you the opportunity. After the invasion, you weren't fighting for the corporation, you fought for your independence. You won the right to this day—this hour. It is yours. Never let anyone take it from you."

The crowd broke into cheers—the racket of blowing horns and people's shouts was almost overwhelming.

He turned toward Hulk seated a few meters behind and beckoned him to the dais. He shook his friend's hand.

"Admiral Ashcroft named the operation to free Saragosa Prime, 'Freedom's Dagger.' This was the Admiral's sword." He handed Hulk the saber and then stepped away. With that handshake, the day's events ended. If the crowd was crazy before, it was now berserk with joy.

Winner stood clapping and taking handshakes for at least thirty minutes. Finally, he turned to Celia. "It's their moment and it's time for us to leave." He loved the beautiful smile it brought.

Celia put her hand on his arm and stood. "Whatever you say."

"Hey, I like the sound of that. It even had some ring of obedience."

Celia pinched his arm. "Don't push it." She gave the same arm a hug.

"Do you mind if I admire you?" she asked.

Putting on his best haughty act, Winner struck a mock pose, raised his chin and said, "If you must."

"You're pushing it again."

Winner turned to Hulk. "Mr. President, Colonel Henderson will remain here with a two thousand man garrison for as long as you want. Your new congress is in session, and the mines are working. And it's time for me to leave."

Hulk placed his huge hand on Winners shoulder. "Four months ago, if someone had told me what was in store—for all of us, I would have dismissed them without a second thought. Four months ago, I was plotting my retirement."

Winner laughed.

"Where are you going from here?" Hulk asked.

"Namaycush," Winner said. "Claim my prize. See for myself what's there to work with. My thinking is to make Colonel Hornblower military governor and set about putting some civilian structure in place.

"From there, I'll head to Earth. That's going to be the fun part. Some of the banks were up to their butts with Bartok's loans, betting I would lose. They're going to have to eat Bartok's debt. It means WMC will take over a few banks. Some of them are the same ones who demanded a seat on our board of directors when it looked like we were going to lose." Winner extended his hand to Hulk and left the room. "Goodbye my friend."

With Celia on his arm, he'd only taken two steps into the hall when he skidded to a halt. "Melissa. What are you doing here?"

"Stopped to say goodbye." She effectively blocked the hall. Two police and two Marines stood just outside the president's office, the Marines assigned as security for Winner. All looked straight ahead.

"I said my goodbye to Derka earlier this morning. How's your marriage going?" Winner wanted to comment on the blue police suit and how nicely it fit but it was way too late for that.

"Just fine. I couldn't be happier. He isn't very pleased with my heading up Saragosa's police and security forces. He would like some kids. But even he admits it's better than me following you around the galaxy. No offense."

"None taken," he laughed. "I want to thank you for everything you did. And don't tell me you were just doing your job."

Melissa stuck out her hand. "Goodbye Mr. White."

Winner reached to shake her hand, somewhat surprised at such a quick dismissal.

Melissa grabbed him and kissed him hard on the lips. "I'd never forgive myself if I hadn't done that." A grin covered her face. Celia, hands over her mouth, seemed delighted.

Winner said, "Thanks. I'm glad you did."

Melissa turned and walked down the hall. Winner watched until she looked over her shoulder then turned the corner.

* * * *

In the co-pilots seat, Winner watched the image of Deliverance grew.

The pilot pointed to the battlefield repairs just completed.

When Winner saw the panel covering the hole blasted by the torpedo that killed Admiral Ashcroft, he silently lamented the man's passing. Once they reached Earth, Deliverance would go into refit and repair. The shuttle settled into the hanger bay.

He accepted the boarding honors, and stepped onto Deliverance with Celia immediately behind him. The 'boson's whistle ended its shrill attention on deck. As many as could of the thirty-five hundred-man crew lined the catwalks and crowded the hanger deck. As the ceremonies concluded, three cheers went up. Winner and Celia both waved to the spacemen and marines.

Captain Davenport motioned them toward the gravlift, "Sir, Ma'am, if you'll follow me, I'll show you to your quarters."

The passageway was coated with gray paint and multicolored placards stating the purpose of each entity. The ceiling tiles had been removed to show the proper overhead with lengths of pipe and conduit that ran throughout the battle cruiser. All of the pastel colors and other amenities that had been the travel ship Galactic Star were gone, replaced with the battle gray of Deliverance.

Davenport stopped in front of a bulkhead. With a sweeping arm gesture he said, "Ms. Markham, your quarters." He opened the hatch and stepped back.

"Dinner at nineteen hundred?" Winner asked.

"I'll be ready," she answered. "Where are your quarters?"

Winner pointed up the passageway and said, "Next door."

"Very convenient."

"I thought so. It sometimes pays to be boss," he laughed and then winked at her.

Davenport followed Winner into his cabin. "You received a message from Richard Hastings. It's on a secured telecom channel."

A new wall plaque drew Winner's attention. He walked over and read it. "The Preamble To The Constitution of The Republic of Saragosa Prime. Presented to Winner White.

Winner retrieved the card leaning against the lamp stand and read it. "Thank you. The people of the Republic of Saragosa Prime."

Davenport said, "We found the SGL launch Masten escaped in. it was empty. No signs of violence or forced entry. Looks like he had a deep space vessel waiting. It explains why we couldn't find him."

"A talented but dangerous man." Again, the feeling came that he'd not heard the last of him.

Davenport turned to leave.

"Captain, Archimedes isn't too far off our course to Namaycush. Don't you think the crew could use a little R & R? Say a week?"

Davenport smiled. "Thank you sir. I'll pass the word. And that does explain the reservation confirming two rooms at the Harbour Lodge."

After Davenport left, Winner showered and lay down on his bunk. "Computer, wake me up at eighteen thirty."

* * * *

A few minutes early, Winner palmed the entry to Celia's cabin. The hatch opened and a breath whistled lightly through his lips.

Her plain high-necked gray dress glistened. The dull gray color of the ship created, instead of ambiguity, a startling contrasting background.

"Stunning," he said.

Celia stepped back from the hatch entry and said, "Thank you kind sir. Please come in."

Winner cleared the entry, closed the hatch and pulled her into his arms. The press of her body, the gentle kiss of her lips washed away every other thought.

Richard Hastings and the Tri-Lateral Council couldn't interfere with tonight.

2547000